TRAPPED IN THE HOLD OF A FERENGI SHIP . . .

. . . by two hulking bodyguards, Wesley Crusher tucked the small device he had come for—the device with the potential to destroy the Federation —under one arm.

Wesley charged toward the man on his left, then head-faked to the right. The man was fooled, but his partner was not. He pushed the other man out of the way, and in seconds Wesley's head and neck were immobilized, wrapped in muscular arms that felt like iron.

Tunk, the Ferengi owner of the ship, reached out and took the device from under Wesley's arm.

Wesley opened his mouth to protest, then shut it without a sound. A Ferengi who would kidnap a Starfleet cadet might not draw the line at murder. . . .

Look for STAR TREK Fiction from Pocket Books

Star Trek: The Original Series

Star Trek: The Next Generation

Star Trek: Deep Space Nine

STAR TREK
THE NEXT GENERATION®

BALANCE OF POWER

DAFYDD AB HUGH

POCKET BOOKS

New York   London   Toronto   Sydney   Tokyo   Singapore

An *Original* Publication of POCKET BOOKS

POCKET BOOKS, a division of Simon & Schuster Inc.
1230 Avenue of the Americas, New York, NY 10020

This book is published by Pocket Books, a division of
Simon & Schuster Inc., under exclusive license from
Paramount Pictures.

ISBN: 0-671-52003-2

First Pocket Books printing January 1995

10 9 8 7 6 5 4 3 2 1

POCKET and colophon are registered trademarks of
Simon & Schuster Inc.

Printed in the U.S.A.

Chapter One

LIEUTENANT COMMANDER Geordi La Forge strode quickly out of his temporary quarters aboard the Klingon scoutship *Strange Legendary Klingon Fish That Hides in Rocks and Spies on Enemies of the Warrior Gods*—Geordi could not pronounce the actual Klingon name.

As he rounded a corner into the main, peak-roofed corridor, heading toward the bridge, a meaty hand clamped on his shoulder: It was Lieutenant Worf. The pair were temporarily assigned to the Klingon ship, commanded by Worf's brother Kurn, until they finished retrofiting the *Hiding Fish*'s sensor to detect the subspace damage done by traveling faster than warp five.

"Commander," said the Klingon in his best approximation of a sympathetic tone of voice, "I sorrow for your loss. I know what it is like to lose a comrade. It is sad that he could not have died in battle as a true warrior."

Geordi stared. "Worf, what are you talking about?"

Now the Klingon was puzzled. "Did you not read the message traffic from Starfleet this morning?"

"Whoops. No, I was running late and I skipped it. Did somebody die?"

Worf took a deep, sympathetic breath. "Yes, sir, your mentor from the Starfleet Academy has died. I sorrow for your loss. I understand that humans consider death a great tragedy. I know what it is like to lose—"

La Forge massaged his temples; his visor hurt even more than usual this day. "Worf, I didn't *have* any mentor at the Academy. Whom are you talking about?"

"Why, Doctor Zorka, of course. He died two days ago, but nobody discovered the body until yesterday."

Geordi shrugged. "Thanks for the concern, but I barely knew Doctor Zorka. I took a couple of classes from him, but that's about it."

Worf nodded. "I, too, have suffered the pain of seeing one of my instructors from the Academy die in bed like a shopkeeper. I understand how you must feel."

Helplessly, Geordi tried to clarify. "Worf, believe me; I didn't care one way or the other about the guy. He was a crank at the Academy, and he's even more of a crank now—well, *was* a crank. Come on, we're supposed to meet Captain Kurn on the bridge."

They marched into the lift, and Worf called out "bridge" in Klingon. As they passed deck after deck, then headed out the long neck of the scoutship toward the bubble section, Geordi could actually feel the waves of sympathy emanating from Worf, discomfiting the young lieutenant commander.

The doors slid open with a whoosh. Kurn lounged in his command chair, legs crossed, staring at a tactical display of the historical battle of Gamma Amar IV, in which the Klingons soundly routed the Federation forces seventy-five years before.

"Captain," said Geordi, "we're a few hours ahead of schedule on the retrofit. So far, we've synched the Doppler on your sensors to the tachyon emission belt frequencies of the new cloaking field; but we still need to modulate your shield and disruptor projection points to match the hole in the spectral . . ." La Forge paused, noticing that Kurn stared blankly, not understanding a word Geordi had said.

"You said you are ahead of schedule, human?"

"Yes. Three hours."

"Fine. That is your report. Now leave me alone; I have important duties to attend."

Worf leaned close to Geordi and whispered, "Kurn has a commodore examination to take in a few days. He will not be disposed to listen to details about anything."

The executive officer of the *Hiding Fish,* Commander Kurak, cleared her throat. When Kurn did not respond, she did so again.

"Oh, yes," Kurn said at last, "the *Enterprise* first officer is waiting to speak to you."

"Shall I put it on screen?" suggested Kurak. Kurn glared furiously at her, then savagely gestured at the viewport. The tactical map vanished, replaced by a view of the *Enterprise* bridge.

Geordi felt peculiar, standing on the deck of a strange Klingon ship, watching a communication *from* the *Enterprise;* he had so often seen the reverse.

Commander Will Riker, first officer of the *Enterprise,* sat in the command chair; Dr. Beverly Crusher stood behind, leaning on the rail. Commander Data noticed the transmission and turned back toward Riker.

"Sir, Commander La Forge has reached the bridge on the *tlhIngan bIQDepHey Huj So'bogh naghmey 'ej veS qa''a' jaghpu' ghoqbogh 'oH.*" Geordi was absurdly annoyed that Data, programmed with every known language, pronounced the Klingon name perfectly.

Riker looked up. "Geordi, have you heard the news yet?"

"Which news?"

"The news about Doctor Zorka."

"Oh. Yes, sir. Would you like a report on our progress so far?"

Riker raised his brows, somewhat surprised. "No, that's all right. If you need some time off to deal with the loss, just let us know. The captain is resting right now, but he said if you needed to talk to someone . . ."

"No, sir," said Geordi, trying not to look annoyed. "It's really all right. I barely even knew—"

Beverly interrupted, looking into the viewscreen with a face that would have broken the Devil's heart. "Geordi, I . . . I lost my residency advisor just a year ago. I know how much it hurts."

"It doesn't hurt, Commander. Really. I only took three classes from Zorka, and he even gave me a B in one of them."

On the screen, Data did his best to make his face show concern. "Geordi, you said much the same things when your mother vanished. Most therapists agree that it helps ease the pain to talk about it. I do not think it a good idea to hold your grief inside."

"This time I'm not holding anything in!" exclaimed Geordi, becoming seriously annoyed. *Why does everyone keep offering me tea and sympathy?* Captain Kurn and Commander Kurak snickered, and La Forge felt his face flush. "I really don't care whether Doctor Zorka died. I didn't wish him ill—well, maybe when I saw that B—but he was *not* my mentor! He was a lunatic."

"But . . ." began Riker, "but you always said you hated him."

Embarrassed, Geordi realized the commander was right. "All right, I did say I hated him."

"You mean you really *didn't* like him?" Riker turned to Beverly as if to ask *how could this be?*

"Yes!" admitted Geordi, exasperated into the honest truth. "I confess! I hated everything about him, the old fraud. I hated having to rewrite papers to support his idiotic obsessions, and I hated answering questions wrong just to get a good grade on his tests. If it hadn't been for tenure, the real engineers at Starfleet would have fired him before I even arrived!"

Beverly answered, confused. "I thought . . . well, you

joked about him so much, about how crazy he was, that we all thought you really loved him."

Data cocked his head quizzically. "Were you not being gruffly humorous when you spoke of Doctor Zorka's mental imbalances?"

"No, Data, I was not being gruffly humorous. I would have been perfectly happy if he had, well, retired or something years ago. I didn't want him to die, but he had no business instructing at the Academy or receiving Federation grants.

"He was always in the news, each time with some grand new invention he was supposedly perfecting that he never quite finished, of course. I kept asking, 'Why does the Federation keep funding this doddering, old mental patient?'

"But that *wasn't* my subtle way of saying, 'Gee, I sure wish I were back in his Engines 313 class, slaving away over a hot warp coil and pulling Bs again!'"

Kurn interrupted. "The Klingon Empire does not have time to waste on such frivolous banter!"

"But you chose him as your dissertation advisor," countered Data.

"No—he chose *me!* I wanted Crystal Estes. I worked my whole senior year at the Academy on that dissertation, and Zorka *rejected* it! I didn't take into account his new theory on mystical subspace nonsense. He made me rewrite it over the next five months."

Kurn leapt to his feet. "Enough! I have important tactics to consider for the exam—for the greater good of the Klingon battle fleet! I shall not tolerate this foolishness any further!"

"Guys, please," said Geordi, "I'm not fooling. I'm not broken up; I'm not hiding any pain; I don't care! His papers were garbage, his discoveries nonexistent, and he was an irritating son of a . . . son of a bachelor. Now will you *please* let me get back to work on the retrofit?"

Riker looked at Beverly, then Data; Dr. Crusher pursed

her lips; and Data deliberately raised both eyebrows. "Sorry, Geordi," said Commander Riker, sounding distinctly miffed.

"I'm sorry, sir; I didn't mean it that way. It was really nice of you all to worry about me . . . but I'm fine. Really."

"Yes, right, fine!" snarled Kurn. "Good-bye, good-bye; Commander, terminate communication." The screen went blank; after a moment, it was replaced by the tactical map again. "Now get off the bridge, human, and take that . . . take my brother with you back to the engine room. Get busy with that cloak detector!" Kurn turned back to the map, staring at it with such intensity that Geordi would not have been surprised to see it burst into flames.

"Um, maybe we'd better head back down to the engineering section, Worf."

"I think that is a good plan."

As soon as the doors closed behind them and they started back along the neck of the *Hiding Fish,* Worf added, "After all, we would not want to cause my brother's second attempt at the examination to go as badly as his first."

When they arrived back in the beehivelike catacombs of the Klingon engineering "department," Lieutenant Dakvas pointed at a small screen. "Message for Lieutenant Commander Geordi La Forge from the *Enterprise.*"

"Again?" Frustrated, Geordi jabbed the comm link button, activating the screen.

Commander Deanna Troi, the ship's counselor, stared at him from the viewscreen, her face dripping concern and understanding. "Geordi," she said, "I understand how you feel. I can sense your stress. We all feel stress and apprehension when someone near and dear to us passes on. Would you like to talk to someone about it?"

Chapter Two

IT TOOK GEORDI A WHILE to shoo Counselor Troi off the comm link. *No, Doctor Zorka was not my mentor; yes, I'm fine; yes, I know I'm agitated; no, it's not because of Zorka's death, it's because of all the sympathy I don't need!* At last, Deanna seemed eighty-five percent convinced and signed off.

He shook his head in amazement. "I never realized how much I must have mentioned Zorka," he said to Worf.

"You brought him up more than you think, Commander."

"Did you think I really liked the guy?"

Worf grunted, considering. "I thought it was some strange human custom, speaking ill of absent comrades to ward off evil. Some Klingon families have taboos against excessive praise."

They had barely resumed working on the retrofit when Geordi received a third transmission from the *Enterprise*. This time, it was Captain Picard himself.

"I'm very sorry for your loss," said Picard. "Doctor Zorka was a fine man."

"Thank you, sir," said Geordi, striving not to allow a tone of exasperation to enter his voice.

"I would like to speak with you, Mister La Forge, in private. Please contact me at your convenience."

"Um, sir, if this is about Zorka, I'm fine. I really am. I don't need to talk it out, sir. But thank you for your concern."

"I'm afraid you don't understand, Commander. *I* need to speak to *you* about Doctor Zorka. When would be convenient?"

"Let me check, sir."

Geordi turned to Worf and spoke too quietly for Picard to hear over the comm link. "Did the captain sound urgent to you, or is it just me?"

Worf spoke quietly. "All transmissions to and from Klingon ships are monitored. I believe the captain wants you to return to your quarters and reestablish contact on a private channel."

"That's what I thought. Can you take over, Worf?"

Worf nodded. "I can finish remodulating the shields, but you will need to return and help me tune the disruptors."

Geordi turned back to the viewscreen. "Captain, I'm on my way back to my quarters. I'll contact you as soon as I get there."

"Thank you," said Picard.

"La Forge out."

Geordi looked around, trying to find the engineering watch-stander to tell him he was leaving. But the Klingon had vanished.

"Worf, what happened to Dakvas?"

"He hurried away abruptly as soon as Captain Picard said he needed to speak to you privately. He has probably gone around the corner to call Kurn."

Geordi hurried back to his quarters, reluctant to leave the retrofit project at such a critical phase. However, the hardness in Picard's voice had told Geordi more than the words themselves: The captain, and probably the *Enterprise,* had some serious problem related to Zorka's death; and Picard needed to pick Geordi's brain about the enigmatic instructor and inventor.

Geordi and Worf's temporary quarters were decorated in old, "High Klingon" style with various bladed weapons hanging from the walls amid harshly representational paintings of socially useful activities. Geordi quickly popped open the communications viewer. He took several moments to figure out the innards, then disconnected a particular fiber and plugged it directly into his data-reader. He connected the data-reader output back into the viewscreen.

He sent the initial search string unencrypted to establish the link with the *Enterprise* computer. Then he shifted to scramble mode, encrypting the transmission by a specific pair of 900-digit numbers. After a moment, Captain Picard's face appeared onscreen.

The captain's normally spotless desk was piled high with data clips labeled "Zorka—moment trans beam," "Zorka —phasr rfl screen," and so forth . . . all inventions that Geordi remembered seeing announced in engineering and physics journals at one time or another over the past ten years—and not a one of which he recalled ever being actually demonstrated.

Captain Picard did not look up; he contemplated the pile of data clips on his desk. "Commander La Forge," he began at last, "I'm glad to hear back from you so soon."

"This line is secure, sir."

"Good. Geordi, Will has given me a brief report on the discussion of a few minutes ago."

"I'm sorry, sir; I didn't mean to be rude. I know they were all trying to be helpful."

"That's not what worries me. I need your unbiased judgment about a matter related to Doctor Zorka, and I'm concerned you may have such strongly negative feelings about the man that you cannot be impartial."

"Well . . . I can try, sir. But I can't guarantee anything. I really didn't like that old crank."

Picard finally looked up, fixing Geordi with his eyes. "Are you aware of what Zorka's son has done upon his father's death?"

"I—I didn't even know he *had* a son."

"You'll see it in tomorrow's message traffic. Doctor Zorka's son is a middle-aged artist who has never achieved the level of success to which he believes himself entitled. He has received three grants from the Federation Arts Council, but the last one was on stardate"—Picard glanced at his screen—2358."

"Twelve years ago."

Picard nodded. "In short, he's broke."

"Why is Starfleet so interested in Zorka's son?"

"That, Geordi, is what I want you to tell me. You told Will that Zorka was a complete fraud . . . I think that was the word you used. However, in reading his file, I find no doubts expressed by any Subcommittee members or fellows of the Federation Association for the Advancement of Science about Zorka's bonafides. I cannot quite reconcile these two views of the same man."

"Is there a particular reason you have to, sir?"

Picard nodded. "Zorka's son, um, Bradford Zorka, Junior—"

"Doctor Zorka's name was Bradford? I thought it was Jaymi."

"It was Jaymi. I don't know why his son calls himself 'junior,' but he does. Now Bradford Zorka, the son, has decided to raise funds for a new art project by holding an auction of all of his father's notes, inventions, and lab equipment. Starfleet has instructed us to attend this auction and bid on behalf of the Federation."

Geordi stared. After a moment, he realized his mouth was open and shut it quickly. "Sir, I hope they didn't send us a list of things we *must* bid on!"

The captain plucked another data clip from his desk and held it aloft. "A complete list of lots that we must obtain, along with maximum prices we're allowed to bid."

Geordi sighed, tilting his head and shaking it. As he looked back at his screen, he saw peculiar flickering around the edges. He recognized the particular interference pattern.

"Sir, the Klingons are running the transmission through a

pattern-search subroutine, trying to break the encryption. Why are we keeping this secret in any case?"

"Let me know if you think it's been decrypted. Commander La Forge, one of the items we're particularly interested in is a photonic pulse cannon. Zorka claims to have developed it quite recently, about three years ago. His paper in the *Journal of Plasma Extrusions* claimed that it would punch right through our best shields . . . or anyone else's. Now, I haven't actually seen this demonstrated—"

"Neither has anybody else. It's 'vaporware,' another fantastic invention he announced but never released."

"Nevertheless," continued the captain, undaunted, "there are still . . . unresolved problems relating to the succession of Emperor Kahless, and Starfleet is concerned that such a weapon not fall into the hands of some of the more, ah, *exuberant* members of the Klingon High Council who are having trouble accepting the new emperor."

"Well, you don't have anything to worry about, sir. The photonic pulse weapon is about as real as Rumpelstiltskin!"

"Geordi, if you can prove that, or if you can show good evidence that Doctor Zorka was actually mentally disturbed or delusional, you would make a lot of Federation scientists and Starfleet admirals sleep easier."

Helplessly, Geordi spread his hands. "I don't have any specific evidence, if that's what you mean. I had many discussions—well, I guess you'd call them arguments— with Zorka when I was in his class. Every week, he had a new master plan to save the universe: One time, he wanted Starfleet disbanded, since it only encouraged violence. He said the only solution to violence was for all the good people, and he really used the term 'good people,' to unilaterally disarm themselves so the bad people wouldn't feel threatened anymore.

"Another day, he suggested we build an army of androids to do all our fighting for us; then he proposed to the Starfleet Academic Council that we no longer teach basic warp-field engineering principles because they had all been developed from the phase-space equations of Professor Vinge."

"Vinge?"

"The mathematician and philosopher who spent the last eleven years of his life trying to prove that the universe is actually a hollow sphere and you can get across the galaxy by moving in the opposite direction. Zorka hated him for some reason. Personally, I loved Vinge's classes; he was crazy, but *good* crazy."

Picard raised his brows. "Geordi, I hope your opinion isn't mere ivory-tower political intrigue."

"You know me better than that, sir. It's not that Zorka had weird ideas; the problem is that he supported them with crackpot arguments, like the disarmament theory. He claimed there was secret, unpublished research that showed that the Cardassian Empire was a peace-loving utopia until they discovered us—and *then* they turned into a military dictatorship in response! He claimed there was a secret, Federation warehouse on Deep Space Five, at the Cardassian border, where Starfleet had the remains of the first Cardassian ship we encountered: a peaceful trading mission that we supposedly blew out of orbit for no reason."

The captain could not resist a smile. "So, have you actually been to Deep Space Five?"

"Yes, sir. I surveyed their engineering systems on a ship's tour before I joined the *Enterprise*. There isn't room on Deep Space Five for a warehouse to store a Cardassian ship! It's a tiny outpost, nowhere near as big as the other deep-space stations; about the size of the *Enterprise*'s saucer section."

Picard looked back at his monitor and flipped through several screens. "I don't find mention in Zorka's file of any adverse psychiatric evaluation."

"You probably don't find any normal ones, either," predicted Geordi.

Picard nodded. "You're right. There are no medical records at all. I suspect they have been withheld in consideration of his son Bradford's privacy."

"Captain," said La Forge, "Doctor Zorka may have been a crackpot, but he was brilliant, at least when he was young.

He practically invented modern phasers, or at least the solid-state phase amplification, and he cut his teeth developing half the modern medical equipment that we use.

"It's just that when he got older, he couldn't distinguish between a correct brilliant theory and a brilliantly worked out crank theory . . . and frankly, neither can most of Starfleet, myself included.

"All the stuff that Zorka wrote about in the journals sounds workable, until you actually start working with it. His inventions are like ingenious perpetual-motion machines . . . the flaws are subtle, but profound. I can't *prove* he was delusional, certainly not at a sanity hearing. He probably wasn't, in the medical sense: He didn't crack eggs on his head or think he was a potted plant, or anything like that. Sir, I think we've only got another minute or so before the Klingons either decrypt the transmission or give up and have a sudden equipment failure."

Picard considered, glancing from Geordi to the screen and back again. "Commander, you still leave me with my original problem: If I can't prove that Zorka *didn't* invent a photonic pulse cannon, then I have no choice but to head directly toward the auction and begin bidding.

"Because of the dangerous nature of some of his experiments, Zorka's laboratory is located outside Federation space. And Bradford junior has made it very clear that we are not to be the only parties invited to the auction. We expect to see Klingons, Bajorans, Cardassians, Ferengi . . . in fact, everybody but the Borg."

"I'm sorry, sir. I can't tell you any more than I already said. You've trusted my gut feelings before; my gut feeling is that Zorka is a zilch. There's no photonic pulse cannon, no momentum-transfer beam, and no psi-directed transporter. It's like antigravity paint or Vinge's hollow sphere . . . makes a great story, but there's no such thing."

"Very well, Commander. I have no choice. You and Commander Worf shall return to the *Enterprise* as soon as you finish the retrofit. When will that be?"

"Another day should do it, sir."

"Make it so. Picard out."

Geordi reached for the comm switch; but just then, a burst of static swamped the picture and sound, turning the viewscreen into nothing but snow and white noise. Geordi chuckled and turned it off. *I guess Kurn got tired of trying to crack the code,* he thought.

He rose and returned to Worf in the engineering section, but the *Enterprise*'s security officer stood stiffly near the shields console with his arms crossed, two beefy, Klingon "liaisons" at his sides.

"It seems that our retrofiting project has been terminated," growled Worf.

"Temporarily," added the gorgeous Commander Kurak, stepping from the shadows. Geordi consciously noticed her for the first time: She looked like she could bench-press Worf, if necessary. Geordi sighed; what was the chance that a beautiful Klingon warrior and commander of a scoutship would be attracted to a short, human engineer with a peculiar VISOR? He decided the odds hovered somewhere between "Earth's moon is actually made out of ice" and "every air molecule in the engineering deck simultaneously decides to crowd into one corner of the room": *slim* and *quite a bit slimmer.*

Kurak explained. "We received emergency orders to journey to a particular spot at maximum speed. We cannot afford to shut down the power grid while you two work on the shields and disruptors."

"How did you know we were going to have to shut down the power grid in a few hours?"

She smiled, looking deadly and amused at the same time. "I began in the engines section myself. I have followed your project from the beginning."

Mmm . . . Geordi sighed for the second time in ten seconds. "All right. We have to return to the *Enterprise* anyway. How soon can you rendezvous with our ship so we can beam over?"

Worf snorted; "I already made that request, Commander. It seems that a rendezvous is impossible."

"Ah," said Geordi, nodding. "Did your navigational computer suddenly break down? How inconvenient and coincidental."

"Of course it did not break down," said Kurak, "we are not stupid, and we do not think you are stupid either. We simply do not have the time to travel halfway across the sector to beam you back. We have urgent orders to report, and 'urgent' means no time for passenger service or sight-seeing."

"But *we* have to get back to *our* ship urgently, too!"

"Geordi—may I call you by your familiar?—let us not play games. We are both going to the same place: the auction of the estate of that Federation scientist who just died. Does it matter whether you go there in our ship or yours? We will beam you down with our negotiation team and you can find your captain and join up with him then."

She stepped closer to the *Enterprise* engineer. "Besides . . . is it really that harsh a penalty to have to spend a few more days with me? It is so rare that I meet anyone, human or Klingon, who knows enough about engines to have an intelligent conversation."

Geordi gulped, glancing from Kurak to Worf. His Klingon friend and colleague stared in fascination at a piece of shield equipment that he had taken apart and put back together a dozen times in different spots along the hull.

Kurak grabbed Geordi's arm, dragging him next to her. "Let me show you a little something in my quarters," she breathed. "It is a holomorphic model of an antique warp coil. I made it myself."

"I . . . I . . ." Geordi tried to lick dry lips. "I—"

"Sir," barked Worf, "I need your help briefly before you depart. Perhaps the commander can return to her quarters and you join her there in a few minutes?"

She gazed speculatively at Worf. "By all means," she said, "I would not want anything to break because of a lack of preparation." She left them.

"Worf, what are you doing?" demanded Geordi. "I think I really have a chance with her!"

"Do you know what her job is on this ship?"

"Um, first officer?"

"No, Commander. Kurak is the political officer. She watches the rest of the crew, including Kurn, and reports on any deviations from the political orthodoxy of the homeworld. She is most certainly a member of the security service and a trained killer."

"I won't hold it against her that she's a state torturer," said Geordi, trying for lighthearted banter.

"Klingons do not torture!" snapped Worf. "It is not honorable."

"Sorry, I apologize. Worf, I'll . . . I'll see you back at the quarters in a couple of hours."

He could not quite catch Worf's response, but he could swear the Klingon muttered "not likely." Then the massive doors to the engines department rolled shut behind Geordi.

Chapter Three

CADET WESLEY CRUSHER stared in dismay at his dorm room at Starfleet Academy. The left half, his own, was spotless; it could have been a stateroom aboard the *U.S.S. Enterprise.*

The right half could have been a combined clothing store and electronics warehouse that went bankrupt after a devastating earthquake. Alas, some of the junk from the messy side seemed to be creeping inexorably across the line into Wesley's territory.

Cadet Crusher had just returned from morning chow, and despite the lateness of the morning—nearly 0900—his roommate had not awakened, not risen, not drawn the blinds to let in the dim morning light reflecting off the blank wall of the dorm building next door.

He spent a few moments kicking things back across, then decided to confront the owner/occupier, instead of simply going to the library and forgetting about it, his usual nonresponse.

Somewhere among the heaping piles of uniforms, fiber-optic cables, holovision remote controllers, wind-up toys, half-finished inventions, half-eaten food, and other bric-a-brac, lurked his roommate, Fred Kimbal, dead to the world.

Or perhaps not; it was hard to tell. Wesley heard no snores. Fred was generally early-to-bed, late-to-rise.

"Fred?" demanded Wes. "Are you in here? Are you under anything?"

One of the clothing heaps grunted. Wishing he had a pair of radiation gloves, Wesley began digging, finally unearthing Kimbal.

"I'm sleeping," grumbled the disheveled cadet, a year Wesley's junior. Kimbal's hair was unkempt, he smelled of garlic, and he still wore his cadet's uniform. In fact, it was the same uniform he had worn the previous day, and he had not even had it replicleaned.

"Not now you're not," observed Wesley.

"I'm *trying.*"

"Very."

"Har-de-har-har. So what if I missed a class? I've got the top grade in every class."

"Really? Every class?"

Kimbal grinned, his chubby face looking distinctly baby-ish. "Well, every class that counts." It was Fred Kimbal's running joke: every class that *counts,* meaning all the classes that involved mathematics. In that sense, the statement was true; Kimbal was frighteningly brilliant at any activity that involved mathematics, physics, or engineering. Even Wesley Crusher, no slouch in the math and engineering department himself, could barely keep up with Kimbal in full-yell, despite being a year ahead.

In the more complete sense, however, there were many classes that "counted" toward graduation in which Kimbal was close to flunking . . . notably the class in Starfleet Leadership—which most officers in the fleet considered the most critical course at the Academy.

"Fred, do you remember when I painted that white line down the middle of our room? Do you remember what it means?"

"You must have been drunk, Wes."

"I don't drink."

"Then *I* must have been drunk."

"Don't be a jerk. Do you remember what it means?"

Fred rolled his eyes. "My side is the west side, and I'm not supposed to cross the line. Hey! How come the bathroom's on your side?"

"Fred, this isn't some stupid holovision situation comedy. I just said you can't keep your junk on my side of the line."

Fred peeked out. "I don't see anything on your side."

"That's because I just kicked it back! Look, you're going to have to do something about this; there's going to be an inspection tomorrow, and the drill chief isn't going to care whose side this crap is on."

Fred sat up woozily, keeping the blankets tucked around his neck. Wesley wondered what Kimbal did not want him to see.

"It's not crap," argued Fred, "and not junk either! These are delicate experiments. There's my latest one, on the counter."

Wesley stared at the shelf until he spotted the newest bundle of fiberoptic cables and data clips. It looked too small to be particularly useful, including only five processors total.

"What does it do?" asked Wesley, intrigued despite himself. Kimbal built the most outrageous, tiny machines, advanced designs light-years away from the simplistic projects assigned in even the upper-division engineering courses.

Alas, Kimbal had a disturbing tendency to *half*-finish his inventions; then, when he finished solving the tough parts in his head, he would lose interest in the invention and leave it lying around as . . . junk.

Fred thought for a moment. "I don't know. Honest. I was playing around with the properties of chaseum, which is very similar to gold-pressed latinum. *Very* similar."

"Except you can replicate chaseum, so it's no good as a currency."

"Yes, yes, yes," said Fred, waving his hand dismissively. "I don't care about the economics and all that nonsense," continued Cadet Kimbal. "But the properties are so much alike because the molecules are the same except for leg orientation. Did you know that chaseum and latinum have two key sets of Balmer spectral lines that are identical, just phase-shifted with respect to each other?"

"No. What do you mean, key *sets* of spectral lines? I didn't know they came in sets."

"Oh, I forgot to mention. I've been burning things in the lab and reclassifying spectral signatures by my own system."

Wesley shrugged. "So what does this thing do?"

"I told you, I don't know. I had a problem and I solved it. If you want to finish it off, it's yours." Kimbal yawned and pulled the blankets tighter, despite the comfortable temperature of the dorm room.

"Thanks. Hey, I almost forgot why I came in here to hunt you down. I got an invitation today. La Fong invited me to the big game tomorrow night."

"La Fong?"

"Yes," said Wesley, shaking his head in exasperation. "Don't you remember? Capital-*L*, small-*a*, capital-*F*—"

"Oh, you mean *Carl* La Fong?" For the first time in the conversation, Fred Kimbal showed definite interest. He wriggled out from under the covers and sat up, rubbing his left eye vigorously.

Wesley cringed. "Why? Do you know another batch of La Fongs in the next dorm? Of course Carl, the guy who runs the big poker game every term break." Wesley rolled his eyes. "It's a gift, Fred."

Fred blinked, trying to bring his left eye back into focus. "He's not all that bright, is he?"

"Yeah, well, he may not be able to solve partial differential equations in his head, Fred, but he's a god, as far as the CO is concerned. Even Captain Wolfe leaves him alone. Have you noticed there's not much relation between math ability and success at the Academy? This is Starfleet, Fred, not a technical college."

Fred put up his hands in surrender. "All right. Don't bite my head off."

Wesley gravitated to the shelf and began poking at the new device. *I'm going to have to use a logic board on this thing to even figure out the gateways.*

Wes continued his lecture. "La Fong is exactly the kind of guy they like to see here. Everybody trusts him—he's like Locarno, but he started a year after I did. Now we're the same class, and even though I've been here for a year longer, he's the odds-on favorite to be class leader at graduation."

"Yeah, but you had that little problem earlier."

"Thank you, Fred. I'm sure I would have forgotten all about that if you hadn't reminded me." As soon as Wesley said it, he felt guilty. Fred looked away, embarrassed, his face paling slightly.

"Hey, I'm sorry, Fred. I didn't mean it like that. I know what you mean: If I hadn't been reprimanded and sent back, I'd be in contention for class leader. Tell the truth, at this point, I really could not care less . . . I've been treated like a prisoner here for the last three years, and I'm sick of it.

"All right, it was a terrible mistake! But it was *one mistake.* You know, I would never say this to anyone else, but if Joshua Albert hadn't panicked, he'd still have had time to punch out."

Wesley stepped away from the shelf, angry . . . mostly at himself for being angry. What right did Wesley Crusher have to object to anyone reminding him of what he did? He *did* inadvertently kill his wingmate.

His throat and stomach hurt suddenly, as if he had eaten a *habanero* pepper straight.

Fred shrugged. "Wes, nobody else will say it either—not publicly. But everybody knows it. It wasn't your fault."

"They *act* like it was my fault! Do you know it was a solid year before anyone would work with me, ride with me, talk with me, or even stand next to me?" Wesley felt himself losing control, as he had more and more lately. He stopped himself, took a deep breath. When he let it out, he still felt cold fury, but he knew he would not have another outburst.

The room was too dark. It was too hot. Fred should have gotten up two hours before, and Wesley had no right telling anybody else when to get up from bed. Using his foot, Cadet Crusher nudged Fred's clutter even farther west, aiming to get some of it under Kimbal's rack.

"Sito died on her shakedown cruise."

"Yeah, I heard."

"I think she took that Cardassian mission because she knew it was almost the only way she could ever live down what happened here three years ago. You understand? The only way for her to live it down was to *die.*"

Fred opened his mouth, then closed it again. Whatever he was about to say, he had thought better of it.

Wesley smiled; a year ago, when they met, Fred would have simply blurted out the first thing that popped into his head. *Maybe we are ready for the next step in the socialization of Fred Kimbal. . . .*

"Look, Fred, this thing is going to haunt me the rest of my life; I accept that. Even if I ever leave Starfleet, I'll still know that a stupid decision I made cost a friend of mine his life. But La Fong is the only cadet here in the directory, the inner circle, who seems like he cares about me.

"Face it, the guy has really bent over backward to 'rehabilitate' me, so to speak, and I know he's taken a lot of phaser fire over it from the brass. Captain Wolfe practically ordered him to stay away from me, but La Fong stared him down and as much as dared Wolfe to make an issue out of it. La Fong's still here, so I guess Wolfe backed down."

Wesley sat on the bed, staring at the window. The weak morning light painted bright-gray streaks across the blackness of the venetian blinds. The dingy light was depressing; not until afternoon would the sun shine directly into the room. Wesley hoped it would shine upon an awake Fred Kimbal.

Crusher continued. "Now La Fong's invited me to the big, end-of-term, directory poker game. *Everyone* will be there! Nanci Lees, Cadet Axel, Cadet DuBois—that's Captain

DuBois's daughter—even Lieutenant Allende, who graduated two years ago and just got back from her first tour. She's friends with Lieutenant La Fong, La Fong's brother, who just rotated from the *Lexington* to the *Constellation*. Some rich Ferengi kid studying economics over at Keynes; the son of Ambassador Daxal from Betazed . . ."

"They let a *telepath* play poker?" Kimbal groped for the touchplate to open the blinds, but failed to find it by blind touch.

"Hm. The way he loses, everybody knows he's honest enough not to use his advantage. Or that's what La Fong says. Anyway, the point is it's a great honor to be invited . . . and damn it, I'm going to go and *not* make an ass of myself if it kills me. And I'll make sure I don't win too much, too. If I lose a lot, that's okay; but if I'm winning, I'll start throwing hands."

Wesley crossed the room to his own bed. He lay back, hands behind his head. "I can't believe I really said that. It's the truth, though."

Kimbal finally found the touch plate. He pressed it, letting in the morning light, such as it was.

"Wouldn't that count as cheating?" Fred smirked. "As in, 'I will not lie, cheat, or steal, nor tolerate those among us who do'?"

"Sometimes I feel like the directory has its own version: I will not lie, cheat, or steal, except to advance my career or pump up the ego of some aging admiral. No, that's not fair; they don't really ask anyone to lie. It's more like the occasional 'judicious silence' when some commissioned officer is acting like an ass."

"Um, Wes? Buddy, pal?" Fred hesitated, not used to thinking in terms of politicking. He licked his lips and continued. "You're going to think I'm mental, after everything I said about the stupidity of gambling. But do you think there's the slightest chance that I might be able to come along? I'd be willing to just watch if they won't let me play."

"I already got you a slot, Fred."

"I didn't think so. All right, it was worth asking. Thanks anyway."

Wesley turned his head, waiting for the token to drop. *One hippopotamus, two hippopotamus, three hippopotamus, four hippopotamus, five hip—*

"What did you say?" Fred sat bolt upright, dropping the blankets and staring at his roommate.

"I said I got you a slot. When La Fong first mentioned it to me, I didn't say anything about you. I'm sorry, I didn't want to jeopardize my chances because of guilt by association. You're not exactly the most socialized cadet in the Academy, Fred."

"Well, I'm better than I used to be," he said defensively.

"True. I thought of that. I also thought about what it felt like to always be the one they *don't* invite to the big poker game. So I raised the point with La Fong and managed to talk him into including you in the invitation . . . but I had to promise you would be on good behavior, which in your case means on your best behavior. You can manage, can't you?"

Fred raised his left hand and put his right across his heart. "I won't be a weasel, Wes."

"No inappropriate laughter? No stupid jokes? No trying to look down Nanci's shirt?"

"What if she doesn't catch me looking down her shirt?"

"Don't do it at all!"

"I swear," said Fred, nodding solemnly.

"I don't want you eating anything. You get crumbs all over yourself and greasy fingers. You'll mess up the cards."

"Nothing?"

Wesley frowned, considering. He stroked his chin, then stopped when he realized it was an unconscious imitation of Commander Riker stroking his beard.

"All right," he said, "you can eat a little; but use a fork, not your hands."

"Even for pretzels?"

"Stay away from the pretzels! You can't handle them. How good are you at poker?"

Fred grinned. "I'm perfect! I know the exact odds of every possible hand, with every possible variation."

"Draw? Stud? High-low?"

Fred nodded vigorously. "I know exactly which cards to throw and how much a hand is worth."

"Suppose I dealt you four jacks."

Fred's face lit up like a light panel; his eyes grew as big as saucers.

Wesley frowned. "That's just what I was afraid of. Have you ever met a Vulcan?"

"Once, I think."

"Think Vulcan. Think utter rationality and no emotion. *Be* a Vulcan. Fred, you can't show even the slightest hint of your hand or they'll eat you for lunch in there. I've seen the best: Commander Riker on the *Enterprise*. He could pick up a straight flush in one hand and straight trash in the next, and you'd never be able to tell the difference from looking at him. It's not just a game of making the best hand and placing bets; it's a psychological game. Riker says he can tell a person's officer potential just by playing poker with him one night."

Fred grimaced. "Uh-oh."

"'Uh-oh' is right. Here, try this: When you're not under the phaser banks—that means first to bet—watch the other players while they look at their hands and make their bets. Try to figure out what they have before you even pick up your own hand to look at it."

"Okay, Wes. I won't embarrass you."

"And don't be afraid to take a break if you're porting out. These games go on for hours."

"How much should I bring?"

Wesley blinked. He suddenly realized he had forgotten to ask La Fong that very question. "I don't know. I should have asked. How much do you have?"

"I already paid next term's dorm fees and food; we get

paid again about a month before graduation. I guess I could afford to lose a bar of latinum, or maybe two."

"A bar! Well, that's more than I'm taking. If the game is *that* hot, it's out of my price range anyway, Fred."

"Just don't lose; then it doesn't matter how hot the game is."

Wesley stood and folded his arms again, trying to look stern. "Bad attitude, Kimbal. Are you sure you can afford to lose two bars of latinum?"

"What else have I got to spend it on? Dancing girls? Dinner at the Captain's Log?"

"Okay, Fred. Get lots of sleep tonight, for tomorrow, we die."

Wesley need not have worried. Within five minutes, deep snores emanated from beneath the pile of bedclothes across the room. Fred was out like a discharged nacelle.

Instead, it was Wesley Crusher who could not sleep. He lay on his own, immaculate bed, which he carefully made each morning out of habit from many years on the *Enterprise* (under his mother's critical gaze: Starfleet tautness *and* hospital corners—the worst of both worlds).

Despite all his brave advice to Fred, Wesley was, in fact, terrified of making the Big Mistake that would confirm what everyone knew all along: He simply did not fit. No matter what he did, he would never quite make it into the inner circle, the directory, the invisible hand of Starfleet.

I'm just not career material, he thought miserably.

Beverly Crusher, his mother, would have vigorously denied the charge; but she did not quite fit, either. It was different as a doctor: When a person saved lives and made patients well, nobody really cared whether she was "in" or "out." A doctor could get away with being anything, even a slovenly, underdeveloped misanthrope, like Fred . . . so long as she or he brought people back from the afterlife.

God, I wish I were more like Dad. Wesley's father had been the perfect insider; had he not died, he would surely command his own vessel by now. He was . . . he was Will Riker.

Wesley scrunched up his face. Was Riker his surrogate father? It was a disconcerting thought. Certainly his father was not at all like Picard . . . unless it was Picard thirty years before Wes had ever met the captain. Today, Picard was too restrained, too serene. Somehow, Wesley could not imagine his father—or Will Riker, for that matter—ever saying "make it so."

Too many thoughts swirled around Wesley's head. Aware that he was violating the advice he had just given Fred, he rose from the bed and padded over to Fred's workbench, stepping carefully in the dark to avoid treading either on something sharp or something squishable.

Faint starlight filtered through the tightly packed rabbit warrens of Garth Dormitory. Directly opposite Wesley and Fred's room was the ancient brick wall of Ionesco Dorm; but between the two buildings, when Wesley craned his neck at just the right angle, he could see a small piece of the sky with Ursa Major.

Gleaming in the faint light, as if lit by an inner glow, was Fred Kimbal's newest invention. *I don't know what it does . . . if you want to finish it off, it's yours.*

At this point in its birth, the toy was nothing more than a collection of one main processor and two satellites, a dozen data clips, enough fiberoptic cables to connect everything to everything else (twice), and even a pair of copper wires . . . though what Fred needed the last for, Wesley could not imagine, unless the genius simply ran out of cable.

Wesley gingerly scooped up the collection of junk and moved it to his own bed. He could not work in the unrestrained clutter of Kimbal's side of the white line; Wesley constantly had the feeling that the mess was creeping up on him when he was not looking.

He set a directional lamp to shine onto the invention, making sure his own body was between it and Fred, to minimize the chance of high-intensity light reflecting into Fred's eyes and waking him . . . as if anything could stir the third-year cadet once he had stumbled into the land of Nod. Wesley attached an engineering tricorder to his full-size monitor and drew out a pair of leads. Systematically touching the tricorder leads to paired cable junctures, he began mapping the logical pathways of the main processor.

Four hours later, Wesley still mapped, sleep long forgotten. He worked with feverish intensity—he was still unsure exactly what Kimbal's device did; but whatever it was, it was the most astonishing thing the boy had developed in a year of astonishing developments.

Fred had obviously ripped the two satellites from replicators (Wesley did *not* want to know from where!), but the main unit was custom-built, negotiating between the other two. The data clips simply stored data bases that represented the Dirac numbers of the chaseum crystals, their "quantum state."

With everything that Wesley now knew about the toy, however, he still had not the faintest idea what it did . . . except it rearranged the surface crystals (and some of the interior structures) in a complicated, devious dance.

Sometimes, Wesley would have to give up in frustration trying to understand or complete one of Fred's "puzzles," as he came to think of them. The basic principles may have been as clear as the skies of Trillby 13 to Fred Kimbal, but they were clear as mud to Wesley Crusher.

This time, however, completion of the logic circuits and final assembly were obvious, so clear they might even have been obvious to Carl La Fong.

Without a second thought, the young cadet popped open his personal computer (a present from his mother) and stripped it of fibers and a few more processors. He wrote a short sequence of routing instructions in the processors, then connected them into the growing octopus on his bed.

The disorder offended him. Without looking, he plucked an old chronometer off his wall and plopped it down on the bed next to the mess of clips and cabling. He eyeballed them both and decided the clock case was large enough. Wesley opened the clock, scooped out its guts and tossed them into a drawer, then carefully arranged the device into the now empty case, tacking everything down with adhesion clamps.

28

When he finished, he had a pie-plate-size oblate spheroid with a knob sticking out.

"Okay, Kimbal, let's see what you've gone and done." Wesley opened the plastiglass face and deposited a commemorative medal inside. The medal was made of chaseum, replicated in honor of the twenty-fifth anniversary of the development of the highly useful metal. He twisted the knob that once had been used to set the hologrammatic clock hands.

The medal rippled as if made of melted butter swirling in a pan. The bottom of the "pie plate" rapidly grew too hot to touch, and Wesley dropped it onto his bed with a stifled yelp. The plastiglass face cracked loudly, but Fred did not stir.

Wesley gently touched the erstwhile clock; it had cooled considerably. He opened the face again.

The chaseum now sparkled with a different, distinctly yellowish hue. Wesley Crusher stared. The medallion had turned into *gold-pressed latinum*.

Chapter Four

"LAY IN A COURSE for Novus Alamogordus," said Commander Riker. Zorka had been granted half a planetoid for his laboratory; many of the items he had been developing—*allegedly developing,* corrected Riker to himself, recalling Geordi La Forge's skepticism—could be extremely dangerous over a very wide area if experiments went awry. Curiously, the opposite side of the planetoid, separated by a midsize ocean, contained a ritzy hotel and casino.

"Sir," said Commander Data, "that course will take us out of Federation space."

A silly ritual, thought Riker. He certainly knew Novus Alamogordus was in neutral space; Data knew it; probably everybody on the bridge knew it. Captain Picard knew it, but he was in his cabin, studying the specifications of Zorka's (alleged) inventions. Still, the Federation Space Training and Operating Procedures Standardization manual obliged pilot and acting commander to speak the ritual aloud. Thus, both officers were clearly identified as responsible parties if the *Enterprise* were destroyed outside Federation territory.

"Advisement acknowledged," said Riker, completing the magical formula.

"Course laid in, sir," said Data.

"Engage, warp factor . . ." Riker paused, scrolling through the mission profile sent from Starfleet by subspace communications.

Commander Will Riker was silent a long time.

Data turned to face him, raising his brows quizzically. "Sir? What warp factor do you wish?"

Riker shook his head. *It must be in here somewhere— must be!* No matter how many times he scrolled back and forth, however, he could not find the authorization to exceed warp five, the maximum allowable warp under General Warp Speed Limitation Standing Order Number 44556–34.

Riker searched on the keywords *warp, speed,* the number 5, and 44556–34.

"Commander Riker?" asked Data.

"Stand by," said Riker. "Computer: Search the most recent subspace transmission from mission command. Do we have authorization to exceed warp five?"

"Negative," responded the computer voice immediately.

"Damn it," muttered the first officer, folding his arms and tilting his head back in annoyance. "How are we supposed to get to the auction if we can't exceed warp five?"

Silence. Riker tilted his head forward again, opened his eyes. "How the hell are we supposed to get there on time at warp five?"

Data continued to watch the commander placidly.

Annoyed, Riker snapped, "That was not a rhetorical question, Data!"

"It was not? I am sorry, sir; I assumed it was another one of those questions I am not supposed to answer." Data furrowed his brow, the positronic pathways in his "brain" firing in all directions at once. "At the maximum warp allowed by the general standing order, we shall arrive at the auction on Novus Alamogordus in approximately six days, thirteen hours. The auction is not set to begin until three days from now; it is possible it will still be in progress when we arrive, sir."

"It will have been going on for three and a half days. Will anything be left but the desks and chairs?"

"I do not know, sir. Possibly Bradford junior will auction the chairs first, leaving the important lots until the end. In that case, we might still be in time to bid on the photonic pulse cannon and other vital technologies."

Riker stroked his beard. "This is ridiculous. Didn't the Federation Council say this auction was of the highest priority? Surely that implies we should proceed with all deliberate speed!"

"I cannot advise that line of reasoning, sir. Our orders come from Starfleet, not the Federation Council; they are not in the chain of command. The council must advise Starfleet Command of the urgent necessity of violating the general standing order, and Starfleet must convey permission to us. In my official opinion, sir, we cannot simply take it upon ourselves to second-guess Starfleet's motives in not including such permission in the subspace transmission."

"You're saying our ass will be hanging over the line if we just assume that permission."

"I would not have used such a colorful expression; but you are essentially correct, sir."

"Send a subspace transmission to Starfleet, Data. Wake them up down there. I want that permission! In the meantime, engage preset course, warp factor five." Riker shook his head; he never ceased to be amazed at the boneheaded lapses of bureaucracy.

"Riker to Picard."

"Picard here," said the captain's disembodied voice. "What is it, Number One?"

"Sir, we have a very delicate question."

"Come to my quarters, Will. We'll discuss it here."

Will Riker sat across from Captain Picard while the latter pondered the implications, frowning. After a long silence, during which Riker refrained from interrupting with more arguments for simply ignoring the prohibition, Jean-Luc Picard finally spoke.

"Will, try as I might, I can find no reasonable argument around Data's point. We must presume that if Starfleet wanted us to exceed warp five, they would have included permission."

"They probably forgot."

"Possibly. But we cannot presume that."

"At this speed, there is an excellent chance we won't arrive at the auction until the important lots are sold."

Picard grimaced. "I know that, Will. And I agree with you that this situation merits an exception to the general standing order. It's absolutely critical to Federation peace efforts that the Cardassians—or worse, the Romulans—not get their hands on the sort of weapon described here . . . presuming it works, of course. This may well be the most important mission underway by any vessel at the moment."

"Then surely it's worth a little risk."

"Exceeding the maximum safe warp speed is hardly a little risk, Number One. You saw what happened in that subspace corridor; imagine if the mainstream of Federation space began to erupt into subspace singularities . . . we might have to give up the entire alliance."

"It's just one case!"

"Every case is 'just one case,' Number One. But I agree . . . this time, I think it's worth the risk."

Riker opened his mouth, but Picard continued. "However, Will, it is not our decision to make. Only Starfleet Command can authorize an exception to a general standing order." He smiled ruefully, picking up a data clip and rolling it before his eyes. "Let's wait until we hear back. I'm sure they'll tell us it was just a mistake and authorize maximum warp. If even a tenth of these inventions actually work, then Novus Alamogordus may turn out to be a latinum mine of scientific advances for us . . . or for whoever outbids the other interested parties."

Picard's annunciator chirped.

"Come," said the captain. The door slid open and Commander Data entered.

"Sir, we have received a response from Starfleet regarding our request to exceed warp five." The android hesitated for a moment, then plunged on. "I am afraid permission is temporarily stayed, sir."

"Stayed?" exclaimed Riker, incredulous. "You mean *denied?*"

"Starfleet says it is only a temporary stay. They say they will give us a final answer within twenty-four hours."

"Data," said Picard, "did they say what the problem was?"

Data nodded. "According to Captain Blut, Admiral Vernor's aide, the Federation Association for the Advancement of Science is not speaking to the Federation Exo-Vironmental Research Council. The latter was formed specifically to study the effects of warp-field operations, and apparently this decision was unpopular among the scientists of the FAAS. They felt their own subcommittee which is studying the effect should have been given policy responsibility. Instead, they were made advisory only, and the FEVRC has complete control of Federation policy-making."

Picard and Riker looked at each other, then back at Data. The first officer spoke first. "A turf war? We're going to miss the auction because of a stupid turf war between different groups of scientists?"

Data nodded. "That is the gist, sir. The FAAS understands the immense implications of this auction to peace throughout the quadrant, but they have no power to grant an exception to the general standing order; they also refuse to communicate with the FEVRC . . . who have the power to authorize high warp speed but know nothing about the importance of the auction."

"Data," said Picard, "send an emergency subspace transmission to the Exo-Vironmental Council apprising them of the urgency of this auction. Include a copy of the FAAS

analysis of the strategic importance of the Novus Alamogordus development center."

"Aye, sir," said the android.

"Dismissed." Data went off to send the message.

For a long moment, neither captain nor first officer said a
word. Then suddenly, both spoke at once.

"Geordi!" said Riker.

"La Forge," remembered Captain Picard.

"I'll contact him immediately, Captain. The Klingons
have agreed in theory to the warp speed limitation, but they
routinely violate it. I'm certain that Kurn will interpret his
orders literally and run for Novus Alamogordus at the
scoutship's top speed, which is . . ." Riker thought for a
moment. "Warp eight point three, I believe."

"Picard to Data."

"Data here, sir."

"Assume Captain Kurn heads for the auction at the
maximum speed of his vessel. When will he arrive?"

After a moment, Data responded. "I calculate he will
arrive on Novus Alamogordus nearly four hours before the
auction is scheduled to begin."

"Perfect," said Riker, rising. "I'll get Geordi on subspace
immediately."

Picard smiled. "Assuming Kurn has fixed those 'faulty
circuits' by now. Make it so."

Moments later, the first officer stood on the bridge,
talking to the image of Worf and Geordi in their "cabin," a
tiny room just two decks up from the engineering department.

"You want me to *what?*" asked Lieutenant Commander
Geordi La Forge.

"You heard me, Commander."

"Yes, sir, but I don't think Kurn is going to allow us to talk
as long as last time. He's still pretty grumpy about being
unable to decrypt the transmission."

"We might not be able to arrive in time for the auction."

"Sir? At warp nine, you should arrive at—"

"We can't *go* warp nine." Tersely, Riker explained the entire situation to Geordi.

Geordi stared at Commander Riker. "You can't be serious. Me? Bid on a bunch of Doctor Zorka's fictitious inventions?"

"Geordi, that was not a request." Riker held his breath; Geordi could respond one of two ways.

"You're kidding!"

"It wasn't a joke, either. I am serious—you're going to arrive three days before we do. You're the senior officer; you get to bid on the photonic pulse device and anything else of note."

Geordi pursed his lips. "I'm sorry, sir," he said at last, "but I can't do that."

"What do you mean, you can't do that? This is a direct order!"

"All right; then I'll have to bid what I think the toys are worth: nothing."

Will Riker clamped his mouth shut. He silently counted to eight before calming himself enough to respond. "Mister La Forge, you *will* bid on Zorka's experimental devices, and you *will* bid seriously enough to buy them. We cannot allow a photonic pulse cannon to fall into the wrong hands— which means anybody's hands but ours!"

Geordi slowly shook his head. "I'm sorry, sir. I took my oath to the Federation and Starfleet, not to any one person in particular; I have to support and defend the protocols of the alliance . . . which means in this case I must bid what my best engineering opinion tells me these items are worth: exactly zero. Bidding anything higher than nothing would violate my oath as an officer of Starfleet."

Riker stared, lip curling. *If Deanna were here,* he thought, *she would have said* I sense anger. . . .

"Very well, Lieutenant Commander. You must bid as you see fit. Riker out." Without further ado, he severed the connection.

Lieutenant Commander Geordi La Forge began to respond, "Aye, sir," but realized he was speaking to the

Starfleet logo; Commander Riker had faded into sudden existentialism with an irritated flick of his finger.

"La Forge out," finished Geordi lamely, gently clicking off the monitor.

Ooh, boy, he thought, *there goes any chance at my own command this millenium!* Still shaking, but subsumed by an overpowering sense of righteousness, Geordi turned to his Klingon companion.

"Now what, Worf?" he asked.

"I cannot advise you, sir. You must bid what you think the equipment is worth."

"Yeah. Easy for you to say . . . you don't have to face Riker when this thing is over and we end up with a fat lot of nothing."

"But if your assessment is correct, and the experimental designs are actually worth nothing—"

"But how can I ever convince the commander of that? For that matter, how am I going to convince Starfleet? If the Cardassians waltz away with the photonic pulse cannon, do you think they're going to admit to us that it's a piece of junk? Worf, I'll *never* be able to prove to anybody that I was right!"

Worf frowned. "Commander, you must perform your duty as best you know how. If you are unfairly blamed for a bad situation, you will still know in your heart that you served your command with efficiency and distinction.

"If a Klingon warrior is given an impossible task, he does not complain about things he cannot change."

"Yes, yes, I know that . . . but can't you think of any way I can perform my duty without ending up busing tables in Ten-Forward for the rest of the cruise?"

Just as Worf opened his mouth to respond, the harsh clang of the ship's intercom shattered their thoughts.

"Lieutenant Worf will report to the bridge immediately," snapped the curt voice of Commander Kurak.

Worf closed his mouth, put on the official Klingon warrior's scowl, and departed smartly, leaving Geordi La Forge alone to brood.

Lieutenant Worf marched stolidly onto the bridge of the *tlhIngan bIQDepHey Huj So'bogh naghmey 'ej veS ga''a' jaghpu' ghogbogh 'oH.* "Lieutenant Worf, United Federation of Planets," he announced formally.

Kurn sat on his command chair in the posture of the hu-man statue *The Thinker,* leaning forward to rest his chin on one balled fist, elbow on knee.

Worf waited but received no response; when he decided that his younger brother had exceeded allowable familial rudeness, he shifted to Klingon.

"Must I call the Emperor Kahless himself to announce me?" he asked; it was quite a snotty Klingon insult, since of course seniors did not "announce" juniors.

The effect on Kurn was startling. He leapt to his feet, staring wildly at his brother. "How did you know about that? You were *spying* on me!"

"Know about what? What are you talking about, you theoretician?"

Kurn bristled at the new insult; but it was within limits allowed by their close relationship. Kurn sneered, said, "I am too busy doing warrior's work to explain horticulture to a nonreproducing minor." He gestured at the commander. "My female assistant will instruct you."

The frighteningly enticing political officer explained. "The Klingon High Council has decided that Lieutenant Worf will represent the Klingon Empire at the auction, bidding on all military equipment and all scientific equipment of value."

Worf's eyes widened; but true to his heritage (and mindful what he had just said to Commander La Forge), he did not complain or object. Stoic as the warrior he was, he bowed his head. "I accept the great honor which the Emperor Kahless has bestowed upon me through the High Council, and I will faithfully represent the empire at the auction."

Worf snuck a glance at his brother; Kurn had resumed his statuesque pose, obviously hurt and offended that the Council selected Worf rather than Kurn—a Klingon who had joined the human Federation over a Klingon who had faithfully risen through the ranks of the Klingon fleet itself. Kurn ignored the fact, or deemed it irrelevant, that Worf was the elder brother, and as such (since the restoration of his family's honor) was obliged to represent his family at all formal occasions.

After a few moments, Worf diplomatically withdrew, not even offering a parting shot. He decided that in Kurn's present mood, he might forget family obligation entirely and announce his brother to the airlock.

Back in their temporary "quarters," Worf and the engineering officer stared glumly at each other. "So, Worf . . . what are you going to bid on the devices as they come up?"

"I shall observe the actions of the other participants and make my bid accordingly."

"On the theory that if the Cardassians and Romulans throw latinum down a rat hole, it would be undiplomatic for the Klingons not to follow suit?"

Worf rolled his eyes.

"Take my word for it," continued Geordi, "not a single thing that Doctor Zorka ever built, if he even built any of it and didn't just make it up, is even worth the time spent reading about it in the journals, let alone hard latinum. I'd rather spend my time reading about real research, not bidding on vaporware!"

"I am well aware of your opinions of Zorka's work, Commander. But I must make my own decision."

"All right! Don't get touchy. I was just offering a suggestion."

"Thank you, sir. Now may I please get some sleep? It is a long trip to Novus Alamogordus, even at warp eight."

Geordi lay on the upper bunk. "Lights," he said.

Nothing happened. For a moment, he was confused; then he remembered where he was. Before he could rise, however, Worf's enormous hand reached up from the lower bunk and pressed the touchplate, casting the room into blackness.

After a moment, La Forge changed the subject. "I, uh, guess I should tell you what happened in Kurak's room."

"I have no wish to pry into your private affairs, sir."

"Affairs! I only wish."

"Commander, I do not wish to intrude on your privacy." The Klingon could not quite keep a slight tone of curiosity out of his voice, though he never would have expressed it in words. Geordi took it as an invitation to continue.

"You remember she said she wanted to show me a holomorphic model?"

"Of an antique warp coil. Yes, I remember."

"Well, she did. Showed me her model."

Worf said nothing.

"And that's it!" continued the lieutenant commander. "She showed me her model. It wasn't even that good."

Geordi heard a strange, rumbling cough from the lower bunk. "Commander Kurak may have too sharp a blade for you, sir."

"Too sharp a blade? You mean she's not really interested?"

"Perhaps, perhaps not. Now, please, may I sleep, sir? We have much to do tomorrow."

After a moment, Geordi began to chuckle. He continued to chuckle quietly for several minutes; then he suddenly became aware of a monstrous figure looming over him, deeper black against the faint light of the luminescent chronometer face.

It was Worf, rising up over Geordi's rack.

"Oops," said La Forge, "didn't mean to wake you."

"Will there be anything else, sir?" Worf's voice had more of a Klingon edge than usual.

"Heh. I was just thinking about Commander Riker, sitting in the command chair and positively fuming about that damned speed limit."

"I fail to see the humor. He is just following orders."

"Yeah . . . but I'll bet he's so hot under the collar that he's creating warp field vortexes all by himself!"

After a moment, Worf snorted. Then he climbed back into his bunk and began to snore, rasping like an old-fashioned, ion-drive engine.

Chapter Five

WESLEY CRUSHER BLINKED to conscious awareness, realizing that the dorm room had suddenly become as bright as the interior of a nova.

He sat up groggily. Fred Kimbal stood before the east-facing window, having just defiltered it to allow the brilliant sunrise to enter.

Wesley rolled over and stared at an empty spot on his wall. Somebody had stolen his clock! Abruptly, the events of the previous night flooded back.

"What time is it, Fred?" he asked, voice thick with the drunken slur of sleep deprivation.

"Zero six thirty," answered Kimbal, sickeningly chipper and bright. "Come on, Wes, daylight's a burnin'!"

"No classes. No PT. Break. Remember?"

"Come on, sir. Rise and shine!"

Wesley glared balefully. "If you say up and at 'em, I'll bend your nose back."

"Hey! What happened to my toy? I was going to show it to you. Did you find it last night?"

Wesley rubbed his face, waking fully. "Fred, we've got to

41

talk. I started fooling with your invention last night, and I kind of got caught up in the excitement. I, um, I finished it. It's in this clock case, here."

"Already? What does it do?"

"How can you not know?"

Kimbal shrugged. "I spent a few days mapping properties and matching them between latinum and chaseum. I tied a couple of replicator processors together to morph from one to the other, just to slide the Balmer lines back and forth. I wanted to see if the ratios were really the same, or if there were some subtle differences that threw everything off. Why, what does the thing do?"

Wordlessly, Wesley slid the commemorative medallion, now seemingly made of latinum, from his bedside table and tossed it to Kimbal.

"Heavy," Fred agreed. "Is this part of your stake for the big game?"

"Look closely at it, Fred."

Fred glanced, then studied, then stared, eyes widening as big as millstones. "Jesus!" he yelped, "you've turned it into latinum!"

"No, *you've* turned it into latinum. And not really; in theory, it's still chaseum, though I'm damned if I can spot any deviation from latinum, even scanning with the tricorder. It just looks and senses like gold-pressed latinum."

"So what do we do with it?"

"I've got a good idea. Let's bury it, and I mean literally, Fred. Phaser it out of existence. Things like this are too dangerous for young boys like us."

Kimbal looked up speculatively at Wesley. "You don't suppose we might, you know, test it a bit first? I know a really sleazy joint on Moneyshine Lane in the Ferengi Quarter that has the most gorgeous . . ."

The look in Wesley's eye shut Kimbal's mouth.

"Um, I guess not, Wes."

"See? I told you this thing was dangerous. But I don't

know if I can zap it into limbo either, at least not until we test the limits of the envelope. How long does the chaseum stay altered? Does it change the specific gravity to match latinum?"

"It should; I vaguely remember playing with molecular separation in the crystals . . . density, you know."

"This is really amazing, Fred. You know with this, a person—a criminally minded kind of guy—could become as rich as the Trump family."

"Wasn't he the one who turned everything he touched into latinum?"

"I think so. And basically, that's what we've got here. Fred, don't you understand? We can replicate any amount of chaseum and turn it all into the finest ersatz latinum ever counterfeited! I shudder to think what might happen if this were to fall into . . ."

"What?"

Wesley shook his head, annoyed with his flight of fancy. "Skip it. Let's just test it out then take it apart."

"Actually, we can't."

"Can't what?"

"Replicate any amount of chaseum we want. Or any amount at all, actually."

"Why not?"

Fred grinned, pointed at the clock device. "Because there sit the guts of the only two replicators in this entire dorm." He laughed. "I borrowed them last night after chow."

Wesley stared. "You didn't. You *did!*" Wesley grimaced, put his head in his hands. "Fred, did it ever occur to you that thirty-eight hungry cadets are going to stagger out of their dorm rooms over to the replimats, desperate for a cup of coffee? Then thirty-eight bleary-eyed cadets will discover that the replicators are worthless hunks of junk . . . and they'll remember this peculiar, little habit of yours of borrowing electronics—"

Somebody began pounding furiously on the door. Jenny DuBois's normally dulcet voice rattled their windows.

"Kimbal, you little traitor, open this door! Gimme my coffee, you sneak thief!"

Frightened, Fred looked imploringly at Wesley.

"Don't expect *me* to get that, Kimbal. I'm going back to sleep." Wesley lay back in bed and pulled the pillow over his face. "Wake me when it's over," he mumbled faintly, as Fred lurched toward the door to try to placate DuBois.

That night, Wesley insisted that Fred eat dinner, so he would not be distracted by hunger during the big game, but eat lightly, so he would not fall asleep. Wesley fretted over Fred's clothing, his hair, his mannerisms. Wesley well remembered when he had first arrived at the Academy (after finally passing the entrance exams). He had been pretty much of a geek himself, having grown up on the *Enterprise* with hardly anyone his own age to talk to and no access to popular culture.

For many long years, Wesley studied the phenomenon of "pull," slowly learning what to say, and more important, what *not* to say. Most of his acquaintances would have agreed he was a thousand times more officerlike than when he blew onto campus.

The terrible accident at the end of his first year, however, killed any idea of Wesley ever being considered part of the elite. The best he could ever achieve was to be tolerated, and that was all Wes expected for Fred: So long as Fred did not embarrass him, Wesley would be satisfied.

Somehow, Carl La Fong had arranged official private transportation from the dorms to an eight-room apartment in the surrounding town. The two new kids were impressed. Poker, like all gambling, was officially forbidden to cadets (unless they played "for fun," not for money; and "playing for fun is no fun," as La Fong often remarked).

La Fong had a lot of pull, however. Campus security, normally quite industrious in ensuring that all cadets obeyed the curfew, even during break, were strangely lax with those invited to the big game. Wes and Fred were stopped just outside Garth Dorms; they said they were going "for a walk," and as soon as the security guard saw their name badges, she let them pass unhindered.

The apartment was owned by Tunk, the Ferengi player—or rather, by his father, Munk. Munk apparently had no official position with the Ferengi government; he was on the outs with the Grand Nagus. He had enormous power in the real world, however: according to Pindog, the Ferengi barber who cut Fred's hair, Munk was as close to an "outlaw" as any Ferengi with latinum could be. There were dark stories about murders, smuggling of contraband, secret deals with Cardassia and Romulus, armed robberies, protection rackets, and some devious schemes that even Pindog was unwilling to discuss.

When Munk decided to make another Ferengi an offer for some choice item or service, it would be considered extremely unhealthy to refuse.

When the previous Grand Nagus had died, Munk might have been able to seize the position; however, he could not stomach the cut in income, and the position instead went to Zek, the current officeholder. The two had been locked in a childish feud ever since.

Tunk, Munk's son, was studying human economics at Keynes College, and he offered his apartment for the big game every term. He also liked using his own deck of cards.

Wesley felt distinctly uneasy; but backing out now would be a deathblow to his attempts to inculturate himself and would probably result in a severe blow to his student ranked "leadership" grade. He resolved to be Cadet Conservative in his betting, however.

Fred zoned out whenever they gathered information on the other players, worrying Wesley. It was almost as if Fred rebelled at the perceived necessity of engaging in such logically flawed behavior as gambling on cards, and his rebellion took the form of refusing to pay any attention or prepare himself mentally for the night.

When their cab finally landed on Tunk's roof, Fred almost forgot to greet the beautiful Caraq hatcheck girl who answered the door and took their caps and coats—in fact, he could barely take his eyes off her. Though not a Ferengi, she was "dressed" the way a Ferengi likes to see women dressed . . . stark naked.

With supreme willpower, Wesley forced himself to continue on past her into the living room, where five large card tables had been placed. Obvious bodyguards roamed the room, scrutinizing the guests and making no effort to hide the fact that they were counting the silverware and knick-knacks. A butler or valet silently ghosted around the room, taking drink orders and bringing other refreshments as necessary.

Tunk's gigantic apartment was stuffed to the gills with all varieties of knickknacks; they vied with each other to be the most offensive, the poorest taste, the most vulgar. A jeweled fan dangled from the ceiling, and tinsel-bead curtains sectioned off rooms. The coffee table in the sunken living room was shaped like a kidney bean, and it sported a fabulous collection of grotesquely rude toys, including a wizened old Ferengi wearing a barrel: when the unsuspecting guest lifted the barrel, he got an eye full of water from the old Ferengi's . . .

Wesley shuddered and wiped his eye.

The female guests were all clothed, of course; and if there were any Ferengi females, they were kept carefully hidden in other rooms. On the one hand, Wesley was disappointed that he could not stay upstairs by the Caraq greeter; but he also realized it would be impossible for him to keep his mind on the cards with such distractions.

Rounding a corner, having abandoned Fred by the punch bowl (was that really alcoholic rum in the punch, or just the synthehol version?), Wesley bumped into Ensign Nanci Lees, a senior about to begin her second training tour who would almost certainly end up the valedictorian at graduation, as La Fong would be class leader. As usual, when not in uniform, she wore a tight outfit that had barely more material than the greeting girl wore, except for the flowing, ephemeral cape behind her. She grew up on an earth colony where the ambient temperature ranged around a mean of forty-six degrees Celsius: any clothes at all were a concession, as far as Nanci was concerned.

"Wes, I didn't know you were invited."

"Yes, sir. Last-minute invitation from La Fong. I brought a friend along; Carl said it was all right."

"Oh, I'm not upset; good to see you, kiddo. And don't call me 'sir' here; we're civilians until we're back in class, okay?"

"Sure, uh, Nanci."

"Nance."

"Nance. So how does seating work? There are five tables here, and I have no idea which one I'm sitting at."

Nanci smiled, winked. "If you're a newbie, you'll be sitting with Tunk. Here's a hint for starship loyalty: Bet what you can afford to lose when Tunk is dealing."

"Does he, um . . . ?"

"Let's say he's very, *very* lucky—when he deals."

"Let me introduce you to Fred, my dormmate. He's over by the . . . well, he *was* by the punch." Wesley stared about helplessly, worried about what Fred might have gotten into, aware that he was thinking of his twenty-one-year-old roommate like an overgrown puppy.

"What does he look like?" asked Nanci, staring off to Wesley's left.

"Oh, about one point eight meters, ninety-five or ninety-six kilos, black hair a little long in the back, wearing a maroon, triple-breasted shirt with . . ." Wesley paused; Nanci was already pointing in the direction she had been looking.

Turning his gaze thither, Wesley discovered Fred sitting on a long couch surrounded by four female cadets who were oohing and aahing as he explained about his new invention: the device that disguised chaseum as latinum.

Wesley rushed over, waving to attract Fred's attention.

"Hey, Wes! I was just explaining to these lovely, young officers how I—"

"Fred! Good to see you, pal! Come over here, I want to introduce you to someone."

"But I'm fine where I am with these three beautiful young off—"

Wesley darted his hand between the cadets, snagged Fred by his biceps, and bodily dragged him from the cozy little quadrangle. He pulled his slack-jawed friend into a quiet corner. "Cut it about the toy, Fred. I mean it."

"You think so?"

"You want to spend the next three weeks in a Federation interrogation center, explaining to the nice security officers why you built a latinum-forging device?"

Fred rolled his eyes disgustedly. "But I *didn't* build a latinum forger. At least, I had no intention of ever using it to . . . I mean, I know I could counterfeit latinum if I really wanted to, but why would I . . ." Fred petered out, pursing his lips.

"Ah, you see what I mean, pal. I'm sure you'd finally be able to explain it to them—eventually."

"All right, Wes. Your lead."

Suddenly, a heavy hand clamped across Wesley's shoulder. He jumped, fearing it was one of Tunk's bodyguards asking him to kindly leave the premises before the Federation Bureau of Investigation kicked the door down.

It was Tunk himself, and he had a death grip around the shoulders of both cadets. "Friends! My young friends! Come, sit, play! I insist you sit at my personal table . . . to refuse me would be quite rude, don't you agree?" The Ferengi grinned, his sharp, crooked teeth lending a faint air of menace to his otherwise innocuous words.

Tunk was surprisingly strong. He wheeled them around, maneuvering them expertly through the swarming mob, then plopped them down at a table at the edge of the room.

Taking their cue from their host, the rest of the mob began finding seats. The bodyguards stood near Tunk, gently steering away all but the most honored of the honored guests from the Ferengi's "personal table." La Fong ended up at

48

Tunk's table, along with Nanci Lees and a cadet that Wesley vaguely remembered from his military history class last term, Georges St. Jean.

The Betazoid was carefully seated all the way on the other side of the room, he noticed, despite La Fong's assurance that the man never used his telepathic powers and always lost. *Tunk's probably afraid the guy will spot his cheating,* thought Wesley.

Cadet Crusher tried to sit next to Fred, but a bodyguard clumsily got in his way, then stepped on his toe. By the time Wes finished hopping around and swearing softly, the only seat left was directly opposite Kimbal. Around the table clockwise were Tunk, Carl La Fong, Wesley, Nanci, Georges, and Fred Kimbal.

Tunk spread the deck. Each participant drew a card; Georges picked a king, so he started the deal.

While Georges shuffled, Tunk brought out the bank of professional-quality chips. The Ferengi slapped a full bar of latinum on the table and drew himself a huge pile of black, silver, and yellow chips. In turn, each participant bought his way into the game. Momentarily, Wesley thought of holding back some of his money, just in case the bank mysteriously disappeared at payout time; but then he realized that was silly. . . . La Fong would certainly not return to the game again and again if Tunk pulled such clumsy tricks.

Georges, who seemed to know what he was doing with the cards, laid them on the blue felt tabletop. Everyone stared at Fred, who simply played with his pile of chips.

Nanci reached across the table, picked up a green, card-shaped piece of plastic from in front of Fred, and cleared her throat loudly. When Kimbal looked up, she inserted the plastic into the deck around the middle, and Georges cut the cards there, careful not to show the bottom card.

Leaving the plastic cover over the bottom of the deck, he dealt out the cards until each person had five. "Five-card draw," he muttered, with a noticeable accent.

The game progressed mechanically for the next hour and

a half. After his initial *faux pas,* Fred found his groove, never forgetting to shuffle or messing up the cut. Wesley began to relax; at first, he had feared that Fred would pick something completely inane, such as five-card stud, deuces, treys, one-eyed jacks, and suicidal kings wild. However, Fred always announced the same game as the person two deals before his, and nobody seemed offended or annoyed.

Wesley was proud of his own performance. After innumerable hands of play, he was only down by a few grams . . . all lost while Tunk was the dealer. The Ferengi was extraordinarily lucky when he dealt, almost as if he knew everybody else's hand. Nobody said a word about it, of course; but Wesley noticed that nobody bet heavily at those times, either.

Nobody, that is, except Fred Kimbal. Wesley realized many hours into the game that Fred's finances had dwindled almost to zero. But then, a few minutes later, they were back up to where they had begun.

Wesley did a double take. He could not remember Fred winning any major hands in the interim . . . how had he suddenly gotten chips again?

On several more occasions, Wesley managed to miss some big upturn in Fred's finances, or at least the stack of chips before him. After the third time, Cadet Crusher finally caught the transaction: Tunk, the Ferengi, was actually *pushing* chips over to Fred.

Wesley stared, nonplussed. A Ferengi finance a losing session at the poker table? It was impossible. Sweating, Wesley suddenly understood: Fred had talked Tunk (or perhaps the other way around) into running him a tab.

Fred Kimbal was slowly accumulating a monstrous debt.

Judging from the piles of chips, Fred was already into the Ferengi for at least three bars of gold-pressed latinum, and the Academy cadet showed no signs of slowing down. Wesley signaled frantically to Fred, but the latter either did not see him or pretended not to notice. Wesley quickly wrote a note while Tunk shuffled; but when Wes tried to pass it to Fred, one of Tunk's bodyguards intercepted it.

"Now, now," said the Ferengi in polite tones that never-theless spoke a subtle threat; "wouldn't want the other players to think you're conspiring, the two of you!" The note vanished; Fred did not catch the exchange, staring intently at his two face-up cards.

After several more minutes, Tunk dealt again, five-card draw. Wesley picked up his hand and spread it . . . and almost yelped aloud.

From every card, La Fong's smiling face beamed up at him.

The players all chortled, except for La Fong, whose face turned beet red—and except for Fred, who howled with glee. "Carl!" exclaimed Tunk, "I had no idea you were so famous!"

"Hah-hah-hah, you contract jumper," said La Fong, more shaken than he had a right to be. "Now get rid of them."

"Oh, where's your sense of humor, hu-man? It's just a harmless little phrank to break up the tension."

"You mean 'prank,'" corrected Wesley, too tired to be polite.

Tunk smiled dangerously, narrowing his eyes at Cadet Crusher. "I call 'em *phranks;* any questions?"

"No. Never mind."

Ensign Lees leaned over to Wesley, asking in a loud voice, "Wes, these cards are all wet from certain people's sweaty hands."

He guiltily wiped his hands on his pants.

"Will you be a dear," continued Nanci, "and get me the rubber ones?"

"Sure," he mumbled, rising and heading toward the bar. Halfway across the room, he heard more laughter from the Tunk table and realized he had fallen for one of the oldest "phranks" in the world: the "sleeveless errand." Face crimson, he returned to the table wide-awake and dove into the game with vigor.

Wesley managed to regain the three grams he was down and even get ahead by a gram; but he watched in horror as

Fred's mountain of chips diminished, disappeared, then magically stacked up again, over and over.

The game stretched into a seventh hour, then ten. Wesley began taking long breaks; but Fred, mesmerized by the quick flick of the cards, the tick of the chips as they clattered together in the center of the felt, the rapid-fire up-and-down flash of his finances, never left the table, never sat out a hand. He danced every dance, finished every course. Fred ordered a drink whenever the waiter ghosted by; Wesley was quite certain Tunk served drinks a bit harder than synthehol.

The guards found an infinite variety of subtle and blunt ways to keep the two cadets apart, ranging from crowding around Fred to "watch his hand" to taking Wesley by the elbow and escorting him out, saying "spectators must wait in the billiards room."

After a time, Wesley slunk back to the table; so long as he was actually playing—at his spot, on the opposite side of the table from Fred—he was allowed in the game room. He watched in morbid fascination as Fred Kimbal gambled his entire future life away into Tunk's gnarled, pink hands.

Fred's face grew paler with the sky; outside the window, night's black gave way to dawn, and Fred finally collapsed.

He fell facedown onto the table, yet another wretched fistful of cards dropping faceup on the felt. Only Nanci expressed any real concern, reaching over and feeling for Fred's carotid pulse. Georges's only comment was, "Damn, faceup . . . we'll have to play the hand over."

"Is the hu-man dead?" asked Tunk, alarmed—more likely at the possible demise of his account receivable than because of any real concern for Fred's welfare.

"No," said Nanci, "I think he needs some sleep. And no alcohol for a couple of weeks, until he dries out."

Wesley stared at Fred, unable to tear his eyes away. After a moment, his roommate began to snore faintly.

Wesley was somewhat relieved that Fred sounded all right, physically; his relief was tempered by the realization that when Fred woke up, he would find that his career plans had taken an abrupt left turn: Unless he had very rich, *very* indulgent parents, Fred Kimbal now owed his soul to a Ferengi gangster's son.

Wesley felt his stomach tighten and his throat clench. There was no way Fred could ever pay such a debt, which amounted to at least a dozen bars of gold-pressed latinum, probably more money than either of the two cadets had ever seen all in one place. Tunk would complain to the commanding officer of the Academy, and Admiral Boxx would relay his embarrassment downstream to his commander.

Wolfe, of course, would gleefully dismiss Cadet Kimbal, probably with a dishonorable discharge for "Conduct Unbecoming." With a DD on his record, Fred's life was simply over.

Wesley, however, could comfort himself with the thought that the troubles were not all Fred's fault.

At least fifty percent of the blame could be laid squarely at the feet of Cadet Wesley Crusher.

Wesley tossed his hand into the center of the table, folding. He rose. "I think we had better be getting back," he said, not meaning for his voice to squeak. One of the bodyguards quickly cashed Wesley out.

Grinning nastily, as only a Ferengi can do, Tunk handed Wesley a data clip. "Please give the hu-man this message when he wakes up; and tell him he should come see me tomorrow at his earliest convenience . . . say not later than noon."

Noon. He has six hours to live. Wesley gulped, nodded. He wrapped Fred's arm around his shoulders and stood him up. Someone took Fred's other arm: Nanci Lees. She looked as if she were just starting to realize what Wesley had already figured out. "How much did he lose?" she asked.

Wesley shook his head. Between the two of them, they managed to maneuver Fred up the stairs to the entry hall; the unclothed greeting girl handed back caps, coats, and Nanci's leather jacket. Wesley felt embarrassed, standing next to the naked girl with Ensign Lees at his side; watching Nanci, he saw her throw several dirty looks at the typically crass, disrespectful symbol of Ferengi attitudes toward women in general.

"I don't think this is the best place for Starfleet cadets," Nanci suggested.

Right, thought Wesley. *Where was your Puritan ethic twelve hours ago?* "Guess we'd better call a taxi," he said aloud. "Looks like the limousine had a one-way contract."

Chapter Six

WESLEY HEARD A TERRIBLE ROARING in his ears, like a Klingon snoring. It pulsed again and again, rhythmically, shattering the oblivion of his sleep.

He blinked his eyes, slowly struggling back to consciousness. The roar faded; it appeared to be his own pulse, pounding in his carotid artery.

Opening his eyes fully, Cadet Wesley Crusher was blinded by a brilliant flare; the sun had risen to find the crack between his own Garth Dorm and Ionesco.

At first, the significance escaped him; then abruptly he realized and sat bolt upright in bed.

Wesley's dorm-room window faced *southwest*, not southeast. It was afternoon.

Intense pain lanced through his head. He grabbed his temples, squeezed at the agony. After a few moments, the pressure receded, leaving him with nothing worse than a queasy stomach and a serious (but normal) headache.

He rose, poured himself a drink of water, then another. After the third glass, he felt strong enough to try orange juice from the newly repaired replimats in the passageway. While there, he replicated an Academy Standard Breakfast.

He returned to the room; as he feared, Fred's bed was rumpled but empty. The space cadet had apparently left to keep his tryst with the Ferengi, Tunk.

Wesley frowned, worried; Fred Kimbal slept like the dead . . . once his head hit the pillow, he was lost to mortal view for a minimum of nine hours. The only viable explanation was that Fred had not slept.

Must have swum back to consciousness in the middle of the night, Wesley reasoned; *then he remembered what happened or he read the note. Either way, he probably just lay there all night in shock.*

Wesley had left the note propped up against Fred's chronometer. Cadet Crusher had intended to set a wake-up call with the computer to get up in time to wake Fred but had fallen asleep instead, fully clothed.

Feeling an icy hand clutch at his stomach, he sat at the small breakfast table, uninterested in the food, barely picking at his replicated bacon, eggs, ham steak, pancakes, muffin, toast with peach preserves, coffee, and soda. There was absolutely nothing he could do until Fred returned . . . eventually, Cadet Kimbal had to learn to solve his own problems.

Besides, what help could Wesley offer anyway? He did not have the kind of money Fred owed. He did not even know any good lawyers. For good or ill, Fred Kimbal was on his own.

Footsteps approached. Wesley quietly collected the dishes, all that was left of the breakfast, and dumped them into the replicleaner, which disposed of them. The footsteps hesitated, then receded. They returned, pausing at the door.

Wesley waited, becoming increasingly annoyed. It was obviously Fred; Cadet Crusher recognized his roommate's lurching gait. After another long pair of minutes, Fred must have touched the fingerplate, because the lock snicked back. Still, Kimbal neither opened the door nor activated the annunciator.

Finally irritated beyond politeness, Wesley stalked to the door and thumbed it open.

Fred jumped, then guiltily stared at Wesley's boots. "Um, hi, uh . . . uh, Wesley."

"Right, I haven't changed my name recently. What happened? Did you see Tunk?"

"Tunk?"

"The Ferengi!"

"Oh, *that* Tunk. Well, yeah. Yes. Yes, I saw him."

"What did he say?"

"About what?"

"This is getting tedious, Fred. Can't you just skip all the part where I drag the story out of you, sentence by sentence, and just spill it? You know you're going to eventually."

Fred fidgeted, clearing his throat and looking uncomfortable. At last, he seemed to deflate like a punctured balloon. Wesley stepped aside, and Fred Kimbal entered, plopping down on a chair and staring at a fixed spot about a kilometer south of the south wall.

"Yeah, I saw Tunk. He seemed, um, oddly insistent that I pay off that ridiculous tab. You know, heh-heh."

"Fred, you don't have that kind of money, unless you've forgotten to tell me about some filthy rich uncle of yours."

"No, no uncle."

"You didn't tell Tunk that *I* would pay it off, did you? Because I don't have anything like a dozen bars of latinum, either."

"A dozen? Oh, ah, actually closer to twenty. No, I didn't try to shove the debt off on you; you can rest easy."

"I didn't mean it that way. Well, maybe I did; but I'm sorry. So what happened? Do we have to ship you out of the sector?"

"Well, heh-heh, actually, you're not going to believe this. We managed to, as it were, work it out."

"Work it out? What, you got Tunk to set up payments? A *Ferengi?* That's amazing!"

"No. No payments. I, ah, swapped him my m-most valuable possession."

Wesley stared at Fred, unable to parse what the chubby junior had just said. Crusher's brain shifted to warp drive as he quickly sorted through, and discarded, every possession of Fred's he had ever seen. He could not see how Fred Kimbal could possibly be worth more than twenty grams of latinum—clothes, pocket change, blood chemicals, and all—let alone twenty bars.

Then, aeons later in Wesley-time, but a bare instant later by the standard chronometer, the most horrific thought occurred to him.

"Oh, no, Fred. Don't tell me you . . . you know!"

"Heh-heh-heh, funny world, eh?"

"Kimbal, *you didn't!*"

"Didn't I? I think I did. I have a horrible memory of doing so. He liked it, said it was definitely worth tw-tw-twenty bars."

Wesley tried to swallow, but his throat was too dry. He licked his lips, but his tongue was sandpaper. His words came out as separate granules of sentence fragments: "Fred . . . you—swapped—the latinum forging—device— to *Tunk?*"

Fred sunk lower into his chair, apparently trying to curl up into a ball. "Yup. Brilliant, wasn't I? Now, instead of a civil judgment against me and possibly being expelled from the Academy, I can go to the brig for fifty years! Boy, when I crumble, you can hear the squish of my spineless collapse all the way to the Delta Quadrant. Well, it's been nice knowing you, pal. Try to drop by the prison colony once every few years, when your ship is in the sector."

Wesley stared at Fred, having been stunned to silence since Kimbal admitted his horrific gaffe. Cadet Crusher backed up slowly until he bumped into a bed—Fred's—and collapsed backward onto it.

He stared around the room, noticing the darkness, the stench of Fred's clothes and sheets that he rarely rep-licleaned, the clutter. Everything seemed to be inexorably marching inward toward Wesley, choking him.

Finally, he spoke, his voice cracking. "Oh, I doubt you'll

be lonely, Fred. No, you'll have at least one friend to chat with, there in the Federation prison colony."

"Who?"

"Me, you brainless—! I helped you build the damned thing, remember? You're in this thing up to *my* neck . . . they're going to fry us both for counterfeiting!"

"You?"

"Yes, me. Funny world. Heh-heh."

Kimbal opened and closed his mouth like a grubfish. "Wes, believe me, I never thought—"

"Oh, I have no trouble at all believing *that."*

"I never thought you'd get in trouble, too."

"But why not? It's perfect, Fred. Here, I put the finishing touches on the working model of your invention; I didn't destroy it when I figured out what it did; I dragged you into the poker game in the first place. No reason I shouldn't share in the fruits of my own labors."

Fred shifted uncomfortably. "Come on, Wes. You didn't mean for this to happen, and neither did I. We're just vic—"

"I'll break your arm if you say we're victims of circumstance, Fred. I'm not kidding."

"Well, what do you want me to say?"

"How about coming up with some way to get that thing back from Tunk before he redlines it to his father, the gangster?"

"But then he'll say I still owe . . ." Fred faded into silence, seeing the homicidal glare in Wesley's eyes.

"We're going to get that thing back if we have to break into Tunk's apartment." Wesley stopped, rolling the idea around his head. "Hey . . ."

"No good."

"Why not? Are you worried about the ethics, for heaven's sake? You know he was cheating."

"How do you know he was cheating? Did you see him?"

"He cheats every day and twice on Sundays. He's a Ferengi and—"

"What, all Ferengi cheat? That's not like you, Wes."

"And," continued Wesley, "the son of a Ferengi so

crooked that even the Grand Nagus avoids him. In any case, didn't you notice that Tunk always won when he dealt the hand? Or nearly every time; he won much more when he dealt than when any of the rest of us did?"

"All right, all right. I wasn't worried about the ethics anyway. I meant it was no good to break into Tunk's apartment."

"Why not? Wait, didn't we just go through this?"

"Because he's not there."

"All the better. I hate burglarizing flats when the occupant is present."

"He's moved out."

"What!"

"To his yacht. I heard him on the comm link transferring a month's rent to the landlady in lieu of notice."

"How do you know he's moving to his yacht?"

"He called the garage and ordered it washed and fueled up. I deduced the rest."

"Why didn't you tell me this in the first place? He could be off-planet by now . . . he could be halfway to . . . to wherever Ferengi gangsters hang out!"

"Not unless he can get there in a yacht whose fuel tanks have been drained for garage storage. I only left him half an hour ago."

"Of course, it would take . . ." Wesley made a quick mental calculation. "I have at least another fifteen minutes, figure another ten to file a flight plan—he has to file one even if he plans to deviate as soon as he's out of controlled orbit—then if I'm lucky, he won't get immediate departure permission."

"What are you going to do, run out onto the pad and flag him down?" But Fred was shouting out the open door after Wesley, who pelted toward the turbolift en route to the pad.

He whistled for a cab, waved his hands, and finally dashed out into the right-of-way directly in front of one. The alert driver pulled up and over Wesley's head, the mag-lev field forcing the cadet's hair to stand endwise.

"You crazy cadet son of a . . . !" shouted the irate hackie.

She hopped out of the cab, intending to punctuate her ire by poking Wesley in the chest. When the woman got close enough, however, the cadet held up a decigram coin, snapping it in her face.

She stopped, staring at the bill. "Yes, sir," she amended, her entire attitude undergoing an instantaneous sea change. "Where would you like to go?"

"Hawking Field, the commercial pad complex. There's another one of these if you get me there in ten minutes."

The hackie's eyes widened like black umbrellas. She smiled, darted a hand out to snag Wesley's uniform jacket. The cadet was pulled off his feet, fluttering along behind the woman like a flag behind a pace vehicle. She dragged him at a sprint to her cab, flung him inside, and took off with an electromagnetic flare that vibrated every hair on his body.

Wesley braced himself against both sides of the vehicle, staring at the woman's license to avoid glancing out the windows and scaring himself: S. Muldowney. S. instantly swerved off the official right-of-way, cutting directly across the Quadrangle as cadets scattered like fleeing antelope.

She pulled hard to starboard, aiming for a walkway between Ionesco Dorm and the Medical Science building. The hack fit, practically scraping the walls on either side.

With supreme willpower, Wesley finally forced himself to blink, then exhale.

S. pushed her rig to redline but missed the deadline by two minutes. Wesley gave her the extra decimal anyway. She dropped him just outside the tower annex, and he dashed inside to check the hot board.

He touched the screen, bringing it to life, then said, "Tunk, Ferengi, location."

After an instant of lookup, the screen displayed a schematic map to Slip 9. Wesley ignored the map; he knew the field almost better than the architect who had built it.

Cursing the lack of transporters under his breath, Wesley hopped the slidewalk, shifting to the fast lane. He did not bother to slow down as he approached Slip 9, merely grabbing the rail and hopping over the side. He hit the sod, turning his fall into a forward roll back up to his feet, then dashed to the slip.

At the door, Wesley paused, catching his breath. He closed his eyes, listening to the activity inside the garage. The yacht was apparently finished fueling, for he heard Tunk and his bodyguards loading his possessions onto the cruiser.

When calmer, Wesley steeled himself to take a quick look around the corner. Tunk was only "helping" in the loosest possible definition of the term; in fact, he stood in front of the ship with a clipboard, barking incomprehensible orders that his bodyguards and a pair of stevedore robots appeared to ignore as they performed the grunt work of transferring Tunk's worldly goods into the cargo hold of the *Write Off*.

Grunt work it was, for Tunk shunned the transporter pads on the loading dock . . . probably because the rather steep fees offended his miserly soul; his bodyguards and the robots were cheaper.

Wesley stared in horrified fascination at the heaping pile of junk that the crew was slowly injecting into the yacht. Tunk apparently had more possessions than the Federation Museum of Earth Artifacts; and those that Wesley could see made the Treasures of Inner Mongolia and the Eugenics Wars Bas-Reliefs look pallid and sedate. Ferengi ideas of good taste were frightening enough as it was, and Tunk's collection was garish even by Ferengi standards . . . which meant any Ferengi who saw it would have been consumed by envy.

There were far more pieces than could possibly have fit into the apartment where Wesley had played in the big game, as large (and stuffed) as it had been. He was certain, moreover, that he would have noticed the two-meter-tall brass bird cage filled with some vile teal fluid, through which bubbled rainbow-hued globules of glowing goo, the whole surrounded by eight holovisions of dancing angels wearing skimpy, two-piece swimsuits; it was the sort of *objet d'art* that was impossible to miss even if it were in another room, covered by a drop cloth.

It sat between Wesley and Tunk's yacht now, and it was

difficult to even drag his attention past it to observe the proceedings.

Other items that would have been unmissable were a fluorescent yellow chair with legs like a praying mantis; a jewel-encrusted leather jacket with the words *Boomba Jamak the Quadrant Tour* emblazoned in neon; and a woven-rattan suit, complete with cork tie, dangling from a chaseum "rib bone" stand—an "original" *(thank God,* thought Wesley) by an artist known only as "Huck."

The only explanation was that Tunk kept a warehouse nearby and swapped the pieces he displayed in the apartment as they got old or were replaced with some new monstrosity, even more hideous.

Tunk began howling in outrage that one of his bodyguards had broken some priceless gewgaw. The huge man fled down the corridor leading to the moving van, frantically searching for the missing tusk, and Tunk followed, shouting imprecations that curled Wesley's ears.

It was an opportunity he could not afford to miss.

Wesley Crusher slipped from his hiding place and dashed to the goo lamp. He peeked between a pair of nearly naked angels, assuring himself that nobody stood between him and the cabin door. The remaining bodyguard crawled among a pile of fathomless stuff in the corner, toe-tagging the crockery.

Heart pounding, Wesley stood and strode casually toward the yacht. His knees shook, and it was all he could do to keep from breaking into a panicked run, either toward the cabin door or (more likely) back the way he had come.

There was no option of fleeing, however; he had to steal back the Kimbal Clock!

Wesley almost whistled casually, but stopped himself, realizing this would surely attract the bodyguard. He heard Tunk's voice grow in volume as the Ferengi verbally lashed his lackey back toward the task at hand. Wesley swallowed his fear—*now or not at all!*—ducked his head, and raced up the gangplank.

He paused just inside the door, crouching in the shadows;

he was in a cabin that resembled a living room, with fold-down couches, chairs, and a card table. A miniature Dabo machine crouched menacingly against the inner bulkhead.

The room was ill-lit, but a harsh light filtered down a corridor from a room beyond . . . presumably the treasure room where the Ferengi packed his priceless, or unpriceable, toys.

Now what? Where would that damned Ferengi hide the clock?

Wesley blinked his eyes, waiting for them to adjust to the darkness. He was not worried about being spotted in the living room; the light difference between the bright cargo slip and the dim room meant the guards and even Tunk himself would cruise through the living room and head directly toward the light, like moths, without a sideways glance.

This brief interval might be Wesley's only chance to hunt for the clock, however; when Tunk and his clumsy bodyguard returned, there would be too much activity for much of a search.

The robots would probably ignore the cadet, if they were simple stevedores; the Ferengi might have hired one or two "watchdogs," however, which would sound an alarm and attempt to apprehend Wesley.

He rose from his place, scanning quickly. Boxes filled the living room, shoved into the darkness in lieu of actually stowing them away.

Would Tunk have dumped the clock in his treasure room? Wesley stared down the corridor, aware that he would be finely silhouetted all the way down the ten-meter-long passageway, ultimately entering a room so brilliantly lit that he could not be missed. He dreaded the attempt; if he were caught, Tunk would still have the clock, and Wesley would have a trespassing charge on his record.

A thought occurred: All the tasteless gimcrackery that Tunk was transferring to the treasure hold was undoubtedly old stuff, toys of which he had long ago grown tired.

The clock was his newest acquisition . . . and almost certainly the overriding reason for his sudden departure. Surely he would keep it in a special place! Wesley began scanning the walls for a "hidden" safe.

There were four ugly pictures on the walls: two holovisions of Ferengi women, suitably unclad (and posed in most unsavory positions that Wesley found repellent), an oddly out-of-place seascape, and a view of the purple sands and violet setting (or rising) sun of a world Wesley did not recognize.

One of the girlie paintings looked suspiciously thick.

The voices had stopped outside the door; Tunk found it a convenient moment to chew out his bodyguards and one of the stevedores—though what he expected the mute robot to answer was unclear.

"Lift it, don't drag it! Lift it! These are priceless works of high art. . . . I could replace any of you three for a tenth the cost of even one of these pieces!"

"Sorry, boss." The guard did not sound sorry; he sounded weary, as if he had been through it all before.

Wesley pondered for an instant: *I wonder what the Ferengi pays them to take such abuse from a man they could pound into the deck with a single blow from their ham fists?* He moved to the suspicious pornography, trying not to look at it while he inspected it—a difficult task.

With no tricorder, Wesley could not tell for certain whether it was just a holoimage with an extra-thick frame or whether it hid a wall safe. He hesitated to touch; it might have a pressure- or heat-sensitive alarm trigger.

The air smelled stale, exactly as he would have expected from an unrecirculated enviro system that had remained dormant for many months, while Tunk studied (and partied and gambled and womanized) at his own university. Did this mean the security systems were likewise disabled, perhaps not having been activated yet?

"Oh, what the hell have I got to lose?" he whispered to himself. Wesley touched the frame, then ran his fingers around it. At the top, right corner, he felt a tiny, anomalous bump; it did not feel like an imperfection in the wood (which was probably replicated anyway, and would not have any imperfections unless specifically ordered).

Holding the frame steady with his left hand, he gingerly pressed down on the bump, simultaneously pulling the holoimage away from the wall. It swung open noiselessly, revealing a titanium safe with a touchplate.

Okay, Wes . . . got any bright ideas? The touchplate undoubted wanted the pawprint of Tunk himself to open, presuming Ferengi even had "fingerprints" in the normal sense of the word. Wesley examined it visually, switching between staring at the safe and peering anxiously back toward the open cabin door. The argument still raged outside, though now the bodyguard was responding a bit peevishly himself. Wesley decided he might have a few minutes, but he would have to close the safe instantly and shrink back into the shadows at the first hint of a footfall on the gangplank, which, fortunately, was metallic and would clank when trodden on.

He closed his eyes to think . . . and remembered a data clip he had read ages ago about the life and exploits of Bophur the Unholdable, the most famous escape artist of the 2350s. He once saw Bophur, in the last year of the Unholdable's professional career; Wesley was so astonished at age nine that he rushed to his data library and downloaded the only text ever written about the man.

Bophur used to pick thumbprint locks. His technique depended upon a "wire," an ancient term of unknown origin for a miniature parawave generator. Apparently, thumbprint locks used positronic circuitry; parawaves, with a short enough wavelength to pass through the metal exterior, which played merry hell with the circuits, often triggering the unlock program.

Wesley opened his eyes, grinning; replicators used parawaves to monitor the replication process.

He took two quick sidesteps to the kitchenette and found the replicator. "Uh . . . uh . . . a chaseum disk, smooth on one side to an accuracy of ten microns," he ordered. In a moment, a dull, lusterless "mirror" materialized. He replicated a second mirror, but left it in the machine, angled outward.

Wesley Crusher held the second chaseum mirror to catch the parawaves reflected off the first, reflecting them a second time onto the thumblock safe; chaseum was one of the few metals whose semicrystalline structure actually reflected parawaves. Gold-pressed latinum was another, but he could not replicate that.

"Self-diagnosis," he commanded. As the monitoring equipment sprayed parawaves around the interior of the replicator, Wesley fooled with the chaseum mirror in his hands, playing the waves across the safe. After two seconds, the safe clicked and slowly opened.

He had done it! He saw the clock inside, unharmed and ready to be returned to nowhere.

As he reached for it, he heard three people burst into applause behind him.

Wesley spun around, aghast. Watching the performance with obvious appreciation were Tunk and his two bodyguards. The Ferengi shook his head. "I never knew you could open a safe that way," he said in amazement.

"Ah—ah—Tunk! You're probably wondering what I'm d-doing in your . . ."

"In my safe? No, not at all. I'm merely surprised at your ingenuity and audacity; most hu-mans are so fatalistic about property they don't own."

"Well, sir," Wesley began.

"You aren't going to tell me you were returning that clock to its rightful owner?"

"No, sir. You are in possession of an illegal device. . . ."

"Rule of Acquisition number two hundred nineteen: Possession is eleven-tenths of the law. And as I seem to have possession, *you*, human, would appear to be the *other* tenth: a burglar."

"Tunk, you've got me all wrong!"

"Hah! I have you dead to rights, hu-man. Alas, I'm in a bit of a hurry now, so I think I'll have to take this up with the highest tribunal."

Wesley frowned. "The disciplinary committee?"

Tunk smiled nastily. "My father. He'll know what to do with you, I'm sure."

"But—your father is in—"

"Sector delta-alpha-hotel, about four days from here."

Wesley had edged close to the safe during the dialog; snakelike, he darted his hand into the open cavity and seized the clock. He tucked it under his arm and charged toward the open cabin door.

Tunk skipped nimbly out of the way while his two bodyguards set their legs and spread their arms. Wesley charged directly toward the man on the left, then head-faked to the right. The younger man was fooled, diving to intercept the new course.

Unfortunately, the older man, a squat, muscular human with a "d'Artagnan" mustache and goatee, spotted the fake. He slapped his comrade out of the way, knocking the half-Klingon, half-hu-man headfirst into a bulkhead; then d'Artagnan caught Wesley about the waist.

Cadet Crusher tried to elbow d'Artagnan in the face, but the man ducked his head behind Wesley's back, hooking his left arm around the cadet in a half nelson wrestling hold. After a moment's struggle, Wesley realized he was going nowhere.

Tunk stood to one side, capering and clapping his hands like a gleeful goblin. The half-Klingon bodyguard climbed to his feet, smacking his head to clear the stars. Soon, each of the pair held one of Crusher's arms, turning him to face Tunk.

"You can't . . ." Wesley faded into silence; he had been about to say "You can't get away with this," but he realized after two words that it was silly bravura: *Of course* Tunk could get away with kidnapping; who would search the yacht of the rich, politically powerful son of a Ferengi crime boss?

Tunk held out his pink paw. Without warning, Wesley let

go of the clock, hoping it would drop to the floor and smash itself into a hundred pieces against the deckplates. However, d'Artagnan, with his lightning-quick reflexes, caught it without trouble and returned it to the Ferengi. "All yours," said the mustachioed guard smoothly; he had definitely not been the oaf that Tunk chewed out about dropping pieces of kitsch in the corridor.

Wesley opened his mouth to protest—then shut it without a sound. A Ferengi who would kidnap a Starfleet cadet might not draw the line at murder.

The yacht shuddered, lifted from its pad, and glided along the launch bay, the front door still hanging wide open. Wesley Crusher watched the tarmac slide past the portal, accelerating faster. He swallowed; this was no run on the *Enterprise,* and there was no Captain Picard, Commander Riker, or Lieutenant Commander Data to rescue them when plans went sour.

One leg of Tunk's yacht knocked over a pile of boxes still neatly stacked in the bay. The ship tumbled the glowing-globule lamp, sending it spinning into a corner where it shattered, spraying noxious teal liquid across the Ferengi's remaining objets d'art.

Tunk shrugged. "It's of no matter, hu-man. Everything's carefully catalogued; some slow afternoon, I'll replicate it all again." He leaned close, his fetid breath gagging Wesley. "I've more important cargo. Heh! Heh!"

One of Tunk's ragged teeth was loose; it swiveled when he shook his head.

Oh, brave, new world, thought the cadet, *that hath such Ferengi in it.*

Chapter Seven

LIEUTENANT COMMANDER DEANNA TROI sat in Ten-Forward, desultorily picking at a chocolate truffle. Like every other officer aboard the *Enterprise,* she was simultaneously outraged that the ship had been reduced to a crawl because of bureaucratic infighting and resigned to a future of such plodding. After all, when the survival of the universe itself was at issue . . .

Still, strange as it seemed to her . . . she missed it; she missed the derring-do, the carefree way they once had charted a course toward the Unknown at warp nine. Warp five seemed so pedestrian, almost "walking speed."

A strange sense of unease pervaded her, haunting the Betazoid corridors of Deanna's mind. Something about a dog, a child in the water. She shook her head, remembering the time her mother, Ambassador Lwaxana Troi, was "lost" inside her own head, fleeing the memory of the little sister that Deanna had once had.

"Now why, of all people, am I thinking of Mother?" she asked of all people; no one heard her.

Guinan, the enigmatic bartender in Ten-Forward, was experimenting with variants on her infamous Sommerian Sunrise, the clear drink that suddenly flushed crimson when the imbiber sharply rapped the rim of the glass. The monk-cowled bartender looked up from her task, gazing speculatively at the counselor.

Guinan rose, bearing one of the drinks. "A Gray Dawn," she explained. She tinged the glass with her fingernail, and it swirled with sudden clouds, gloomy and overcast. "For patrons who are morose and brooding."

"Thanks anyway," said Deanna, "the chocolate is fine."

Deanna's comm badge beeped.

"You'd better answer it, Deanna."

"Answer what?"

Her communicator beeped again; the impersonal voice of the computer announced, "Communication for Commander Troi from Ambassador Troi."

Deanna sighed. The bartender shrugged, a comical expression of exagerated, *don't-blame-me* innocence. "I'll take it in my quarters," said Deanna, clipping the words carefully.

She rose. Guinan glanced down at the Gray Dawn; clouds still rolled through the drink, but they were beginning to dissipate, the gloom fading toward invisibility again as the ripples damped.

"Mother," muttered Deanna Troi. She plucked the glass from the table, swirled it to restore the thick fog, and downed it quickly. It burned her throat; she was not used to such strong drinks. Then her stomach caught fire, and she blinked tears from her eyes. A sickly, syrupy tang stung her mouth, and she swayed slightly as the synthehol was quickly absorbed into her system; it would fade in a few minutes.

Fortified, she left the truffle mostly untouched on her plate, trooping into the corridor to head for her quarters. Smiling, Deanna realized that her mother was undoubtedly pacing in annoyance at the wait.

Deanna sat at her desk, waited one last delicious moment

to allow Lwaxana Troi's fuse to burn down another centimeter, then stabbed the link touchplate to accept the communication.

Mother stared at daughter, raising her brows. "Well! Did you finish redecorating the bridge? Playing a game of chess? Reading a Vulcan philosophy book?"

"I don't know what you mean, Mother," said Deanna in as neutral a voice as she could manage. She tried to hold her thoughts proof against Lwaxana's prying, but it was no avail.

"Don't give me that innocent air, young lady; you haven't been able to hide your emotions from me since the day you were born."

"All right. What do you want?"

"Is that any way to talk to your mother? Here I spend some last, precious moments of my diminishing life contacting my only daughter, just to inquire about *her* life, since she hasn't seen fit to communicate with me in weeks and weeks, and instantly she assumes I must be up to something! What did that Federation poet write? 'Oh, sharper than a brief candle it is to bury a thankless child!' "

Deanna felt a wave of guilt; as soon as Lwaxana sensed it, she allowed a smile to flicker across her lips for an instant.

"I'm sorry, Mother. I should be a better daughter, I know. I should communicate with you more often . . . but my duties can be overwhelming."

"If you had listened to me and found yourself a nice man, you would have a helpmate to turn to who would comfort you. You'd bear up much better, you know. Oh, how I remember the days when my own *imzadi* and I—"

"Mother, I can't get married right now. I'm simply too busy! Besides, there have been some . . . ah, complications." Flushing, Deanna realized her mother would never understand about Will—and how he had returned as his "transporter twin," Thomas Riker. All her old feelings had surfaced once again; yet the new Riker was as exasperating as the old.

72

And then there's Worf...

Lately, she had begun to suspect that the ever-efficient, growling-bear Worf had designs on her, designs she was not completely averse to exploring. It was all too confusing; and the last thing, the very last thing Deanna needed at that precise moment was for her mother to start dropping hints about how constricting her clothes were, and was it not about time she shed them for a small, tasteful, little wedding?

"What complications?" demanded Lwaxana, rolling her eyes; "you find a man, find your darling captain—"

"Mother, what did you call about?"

"Can't a mother simply call to pass the time pleasantly with her daughter?"

"Not when you're the mother. Now come on, you want something."

Lwaxana Troi sighed. "Oh, it's such a little thing. Hardly even worth bringing up. Not that I don't think you're not *up* to it, not exactly."

"Not up to what?"

"Well, the senior plenipotentiary suggested . . . no, it's silly."

"What's silly? Mother!"

"Oh, he just thought that since I'm rather, er, tied down here on Adelphus-B, and since you are related to me . . ."

Deanna Troi closed her eyes and counted slowly to eleven. "Mother, *what* did the senior plenipotentiary suggest?"

"He suggested that you might turn out to be a petal off the old flower."

Deanna let her mouth fall open. "Doraxi wants *me* to be an ambassador?"

"Never mind, dear. I told her it was impossible. Not that I don't think you can do it; it's just not exactly . . . well, we each have our own talents and directions."

"Mother, I *am* a trained diplomat. What makes you think I can't do it?! I—" Deanna suddenly stopped.

Lwaxana shrank from the outburst, blinking rapidly. "Oh

dear, I never meant that you weren't capable of it! I'm sure you would be just as good as your mother—even better!—if only you were interested in trying."

"You, um, do you want me to do it? Oh, Mother, I'm sorry I snapped at you."

"It's all sand along the seashore. If you're sure you want to try, I'll call Doraxi back and tell her you've changed your mind."

"Well, I didn't refuse in the first place! You did it for me without even asking."

"Well, I didn't mean to insult you."

Suddenly, the enormity of her mother's trickery burst upon Deanna. With a flash, she realized that once again, Lwaxana Troi had managed to trick her daughter into *volunteering* for some unpleasant and distracting task!

Unfortunately, Deanna *had* volunteered; she could not deny it or go back on her word, not after giving it to her own mother.

Astonished at the ease with which Lwaxana could still wrap her around the dinner spoon, Deanna could only stare in amazement at the viewscreen.

Lwaxana smiled, magnanimous in victory, now that she realized Deanna understood what had happened. "Don't fret, dear; it's a lovely little assignment that won't even take you afield. You're already on your way to that silly auction, right? Well, all you have to do for Mother is bid on behalf of Betazed. But you're not doing it for me, really; you're doing it for Doraxi, for Betazed, for the Federation itself.

"We must keep those inventions away from anyone else, even Starfleet. Just think of the damage those immature races could do! You don't let children play with guns, Deanna! Must protect them from themselves!"

Lwaxana spoke urgently. "Do you really think that humans and especially Klingons are emotionally stable enough to handle such a treasure trove of powerful devices? Perhaps the Vulcans would be, but they're not interested."

"Well, now that you mention it, I guess not." Deanna

remembered when Captain Picard had discovered just such a device. The result was not inspiring.

Deanna fumed, grasping at straws; she definitely did not want to become involved in another of her mother's schemes. "But . . . but, Mother, I'm a Starfleet officer. I can't bid against Starfleet!"

"You may be a Starfleet officer now, but you've been a Betazed ever since you were born."

"But they won't even let me bid against Starfleet—I'm sure that it would be considered a violation of . . . of something!"

Lwaxana smiled, brightening considerably. "Actually, dear, I already had a chat with Admiral Boom. He seemed most anxious to please me . . . of course, considering the circumstances, that's quite understandable. We were hiding in the bushes outside his son's apartment, watching the most shameful exploits—"

"Mother!"

"I was only going to say that he was hardly in a position to object to anything reasonable I might ask. He didn't seem to think it such an odd request that Betazed be represented by a Betazoid; and since I couldn't possibly make it to the auction on time, you're nominated."

"I . . . I . . ." Deanna gulped. "I'll have to ask the captain."

"Of course, dear. You just tell that gorgeous hunk of man, Jean-Luc, to send a subspace message to Admiral Boom of the Starfleet Diplomatic Corps. I'm sure Bucky will explain everything."

Numbly, Deanna grunted her way through the remainder of the conversation; when Lwaxana finally signed off, Deanna could not remember a thing after she had been drafted, completely against her will, into volunteering to bid for Betazed at the auction.

She had only one faint hope: Perhaps Captain Picard would be completely unreasonable and refuse to allow her to bid against Starfleet. And if he would not, perhaps a long, quiet appeal would persuade him to be completely unreasonable.

Soon Deanna Troi sat in Captain Picard's quarters. The captain looked right at her; but she could sense that he was a dozen sectors away, already at the auction, in spirit.

"Captain, I just had the most disturbing communication from my mother."

He nodded distractedly. "Yes, Counselor, I know."

"You *know?* Did you know she wants me to represent Betazed in the bidding?"

Picard raised his brows. "I just received a subspace communication myself, Deanna, from Buckminster Boom. His brother Phillip was my department head on my shakedown cruise at the Academy."

"Captain I think I would make a terrible representative for Betazed. I don't know what any of Zorka's inventions are worth; I'm not even an engineer! How could I bid against *you,* anyway?"

"I won't be bidding, Deanna."

She looked puzzled, and Picard continued.

"There will be Romulans and Cardassians at the auction." He smiled weakly. "Standing orders require me to remain on the bridge in full command when in the same sector as either one of them. I'm sending Will down to the auction."

"Oh. Well, I can't bid against Will, either. I can't bid against Starfleet. I'm more Starfleet than I am Betazoid."

Captain Picard shrugged. "I'm sorry, Deanna, but there is not a single admiral in Starfleet who is proof against Ambassador Troi when she's on a crusade. Whatever Lwaxana Troi wants, Lwaxana Troi gets. But you know that, don't you?" He smiled at the memories.

All too well, she agreed; but she said nothing aloud.

"There is another point," said the captain. "I was very pleased recently to put you in for promotion to full commander. You worked very hard; Will worked you very hard . . . and all to learn the most important part of command: You must accept your duty, no matter how unprepared you may feel, no matter that you have a personal repugnance to perform it."

"Captain, with all due respect, it's not the same thing. This isn't an order from you or from Starfleet . . . this is my mother pulling strings, as usual, sticking me with some unpleasant assignment because *she* doesn't want to do it!"

Picard shook his head. "Duty is found in many places. You owe a duty to your home planet, which is as much a part of the Federation as Starfleet or this ship. You cannot put your duty on and take it off like an overcoat; you must wear it always, on watch, on the ship, or even on leave.

"Anything less is unacceptable in an officer under my command."

Deanna looked down at the deck. She knew in her heart that Picard was right. She took a deep breath and looked up. "I understand, sir. I'll coordinate with Will; he'll have to help me decide what to bid."

"Ask Ambassador Troi for a wish list, Deanna. Betazed owes you that. You have to know the maximum they can afford in order to allocate your resources."

"Thank you, Captain. I hadn't thought that far ahead yet." Counselor Troi was glad Picard was not a Betazoid. She would not have wanted him to read what was on her mind at that moment.

Captain Picard smiled. "I do not envy your task, Deanna. I doubt I would be any better at it than you, and my pride might suffer a mortal blow. Good luck."

She stirred restlessly; taking the hint, the captain said, "Dismissed, Commander."

"Thank you, sir," she said, rising. Deflated, Deanna exited as politely as she could, returning to her office. There she discovered that she had mistakenly scheduled two different crew members for the same time slot. This was not going to be her week.

Chapter Eight

FOR TWO DAYS, Tunk's small yacht chugged along at warp two, its fastest speed. Wesley Crusher spent the time scouring every surface on the ship, despite the presence of two scrub-bots who could have done the job more effectively and a dozen times faster.

The Klingon bodyguard towered over the cadet, arms folded, wearing a scowl that might have been truly terrifying —but not to a boy who had practically grown up tripping over Lieutenant Worf on the *Enterprise*. Wesley scrubbed with an air of resignation, knowing that if Worf were present, he could roll the bodyguard into a ball and pitch him out a porthole.

Several times each day, Tunk strolled over to gloat over his "citizen's arrest," as he insisted upon calling Wesley. The only other thing Tunk called him was "human," indicating that he did not remember Wesley's name. Cadet Crusher chose not to enlighten the Ferengi, and Tunk did not ask.

At last, the *Write Off* hove into view of his father's cruiser, whose one-word Ferengi name translated, as best Wesley could make out, as "A Ferengi Indulging in All Possible Vices Simultaneously With Tremendous Satisfaction"; he decided to call it *The Glutton,* which conveyed a similar feeling but was less of a mouthful. The *Write Off* matched orbits and docked with *The Glutton.*

The Glutton was a bipolar, impluse/warp-coil light cruiser of the Madison-class, Starfleet surplus. A dead one orbited Earth and was used for early phases of Academy training; forty years earlier, it had been a top-of-the-line resupply ship, capable of long hauls at a maximum of warp five.

Cadets and pilots called the Madison-class ship a "tuning fork," which it resembled: two side-by-side "tines," 250 meters long, which eventually joined into a point (the bow). The tines contained antimatter and impulse-fusion fuel. Theoretically, the ship could operate for fifteen years without docking anywhere . . . twenty years, if the captain were anal-retentive about rationing.

The *Write Off* docked near the aft end of the starboard tine, but Munk, Tunk's piratical father, insisted upon receiving them in his cabin, just abaft the bridge. The four of them trooped the entire distance, almost three hundred strides, despite the monorail track to their left. At Munk's quarters, they finally found the monorail itself, which seemed in perfect working order. Munk had simply not thought of sending it, or had considered and rejected the option.

Munk himself sat behind a pagodalike desk that looked like the person who designed it had gone mad from eating too much replicated Earth-Chinese cuisine; it was mahogany laced with bamboo, completely covered with jade bas-reliefs, carved ivory "pilgrimage" scenes, and whalebone scrimshaw. A yin yang symbol assembled from obsidian and ivory dominated the front of the desk. On the opposite side of the cabin lurked a jade statue of the chubby, laughing, Ferengi-god Roqadox, fully four meters tall. Every wall of the cabin was hung with tapestries, menaced by martial weapons and shields, glittered with gold-pressed latinum, and graced with explicit paintings and holoimages of unclad Ferengi women, along with females of other species.

Yet Munk himself dominated the room.

The squat Ferengi was barely a meter tall and looked older than the Grand Nagus; Wesley would not have been surprised to learn that Munk was older than Guinan, despite the fact that Ferengi do not measure their life spans in centuries, as Guinan's people did.

Munk was quite literally wider than he was tall, the most enormously fat Ferengi Wesley Crusher had ever seen. His warty, hairy skin, mottled pink and orange, looked like a Bajoran Vedek's warning of the dangers of excess. His ears twitched and flapped as he cackled obscenely, the laugh emerging as a hoarse wheeze that would not stop.

Wesley could not move; he was mesmerized by the sight and sound of the man. Then the cadet remembered to breathe for the first time since entering the room and discovered the incense.

Pungent smoke swirled through the room. Clearly a Ferengi scent, it smelled partly like bananas, like rotting flowers, like sweat-soaked running shoes, and partly like nothing Wesley ever smelled before. The cadet clenched his teeth and talked himself out of gagging, forcing a near-smile onto his lips.

He swam through the cloying aroma to stand before Munk's desk, Tunk and the human guard at his back. Tunk bowed and cringed in a truly obsequious manner.

After a moment, iron fingers gripped the back of Wesley's neck; the short, powerful guard with the "d'Artagnan" mustache forced the cadet to his knees, then pulled him back to his feet.

"Certes, m'boy," squeaked Munk, "what have ye brought nigh?"

What a tiny voice to come out of such a monstrous personage! wondered Wesley.

Munk hopped down from his chair and wobbled toward the hu-man cadet, clutching a small, gnarled walking stick in his spiderlike fist. He raised the shillelagh and without warning, bopped Wesley in the head with the weighty brass knob.

"Don't do that!" Wesley rubbed his stinging brow, wondering how far respect for alternative cultures had to extend . . . and how Ferengi treated stowaways and burglars.

"So, it boasts a salty tongue in its noggin? Splinter me mainmast! I'll warrant it's a strong back and brave right arm, too."

Munk spoke as if he had learned Federation Standard from watching pirate adventures on holovision.

From his cringing position, Tunk called out, "This human burgled my ship and stowed away, Cap'n Munk, Chairman of All Sectors. We only discovered him a day into the journey."

"That's a lie," retorted Wesley. "Tunk kidnapped me, and you're going to be in pretty severe trouble with Starfleet if you don't return me immediately."

"Eh? What? 'Zounds, but which lubber to believe?" Munk turned to the hu-man guard; Tunk rose slightly from his cringe and fixed his calculating eye on the man.

"Stowaway," lied the guard without a moment's hesitation. Wesley Crusher rolled his eyes; had he actually expected honesty from one of Tunk's own employees?

"But a beastly liar," added Tunk, "as you saw yourself, venerable one. Very dangerous. Talks too much."

"But anon, the Philosopher's Stone! The sacred alchemy, the marriage of heaven and hell . . . bring me out my Djinn lamp!"

Tunk leapt to his feet, dancing and capering. He clapped his hands; from the corridor, the Klingon guard appeared with the Kimbal Clock.

Wesley chewed his lip. He tensed, waiting for an opportunity to dash forward and slap it from the Klingon's sweaty hands. Once on the floor, a single, quick stomp with his flight boots and the latinum counterfeiter would be history.

The mustache-guard clamped a hand on either one of Wesley's shoulders, however; the man must have sensed

Wesley's intention, or else he simply thought it prudent. D'Artagnan hauled the cadet back out of range as the Klingon brought the clock forward and handed it to Tunk.

Tunk opened the cracked clock face and dropped a small, chaseum wrench inside; he closed the case then twisted the stem.

"Let me see!" screamed Munk, snatching the clock from his son.

The bright light lit both their faces to a sickly, fiendish yellow. After a moment, Munk yelped and dropped the burning hot clock on the floor. It did not break.

Gingerly, Munk opened the clock face; he reached inside and pulled out what appeared to be a wrench made of solid latinum.

He frowned, shaking his head. "Nay, nay, but 'tis a mistruth. Ye cannot replicate latinum; we've kenned that for ages."

"It's not replicated latinum," whispered Tunk reverently; he was in the presence of his god . . . the greatest fraud in history. "It's all an illusion, a counterfeit."

"Fairy gold!" declared Munk in triumph.

"Fairy gold; that's perfect, Father! That's exactly what it is."

"And that be exactly what we shall use at yon sales auction—with this witchery shall we lord it over that pox-riddled, wizened, putrescent knave, the so-called Grand Nagus. Avast, exeunt! Leave me to mine own company and drag this sack of dung with thee—" Munk suddenly walloped Wesley with the knobkerrie again, producing yet another startled outcry and very unofficerlike oath—"I would fain be alone with my Djinn."

The guards dragged Wesley Crusher behind Tunk, depositing the cadet in a holding cell in the brig.

Wesley fidgeted, pacing back and forth for a time. Then he finally shrugged and climbed onto the single bunk, exhausted from two days of crawling on hands and knees, scrubbing at years of accumulated Ferengi grime.

I'll just rest here for a moment, he thought, *then devote my full attention to figuring a way out of this mess . . . and a way to warn Starfleet that a pair of Ferengi have a latinum-counterfeiting device.*

He closed his eyes and fell into a deep, dreamless sleep, waking himself up twice with his own snores.

Cadet Crusher was washed awake by a bucket of ice water splattered across him. He flew up off his rack, sputtering, and promptly slipped in the water puddle. While he regained his balance and his temper, d'Artagnan placed the bucket back on the replicator pad, where it promptly vanished.

"The boss wants to see you, mister."

"Great. I want to see him."

"After you." D'Artagnan politely flourished, and Wesley walked through the empty space that had been a force shield a few moments before.

Munk received the cadet in the same room as last time, dashing Wesley's hopes that the room was ceremonial, and Munk did his real work in a small, tasteful office. The cadet sighed, looking for a chair.

"Ye won't find one," cracked the ancient Ferengi.

Wesley jumped; had Munk read his mind or his actions? "I can stand."

"I see three bonny reasons to fling yer out the airlock and none to hold ye. *Primo,* ye're evidence; *secundo,* ye can talk and might cast a subspace signal to yer friends; *tertio,* me own kith and kin tells me ye're an altruistic little philanthropist, and ye make me nervous for I nae can fathom ye."

Cadet Crusher licked his dry lips; the first step in resolving the problem was to avoid sucking vacuum. Dead cadets tell no tales.

"First," said Wesley, "you need me to fix the clock when it breaks down. . . . I . . . uh . . . I built it, and I'm the only one who can fix it. Second, ah . . ." He thought furiously. "Second, if you're worried about me contacting anyone, I'll . . . I'll sign a contract saying I won't. Third, I'm a realist, not an altruist; I don't buy into Federation propaganda; I don't even belong in Starfleet!"

He blinked. Had he really meant the last affirmation to come out so positive, so forceful? *I'm just dancing,* he thought, *saying whatever the Ferengi might want to hear; that's all.*

Munk smiled, a horrible, vicious sneer. "Heh! Me own brand o'scallawag! Come, boy; take me hand; lend me yer word on't!"

Munk extended a frail paw. Wesley gently took it, not wanting to damage the Ferengi (not yet). Then Munk squeezed with an unexpected grip of iron, crushing Wesley's hand like an eggshell.

The cadet managed to stifle his yelp this time, biting his teeth together so hard his jaw nearly locked. Off balance, he was easy prey for Munk to yank over to his desk.

"Now *sign,* boy! It's a standard, Ferengi nondisclosure agreement, binding ye and yer future generations, agents, employees, handlers, lawyers, accountants, associates, acquaintances, relatives, and nonorganic recording or broadcasting media to silence 'pon whatever issues be raised in the scope of yer employment by meself."

"Employment?"

Munk let go Wesley's hand and slapped him on the shoulder, staggering him. "Ye're the new cabin boy, human!"

Stunned, but seeing no alternative, Wesley quickly signed the document, affixing his thumbprint to the ID box.

"All right, ye swabbie, uh"—Munk scowled at the signature—"Fred Kimbal . . . say, be that in sooth yer name? I recall a different moniker betimes . . . are ye not Westlake Kimbal?"

Fred Kimbal? Wesley blinked; he had not consciously taken the pseudonym, but it was a good move nonetheless: Fred had, as usual, encoded his name all through the programming of the device; if Tunk or Munk bothered to check, it would reaffirm Wesley as the "designer" of the clock.

Then, too, perhaps he would be able to weasel out of the contract later by having signed a false name; it clearly showed he had no intent to make a contract. Of course, since the matter would necessarily be heard in a *Ferengi* court before *Ferengi* jurors, it was highly unlikely that anything Wesley Crusher said in his own defense would carry much weight.

"No," he answered, "that was the other guy."

"The other hu-man?"

Wesley nodded. "That's the one."

Munk stared hard at Wesley Crusher. "Ye speak sooth?"

"Sooth."

"Well, for a certain, we Ferengi can tell none of ye hu-mans apart; ye look all of a kind to us. This other Kimbal; be ye related?"

"He's my brother—my cousin—my brother!"

"Which?" Munk's eyes narrowed suspiciously.

"Well, both, actually. My, ah, my father's brother married my mom when my father was—arrested for trading a cargo of Cardassian relics." *Ladle it on thick,* he told himself; *may as well be hanged for a sheep as a goat.*

Munk grinned even more broadly, exposing his mangled, pointy, yellowing teeth. *"There's* the lad! Ye're after me ain heart, and no mistake."

They were the last friendly words that Wesley Crusher ever heard from Munk, for in the next breath, the Ferengi shouted his new cabin boy below for "sech duties and urgencies as may betimes be commanded by the ship's master," which presumably was Tunk, second in command.

In addition to Cap'n Munk and Master Tunk, the other three crew members were Lotriati who managed to imply that they had come with the cruiser—and would disappear with it if Munk ever sold out. This "crew" comprised a female engineer, a female chef, and a male navigator.

Wesley discovered that Munk's Lotriani crew treated their cap'n the way Tunk's bodyguards treated Tunk: They took their destination from Munk, then aye-aye-cap'ned his subsequent orders and did whatever they planned to do in the first place.

Unfortunately, this left Munk and Tunk quite free of

responsibility and starved for personal contact, which to a Ferengi meant personal abuse. They followed Wesley around or summoned him to their respective quarters and gave him what-for.

After a few hours of not seeing d'Artagnan or the Klingon around for a while, Cadet Crusher decided to make a run for the subspace transceiver.

There he found the guards. They sat comfortably between Wesley and the equipment, lips curled in an identical pair of nasty grins. Wesley made as if he were counting transceiver coils, tapping the answer into a notepad. The guards were not fooled, but they let him continue unmolested.

A few minutes later, as Wesley replicated dish after dish for the chef, Charteris, who rejected each offering and suggested something different, he felt a presence loom behind him.

Master Tunk gloated. "I guess you haven't read your contract, Kimbal! Don't you know this is a *Ferengi*-flagged vessel?"

"So?" Wesley was annoyed by Charteris's punctiliousness —was there really a difference between mashed or whipped *mookatatoes?*—and he allowed the irritation to creep into his tone.

The slip bought him a kick in the shins from Tunk. "Insolent hu-man! By the treaty of your own Federation, Ferengi-flagged vessels operate under Ferengi law. That means that any breach of your contract will be adjudicated by a *Ferengi* court on the nearest *Ferengi* outpost." He leaned close, breathing his fetid breath on Wesley. "Have you ever seen a Ferengi prison?"

The point was clear: If he entertained any hopes of simply waiting until the guards fell asleep or slugging them to have at the subspace communicator, he might bear in mind that regardless of how grateful the Federation and Starfleet might be for his information, they could not extricate him from the Ferengi injustice system.

In fact, Wesley was in just a cynical enough mood to brood that if he did escape, Starfleet would undoubtedly return him to the Ferengi . . . in the interest of diplomatic relations, of course.

Pro forma threats out of the way, Tunk seemed anxious to talk to somebody other than his pompous father and the taciturn guards. Wesley drew the ship's master out, desiring to learn the plan. Tunk was only too willing to be drawn.

"In case you haven't heard about it, hu-man"—Wesley had not—"one of your own great scientists has died and specified that his inventions are to be auctioned to the highest bidder. Everybody is turned against his neighbor . . . it's the first sensible thing we've ever seen your people do!"

"Yes, of course," said Wesley, being agreeable, "Rule of Acquisition number, ah, now what was that number again?"

Tunk's eyes widened. "You must be thinking of the Sixtieth Rule of Acquisition: Let's you and him fight. I'm astonished that you know our culture so well."

Wesley shrugged nonchalantly. "I try to keep up. I take it you intend to . . . well, you know. Let's not dwell on your successful schemes."

"Why not? I mean, we ought to at least examine them for flaws, right?" Drawn to his favorite subject, Ferengi cleverness, Tunk became impossible to turn off. He needed no more prompting. His face lit up, and he rubbed his hands as if washing them under an old-fashioned faucet.

"We'll replicate hundreds and hundreds of bars of gold-pressed latinum—only it won't really be latinum! It'll be—"

"Chaseum."

Tunk glared reproachfully, and Wesley shut up; he did not enjoy being kicked, punched, bopped on the head, or any other examples of Ferengi annoyance.

"They'll be chaseum. Then we use your device, and *radrabat!* We have more latinum than anyone has ever seen . . . more than enough to steal—to snap up every lot at the auction. The only dress on the female is that Hatheby's, the human firm running the auction, might subject our latinum to some sort of test. Everybody's so suspicious of

Ferengi these days! It's just not fair . . . they don't go around calling other races crooks and thieves, just because they use aggressive and inspired sales pitches. Everybody always picks on us!

"But I suppose it doesn't matter; unless they subjected the bars to a replicator—and who would think to put latinum in a replicator?—your accomplice tells me they won't be able to tell the difference . . . you saw to that, eh, Kimbal? Heh! Heh!"

Wesley smiled. He had a photon torpedo to deliver. "Well, there's one tiny detail you all may have overlooked."

"What? Don't be impertinent! There are *no* details that we've overlooked."

After a long pause, during which Tunk hummed and whistled and stared at his fingernails as if inspecting for graffiti, his iron resolve broke down. "All right, Kimbal; what have we overlooked? The plan is perfect!"

"If you say so."

"No, really, it is. What's the problem?"

"If your plan is perfect, there's no problem. I guess I was mistaken."

Tunk stared hard at Wesley, obviously not convinced. Something still bothered the Ferengi; but he could not quite bring himself to believe that a mere human might see a possible loss in a venture before a Ferengi did. After a typical Ferengi sneer, Tunk stormed off, grumbling below his breath.

The point that Wesley had seen at once, with his Starfleet navigational training, was that of propinquity, or the lack thereof: *The Glutton* was so far away that at its maximum speed, warp five, it would not even reach the auction site until the auction was nearly over.

The Lotriati navigator and engineer (and probably even the chef) obviously knew this; but since neither Tunk nor Munk had bothered asking them, they chose not to volunteer the information.

There was, however, a ship patrolling in the sector that could easily reach the auction in time, a Galaxy-class vessel that could travel at warp nine, several times the rate of *The Glutton.*

If Wesley remembered his assignment schedule correctly, that ship was the *U.S.S. Enterprise,* under the command of one Jean-Luc Picard.

Cadet Crusher waited patiently; sooner or later, the Ferengi's stubborn, monkeylike curiosity would get the better of his pride, and he would come back and demand to know the "flaw" in the plan. The longer Wesley delayed, the later it would get . . . and the more likely that Munk would grow desperate enough to throw caution to the winds and try to hitch a ride.

Wesley was not sure what he would do, or even could do, under the circumstances; he was still bound by the Ferengi contract, and it would still be judged by Ferengi law. But at the very least, he would be among friends; and due to his "farsightedness" in giving the name Fred Kimbal instead of his own, neither Munk nor Tunk would realize that everybody on the *Enterprise* crew knew Wesley.

Whoops . . . He suddenly realized the flaw in his *own* plan: He would have to make quite sure that he introduced himself as Fred Kimbal (nod, wink) before anyone saw him and called out, "Hey, Wes, how's the boy?"

Tunk managed to hold fast to his pride for two hours; then, just as Wesley predicted, he sidled back. After several minutes of tooth-pulling, Crusher allowed the Ferengi to "drag" the point out of the cadet.

In a moment, Tunk raced off to his father as fast as he could waddle (the young Ferengi was well on his way to developing the spherical look popularized by Munk). Unsupervised in the excitement, Wesley strolled to the bridge in time to hear the hurried orders to find the *Enterprise* and rendezvous.

When Tunk had given the orders, in the absence of Munk (who was annoyed at being interrupted while counting his collection of bona fide latinum—itself quite impressive), he turned to find Wesley Crusher sitting on an instrument panel.

"You lazy, good-for-nought, hu-man dog! Get back to work!"

"You didn't order me to do anything."

"Well, *find* something. Then do it!"

"If you insist. Except . . . there might be one, teensy, tiny flaw in your plan. How do you plan to . . ." Wesley shook his head. "No, I'm sure you have it under control."

If Ferengi could make smoke come out their enormous ears, Wesley decided it would have happened right there and then.

Tunk sucked in a huge lungful of air and held it, his face slowly turning whitish pink. He looked ready to explode if someone would only poke him with a fork. Then he slowly expelled the breath, regaining his cold composure.

"All right, Kimbal; you win. *What* is the flaw this time?"

"Once you catch up with the *Enterprise* . . ."

"Yes?"

"How do you intend to get aboard?"

"Why, I presumed we'd just . . . ask . . ." Tunk trailed into silence. It was hardly likely that the *Enterprise* would cheerfully contract herself out as an interstellar taxi service for itinerant Ferengi, especially taking them to an auction where they would bid against Federation interests.

"Fine, hu-man. I presume you have a plan for getting us aboard?"

"Haven't a clue. Sorry."

To his credit, Tunk did not fly into a rage. Ferengi were not fairy-tale goblins. Instead, he pondered deeply, pacing up and down, his Klingon bodyguard loyally if absurdly shadowing his every step.

At last he looked up with the air of a man who had solved a difficult puzzle, but did not like the solution.

"The only way I can figure is if we're in distress. Starfleet ships *must* stop for distress calls—it's one of their rules of acquisition, or altruism, or whatever they call them. All we have to do is send a distress call."

"Don't you think they'll scan you? They'll find out you're not really in distress."

"I know, I thought of that," admitted Tunk ruefully. "The solution, of course, is to really *be* in distress. Which means in imminent danger of total destruction, since I doubt your precious Starfleet would stop for anything less for us Ferengi."

"Don't tell me you're going to blow up your own father's ship!"

Tunk glared sourly, curling his upper lip in a frightening display of sharp, jagged teeth. Then the snarl turned into a grin as Tunk thought of his father's ship vanishing into a white-hot ball of superheated gases. Wesley knew the meaning of that grin; the Ferengi was thinking *yeah, the old philanthropist has it coming to him!*

Tunk stared at his father's cabin. Having just disturbed the Great Man a moment before to persuade him to rendezvous with the *Enterprise,* Tunk was a bit nervous about trying to persuade Cap'n Munk to blow up *The Glutton.* But the payoff was so huge—the greatest "phrank" of all—that Tunk finally resolved himself to do it.

Calming himself, he slowly began to walk toward the door, practicing various degrees of cringing along the way.

Wesley tried hard not to laugh, which would have given the game away.

At the very least, once aboard the *Enterprise,* all the abuse he had suffered would cease. The contract he had signed might still be adjudicated under Ferengi law; but treatment of employees, including cabin boys, fell under the jurisdiction of the Federation aboard a Federation ship.

And maybe, just maybe, he could goad the Klingon guard into giving some sort of offense to Lieutenant Worf. Wesley was not above wanting to see the brutal guard knocked onto his hard-as-chaseum Klingon posterior.

Chapter Nine

THE BRIDGE WAS SILENT for a few moments. Then an explosion of unintelligible imprecations burst from the captain's quarters. Wesley recognized Munk's high-pitched voice, but the walls mercifully muffled the actual words.

Mercy did not last long on the Ferengi ship. The door to the captain's quarters slid open and Munk stormed through, waving his knobkerrie over his head in utter outrage. He spied Wesley and beetled directly toward the cabin boy.

Cadet Crusher stood his ground, refusing to be bullied by a Ferengi. He kept a sharp eye on Munk's walking stick, however.

"What suggest you, you pox-ridden, deal-breaking, earless philanthropist? Think you I'll cast me ship into yon star for yer amusement?"

Wesley folded his arms. "All I did was point out that the *Enterprise* won't stop for you unless you claim your ship is breaking up; and they won't believe your ship is breaking up unless it really is . . . they've got sensors, you know. These are the facts; if you don't like them, then limp along to your auction at warp five—*I* don't care!"

Munk's face turned as dark red as a Russet potato; then he held his breath. After half a minute, his breath exploded out in a rasping cough.

Deflated, Munk lowered his head but maintained his cold, reptillian gaze at Wesley. "If this be unworking, hu-man, the cost of ye *Glutton'll* be added to yer already considerable debt: faulty consultation fee."

"Debt! What debt do I have? I haven't bought anything!"

Munk looked up again, smiling to show his rotting, pointed teeth. "Certes, and ye have! Mass, air, water, food, transportation, tour-guide services—"

"Tour guide!"

Tunk responded. "I led you on a tour of the entire ship from the stern to the bow when we first docked. I remember it distinctly."

Wesley Crusher threw his head back, exasperated. "Fine. Whatever you want. Rack it up." He realized he could never work off the Ferengi debt *legitimately* anyway; he would have to think of something.

Three more hours passed as they drove along the path charted by the Lotriani navigator that led to rendezvous with the *Enterprise*.

At last, she reported the starship within hail; a few minutes more and they could see it on their forward monitors.

Munk wandered helplessly back and forth on the bridge, mumbling, "Alas, alack!" and "Woe is me!", gripping his ears in anguish. He approached the communications station twice, each time veering off into yet another useless orbit around the bridge.

Wesley watched, worried that the Ferengi had walked the mental plank into the drink. Nervously, the cadet tried to edge away from Munk, in case the cap'n decided to run amok, or whatever it was the Ferengi did when they went loopy.

Tunk, however, could not care less about *The Glutton*. After all, it was not his ship. He stomped purposefully to the station, composed himself, and hailed the starship.

"Enterprise," responded Commander Data.

"Ah . . . ah . . . *U.S.S. Enterprise?* This is, um, Captain Tunk of the Ferengi trading vessel *Glutton.* We're having some difficulty with our antimatter flow control. Stand by; we're sending a—" Tunk grinned. "Our human engineer is attempting to correct the problem, but we may need assistance."

Wesley opened his mouth, then shut it, realizing that Data would surely recognize the cadet's voice patterns and might accidentally alert the Ferengi. Cadet Crusher slid into the shadows, hoping that his image would not be broadcast on the *Enterprise's* viewscreen.

Data's voice responded without hesitation. "Captain Tunk, we suggest you do *not* attempt to adjust your own antimatter flow control. We shall be happy to beam a technical crew to your vessel to—"

Tunk abruptly interrupted with a blood-curdling shriek: *"Gods of profit!"*

He quickly yanked the sliding control circuit panel out of the subspace transponder; it would produce pure static on Data's end of the channel.

"Hurry, you lazy swine!" shouted Tunk at the Lotriani engineer. "Set those antimatter pods to overload in twenty seconds . . . if they haven't beamed us aboard in ten seconds, eject the pods!"

"Ten seconds!" shouted both Wesley and Munk simultaneously, though the latter added an "arr."

Wesley was paralyzed; he would have been fine had there been anything for him to do . . . but he was depending on Ferengi, Lotriani, and how fast the *Enterprise* crew might react, not his own considerable abilities.

The engineer said not a word; she bustled around the bridge from one station to another, overriding fail-safe circuitry, then finally announced, "Ship detonation in twenty seconds . . . nineteen . . . eighteen . . ."

All of a sudden, Wesley wondered whether it had been such a brilliant scheme of his after all. What if the *Enterprise* were not prepared to beam them out? What if Data were distracted or had left his console? *What if the Lotriani could not eject the pod?*

As the engineer passed twelve seconds heading for ten, sweat began to drip into Wesley's eyes. At ten, she began fiddling with the console.

At six seconds, she turned back to Tunk and shrugged, fatalistically. She was unable to eject the pod.

Wesley Crusher felt his knees buckle; he gripped a railing, staring at the clock countdown on the screen. He had five seconds to live.

Four . . .

Three . . .

Two. He blinked. He had been so fascinated by the clock, he had not even noticed the telltale fuzzing of the transporter. He silently counted *two, one,* and *boom!* in his head while standing in the transporter room aboard the *Enterprise.*

The beautiful, musical voice of the *Enterprise* computer announced, "Ferengi ship has detonated; all personnel accounted for."

Wesley looked around; indeed, Munk, Tunk, three Lotriani, two bodyguards, and one Cadet Crusher were all crowded around the transporter pad. Tunk had grabbed hold of his father in utter panic, and Munk struggled to extract himself from his son's grip. D'Artagnan's face was as pale as Earth's moon, while the Klingon's pupils had contracted to pinpoints and he looked distinctly dazed. Only the Lotriani appeared unruffled; perhaps their race was incapable of feeling fear.

Wesley stared at the transporter chief. Did he know the man? The man stared back, as if he were about to shout out a, "Hey, Wes!" Or, it might have been Wesley's imagination.

The cadet decided not to chance it. "Fred Kimbal!" he sputtered, racing across the room to stick his hand out. Startled, the man took it as one would grab a squirming fish that had just been yanked from the stream.

"Uh, Senior Chief Heavenly," he stammered.

To cover his odd behavior, Wesley began pointing out the other crew members from *The Glutton.*

"Cap'n Munk, Master Tunk—no, the taller one—Engineer Jina Kef, Navigator Rolt something-or-other, Chef Ming, d'Artagn—" The cadet paused, embarrassed; he realized he had not the slightest idea what the bodyguards' names were.

It made no difference; the Ferengi glared suspiciously at Heavenly, the Lotriani talked quietly among themselves and ignored everyone else, and d'Artagnan and the Klingon watched Wesley like vultures but said nothing.

"Oh," said Heavenly. "Hi."

The transporter doors slid open with a hiss. Commander Data entered with Dr. Beverly Crusher, Wesley's mother.

They barely crossed the threshold before stopping to stare at the familiar face.

"Fred Kimbal!" shouted Wesley, lunging past the Ferengi to jab a hand at Data. "My name is Fred Kimbal! I'm with these fine, honest, Ferengi traders! We're on our way to the auction! The ship exploded! I don't know any of you! Tell me who you are!"

Dr. Crusher looked at Data, who raised his eyebrows and spoke first. "We are very pleased to meet you, Mister . . . *Kimbal.* I am Commander Data of the Starship *Enterprise.* This is Doctor Beverly Crusher, the ship's medical officer. Who are your friends?"

Wesley pointed the rounds again. "Cap'n Munk, his son Tunk, his employees Jina Kef, Rolt something, Ming something—they're the crew of *The Glutton*—and two bodyguards."

Engineer Kef looked up sharply. "We're not crew or employees," she snapped, "there's no ship left, so we're released from our contracts."

"All right, they used to be the crew of *The Glutton.*"

"We've talked it over, and we've decided to allow you to convey us to the auction. We'll bid for Lotri."

"Are you all right?" asked Dr. Crusher breathlessly. She stared straight at Wesley, as the cadet flicked his eyes at the Ferengi, trying to get his mother to act a little more natural.

Again, the door slid open, this time disgorging Commander Riker and a pair of security guards disguised as a welcoming committee.

"Fred Kimbal," said Wesley nervously.

Data pointed at Wesley. "This is Fred Kimbal," he said.

"Kimbal," said Beverly simultaneously, "here with a couple of Ferengi."

Riker looked from Data to Beverly to Wesley, the last holding his breath. "Welcome aboard the *Enterprise,* Mister Kimbal," said Riker in as supercilious a voice as he could manage. The left corner of his mouth turned up as he labored to suppress a laugh.

Great! thought Wesley, *Riker is never going to let me forget this.*

"Who are your friends, Mister Kimbal?"

Sighing, Wesley pointed the round again. "Munk, Tunk, Kef, Rolt, Ming, Thing Number One and Thing Number Two. The Ferengi own the ship that just blew up, and the Lotriani used to crew the ship."

"Who are they?" asked Riker, indicating the bodyguards.

"Muscle," said Tunk proudly.

"Speaking of which," added Wesley, "where is the security officer of this ship . . . the *Enterprise,* isn't it?"

"It is," said Riker, having a harder and harder time hiding his grin. "Lieutenant Worf, the security officer, and the chief engineer, Lieutenant Commander La Forge, are on another ship; they'll join us for the auction. Am I to understand that's where you're all headed, too?"

"Yes," declared Tunk, "our ship developed mechanical problems, as you saw. Well, what are we waiting around for? Ahead, hu-man! Warp factor twelve! We must arrive before the bidding begins!"

Riker immediately lost his smirk. "We're moving at top speed already, Mister Tunk."

"What? Nonsense! Kimbal, how fast are we going?"

Wesley stared at Riker, trying to figure out the first officer's game. "When we were beamed aboard, the *Enterprise* was making warp five."

Riker drew himself up to look as "Starfleet" as possible.

He yanked down on his uniform jacket, straightening out a couple of proto-wrinkles. "Perhaps you're not aware of current Starfleet regulations, *Cadet Kimbal,* but warp five is the maximum allowable speed inside Federation space."

Wesley waited for the punchline. After a moment, during which nobody said a word, he broke the silence. "You're *serious?* You don't have authorization to exceed the environmental limit?"

In his huffiest voice, Riker said, "Starfleet considers the damage caused by excessive warp speed to be of the highest priority; I presume the Starfleet Academy still teaches respect for the environment and the Prime Directive?"

"Yes, of course it does! I just meant—"

"If we casually exceeded the maximum limit every time some mission of the moment seemed important, we may as well not even *have* the limit."

"That's not what I meant. You're taking it all wrong, sir! I just—"

"This ship is proceeding with all allowable speed toward the auction . . . at warp five. If you have a problem with that, we can put you off on Starbase Thirty-Eight and you can arrange your own transport."

Wesley shut up; if he kept babbling, he would undoubtedly say something like "hooray," and the Ferengi would deduce that he still sought to thwart their plans.

Munk had been sputtering and squawking throughout the entire exchange; he finally managed to put his outrage into words.

"Blackguards! Villains! Ye'll *bankrupt* me, tear me beard out by the roots! See here, me fine bucko, ye'r obliged to ferry us to the auction in all fairness by the Federation-Ferengi Treaty of—"

"By that treaty," interrupted Data, "the Ferengi also promised to obey Federation law in Federation space. That includes the law against sending false distress signals and deliberately endangering Federation passengers by sabotaging a ship."

Munk clamped his mouth tight, puffing out his cheeks as

his good sense won out over the desire to defend himself against such an outrageous attack, particularly a truthful one. Tunk stepped between the Ferengi and android, oiling over the acrimony.

"Gentlemen, gentlemen! What use are recriminations and might-have-beens? So the ship is going to drag its feet—ah, you know what I mean—getting to the auction, delaying us until nearly everything is gone. So what? We're used to such treatment from the Federation. It's nothing to get upset about.

"It's no problem . . . you say your other two crew members are going to meet you at the auction?"

"Yes," admitted Riker, somewhat reluctantly. He scowled at Tunk, trying to figure out the Ferengi's angle.

"I take it they're already en route, on this other ship you mentioned?"

"A Klingon vessel," clarified Data.

"As I recall," continued Tunk, "the Klingon empire has not yet achieved final agreement on this, what did you call it? Environmental maximum warp limitation?"

"That is correct," said Data, "we are still in the process of negotiating with Emperor Kahless. The emperor's spokesman Dagragas Nai indicates that the main sticking point is—"

"Yes, yes, yes." Tunk waved his hands impatiently. "My point is that your men will arrive at the auction before the bidding begins, I'm sure."

"So?" Commander Riker still did not see the Ferengi's point.

"So, my dear hu-man, they can maintain subspace contact, can they not, relaying a complete description of every item and receiving and entering our own bids on each . . . right?"

"I suppose so." Riker still sounded dubious; but he could think of no good reason to refuse Tunk's request. "It might get confusing," he added. "La Forge is bidding for the Federation, while Lieutenant Worf is bidding for the Klingon Empire."

"Who's running the auction?" asked Tunk.

"Hatheby's of Earth and Cis-Lunar," said Data, "quite a venerable firm, actually. They have been in existence for over five hundred years."

"There, you see? They should have no trouble distinguishing between your La Forge and Worf bidding for the Federation, the Klingons, or us Ferengi. All they have to say is, 'The Federation bids thus-and-so,' or 'Cap'n Munk bids thing-a-ma-bob.' Simple as making book!"

Riker still did not like the suggestion, but there were no valid grounds to refuse. Tunk was right about one point: By the various Ferengi-Federation treaties, the *Enterprise* was required to render any *reasonable* assistance requested by the victims of a disaster out in space . . . unless Data could prove his implication that the Ferengi had deliberately blown up their own ship.

Until then, however, the *Enterprise* and Commander Riker had to play along.

"All right," he agreed, flashing an ersatz smile. "So long as we remain obligated to render reasonable assistance, you can transmit your bids to Commander La Forge, who will bid for the Ferengi."

Tunk turned a deep pink. "Ah, our bids are for Cap'n Munk and son only . . . not for the Ferengi or the Grand Nagus."

"Whatever. Arrange the details with Commander Data."

"Thank you so much," oiled Tunk.

"Bless ye and keep ye," growled his father, still glowering.

"In the meantime, Data will escort you to your spacious quarters directly next to the security office."

"Er . . . thank you, Master Riker." Stiffly, Tunk and Munk followed Riker toward the door. Wesley felt a meaty hand on his shoulder, and d'Artagnan propelled him along behind the Ferengi.

They reached the door, which obediently slid open to reveal Captain Jean-Luc Picard just entering.

For an instant, Wesley stared. Picard saw him, opened his mouth to greet the cadet.

Wesley beat Picard to the introduction. *"Kimbal, Fred Kimbal!"* he exclaimed.

"Captain," said Riker, "say hello to *Cadet Kimbal.*"

"Yes," said Beverly, *"Mister Kimbal* is traveling with these two, fine Ferengi to the auction."

Simultaneously, Data said, *"Sir, have you met Cadet Fred Kimbal?"*

Picard looked from one to the other ruefully. "Really. Well, I hope *Mister Kimbal* and his friends have a pleasant stay here aboard the *Enterprise.* I'm sorry I could not be here sooner, but duties were pressing. Mister Kimbal, will you please introduce me to the rest of the crew of this unfortunate starship?"

Groaning, Wesley ran through the introductions once more; again, the bodyguards did not offer names.

"Am I to understand," queried the captain, "that you are all on your way to the auction as well?" Everyone nodded or grunted agreement.

"The Ferengi want us to relay their bids to Geordi and Worf," said Riker unhappily. "It doesn't seem unreasonable . . . is it?"

"Not unreasonable," said Picard, "but impossible. We just received a subspace communication from Hatheby's outlining the bidding procedure. The only atypical wrinkle is that Hatheby's, having had problems in the past, has dictated that there is to be, quote, *no electronic bidding.*

"They specifically barred any bids sent in remotely by subspace communication. Unfortunately, that means we shall not be able to convey bids from the Ferengi. I apologize for any inconvenience this may cause you; but I assure you, barring unforseen trouble, we shall arrive before the auction ends."

Riker turned from Picard to the Ferengi; he did not appear overly disappointed. "Hard luck," he said, patting Tunk on the shoulder. "Well, I wouldn't worry too much . . . Ferengi interests will be represented."

Tunk stared dazedly at Riker. "They will?"

"Absolutely! We received word earlier today that the Grand Nagus himself has already arrived at Novus Alamogordus."

Once again, Munk puffed up as if he were about to explode more violently than had *The Glutton.* Tunk clapped his hand over his father's mouth, preventing the stream of invective from spraying all over their only hope for getting to the auction at all. He hustled Munk down the corridor behind Data, and the bodyguards ensured that Wesley followed. The Lotriani remained behind.

As they rounded the curve, Riker called out with an innocent smile, "I'm sure the Nagus will be pleased as punch to see you two!"

Tunk shuddered, muttering dark Ferengi curses about bankruptcy and bad credit.

Chapter Ten

"COMMANDER," SAID LIEUTENANT WORF, with an amazing amount of patience for a warrior, "if you have information about Doctor Zorka's state of mind, I request that you share it."

"I don't have any information, Worf."

"The Klingon Empire should have access to all the relevant information required to make informed decisions on how much to bid."

"You mean you want to know how much to bid." Geordi La Forge looked up from the data clip reader, displaying years of back issues of dozens of technical journals. "Worf, I made a copy of the clip for you. Didn't you read it?"

"I am not enough of an engineer to make tooth or claw of it, Commander."

Geordi shrugged. "I'm a damn good engineer, and they're all gibberish to me, too! There are two possibilities from where I sit. First, maybe it's all so advanced and erudite that it's just beyond me; maybe I'm being stupidly blind to Zorka's genius, prejudiced against him because of his megalomaniac tendencies. Or else I'm right, and it's all a bunch of pseudoscientific hand-waving that isn't worth the electronic storage space necessary to publish it.

"How can I say which it is? If it's beyond me, then it's beyond my ability to say that it's beyond me."

"But what do mean, his 'megalomaniac tendencies'?" demanded Worf. "What makes you think he is insane?"

"I never said he was insane; that's too strong. I said he was *peculiar.*"

"But what evidence makes you say *that,* sir?"

Geordi leaned back, rubbing his temples. He removed his visor for a few moments of blessed darkness and freedom from pain. The engineering section was quiet, only a single young Klingon watching a few dials across the room.

"A good scientist always has a touch of monomania about him—tends to focus on a single idea and follow it much further than anyone else ever did. Albert Einstein's theories about special relativity came from his almost religious obsession with the speed of light being constant everywhere, for everybody. In exactly the same way, Zefrim Cochrane invented the warp field a hundred and fifty years later by following the *opposite* idea beyond all reasonable bounds: He wondered what the universe would look like if lightspeed were *not* a constant in normal space."

"But what about Zorka? What makes you think he is . . . a crank?"

"Eventually, the scientist has to put up or shut up. It's like poker, Worf: You have to either fold or lay the cards on the table. Zorka has kept his hand hidden for his entire life! He's written up dozens, scores of inventions; yet he's never demonstrated a single one of them. He claims to have reworked everything from relativity to Cochrane's equations to the Photonic Theorem; but nobody's ever seen the math. But there's more to it . . ."

"Perhaps he is merely secretive."

"Paranoid is more like it. Delusions of persecution; when I was in his class, he accused me of being a spy."

"What? For whom?"

"For the executive officer of the Academy."

Worf growled deep in his throat. *I do not like this,* he thought to himself. Bidding on unknown scientific equipment was bad enough . . . but now, his commander had cast doubt on the trustworthiness of Dr. Zorka's "inventions."

There was nothing Worf hated more than being compelled by honor to undertake an impossible task, knowing he would doubtless fail; but there was nothing he could do. He had been selected by the Klingon High Council, and the duty of a warrior and representative of the House of Mogh was to obey when commanded. The Council acted for the emperor himself.

"Thank you, sir," he said, politely, "you have been a great help to me." *You have been no help at all!* It was not the commander's fault; Worf knew his own ambivalence was mirrored by that of his friend—the more so, since La Forge might even doubt his own perceptions.

The lieutenant commander cleared his throat, looking stern. He found his visor and reattached it: back to business; he resumed reading the publications.

Worf did not envy his department head; the Klingon, at least, was not expected to *know* whether an item offered at the auction actually worked. But La Forge was considered an "expert," and would probably be held subtly responsible if he bid on something that turned out to be junk . . . or did not bid on something that actually worked.

Worf rose silently and returned to their quarters, leaving Geordi La Forge to read Zorka's gibberish for the rest of the night. For his own part, Worf dimmed the lights and sat quietly, imagining himself as Captain Picard; if he could figure out what the captain would do in this situation, Worf might be able to think his way through.

On the bridge of the *Hiding Fish,* Worf's brother Kurn paced nervously. He had to phrase his request exactly right, for the last thing he would want to do was dishonor Worf before the Council . . . first, because to dishonor Worf was to dishonor the House of Mogh, thus Kurn himself! second, because if Worf found out, brother or not, he would tear Kurn's ship (and Kurn) apart with his bare hands.

Kurn honestly believed, however, that he would make a better representative of the Klingon Empire than his older brother; he could not ignore his duty to the homeworld.

He composed himself as best he could. He had donned black leather of the special "Mogh cut," and also the armor of an admiral. The last was a difficult call: Technically, Worf should have been the only one to wear an admiral's rank, being the elder; but Worf was no longer a member of the Klingon Defense Force, having rejoined Starfleet.

Kurn had decided on a bold statement of his central theme: Worf had been absent from the culture for so long, there was no way he could bid with the heart of a Klingon.

"All right, Commander, open the channel."

The viewscreen flickered, then displayed the ensign of the empire while ComSec inspected the transmission for dangerous frequencies or hidden key sequences that might trigger a remote bomb.

Captain Kurn slouched, hands flapping behind his back, waiting for the secretary of the Council to answer the communication.

"Is this how you greet your emperor?" boomed an enormous voice.

Kurn snapped to attention, astonished to see Emperor Kahless himself on the viewscreen! The captain swallowed, mouth suddenly dry. To date, he had seen the returned emperor only at the convocation and at special speeches. Normally, Kahless greeted the full Council, then retired with the representatives of the ruling factions.

Despite knowing the peculiar history of the entity who called himself the emperor, Kurn could not help thinking of him as the real, actual Kahless. In a very real sense, he *was* Kahless: He had Kahless's entire genetic code and all of Kahless's memories . . . the body and soul of a man dead for centuries.

Almost paralyzed with anxiety, lest he speak rudely and

bring dishonor and discommodation upon the family of Mogh (again), Captain Kurn coughed a few times and unconsciously adopted the "inspection stance" he had learned at the Turn War College.

"Your Highness, Emperor Kahless. I must make an application that appears to be against my own brother. But it is not, not really."

Kurn paused, allowing the emperor a chance to cut in if he chose; but Kahless was silent.

"I have great respect for Worf of the House of Mogh. Had he remained in the Defense Force, he would surely be an admiral by now, serving in the High Council instead of me. If that were the case, we would not be having this conversation!

"But it is not the case; instead, Worf has chosen a different path. He has not turned his back on our people and the homeworld; let me not suggest that he has. He has taken an oath to a foreign power, however, and that limits his effectiveness as a representative of the empire. Sire."

"Good point."

"I would not dream to insult Your Highness by . . . what did you say, Sire?"

"I said good point, Kurn of the House of Mogh. I have been thinking about this ever since I appointed him our representative in the auction."

Kurn waited, making sure Kahless was not merely drawing a breath. *Damned strange,* thought the young captain, *I can face death at the hands of a hundred without fear; yet one old man who is not even what he thinks he is causes me to break out in a sweat.*

"My brother is a warrior to make any house proud. He helped put, ah, *restore* Your Highness himself to the legendary throne of the empire. But he has little experience with the delicate negotiations that are required to adequately represent the homeworld at an event of this magnitude."

Emperor Kahless nodded. "Yes, I have worried about that, too. Worf has great honor, and he honors the House of Mogh. Is it fair, I wondered to myself, to ask Worf to bid on unknown equipment invented by a hu-man, a scientist working for Starfleet, with which your brother has only a few years experience?"

Kurn brightened; his plan was rolling along much more smoothly than he had dared hope! "Such an appointment requires a diplomat's touch; it requires the touch of a man who has sat in the highest councils, advising the makers of empires of the delicate nuances of the Federation. The representative of the empire must surely be a warrior! But not *only* a warrior."

"You show surprising wisdom for one so young, Captain Kurn. I shall eagerly await the results of your commodore examination; if you gain the score I expect, I shall take personal pleasure in placing you in command of a true warrior's craft."

"And you will consider my proposal, Your Highness? About the Klingon representative at the auction?"

"I shall do more than consider it, Captain Kurn; I have decided to accept your recommendation in its entirety. This task is beyond Worf of the House of Mogh, though I cast no dishonor upon Worf's house and your own by saying that. One does not use a *Bat'telh* to perform surgery."

Kurn nodded. "You prove yet again, Your Highness, our own wisdom in restoring you to the imperial throne. Your arm is strong and your head is full."

Kahless smiled slightly. "I shall shortly have a new set of orders for you and your brother, Kurn of the House of Mogh. Until then, continue upon your present course."

"I obey, Your Highness."

"Kahless, out."

"May you reign a thousand years, Sire."

Kurn maintained his aplomb until the screen faded back into the forward view from the *Hiding Fish*. Then he let out a war whoop that brought raised eyebrows from Commander Kurak.

"I did it!" exulted Kurn, stalking up and down his bridge with a clenched fist. "I have the appointment!"

"Make sure you do not mount your enemies' heads before you cut them loose," said Kurak. She smiled faintly, amused by the dirty look Kurn cast in her direction.

"Summon my brother," ordered Kurn, resuming his command chair.

Captain Jean-Luc Picard sat uneasily in his own command chair. All day, as the *Enterprise* crawled toward Novus Alamogordus like a Ryan-class slowboat, he had had the most appalling sense of impending doom.

He sipped his tea, Earl Grey, hot, running over a mental checklist of everything that could possibly go wrong on a starship. He had kept the junior engineers busy performing level-one diagnostics on everything he could think of . . . "just for training," he insisted. But in reality, he sorely missed Geordi La Forge's gut-level instincts.

Will Riker sat beside him, making up duty rosters for the next six months . . . something he only did when he, too, was anxious.

So it's not just me, thought Picard. *What catastrophe can be just about to happen?*

Commander Data turned around in his seat. "Sir?" he prompted.

"Yes, Data?"

"A subspace communication has arrived from the Klingon homeworld. I believe it is from the Emperor Kahless himself."

Picard perked up. A message from Kahless? It could be the disaster he had expected.

For a moment, he considered sneaking off to his quarters to receive it. Then he realized that was silly; he would eventually have to tell everyone whatever Kahless had to say anyway, and whether or not he planned to act upon it.

"Put him through," said the captain.

"Aye, sir."

The views of stars vanished abruptly to be replaced by the Klingon coat of arms. Then that, too, faded and the ferocious aspect of Emperor Kahless (the once and future emperor) dominated the bridge.

"Captain Picard, it has been long since we last met."

"Yes, it has, Your Highness; too long. I hope we can meet soon in person, so you can continue the tale of The Warrior Taruf Sadan and the Autocrat in Green."

Kahless blinked in surprise; Picard's unaccented Klingon startled the old emperor.

Kahless grinned appreciatively. "You have a remarkable memory, Jean-Luc. If I do not complete the tale for twice a hundred years, I will not repeat the part you already heard, for you shall still remember it then.

"I have thought long and hard about choosing a representative of the empire for the auction; the obvious choices were Captain Kurn and your own Lieutenant Worf. I sought advice."

"I shall be most pleased to advise Your Highness in any way you wish."

"As this decision affects the both of them, I shall include them in the conversation."

Kahless signaled to an off-screen technician; after a moment, a small window appeared in the screen. Inside this window was an image of the bridge of the *Hiding Fish*. Worf and Kurn could clearly be seen; Geordi was off to the side, barely visible.

Even across the subspace link, Picard could tell that Kurn was gloating and Worf was trying to be stoic in the face of humiliation; the captain did not even have to ask Counselor Troi.

"I have thought long and hard about this decision," explained Kahless. No matter how peaceful the content of his words were, he somehow managed to make each a declaration of war. Kahless was a born warrior.

"In the end, I accepted the analysis that Worf of the House of Mogh has lost touch with the Klingon mainstream . . . however, Kurn, the younger brother, is simply too inexperienced.

"Thus I have decided, Jean-Luc Picard, to name *you* the official representative of the Klingon Empire in this bidding."

For an instant, Picard, Worf, and Kurn merely stared at one another. Then pandemonium broke loose.

Picard nearly leapt out of his command chair. Will stared at Picard, at Kahless, then back at Picard.

Worf turned sadly to Kurn. "My own brother has plotted to dishonor me before the emperor himself?"

At the same time, Kurn was shouting frantically at first officer. "You told me *I* would gain the honor—I will—"

His last words were difficult to make out as he turned away from Worf's accusing look. Then Kahless gestured, and the window vanished from the viewscreen.

Kahless continued. "I recall, of course, your delicate negotiations to put me onto the throne; as well, I read of your expert mediation between Gowron and the sisters of Duras, Lursa and Betor."

"Your Highness," began Captain Picard, "this is indeed a great honor and privilege. But I'm afraid I really must decline. I must remain on the bridge of the *Enterprise* during the entire auction, due to the presence of Cardassians and Romulans. I thank you for your most generous offer, however."

Kahless grinned. "You do not understand my words, Jean-Luc. I did not ask whether you *wanted* to lead the Klingon bidding delegation."

"Your confidence in me is overwhelming; but I must respectfully decline."

Kahless shook his head. "Oh, no, you decline not. I sent a subspace communication to the Federation Council before I contacted you. They were reluctant at first, but then they agreed to order you to immediately begin making preparations; you will bid for the Klingon Empire."

"But . . . but Your Highness! Surely there are other representatives. Are there no Klingon council members more qualified than I to bid for the empire?"

111

Kahless smiled. Then he began to laugh, a booming, warrior's laugh. "Captain Picard, you have such a wicked sense of humor! Are you quite sure you do not have a trace of Klingon blood?

"Which council member would you suggest? Dorak Halfhand? He would suffer a fatal 'accident' from some partisan of the House of Namal. Tivanazt? House Duras would make its objections known most eloquently. Or perhaps we should hunt down Duras's sisters?

"Any Klingon hero who sits on the High Council or owns a ship or two has a dozen other heros who would as soon see him dead! Even Worf was a choice of expediency: There are many on the homeworld who think your lieutenant would look much prettier with a *skat* knife in his chest."

Picard made a glum face. "Klingons have tried to kill me as well."

Kahless shrugged. "All men have enemies, great and small. You are safe aboard your own ship, however, which is more than many council members and generals can boast."

Kahless dismissed the conversation with a hand wave. "Enough. It is decided, and your own council agrees. From now until the auction ends, Picard, you shall consider yourself my representative, bidding for the greater glory of your friend and ally, the Klingon Empire."

Picard said nothing for a moment. When he spoke at last, he did not exactly acknowledge the situation. "Emperor Kahless . . . if you do have some influence with the Federation Council, and even with Starfleet, I must ask a favor of you."

"Anything within the bounds of honor and reason," said Kahless.

"We are hampered by General Order 44556-34, which enacts the warp-speed-limitation treaty. There is a provision to bypass this order in a sufficient emergency, but we cannot seem to get the right hand to stop wrestling the left long enough to issue the necessary authorization."

Kahless's shaggy eyebrows shot up into his lion's mane of hair. "You are reduced to crawling along at warp five? This is intolerable! As the official Klingon representatives, I order you to proceed at your greatest speed."

A voice whispered inaudibly in the background. Kahless turned away, listening for a moment. He interjected angrily —"No!" and "Find a way!"—then turned back to Picard. "It appears I spoke in haste. Belay that last command."

Picard smiled. "I thought it a bit curious for the commander in chief of the Klingon Defense Force to issue orders to a Starfleet captain."

"I shall speak to your council; I am sure we can correct this ridiculous oversight. Kahless out."

"May you reign another five hundred years. Picard out."

Captain Picard sat heavily in his command chair, ruefully stirring his tea, which had long since cooled unacceptably. "Number One, get me Secretary Corrigon, Federation Diplomatic Corps. I think it's time to call in a nice, big favor."

Deanna Troi, who had remained silent during the entire conversation with Kahless, now turned on the captain. "Captain," she said, clipping her words, "may I see you in your quarters? It's a delicate matter of crew morale."

Captain Picard looked at her, surprised by her evident annoyance; it did not take a Betazoid to see that the ship's counselor was ready to chew nails.

They adjourned to Picard's quarters, just off the bridge. Before he could ask her what was on her mind, Deanna fixed him with an icy glare.

"May I speak frankly here, Captain?"

"Of course."

"Then let me quote a well-known philosopher on the dictates of duty." She folded her arms, reciting. "You must accept your duty, despite lack of preparation or personal repugnance. Duty is found in many places. It's not like an overcoat; you wear it always.

"Do you recognize those words, Captain? They are from the speech you gave me just three days ago in this very cabin!"

Picard frowned, recognizing his own words. He turned his head to the side, embarrassed at being caught out. "Anything less is unacceptable in an officer under my command," he remembered. "Well, I'm afraid my pride is about to suffer that mortal blow I talked about before."

Deanna hesitated, thrown off balance by Picard's sudden yielding. "Well, I . . . well, all right, then. Now what?"

"Now I suppose I must bid on behalf of the Klingon Empire, while you must bid for Betazed."

"So who bids for the Federation? Or is it for *Earth?*" She did not mean the word to come out with such vehemence.

"I hope it has not come to that, Deanna. I can understand Betazoids bidding on behalf of Betazed; but I'll be damned if I'll stand by and see the entire Federation tear itself apart over this foolish auction."

"Then somebody bids on behalf of the Federation."

"I had planned to send Will, but the new Hatheby's rules present an extra wrinkle. With Cardassians and Romulans present, a senior command officer must remain on the bridge at all times. I had planned to perform that task myself."

"But now you have to beam down and bid for the Klingons."

"Which means Commander Riker must stay up here."

"Can't he participate by a comm link?"

Picard shook his head. "No electronic bidding, Counselor. Whoever bids must actually be physically present and present identification . . . presumably to avoid the situation where a participant overbids then claims it was someone else impersonating him."

The captain sighed. "I suppose the next in line is Commander Data. I hope he's up to it."

Captain Picard touched his comm badge. "Picard to Riker. Number One, will you come in here, please?"

A moment later, Commander Will Riker sat across from Picard and Troi. "Number One, it appears I shall be down on Novus Alamogordus bidding for the Klingon Empire."

"That means I'll have to stay on the bridge," said Riker with a noticeable lack of sympathy; in fact, he sounded positively gleeful. "Should we just leave Geordi in charge?"

"That is an unacceptable solution, Will. Geordi is convinced, or has convinced himself, I'm not sure which, that none of Dr. Zorka's inventions has any value whatsoever. I cannot order him to make certain bids and simultaneously expect him to take responsibility. If he bids, he must bid as his conscience dictates—which means he'll bid nothing."

"The next logical choice is Data."

"Yes. It will be an interesting experience for him . . . very *human.*" Picard smiled briefly. "Now, on to another subject that concerns me greatly. What in the world is young Wesley doing in the company of an unsavory pair of Ferengi when he ought to be back at the Academy?"

"Wesley?" asked Riker, pretending puzzlement. "I don't know about any Wesley, sir. The only cadet attached to two Ferengi that I've met is someone named Fred Kimbal."

"Very funny, Will. How did Cadet Crusher end up traveling under an alias to this sector? Why is he attending this auction?"

Riker scratched his beard, considering his answer. "Captain, I've tried to get him alone, but one of those two, either Tunk or Munk, sticks to him like a magnet."

"You can't separate them?"

"Well, there's another problem. I can't swear to it, but I think Fred is deliberately avoiding me. He seems afraid to be caught alone with any members of the crew—even his mother."

"I don't like strange, inexplicable events on my ship, Number One. Deanna . . . what emotions have you detected in him?"

"Anxiety, naturally, and a lot of frustration. But there's another emotion hidden beneath the others. Jean-Luc, I would swear Fred—I mean Wesley—is actually enjoying the game. I detect a disturbing sense of . . ."

"Yes? Please continue, Counselor."

"Superiority. Fred is enjoying fooling the Ferengi, even while he's anxious about being with them."

"Wesley," corrected Picard, annoyed.

"Wesley. What did I say, 'Fred'?" She shook her head.

"He's so different from the last time I saw him. I suppose three years at the Academy can do that; but I would almost believe he *is* Fred Kimbal, not Wesley Crusher."

"Will, I'd like you to run a records check for Fred Kimbal; I don't remember any such person aboard the *Enterprise.*"

"Not while I've been first officer."

"Try the Academy. I want to know what's going on between our young cadet's ears. While you're at it, find out who this Munk is; what Ferengi do we know who might give us some information?"

Riker thought for a moment. "The Grand Nagus. He makes it his business to know anyone with enough substance to show up at the Novus Alamogordus auction. I'll contact him and pump him for information. I don't know how much he'll be willing to give, or whether we can trust him . . . he *is* a Ferengi."

"In the meantime, Number One, I think the safest thing is to play along; continue to interact with Wesley as if he were Fred Kimbal, particularly around the Ferengi. Let's assume he knows what he's doing and hasn't merely gotten himself into serious trouble."

"That's not necessarily a safe assumption," grumbled Riker.

"He's generally been able to extricate himself, Will. I have confidence in Wesley . . . rather, in Fred. Counselor?"

Deanna nodded. "I agree. Whether it's for a good reason or some strange reaction to the stress of his studies, it's best we not break the illusion until we understand what's happening."

"Then it's agreed," said the captain. "From now into the forseeable future, the gentleman is Fred Kimbal, a cadet on loan from the Academy who is helping Munk with his bid."

"Data to Captain Picard," said a voice from the ether.

"Picard," said the captain.

"Excellent news, sir. Emperor Kahless seems to have used his influence to good effect."

"We've got the green light?"

"Yes, sir; the green light. Admiral Boom has just sent a

message by subspace: The *Enterprise* is authorized to violate the maximum warp speed limitation."

Picard and Riker exchanged a glance; the captain spoke. "I suppose there are some advantages to being the avatar of an emperor."

"Mister Data," Riker said triumphantly, "increase speed to warp factor nine. Let's arrive in Novus Alamogordus before all the good stuff is gone!"

Chapter Eleven

WHEN THE *ENTERPRISE* finally entered orbit around Novus Alamogordus, the auction had already been in progress for two days. Just as Captain Picard and Commander Data prepared to beam down, Riker opened a comm link from the bridge.

"Yes, Will; what is it?"

"Priority-one message from Starfleet, Captain."

"Proceed."

"The Federation Exo-Vironmental Research Council has just given final approval to your request to exceed warp five."

"Excellent news, Number One. Drop by Ten-Forward and have a celebratory drink for me."

"I've plotted a warp-nine orbit around the planetoid, sir. Shall I engage?"

Picard chuckled; despite serving decades in Starfleet, the glacial speed of the Federation bureaucracy, hobbled by having to weigh the competing interests of literally tens of thousands of planets, never failed to move him to sardonic amusement.

"Keep the comm link open during the bidding; there's no rule against electronically following the action."

"Riker out."

Data turned to the captain. "Sir, I presume Commander Riker was joking about a warp-nine orbit. Despite the apparent seriousness of his tone of voice, the suggestion is incongruous enough that he can not have meant it in earnest."

"It's a special form of dark humor called sarcasm."

"I have several examples of sarcasm in my memory banks. I am working on a program to respond to such humor, but it is not yet ready for testing."

Just then, the transporter door slid open. Beverly Crusher hurried into the room.

"Good, you haven't left yet. I'm coming down."

"Certainly, Beverly. Is there a particular reason? I thought with your son aboard, you would prefer . . ."

Dr. Crusher rolled her eyes. "Oh, you mean Fred Kimbal? He doesn't seem to have time for me. He's too busy with his new Ferengi friends. Jean-Luc, I'm not sure I entirely approve of those two."

"Why are you beaming down to the planetoid?"

"Medical equipment." Dr. Crusher stepped aboard the transporter platform. "I spoke to Admiral Dyreal, who authorized a small budget at my discretion. But you caught me: I'm less interested in bidding in the auction than seeing the Chateau Hotel Casino . . . especially with such a charming pair of guides."

"Energize," ordered Captain Picard. When they materialized in the antechamber of the great hall on Novus Alamogordus, he resumed the discussion. "I have Will checking on Munk and Tunk; so far, however, there seems to be no record of either of them . . . anywhere."

"The most likely explanation," offered Data, "is that someone has purged all records of their existence. It is a common practice among the more affluent Ferengi."

"We may get some answers from the Grand Nagus, Beverly. He'll be at the auction, according to Hatheby's. In the meantime, we did discover that Fred Kimbal is the name of Wesley's roommate in the dormitory at the Academy."

"That's where I heard the name before!"

The great hall was aptly named. Large enough to swallow the *Enterprise,* it included thousands of offices, a dozen recreational facilities, hydroponic farms, its own power plant (an old spiked-antimatter reactor built forty years earlier), two gambling casinos running every game from Dabo to the ancient game of craps, three separate dining halls—one "small" banquet hall that seated a mere three hundred—and two meeting and dining rooms that could accommodate over a thousand each.

The hall was originally built as an actual chateau back when the artificial planetoid of Novus Alamogordus was still called Nouveau Yvelines and was the administrative center of a six-system mining colony. Just twenty years later, with the twenty-three-company dilithium consortium in financial ruin, the "governor" of the system—Viscomte Nicholas Fouquet XI—fled with most of the treasury. The planetoid was abandoned when the colony was withdrawn; four years later, the Federation Association for the Advancement of Science, having inherited the artificial planetoid, granted it to Dr. Zorka, who renamed it Novus Alamogordus, then sold the northern hemisphere (including the chateau) to Novus Business Ventures, a resort consortium.

Fouquet had decorated the chateau in conscious homage to the Louis XIV chateau of Versailles on Earth, in the district of France. Zorka himself never came near the buildings, preferring the desolate southern hemisphere, which had been designed for factories to produce mining equipment. Dr. Zorka turned the factories into laboratories.

Bradford junior, however, lived in the chateau and demanded that NBV retain him as interior designer. He not only kept the original furnishings, he added to them along the same lines.

Jean-Luc Picard strolled happily through the antechamber into the main building, observing the white, wooden furniture with gilt edges, overindulgent mirrors, bejeweled boxes, and full-length portraits framed by velvet curtains. The floor was a good replication of marble tiles, while the walls were white with gold-leaf trim, and appeared to support numerous "hidden" doors.

Beverly continued the conversation. "Wesley has mentioned Fred Kimbal in several of the letters he occasionally sends. Apparently, the boy is a math and engineering genius, but is a little, how does Wes put it? Unsocialized. Wes said he planned to try to get Fred more involved in things."

"He has chosen an odd way to proceed," Data remarked.

Picard looked up, distracted. "Eh? Did you say something, Beverly?"

"No, nothing, Jean-Luc. Go back to your Louis the Fourteenth love seat."

"I'm sorry, Beverly. It's such a treat for me to see perfect replicas of the most important historical artifacts of my own district. Have you ever seen the reconstruction of the real Versailles, about twenty kilometers from Paris?"

"No, actually. But I would love for you to show me someday."

"Consider it a date, Doctor."

"I will."

The auction itself was in progress, according to the agenda handed them when they arrived; however, as far as Data could tell, nobody was actually present bidding. At least, there were 814 people present in the largest ballroom and only eleven physically present in the main dining hall, where the auction actually occurred.

Poking his head into the dining hall, Data saw the auctioneer standing at a podium. Data watched, perplexed; at last, the android decided he had figured out the system: the auctioneer indicated particular lots then harangued the bidders until they became so unhinged that they twitched or made some involuntary squawk, which the auctioneer took as assent to his current figure.

"It seems a peculiar method of negotiating a fair market value," remarked Data; then he noticed that Captain Picard and Dr. Crusher had vanished.

Raising his brows, Data entered the auction chamber and took a seat.

An extremely large forefinger poked his shoulder. "You're sitting on the Bajoran ambassador," rumbled a gigantic Elphasian.

Data quickly stood and looked back at his chair, concerned that he would find a squashed Bajoran. "Sir," he said, "I do not understand what you mean. There is no one sitting in this chair."

"Sure he is," argued the Elphasian. "He's in the lounge chatting up the Grand Nagus."

Data looked at the chair, at the lounge, then back at his conversationalist. "If the Bajoran ambassador is in the lounge talking with the Grand Nagus, how can he be sitting here?"

"You've never been to one of these before, have you?" Data admitted the charge, and the man continued. "It's pre-bid. Understand? This is short stuff; nobody cares much."

"The . . . desks and chairs?" asked Data, remembering his earlier conversation with Commander Riker.

"Exactly. They're bidding on the lighting fixtures now. They were designed by Art/Dexo Studios. I suppose they're worth something, now that Core Bellorus is dead. Anyway, anybody who's interested has already submitted a maximum bid to the bid-boss; then they disappear to schmooze with the other bidders to sound them out for the hot lots."

"Then if the bids are present, why is the auctioneer still calling out prices?"

The Elphasian shrugged, looking like a mountain shaking in an earthquake. "A few folks stay, those that just like the game. Nobody knows when the pre-bids kick in; if nobody submitted a bid on a certain item, you might get it for cheap."

"Are you here to bid on any of the 'short stuff'?"

"Me? Nah. I just needed a quiet place to balance my accounts. I'm an agent; I bid for clients. Say . . . would you like me to bid for you, too? Takes all the worry and trouble out of the transaction!"

"No, thank you. How do I find out when certain lots are being auctioned?"

"They're all on display. Holosuits upstairs; you find the pieces you want, check the time and the minimum, and submit a written bid if you want. Then be sure to show up at least an hour early; all times are approximate."

Data rose, strode to the door. He paused, looked back: all but two people had left the room, the Elphasian and a young Romulan girl, no more than seventeen. Yet the auctioneer still carried on at full howl.

There is a lesson about biological people to be learned here, thought Data. He stored a complete record in his special memory file where he kept all the pieces of the puzzle so far identified—the puzzle that assembled into a "human being."

Outside, Data wormed through the crowd toward the huge stairway, nearly twenty meters wide at the base.

A long, boisterous line snaked along the upper corridor to the second ballroom, which had been subdivided into a number of holovision rooms by Hatheby's. Data was about to join the end of the line when he spotted Dr. Crusher and the captain two bends ahead of him.

For a moment, Data was unsure of the etiquette; then Captain Picard spotted him and waved him over. Data joined the pair.

"We thought you'd been caught and auctioned off," said Beverly Crusher.

Recognizing the joke, Data decided it was time to test his new program. He opened his mouth and expelled air in a simulation of human laughter.

The captain and Dr. Crusher turned to stare—as did everybody within a four-meter radius.

"Data," said the doctor, concerned, "another laughing program?"

"Yes, Doctor . . . I was laughing at your joke."

Captain Picard leaned close, speaking quietly. "I think you had better work on this one a little longer, Data; it sounds a little like a braying donkey."

"Thank you, sir. I will attempt to modulate the sound to make it more natural."

"Where did you go?" asked Dr. Crusher.

"I thought you were headed to the auction room. I was unaware that one must inspect the merchandise before bidding. It does make sense, though."

They waited more or less patiently for another hour before they finally entered the holovision inspection suites. The Hatheby's employee directed them into a single-file line.

As soon as Data passed through the door, he found himself floating in space—except he could feel his feet still firmly planted on the chateau floor. Dr. Crusher hesitated momentarily, causing the captain, busy gawking at the sudden stars, to fetch up against her. They both laughed then moved away slowly, and Data recorded the sound for later analysis and correction of his own laughter program.

A peculiar object floated before them. It was shaped like a tubular isosceles triangle, colored white. Data took another step forward, studying the object to determine what it did, when he abruptly realized he was moving slowly, apparently on an automated treadmill.

A vocal narration focused on his precise location, describing the first major lot: "This subspace acceleration prototype draws energy from subspace to accelerate mass to near light-speed without drawing any energy from the surrounding continuum. This device, which uses previously unknown properties of protomatter, can completely eliminate the need for costly impulse engines for intrasystem transport."

In illustration, the separate rods of the triangle began to rotate, finally shimmering into an inner red ring and an outer blue ring as the tubes neared light-speed themselves. Then a coordinate representation of subspace appeared, superimposed over the starview; it warped as it passed through the center of the triangle.

A ship appeared, entered the triangle, and promptly vanished in a flash of blue Cherenkov radiation.

Data stared, puzzled. If the invention really worked, it would require a complete rewriting of the universal field equations. *I begin to see what Geordi means,* he thought.

The tour continued past twenty-two more lots that were shown in great detail, with animation, narration, and frequent, three-dimensional diagrams. Data was treated to miniaturization and injected into a human body; he was sent forward in time to observe a bifurcated race of industrious workers below and playful children above; he saw a device that visually projected a person's life as a long, wormlike image, allowing the user to determine the exact future date of death of each person.

At last, the holovision display showed the final lot to be auctioned: the photonic pulse cannon. It was an impressive weapon: a small, artificial planetoid, not quite the size of Novus Alamogordus, but still some two hundred kilometers in diameter, with a gigantic antenna sticking out. Photonic beams of protomatter particles fired from several origin points, joining at the antenna. From there, they burst forth as a single pulse that (in the simulation) punched through the shields of a starship, carefully crafted to match no known ship designs but to be strongly *reminiscent* of ships operated by the Federation, the Klingons, Romulans, Cardassians, and many other races.

After seeing the holovision animation, Data's feet bumped against the stationary floor again. He stepped off the sliding ramp and exited.

The final room in the suite was bare except for static, three-dimensional holoplates of the inventions he had just "seen," along with many others that had had no animation. Beside each plate was an information sheet showing the name of the invention, the time of auction, the minimum bid, and any bids already entered by other participants.

Each of the "hot lots" already had bids entered far above

the minimums, so it appeared the auction would be successful. Data did not enter any written bids; neither did Captain Picard, he noticed.

Along one wall were viewscreens showing the "short stuff," divided into categories, such as power storage, nacelle architecture, and propulsion. Dr. Crusher found the "medical technologies" viewscreen and entered a few small bids on items that did not appear very popular.

Data approached the captain. "Sir, I would like to return to the auction room and practice bidding on some small items. Do you mind?"

"Not at all, Data," said Captain Picard; in fact, Data noted with some surprise that the captain sounded quite pleased at the possibility. He smiled indulgently at Dr. Crusher.

"Jean-Luc," the doctor said, "will you show me around? There are so many fascinating pieces in the chateau that I'd like to understand better."

Without a backward glance at the android, the captain took the doctor's arm and strolled away. Mentally shrugging, Data headed back down the stairs and returned to the dining hall.

The auctioneer had been replaced by another, but he used the same style: rapid patter coupled with exortations to "up the holding a bit" and "keep it going, lads, keep it going." Data sat in a chair far away from anybody else, hoping it was not already "occupied," and waited for an opportunity to bid.

Ten minutes later, the auctioneer offered a small improvement to nacelle architecture. The bidding began.

Waiting for a propitious moment, Data caught the auctioneer's eye and raised his hand, finger pointing toward the ceiling. The auctioneer accepted the bid, and Data felt pleased.

If one accepted the auctioneer's banter, Data was bidding against one person physically present and three others who had submitted maximum lines on the nacelle but were not in the room. It was disconcerting to say the least.

"Who will make it ten bars? Who will make it ten? Thank you, sir, in the front row! Ten is the bid, ten is holding . . ." Of course, there was no one in the front row; it was an absent bidder.

Strangest of all was when *two* absent bidders would begin a bid war between each other! The auctioneer took all three voices—the two bidders and himself mediating—and found it curious that anyone without his positronic brain could follow the bidding.

Data won a bid at three bars of latinum for a force-shield projection tool. The auctioneer called him forward to record his identification.

"Name, client, and race, please," said the bid-boss.

"Commander Data, bidding for the United Federation of Planets."

"Race? Hatheby's follows a policy of full disclosure of all winning bids except in closed, private auctions."

"Android," he said.

The auctioneer paused, stared intently at Data. "Am I to understand that you are an artificial construct, sir?"

"Yes. I was built by Doctor Soong and activated thirty-two standard years ago."

The bid-boss pondered for several moments, then activated a comm link in his podium. "Rules committee to the block," he said.

Several other participants gathered around, curious at the disruption. Word spread, and within two minutes, the room was half full.

"I do not understand this delay," said Data. "I believe I won the bid. What is the problem?"

The auctioneer said nothing, however. A few minutes later, the room was full. The "rules committee" arrived— three senior employees of Hatheby's.

The auctioneer indicated Data. "It says it's an android, artificially constructed thirty years ago."

"Strictly speaking, that is not true," said Data. "I was activated thirty-two years ago, but I was constructed some time before that."

"Can you show that you're an android?" asked the oldest of the three members of the rules committee.

Surprised, Data opened his head plate, displaying the positronic circuitry. The members peered inside, then whispered among themselves. Out of deference for their privacy, Data did not increase the gain on his auditory receptors.

At last, they nodded and returned their attention to Data. "I'm afraid we're going to have to disallow your bids, sir," said the senior member.

"I do not understand. Why am I disallowed from bidding?"

"The rules explicitly stated that no electronic bidding was to be allowed."

Data waited, still not understanding.

"You are an electronic construct," explained the auctioneer.

"My brains use positronic pathways, not electronic."

"It's the same thing; a positron is just an electron with a positive instead of negative charge. I'm sorry, but the decision of the rules committee is final: rule five. You are declared an electronic device, and since electronic bidding is disallowed by principle at this auction, I'm afraid you shall not be allowed to bid."

Scant moments later, Data was "escorted" back to the antechamber by two husky security guards and placed upon the transporter pad. A moment later, Data was summarily beamed back to the *Enterprise*. He did not even have time to contact the captain until he returned to the bridge.

Commander William Riker sat in the command chair, pondering the situation. "Riker to Picard," he said.

After a moment, the captain responded. "Picard here. What the situation, Number One?"

"You may be interested to know that Data is back at the helm."

"What? Why?"

Wearily, Riker filled the captain in on the situation.

"I certainly intend to file a protest about this, Will. They have no right to bar a Starfleet officer from bidding, android or no!"

"I agree, sir; but at the moment, we have a serious problem. The protest will take days—particularly given recent experience with the blazing speed of the Federation bureaucracy."

"Yes, I see your point, Number One. Who is to represent the Federation right here and now?"

"Is there any chance that you could? No, I guess you can't bid against yourself."

"Emperor Kahless would not be pleased."

"I can't leave the bridge; Data is considered an electronic device and isn't allowed to bid; Geordi is convinced that the devices are all worthless and refuses to bid on them. Deanna would be a great choice . . . except she's already been tapped to bid for Betazed! Even 'Fred Kimbal' is busy agenting for our Ferengi chums, Munk and Tunk. What about Beverly?"

Dr. Crusher's voice chimed in. "Absolutely not, Will! I don't have anywhere near enough engineering knowledge to know what works and what's just plain silly. Would you send Geordi down here to bid on microsurgery disphasic forceps?"

Riker grunted; Beverly Crusher had made her point.

"Will, there is only one choice left."

Riker rubbed his beard. "Lieutenant Worf?"

"It's your call, Will. I'm out of the loop on this; I represent the Klingon Empire at this moment."

"Captain, don't you find something a bit bizarre about bidding for the Klingons while Worf bids for the Federation?"

"'Misery acquaints a man with strange bedfellows,' Number One."

"Shakespeare?"

The Tempest, Act two, scene two."

Will nodded slowly, then realized that Captain Picard could not see him over his comm badge. "We have no choice. Worf bids for the Federation."

"I'm certain he'll make an excellent representative, Will. Picard out."

The communications link closed. For a moment, Riker sat silent, contemplating the unpredictable turn of events that had eliminated each possible representative, one by one. "Data," he asked, "what do you suppose the odds are that you have just been selected to represent the Borg?"

Data looked up. "I do not think that is a likely possibility, sir. Or were you making a joke?"

"Joke, Data."

"Ah." Without warning, the android threw his head back and barked with hysterical laughter for four seconds; then he ceased, as if turning off a faucet. When he finished, every officer on the bridge stared in stunned silence.

"How realistic was my response, sir?" asked Data, back to his usual polite tone.

"You sounded like a homicidal maniac about to massacre the entire crew!"

"Hm." The android wore his puzzled expression. "I suppose I still need to work on the program. Thank you, sir."

His heart rate just getting back to normal, Riker added, "Locate Lieutenant Worf and inform him of his new status, Data."

"Aye, sir."

Lieutenant Worf had already located the upstairs holosuite, the only interesting ride on the planetoid. He found the weapons animation amusing, but the rest of the techomarvels were over his head. He exulted that it no longer made any difference whether he understood the devices or not, as he did not have to bid on them.

Worf had never been comfortable with the duty, mainly because he had no idea how to carry it out properly. How did one go about setting a fair price for some item . . . and what should a proper warrior do when the bidding exceeds the price—but only by a little bit?

At what point should one cease bidding? At any moment, bidding a single extra bar of latinum might win the day. On the other hand, one could easily find oneself bidding two hundred bars on an item whose fair price was *one* hundred bars, without even remembering how one got to that point!

Worf was just congratulating his good fortune that Kahless had decided instead upon Captain Picard—a much better choice, Worf believed, far more experienced with this sort of abstract gamesmanship—when his comm badge beeped. It was Commander Data, back on the *Enterprise* for some mysterious reason.

Three minutes later, Worf sat in stony silence, once again the "designated buyer" . . . but this time for the Federation —bidding against his own captain!

He was still sitting and steaming when Geordi La Forge found him; Worf's friend had just finished his fifth trip through the holosuites.

"Man, what a ride!" cried Geordi, as excited as a young boy after his first Rite of Ascension.

"I thought you said these inventions were all . . . 'vaporware,'" grumbled the Klingon, annoyed by Geordi's exuberance.

"They are! But they make *wonderful* science-fiction stories!"

Chapter Twelve

CADET WESLEY CRUSHER sat on his rack, worn-out both physically and emotionally. Physically, he had spent several hours replicating bar after bar of chaseum in the shape of standard, gold-pressed latinum bars in various denominations: dekabars, hectobars, and even some kilobars; the last astonished and frightened him . . . he had never before even *seen* a latinum kilobar.

Emotionally, he had ninety percent convinced himself that he was going to spend the next sixty years either at a Federation prison colony or a Ferengi Acquisitional Educational facility.

Shaping the bars was difficult, exacting work. Ordinarily, to copy some item, one merely popped the original into the replicator and activated the "load object" program; the replicator took the original apart, subatomic particle by subatomic particle, then reassembled it exactly, incidentally determining all the data required to replicate it. Thereafter, infinite copies could be assembled, limited only by the total amount of mass available to the replicator system, the total energy, and the amount of time one was willing to spend.

However, the normal technique was impossible in this case, for gold-pressed latinum could not be replicated . . . hence, the replicator could not take apart the gpl to determine the pattern. Instead, Wesley had to command a chaseum bar replicated, remove it from the replicator nook, visually compare it to a real bar of gpl, then return the chaseum to the replicator with instructions to make the stamp indentation deeper or the starburst insignia crisper, to rework the outer frill or move the portrait to the left a bit.

For the first few minutes, Wesley was afraid that someone would notice that the Ferengi (and "Fred Kimbal") were replicating chaseum bars over and over; then, he began to *hope* someone would notice.

"But why would they?" explained Tunk with a shrug. "What would make them even think to check?"

Wesley had no answer, for of course Tunk was correct: There was no generic "suspicious characters" program that automatically monitored passengers on the *Enterprise* and tattled about anything out of the ordinary. Unless Data or Riker or someone thought to actually ask the computer, "Have the Ferengi been replicating anything?", no one would know. Chaseum was neither dangerous nor restricted.

Of course, chaseum that was altered to look just like latinum was both dangerous and restricted. The Federation even had a fancy name for it: counterfeit currency.

While Wesley hunched over the machine, wiping sweat from his forehead with the sleeve of his shirt, a gigantic pair of boots suddenly stepped to either side of his head.

He looked up; it was the Klingon guard, feet widespread, arms akimbo. D'Artagnan stood at the Klingon's side, arms folded across his chest. Wesley noted with infinite relief that they glowered at Tunk, not at the cadet.

"Ahem," coughed d'Artagnan.

"What-what-what?" stammered Tunk, distracted.

"It's stardate 47283.7, sir."

"So?"

"The first of the month."

"So?"

"So where's our latinum?"

Tunk blinked, then grinned slyly. "Why, here you are! Here's a *hectogram* to split between you . . . that's six months' wages in advance."

D'Artagnan leaned over and spit upon the ersatz bar. "Our contract says *latinum,* not painted chaseum."

"Well, then, maybe we don't even need you anymore!" shouted the Ferengi in a fury. "Go play in the turboshaft, Simon, and take your cheese-headed partner with you . . . why, with our new means, we can buy a dozen like you!"

D'Artagnan smiled, exposing sharp, inhuman teeth. Wesley started—he had simply assumed the man was a human; but unless he filed his teeth to points like a cannibal, he was from some race Wesley didn't know. "Thanks for releasing us, Ferengi worm. We've accumulated a tidy sum . . . which we're about to multiply in that casino downstairs. Have a wretched life . . . I hope you end up in a jail cell."

Tunk snarled right back. "You'd better remember that nondisclosure agreement you signed, if you don't want to be hauled into a Ferengi courtroom!"

Now where have I heard that before? thought the cadet, smiling to himself.

"There's still a little matter of last month's wages . . . in *real* latinum, you bent little gnome, or we'll kill you both."

Grumbling, Tunk rose and padded into the adjoining quarters. While he rummaged, d'Artagnan turned to Wesley. "Hey, kid, no hard feelings, right? I mean, I was just doing my job."

"Yeah, sure. No problem. I get kidnapped and threatened all the time."

"Look, ah, I've never gambled before. Any hot tips?"

Wesley considered. On the one hand, they were simply hired guns; on the other hand, they *had* given Tunk the muscle he needed to kidnap Wesley. On the third hand, the cadet decided he simply did not like the pair of "bodyguards." *Enforcers is a better description,* he thought angrily.

"Sure," he said, "the best game around is old-fashioned Dabo. And remember . . . always bet on double-circles after every run of three blues, and always triple-down whenever all the edges fill with bets." In fact, so far as Wesley knew from reading books on the subject, he had just given d'Artagnan the worst possible bets to take in Dabo. The enforcers would be broke in a matter of hours.

Tunk finally snuck back into the room, grumbling anew when he discovered that the muscle was still waiting for him. He paid off their wages with ill-grace, complaining all the while about how they had cheated him by actually demanding their latinum be paid.

As soon as d'Artagnan had counted both sums, he pocketed them and chugged away, followed by the Klingon. The door whooshed shut behind the enforcers, apparently wiping them from Tunk's consciousness at the same time.

"All right, show's over," snarled the Ferengi. "Back to work, or I'll rouse my father to demonstrate some sharp shillelagh work!"

Just before they departed, Tunk elbowed Wesley aside from the replicator, winking at the cadet. "Just a moment, Kimbal; I have to make something." Tunk leaned close and said, "I want a two-inch diameter ball of pure sodium."

The soft, metal ball materialized; making sure his hands were dry, Tunk picked it up and pocketed it. He grinned at Wesley. "Just a little phrank," he said, as if that explained his mysterious doings. "All right, Kimbal—break's over— hop back to it."

By the time Munk was ready to descend to Novus Alamogordus, Wesley struggled under the back-breaking, guilty burden of fifty-six bars of "gold-pressed latinum," carried in a shoulder bag that caused the cadet to list to the right. The denominations added up to a counterfeit total of 14,060 bars.

"Tools," explained Tunk to the transporter chief who asked what was in the bag; "must examine the merchandise to make sure it's *genuine,* heh-heh." When Tunk laughed, his face split in a goblin grin that gobbled up his eyes between cheeks and eyebrows. His father, Munk, did not deign to answer.

Once on the planetoid and inside the chateau, Munk called a huddle. "Certes, we must proof the gilt to see if it passes muster in sooth. Tunk! Carry a few bars to yon hostelier and take us a twin pair of cabins for the duration."

"Me?" squeaked the younger Ferengi. "Why not the hu-man?"

Munk fixed his son with a frozen glare; its effect was mitigated by the elder's dwarfish stature. "Sure and a Ferengi's going to pass his booty to a *hu-man* servant!"

"Oh. I guess it would look rather funny."

"Har-de-har. Now, get thee hence! Capture a *pair* of rooms; I'll not be bounden to a knave like thee."

Preferring the company of a young knave to an old villain, Wesley tagged after Tunk. Munk leaned on his staff and tried to look wise beyond his years.

"Why does your father talk like that?"

"Like what?"

"Like the duke and the dauphin." Wesley was thinking of the ancient epic novel *Huckleberry Finn,* by Mark Twain.

Tunk grinned, exposing teeth that would have given a small child nightmares. "I see you're finally beginning to warm to the old man a bit. Father never went to the fine schools . . . he's entirely a self-made Ferengi!"

Thereby taking a grievous responsibility off the shoulders of the Prophets, thought Wesley. "Let me guess," he said. "He learned to speak standard English by watching bad Shakespearean holoplays."

"Hah! Shows how much hu-mans know. Father refined his speech by copying a few, negligible points of grammar from your overrated Shakespeare. But he learned originally from a far subtler source: those wonderful pirate holoplay histories they used to produce out of Peter Blood studios. I remember one in particular father loved, *The Treasure of Bludy Sea,* which had a hero named Edward Teach who was very much like a Ferengi—ah, but it's our turn."

Tunk sidled up to the counter with aplomb; he had lost whatever trepidation he had shown earlier. Wesley, on the other hand, was a mass of nerves, squirming, fidgeting, about three seconds from breaking down and confessing everything. All that stopped him was the certain knowledge that Tunk and Munk would put the blame squarely on "Fred Kimbal's" shoulders, claiming that Fred built the counterfeit clock (true) and that Fred had altered most of the chaseum (Wesley, actually). If questioned by the authorities, Wesley would tell the truth, of course, which would put both himself and Fred into Chokey.

"I'd like two of your best rooms," demanded Tunk.

The Fomorian shimmied his shaggy bulk and declared, "That will be six bars for three days, sir."

Without saying a word, the Ferengi suavely tossed a dekabar of "latinum" onto the counter.

"Thank you, sir!" groveled the clerk, handing them a pair of keys.

Tunk snatched them both, not allowing Wesley either one. "The rooms have replicators, of course?"

"But of course, sir. Replicators, dinette nooks, holosuite access, oversize baths—"

"Baths?" asked a puzzled Tunk, as if he had never heard of the invention before. "Wait, what did you say about holosuite access?"

"There is a holosuite at either end of the penthouse corridors, sir; your room keys give access, sir. The libraries contain a wide variation of programs, sir."

"Any programs with . . ." Looking suspiciously at Wesley, Tunk leaned close and put his hand to his mouth; the Fomorian crooked an ear.

Tunk spoke so quietly that Wesley picked out nothing but the word *molasses*.

The Fomorian clerk nodded vigorously. "But of course, sir! We have an entire Ferengi section. Now if that will be all, sir?"

"All? How about four bars change?"

A bit too slowly, as if to register resentment without

making it too blatant, the clerk placed four bars of latinum on the counter. Tunk quickly pocketed all but one bar, then signed in, leaving the bar on the counter.

Wesley scowled, noticing that Tunk signed the name "Brubrak & party." *Why did he do that?* wondered the cadet. Probably just Ferengi cussedness, he decided; *why tell the truth when a lie, plausible or im—, would do?*

"Say," said the Ferengi, staring at the clerk and toying with the remaining bar, "do you have a half-gram piece?"

"Oh, yes, sir!" exclaimed the clerk, wringing his hands obsequiously.

"Really? Then I guess you don't need this!" Tunk quickly swept the last bar into his pocket along with the rest of the change.

He turned and suddenly began hacking, as if he had something caught in his throat.

Spying a huge water fountain in the center of the lobby, surrounded by dozens of representatives, Tunk hurried over. Wesley trailed along behind. *Should I do something?* he wondered, then realized he had no idea how to perform first aid on a Ferengi.

Tunk bulled his way through the crowd with incredible rudeness, then hopped upon a bench. Clearing his throat loudly a few times, Wesley saw him surreptitiously palm something from his pocket.

Tunk hacked one, last, monster time, then spat into the trickling waters; at the same time, he dropped the object, which Wesley recognized as the sodium pellet he had replicated back on the *Enterprise.*

The sodium exploded violently, exactly where Tunk had spat. Yellow-orange flames shot up for a moment, and the water frothed as if it had become a lake of fire. A wave of water erupted from the fountain, drenching the front row of spectators, and, incidentally, Wesley Crusher.

Several persons in the crowd screamed, and the mob surged away from the fountain. They stared in stunned silence as Tunk, ignoring their stunned faces, patted his stomach with his fist.

"Ach, hu-man cooking!" he cried at last.

Wesley tensed, checking himself by main force from planting his foot on Tunk's fundament and launching the wretched "phranker" into the fountain; *it probably violates some term of my contract,* he decided ruefully.

"What the hell you mean, pulling something like that?" demanded a chubby, squeaking representative of some race Wesley had never seen before.

"Oh, it was just a phrank! Where's your sense of humor?"

"I haven't got one!"

"Really. Well, you should at least have a sense of self-preservation."

The long-snouted heckler drew himself up to his full height, a head taller than Tunk. "Are you insinuating that I have anything to fear from *you?*"

Tunk curled his lip. "See this fountain? Why, if I'd a mind to, I could throw you all the way across it!"

Wesley renewed speculation about Tunk flying through the air into the center of the pool; the Ferengi seemed determined to embarrass and humiliate the cadet beyond all rational levels.

But this time, it seemed Tunk had boasted more than he could eschew.

The snouted one stared incredulously; the circular fountain had a diameter of at least twenty meters. "Utter rot!" he exclaimed.

"Can too!"

"Cannot!"

"Can too!"

"Nonsense!"

Tunk stood belly-to-belly with the man. "Oh, yeah? Well, I'll bet you two bars of latinum that I can!"

"You're on!" The man pointed at all the people standing around, who had been gawking at the exchange. "You're all witnesses! He bet me two bars of latinum that he could fling me all the way across this fountain!"

Wesley stared, fascinated; he knew it was some sort of "phrank," but he had no idea what was in Tunk's mind. He did, however, begin to notice a pattern. In each case, Tunk's "phrank" critically depended upon *full participation by the victim.* The crowd, and Wesley himself, had followed close behind Tunk as he approached the fountain, retching in obvious distress ... they had not turned away to give the Ferengi privacy, and they were drenched.

Now, the snouted representative had talked himself into a preposterous bet, one that he could not possibly lose ... thus his greed had propelled him into certain victimhood.

Wesley stepped back, fascinated by his sudden revelation.

The Ferengi pushed his sleeves up, spat on his hands, and asked, "Are you ready to fly like a bird?"

The heckler squatted, hands on knees, facing the fountain. "Let her go," he said.

Tunk grabbed the man by collar and seat; and with a mighty heave and an even mightier yowl, he hurled the man through the air ... all of one meter, right into the fountain pool.

In spite of Cadet Crusher's resolve, he smiled; it was all he could do to avoid laughing out loud as the heckler sputtered and floundered in the water, cursing Tunk in between sucking gasps of air. Before the snout could scramble out, Tunk grabbed him a second time.

"I said I could fling you across the fountain," shouted the Ferengi like a wild man; *"but I didn't say I would do it on the first try! Ready, aim, fire!"*

Once again, Tunk hurled the heckler into the water, face first. Then he reached in and caught him once again by scruff and pant-seat. *"Third time's the charm!"* he hollered.

But the heckler had had enough. "Wait," he cried, struggling in Tunk's grasp; "I concede! I give up! Here!" Dripping water from every square centimeter, the man fumbled into his pocket, extracting two latinum one-gram coins. Hand shaking, he dropped them into Tunk's palm; then he splashed his way across the pool to the other side, climbed out, and bolted into the mob.

Wesley stroked his chin, seeing the pattern clearly. Without the sanction of the victim, none of Tunk's pranks would work.

A thought began to churn in the cadet's mind; if the universe was a huge phrank, was the secret to offer one's opponents the opportunity to become victims of their own greed, vanity, or arrogant pride?

Wesley Crusher filed the subroutine away for further processing.

Tunk turned and strolled back toward Munk, cackling like a dirty young man. He forked over one of the keys; Munk said nothing about the two "phranks."

"Och, 'tis a fine and noble public house in sooth!" agreed Munk when he heard about the holosuites with the complete Ferengi program section. "Anon, young lads, hie ye to yon mummer show, where the barkers hath laid before us all ye prizes we may capture at bid."

"Us? Why, what do *you* plan to do, Father?"

"Meself? Why, this poor, aged relative shall lay to rest his weary bones upon yon feathery nest."

"You're hieing yourself to the holosuite!" snarled Tunk, pointing an accusatory finger at Munk.

"Hold thy tongue, varlet! Fly, fly! Get thee hence! Parting is such a brief candle. Anon, we shall walk again, hand in hand; but for the nonce, *get thine arse into yon demo suite!*" Munk spoke the last with such vehemence and brimstone that Tunk and Wesley both shrank from the old Ferengi's wrath. They hurried away to the animated holosuite to study the lots that would be offered later in the auction.

After passing through the exhibit, Wesley found himself dizzy and confused. Virtually everything he had seen was completely impossible by everything he had learned in his engineering classes at the Academy; what's more, it all seemed like exactly the sort of wish-fulfillment fantasies he would daydream to avoid schoolwork.

Constant exposure to the *real* Fred Kimbal, however, had made Wesley chary of any flat statement "it cannot be done." After all, a week ago, he would have sworn it was impossible to turn chaseum into gold-pressed latinum, or at least into a counterfeit good enough to fool anyone who did not have sensor arrays as good as a starship science lab's.

He shook his head. Who was Wesley Crusher to pass judgment on whether Dr. Zorka, who might well be the greatest scientist of the modern age, was in fact a kook?

As Tunk and Wesley came out of the demo suite, the Ferengi decided he was weary and plopped himself down on one of the numerous benches. He grunted and pointed to the seat next to him with a scowl that clearly said *sit*.

Wesley sat, though he was not particularly tired. He waited impatiently while the Ferengi calculated the anticipated sums required to pick up all the important devices.

For the first time, Wesley began to wonder just what, exactly, Munk and Tunk wanted with such powerful inventions. Having just witnessed a "photonic pulse cannon" as big as a small planetoid blowing apart some sort of starship with a single shot, the cadet's brow began to sweat.

Just how livable would be the Alpha Quadrant if the Ferengi were all armed with shield-puncturing pulse cannons?

Cadet Crusher became aware of a huge Klingon sitting next to him. He edged away, worried about jostling the fellow and getting a demonstration of the traditionally bad temper of Klingons.

"Look, Kimbal," demanded Tunk, shoving his hand-calc in front of Wesley's face. The cadet stared at the gigantic number, and Tunk continued. "That's how many bars of gold-pressed latinum we're likely to need. How long?"

Wesley stared; the number was so phenomenally huge that he had trouble even grasping it . . . *three hundred and fifty thousand bars of gold-pressed latinum!*

His mouth fell open. For an instant, he imagined replicating bar after bar for years to try to amass that staggering amount. There was not enough matter in the entire replication system to produce it!

Then he blinked and realized he was being stupid. They

would replicate *large denominations,* of course, kilobars and hectobars . . . not individual bars.

"How long, hu-man?" insisted Tunk. He apparently wanted an actual estimate.

"Well . . ." Wesley translated his sum into three thousand hectobars and fifty kilobars of chaseum that would be transformed in Kimbal's clock: a total of 3,050 bars. Considering the size, only three could fit at once in the clock case; that meant about a thousand separate transmutations.

"There must be a logical, rational way to set the price," growled the Klingon. Wesley tried to drown out the man's booming voice and concentrate on his estimate.

Each transmutation took approximately ten seconds; but there was also the time spent getting the bars into and out of the case . . . say, another ten seconds. Thus they could make no more than three transmutations per minute, probably closer to two.

A human on the other side of the Klingon said something, and the Klingon again boomed his reply: "Intuition is fine for shopkeepers and money-lenders! How is a *warrior* to know when to drop out of the bidding?"

Something sounded quite familiar about the Klingon, but Wesley continued to ponder his calculation. A thousand bars meant between six and eight hours, assuming continuous work.

He cleared his throat. "I'd guess about twelve hours, if we don't take a single break. But of course we'll have to—"

"Can't you make it eight?"

"Tunk, you don't understand. That estimate is not counting rest breaks, sleeping, eating, or anything else."

"Perfect. Eight hours it is, then. Let's see, if you begin immediately, you ought to have the full amount by morning, yes?"

Wesley sighed. "Sure. No problem."

The Klingon spoke again, drowning out Wesley's thoughts. "Can you at least help me come up with some reasonable estimates if the inventions *were* real, sir?"

Wesley froze in horror; he suddenly realized who sat next to him. Lieutenant Worf gestured expansively with one arm, knocking the cadet forward into Tunk.

"I beg your pardon," rumbled Worf, turning and noticing the boy for the first time. He stared in surprise. An instant later, Geordi La Forge's head peeked around the bulk of his Klingon friend to also stare.

"Wesley Crusher!" declared Worf, "what are you doing so far from the Academy, Cadet?"

"You know my new cabin boy?" asked Tunk in surprise.

"Of course I know Wesley Crusher!" snapped Worf. "He was on board the—"

"The orbital ship!" interjected Cadet Crusher in a rush. "We met aboard the Academy training vessel. Lieutenant Worf was the security instructor my sophomore year."

Tunk sized up the Klingon with evident distaste. "Yes, yes, how nice. We really must be going, however. Very nice to meet you, Lieutenant Whif."

"Worf!"

"But you really must learn to distinguish between different humans if you're going to get along in this quadrant. This is Fred Kimbal, not Wesley Crusher; Crusher is the other one. I know they all look alike to you, and truth to tell, to me, too. But if you go around mistaking one human for another, they get very unreasonably annoyed." Tunk jabbed Wesley in the ribs. "Come on, Kimbal; you've got a good *eight hours of work* ahead of you, if you know what I mean, eh? Heh-heh!"

"Fred Kimbal," said Wesley, staring Worf in the eye and enunciating carefully.

"Fred Kimbal?"

Wesley nodded vigorously. "Kimbal! Please remember, sir."

Worf said nothing as Tunk dragged "Fred Kimbal" away by his elbow.

When the Ferengi and the cadet were out of sight and possible earshot, Geordi spoke. "What in the world was that all about?"

"I do not know, Commander. But one of these days, that boy is going to get himself into a *lot* of trouble."

For a fellow with short legs, Tunk charged so rapidly across the lobby to the turbolift that Wesley could barely keep up. The Ferengi bobbed through the *mobile vulgus* with consumate grace, leaving Cadet Crusher trailing futilely in his wake.

Up in their room on deck thirty-eight—*the thirty-eighth floor,* Wesley corrected himself—the cadet barely had time to toss his kit on the bed before Tunk announced, "Ah, *here's* the replicator! Hurry, hu-man; we've already wasted several valuable minutes."

Wesley moved west to poke at the replicator, an ancient model dating nearly from his own birth; at the same moment, the Ferengi swept Wesley's kit onto the floor with a casual flip and stretched out on the bed.

"Why don't you set up a program to automatically replicate chaseum bars?" suggested Tunk sleepily. "Then you can busy yourself with the tranzzz . . . muuu . . ." The words slurred off into snores; worn-out from a long day of issuing orders, Tunk had fallen asleep.

Well, this is the moment of truth, thought Wesley. *Up to now, I've been at worst a passive accessory. But if I actually start replicating chaseum and disguising it as gold-pressed latinum, I cross the line and become an active collaborator!*

It may not have been a vital distinction, but it was important to Wesley: It was the sin of omission versus the sin of commission. He had allowed himself to be dragged, reluctantly, halfway across the cosmos; he had not resisted sufficiently, perhaps, not been willing to simply accept accountability for his own part in the lark. Now, he could choose to begin actively furthering the crime or else slink out, find a law-enforcement official (probably a Hatheby's employee), and turn himself in.

However, try as he might, he still could not see any way to turn nose, yet emerge with skin intact. The Ferengi could still point the finger at Wesley Crusher, and how could he deny it?

Yet the moment they began to spend any of the counterfeit in large numbers, they would implicate themselves as thoroughly as if they signed a confession. If they got caught, Wesley would at least have the satisfaction of knowing that Tunk and Munk were in the very next rock pile, slaving away.

Besides, if he just fed their greed sufficiently, perhaps they would make a serious mistake; Ferengi were well known for losing all rationality in the shadow of limitless wealth.

Swallowing hard, Wesley programmed the replicator to produce three hectobars of chaseum in the exact configuration of latinum every thirty seconds; after a few minutes, he settled into a routine, scooping the bars out of the replicator nook, arranging them under the clock face, and activating the transmutation field.

After thirty-five minutes, Wesley had a pile of two hundred hectobars of "gold-pressed latinum," or a near enough fake that they would pass even the closest scrutiny—except a sensor sweep in a well-equipped starship science lab. He also had a sweat-soaked tunic and a pair of aching, numb shoulders.

"Pause program!" he gasped as hectobars 201 through 203 materialized on the plate. He forced his hands to transfer them to the clock, nearly dropping the bars onto the device.

For a solid minute, he contemplated the Kimbal Clock without twisting the setting stem. *Do I have the guts to stand up and stomp it out of existence?* he wondered.

Feeling the back of his neck creeping, Wesley looked over at Tunk. The Ferengi regarded him with glittering, lizard eyes. "In case you were thinking of destroying the machine, boy, I'd try to remember everything I'd ever read or heard about Ferengi consolidation camps." Tunk grinned as only a Ferengi could. "The descriptions don't even *begin* to do them justice."

"I couldn't even if I wanted to, Tunk. The explosion

would probably blow my foot off . . . and I'm too exhausted to even drop a bar on it right now."

Tunk's roving gaze caught the pile of ersatz latinum, and he gasped. His eyes widened until Wesley wondered whether they would actually telescope out like in a holotoon. A moth to candle flame, the Ferengi floated up out of bed, across the room, to the pile. He stared, awestruck, then gingerly reached out a paw to touch the glittering dragon's hoard.

"By all the Rules of Acquisition," he breathed. It was not an oath; it sounded more like prayer.

Just then, the lock snicked, and the door slid open, disgorging Munk. The wizened, old goblin looked startled to see them there; then he cringed for an instant in reflexive guilt, presumably having come from the holosuite, not a nap in the adjoining room. Then he remembered who and what he was and strode lustily into the room, waving his walking stick theatrically.

"Anon come I, me hearties! Sure and 'tis a . . ." He squeaked into silence, staring at the pile of latinum. Were it real, it would be equal to *twenty thousand, three hundred bars* of gold-pressed latinum—enough to buy a Miranda-class starship *sans* weaponry and instrument package. It was the most dizzying hoard Wesley had ever seen by far; even Munk was affected.

"Buh-buh-buh-buh-blow me down!" he managed.

Tunk and Munk stood over the pile of loot, rubbing their hands as if warming them over a campfire. They looked like such twins of larceny that Wesley recoiled in revulsion before remembering that he, too, was a nephew in the larcenous family.

"B'dad!" Munk ejaculated. "Sure and 'tis a raw, fresh treasure fit for a space buccaneer, lads! But that ye've seen yer wee rest, 'tis time to strive anew and four-times-double yon heap afore the light of dawn!"

"Aye—I mean Yes, it is," agreed Tunk. Grabbing Wesley's biceps without tearing his gaze from the fraudulent latinum, Tunk dragged the cadet back to his position. "Break time's over, cabin boy. Back to work!" The Ferengi whirled to face the cadet and grinned like a loon. "I'll bet you never thought, when you signed up for Starfleet, that you'd be making ten thousand bars of latinum per hour, did you?"

The two Ferengi brayed with laughter at the *beau* jest, while Wesley wearily reactivated the replicator program and returned to his wretched task.

Chapter Thirteen

WESLEY TUMBLED INTO BED, utterly drained. The grumbling Munk had graciously allowed the cadet two hours sleep . . . two hours during which Wesley Crusher need not make any "latinum." Naturally, Munk directed Tunk to continue the process; and naturally, Tunk objected strenuously (objecting was one of the few activities Tunk ever did perform strenuously).

Munk and Tunk had a terrific row while Wesley held a pillow over his face, blocking out about thirty percent of the noise. In the end, Munk seemed to prevail: When last seen through Wesley's bleary, red eyes, the younger Ferengi knelt hunched over the Kimbal Clock.

However, when Munk prodded the cadet awake with the walking stick in his ribs, the pile of counterfeit had barely grown. Tunk had managed to discover so many "technical problems" that he passive-resisted his way into not actually replicating anything.

Thus, the total amount the Ferengi had was the hoard of bars Wesley crafted: Twelve hundred and fifteen hectobars and one hundred and two kilobars, or two hundred and twenty-three thousand, five hundred bars gpl.

Nearly enough to buy a fully armed scoutship, thought Wesley with a shudder; fortunately, none was on the block.

The cadet stacked the treasure trove into a pile with a base of half a meter by about half a meter, not quite a full meter high. "Are we taking it down with us?" he asked, thinking about the staggering weight of more than two-and-a-half metric tonnes.

"To the auction?" demanded Tunk, incredulous. "Don't you think that would look a bit suspicious, hu-man? We'll leave most of it here and take only a couple of hundred hectos and ten kilos in a satchel."

Wesley gulped; two hundred and ten bars weighed four hundred and twenty kilograms, and he had no illusions about who would be required to wrestle with the satchel. Even with a zero-g pallet, it would still mass the same. *It'll be merry hell dragging it around corners and stopping and starting it!*

"Aye, but what be the scheme for guising it in our absence?"

"Why, we just . . ." Tunk opened and closed his mouth a few times, staring at the pile. It was an awfully big pile.

Wesley rolled his eyes. "For a bunch of brilliant merchants, you sure don't know much about hiding things."

The cadet scooped off the two hundred hectobars and ten kilobars; then he removed a flat, two-dimensional picture of a meter square from the wall, balancing it atop the "latinum." He replicated a white tablecloth and spread it over the picture; it hung to the floor. Then he replicated a Japanese tea service and placed it on the tablecloth.

"There," he said, "a worthless table."

Tunk walked all the way around it, nodding sagely. The table stood three quarters of a meter high and, with the addition of the painting, a meter square . . . perfect for Ferengi.

Tunk's father stood where he was and cackled. "Aye, that

be parfay! What villain or blackguard should squint even twice 'pon such a commonplace stand?"

Munk jabbed Wesley in the back with the knobkerrie again, driving him toward the door. Tunk followed the old Ferengi, carefully setting the locks.

Down the stairs they marched, terminating in the main auction room. The first of the big-ticket items would be offered in a very few minutes, and the room was filling rapidly. Munk hunted until he found two empty seats next to a frazzled Coroustai. The old Ferengi poked Cadet Crusher into one and Tunk into the other, then jabbed and thumped the disheveled Coroustai in the third seat, berating the gentleman and venting his outrage at having "his" seat stolen, until the Coroustai fled to another spot in exasperation. Munk sat down in the liberated seat.

The pair of Ferengi proceeded to ignore Wesley, which suited the cadet fine: It allowed him to concentrate on the curious bidding system.

He was momentarily confused when he realized that the auctioneer was steadily *decreasing* the numbers he called . . . and that nobody was bidding. Eventually, the auctioneer hit a particular point, and a Cardassian toward the front flourished his hand.

"Sold to Gul Fubar, bidding for . . . ?"

"For myself," said the Cardassian.

"Bidding for himself; twelve bars gpl."

For himself—hah! Wesley leaned over to Tunk. "Don't bids usually start low and go up?"

The Ferengi glared as if Wesley's question had been covered in the last lecture. "It's a crutch auction," he sneered, "you start high and keep lowering until someone accepts the bid. After a day or two, the auctioneers get restive and begin playing games to keep everyone interested."

"Why a 'crutch' auction?"

"It's because the auctioneer's own bidding is a crutch for new players, of course!"

For the next fifteen minutes, Hatheby's ran a "crutch auction" for seven different lenses that one of Dr. Zorka's assistants had designed to better focus phaser energy.

On the fifth lens, Wesley jumped when he heard Lieutenant Worf's voice boom out to accept a bid.

"What a dolt!" exclaimed Tunk. "Klingons have no patience . . . he could have saved twenty bars of latinum by waiting another minute."

Wesley looked back and scanned the crowd, spotting not only Worf and Geordi, but also Counselor Troi and the captain himself. Neither bothered bidding on any of the lenses . . . but perhaps they simply thought the price was too high.

At last, the final lens was offered, not moving until its price was down to nine bars of gpl. The auctioneer announced a two-hour recess, after which bidding would return to the "default mode."

"Dinner break," said Tunk. "Come on, hu-man . . . I've just thought of a wonderful phrank!"

Abandoning Munk in the seats—the old Ferengi seemed asleep—Tunk dragged Wesley off to the lobby. They found their way to the banquet hall that was actually serving food. "Stick close to me," cautioned Tunk.

Wesley determined to observe dispassionately, not allowing his own embarrassment to interfere with checking his hypothesis: If the cadet was right, then Tunk's victim would, in essence, make a fool of himself by eagerly stepping into the "victim" role.

The Ferengi strolled through the hall and began following a waiter around, with Wesley immediately behind, playing tail of the dragon. The young waiter finally headed into the kitchen, unaware that he was the front man of a circus parade.

Tunk tapped the waiter's shoulder. "Here, Bud," offered the Ferengi, holding up a decigram, "gimmie the jacket."

"What?" asked the boy, confused.

"Your jacket, hu-man! Hand me your jacket, just for a moment. Here, take this for your trouble!" Tunk shoved the coin at the boy, who suddenly parsed the situation and stripped off his waiter's jacket.

"What—what are you going to do?" asked the cadet; Tunk merely plucked the jacket from the waiter's hand, winking at Wesley.

Tunk struggled into the jacket, but it hung past his knees. Ignoring the incongruous look, he strode pompously back into the dining hall, followed at a discreet distance by a nervous Cadet Crusher.

Tunk wandered among the tables until he found a particularly large party, all dressed in grand, sober style. Tunk gestured Wesley close, whispering in his ear, "Rule of Acquisition number three hundred and three: The sheep *want* to be fleeced!"

Wesley frowned. "Ferengi have sheep?"

"Actually, I just now made it up. Maybe I'll propose it at the next Trade Council meeting!" Tunk wiggled his eye ridges and elbowed Wesley in the gut, doubling the cadet over. Then the Ferengi ambled forward and parked himself at the head of the table.

The host was a venerable, old president of a merchants' corporation. Tunk stood behind the gentleman, eyeing his every move with displeasure.

It did not take long for the rest of the table, followed by the president himself, to notice the frowning gargoyle at the man's side.

Wesley shifted for a better view. *What the hell is he* doing? he wondered, nervously watching for approaching security guards.

Instead, a real waiter approached, bringing the salads; he distributed them around the table according to a complex ritual.

All right, thought the cadet; *now at some point, the target has to give control over to Tunk.*

The president reached for his fork, and the "fun" began. Tunk loomed over the man, loudly clucking his tongue and wagging his finger disapprovingly.

Chastened, the man yanked his hand back, then reached

out to take a different fork; he was nonplussed, having four to choose from.

When he touched one, Tunk snarled, "Not *that* one, you mannerless dolt!" It was almost under Tunk's breath; but in fact, everyone at the table could hear it.

Wesley jumped; *why doesn't he just turn around and smack him one?* Even as old as he was, the president had a great advantage of height, reach, and weight over the Ferengi . . . but Tunk had one attribute that was apparently decisive: *He wore the white coat of a waiter,* thus gaining the sanction of "authority."

"Here!" snapped the Ferengi in apparent exasperation, snatching a fork at random and handing it to the poor gentleman. "This one! Everybody is *watching!*"

Conversation resumed with relief, and the president tried to ignore Tunk; but it was like trying to ignore the Angel of Death hovering at his elbow; the man kept sneaking worried glances back at the supposed waiter. At irregular intervals, Tunk would cluck his tongue, shake his head, roll his eyes, or snort loudly, while Wesley Crusher's face reddened in embarrassment. Once, when the old man reached for his roll, the Ferengi reached over and *slapped his hand!*

At first, the cadet gasped at the audacity; surely now the entire table would rise up in wrath and bean the Ferengi with a soup tureen! But the president cringed, meekly accepting his repuke; and all at once, Wesley understood the true humor of the situation: The president of a mighty company, head of a bidding delegation, was allowing himself to be bossed and insulted by a hotel restaurant waiter *. . . just to avoid making a scene!*

Despite the cadet's stern self-admonition, he had to clap his hand over his mouth, barely suppressing a hoot of laughter.

By the time dessert was wheeled in, the old man was in a frenzy. He shook with terror, afraid to touch a single implement for fear of offending the "waiter" and eliciting another sarcastic comment.

The pastry chef rolled a large dessert cart to the table,

piled high with lucious-looking chocolate cakes that made Cadet Crusher's mouth water. The chef and a waiter served the dessert reverently.

Tunk went into a spasm of exasperation, critiquing everything the poor old president did from his posture to his choice of clothing. *"Really,* sir!" exclaimed the Ferengi, "one would think you'd have the *decency* to change out of your *gardening clothes* before coming to such a fine restaurant as this!"

Wesley shook helplessly with silent laughter, embarrassment forgotten in the beauty of Tunk's performance. He almost began to like the nasty little Ferengi.

At last, in desperation, having been warned away from every other fork or spoon, the president seized the final tool, a cocktail fork, clutching it with both hands. "But—but I must use it! I beg of you . . . *it's the last utensil I have!"*

Tunk fell silent, staring at the president with the eyes of a madman. The table fell utterly silent as twenty-eight eyes stared at the Ferengi, Wesley's among them. The cadet realized this was the climax.

The Ferengi elbowed past the old president, snatched up his dessert, and loudly slammed it down onto the floor.

"Fine!" he cried, a contemptuous grimace on his face. "Then if you're going to *act like a pig,* you may as well *eat like one, too!"*

Tunk delivered the last line in a shrieking falsetto that turned every head in the banquet hall and stopped conversation from one end of the room to the other.

In the stunned silence that followed, the Ferengi grabbed Wesley by the arm, shoving him toward the exit. Snapping out of his stupor, the cadet motored for the door, Tunk storming along at his heels, walking with a stately, stuffy gait.

They made their escape, and Tunk ditched the coat in the concierge's kiosk. Minutes later, still barely a sound emanated from the hall.

Wesley Crusher nodded to himself; his thesis was amply proved . . . without the full participation and sanction by the victim, the president, Tunk's entire elaborate phrank would have blown apart like a depressurized shuttlecraft. *I must remember that,* thought the cadet; the rule was wider than simply a guide to "phranking" people—as Tunk had hinted with his phony rule of acquisition, there was a deep, general principle involved.

Cadet Crusher tucked it away in his backbrain; he had a feeling he would need it before his adventure was ended.

After the two-hour break elapsed, Tunk and Wesley rejoined Munk in the auction room, waking up the old Ferengi. A new auctioneer entered, a much older human; and the crowd fell silent.

"Lot fifty-seven is a subspace acceleration prototype; you have all seen the demonstration in the exhibit hall." The last was a statement, not a question.

The auctioneer fiddled with the controls on his dais and a holoimage of the glowing, isosceles tube-triangle materialized over the audience, rotating slowly.

"The minimum bid was established at one hundred hectobars of gpl by Gul Fubar, bidding for the Cardassian Empire. One hundred and ten. One hundred and fifteen. One hundred seventeen?—I'm sorry, madam, we cannot accept increments smaller than five hectobars."

Wesley stared wildly about the room, trying to catch a bidder in the act of bidding. He did not succeed: Whatever they were all doing to attract the auctioneer's attention and convey the magnitude of their bid, for quite some time, Cadet Crusher could not spot it.

At last, the bidding narrowed to the same four principals; after several rounds, Wesley finally spotted them: Worf, Gul Fubar, Deanna Troi, and Captain Picard.

The Klingon signaled by quickly pumping his fist, Counselor Troi by catching the auctioneer's eye and nodding, Gul Fubar by snorting derisively, and the captain by elegantly holding up one finger for "up five hectobars" and two for "up ten."

The auctioneer noticed quickly that the rest of the bidders

had turned into an audience; he shifted into a pattern, one to the other in order. The tactic worked; each person raised every time his turn came.

Finally, Worf hesitated when his "turn" came around; with a snarl, he shook his head, having presumably exceeded his authority. Deanna was next to fall; it seemed to upset her considerably. Only the Gul and the captain remained in the bid.

The pair shot bids back and forth against each other, driving the price up to thirty-seven thousand, five hundred bars; still, Munk had not opened his mouth.

Then Captain Picard hesitated.

"The bid is held by Gul Fubar, bidding for the Cardassian Empire," warned the auctioneer, "one time, two times—"

A crash grabbed everyone's attention, including the auctioneer. "Is that four, sir?" he asked.

"Four hundred hectobars!" shouted a gnarled old Ferengi in the corner; he looked as old and wrinkled as a bristlecone pine tree. He had produced his explosive bid by flicking a tray of glasses from a waiter's hands.

"Ach!" exclaimed Munk quietly. "A bonny new voice sings a verse!"

Tunk elbowed Wesley in his side, which was already sore from Munk's shillelagh. "The Grand Nagus," sneered the Ferengi. "A Ferengi waits to bid until his opponents have exhausted themselves—Rule of Acquisition number one hundred ninety-one."

"One hundred, fourscore and *fort,*" corrected Munk.

Tunk slunk low, humiliated by his error.

Wesley Crusher had only heard of the Grand Nagus in his political structures class, and he strained for a peek at the infamous leader, or "chief negotiator," of the Ferengi.

"The Grand Nagus raises the bid to four hundred hectobars," intoned the auctioneer. "Mister Picard?"

After a pause, the captain said, "And ten," irritation and worry nagging his voice.

"Four-ten from Mister Picard for the Klingon Empire."

Wesley jumped; had he heard right? If the captain was bidding for the Klingons, for whom was Worf bidding?

The bidding caught fire once more; apparently, sanguine as Picard and the Cardassian may have been about the mass accelerator falling into one of their "superpower" hands, neither was willing to see it go to the Ferengi. They nearly stumbled over each other in their haste to deny the Grand Nagus his toy.

Tunk chuckled. "The Nagus has no interest in that thing," he declared.

"How can you tell?"

"He only bids quickly in between the Klingon and Cardassian bids, never allowing himself to hold the bid for long."

"Well, if he doesn't want it, why is he bidding at all?"

Tunk stared incredulously. "Do you know *nothing* about these sorts of auctions? He cares about one lot and one only—the photonic cannon."

"So why is he bidding for a simple mass accelerator?"

Tunk shook his head, frustrated by Wesley's inability to understand. "The Grand Nagus bids to bankrupt his opponents before the photonic cannon is offered, of course! Every hectobat spent today is one fewer for tomorrow."

"Oh. Of course." It still made little sense to the cadet; it sounded like an incredibly dangerous game for uncertain benefit.

But the bidding suddenly stalled again; this time, the Cardassian Gul Fubar held at four hundred and eighty hectobars . . . so apparently, the Grand Nagus's scheme had worked.

"One time, two times . . ." The auctioneer hesitated, giving plenty of opportunity for anyone insane enough to take the bidding higher.

"Five hundred!" The voice was loud and shrill; Munk raised his knobkerrie and waved it until the auctioneer noticed him.

The man stood a little straighter, squinting at the only

other Ferengi camp in the room. "Five hundred hectobars is bid by . . . may I have your name and principal, sir?"

"Bidding for meself, certes: Cap'n Munk, Chairman of Universal Exports!"

"What!" The Grand Nagus leapt to his feat, then climbed upon his chair for a better look. He shook his own walking stick furiously, his ears fluttering in agitation. Half a dozen Ferengi surrounded the Nagus; each one echoed and amplified their leader's consternation, shouting outraged condemnations and demands to "see the color" of Munk's latinum.

"Now, hu-man!" whispered Tunk, pushing a key into the cadet's hand, "dash upstairs and bring down fifty bars deposit." Fifty hectobars; ten percent as surety against the full amount. Wesley rose, squirmed past the tightly packed bidders and exited the room.

He dodged across the empty, cavernous lobby—the guests were all watching the show in the dining hall—found the concierge, and borrowed an antigravity cargo pad.

He rushed it up to the room, loaded fifty bars onto the pallet, and maneuvered it down the stairs. Wesley had little experience with the antigravity pallets; they nullified gravity but not mass, of course, which meant the bars weighed nothing . . . but still had their full momentum. They did not corner well.

When Wesley returned to the dining hall, he could hear the argument in progress as far away as the reservations desk: the Grand Nagus's Ferengi advisors against Tunk. Apparently, both the Nagus himself and Munk considered such an argument beneath their dignities.

When Wesley entered the room, everyone fell silent. The cadet swallowed as he realized six hundred pairs of eyes stared at him . . . including those of Worf, Geordi La Forge, Deanna Troi, and Jean-Luc Picard.

"Give it to the rules committee," instructed Tunk, pointing at another official who had entered while Wesley was upstairs; but the cadet had a different plan.

Instead, he pushed the pallet toward Tunk.

"No, no, Kimbal! Give it to him, that man standing there!"

Implacable, Wesley Crusher pushed the floating pad at the Ferengi again. The reason was simple: Wesley intended to ensure that it was Tunk, not himself, who committed the more serious crime of actually *passing* the counterfeit. *It might mitigate my sentence at the court-martial,* he thought.

Angrily, Tunk grabbed the pallet, wrestled it around, and shoved it over the heads of the front-row bidders to the low table by the side of the podium.

The rules committee representative deactivated the anti-gravity field, spilled the bars onto the table, and began to count. He counted the fifty, then extracted a mini-data-reader from a coat pocket. He scanned the small pile, scrutinizing the readout.

After an instant, he looked up. "Fifty hectobars of gold-pressed latinum," he confirmed.

Wesley sagged back into his seat, simultaneously relieved, proud, and disappointed that an official from Hatheby's, the quadrant's premier brokerage house and estate disposal firm, failed to detect the counterfeit.

"The challenge is refuted," said the auctioneer pointedly.

After a lengthy pause, during which the Ferengi huddled and whispered among themselves, the Grand Nagus turned back to the auctioneer. "All right, all right," he grumbled, "we accept the debt."

"The Grand Nagus is hereby fined fifty hectobars of gold-pressed latinum."

"Put it on my account."

"Your account is quite steep, sir."

"It is?"

"We require participants to pay off all sums in excess of fifty hectobars within twelve hours."

"It slipped my mind. I must be getting old."

The Grand Nagus and the auctioneer continued back and forth; in the end, the Ferengi's arguments came to nought, and he had to pay down his account. However, the Grand Nagus used even this indignity to his advantage.

"I need to send to my ship for latinum, which may take some time. Since I'm one of the principals here, I demand a two-hour recess."

The auctioneer conferred with the man from the rules committee, and they agreed to the delay.

The Grand Nagus waddled over to his rivals, carefully putting on his "wounded dignity" facade. Tunk and Munk were a dangerous pair, mostly because of their unpredictability; the Nagus did not want to make the mistake of underestimating them ... but he had to discover where they were getting all that beautiful latinum.

He fetched up before Munk, and the two glared at each other like a pair of undead zombies.

"Munk, you old mendicant," greeted the Nagus in a whiny, nasal voice that reeked of threat, "I thought you died in the sack of the Rubilator colony." He grinned, exposing sharp, Ferengi teeth ... *the teeth are the windows of the soul,* taught the great sage Ligwas.

The Nagus, of course, had engineered the sack of the Rubilator colony; and Munk knew that very well. He understood the threat.

"Perchance you dream, Nagus. I be very much hale and hearty, me heartie."

Translation, thought the Nagus; *I ducked you, I ducked you, now I'm going to shuck you!* "Still talking like a holovision buccaneer, I see. All right, we have to talk, Cap'n Munk of Universal Exports. Shall we say my room in ten minutes?"

"Nay, shall we not! Shiver me bones, but I've a strong tremor about staying in your cabin; I've heard tales."

"Lies," objected the Grand Nagus, "spread by people who owe me money ... which is just about *everybody!*" The Nagus cackled with laughter.

"Shall we say *our* room in ten minutes?" offered Tunk.

The Grand Nagus shrugged. "As you wish," he said,

disappointed but not surprised. Anyone who could survive the sack of Rubilator would not stupidly stroll into the Nagus's web.

Fifteen minutes later, Munk's human cabin boy answered the room-door annunciator; the Grand Nagus and a passel of Ferengi breezed into the room.

Although the human Federation recognized the Grand Nagus as a leader of sorts for Ferengi everywhere, in fact he was nothing more nor less than the chief executive officer for a "company" that comprised the entire Ferengi race.

Munk is attempting to buy sufficient power—for instance, the photonic pulse cannon—to depose me, thought the Nagus. He wondered whether he could make the charge stick in a Ferengi arbitration council; if so, it would be treason . . . or worse, a contract violation!

Alas, Munk was undoubtedly too smart to leave an easy trail. "Why, Munk," said the Grand Nagus, "it's so nice to see you again, after all these years! What's it been . . . ten to twenty?"

"You misbegotten scion of a barrow-boy, 'tis merry-met, me bucko; 'tis a rare pleasure tae take ship once again side by side."

"So," said the Nagus, coming straight to the point in an effort to startle Munk, "you're trying to muscle into my territory, eh? Trying to buy power?" The Nagus waited a moment for the words to sink in. "We need to have a little discussion."

Munk curled his lip . . . definitely not the requisite cringe expected when one dealt with the Grand Nagus himself. "Be warned, ye scurvy knave, against whom ye cast such accusatory harpoons. Thar still be actionable causes for damage to reputation in our law."

Acknowledging the riposte, the Nagus retreated slightly. "I've had reliable reports that you have not been paying the proper percentage of your deals to me. Have you no patriotism? I'm a feeble old man; I need my fair cut!"

Tunk interjected smoothly. "Why, Nagus, you wrong us!

162

We've never stinted you of a single bar of gold-pressed latinum that you were actually entitled to."

What audacity! The Nagus almost lashed out with his walking stick, noticing at the last moment that Munk had one as well: the "Ferengi emphasizer," they called such shillelaghs.

"Aaaah," said the Nagus, "and I suppose you think I'm not entitled to the same cut from you that all the other Ferengi pay me?"

"Of course not," said Tunk in his snottiest voice, "we don't need you to control our every deal, like you do for all the other Ferengi. Our operation is completely independent from yours. We don't ask your blessing, and we don't pay any worthless protection money!"

"Oh, really!" exclaimed the Grand Nagus, his eyes wide. "And I suppose you won't mind a bit when you find all your bank accounts frozen, your assets seized, *and your credit records accidentally erased!"*

The direct threat to the competitor's bank accounts. Very effective . . .

"Certes, but we shall not!"

Well—unless the competitor owns his own latinum mine!

"Of course we won't!" Tunk did a double take, staring at last at his father. "Uh . . . we won't?"

"Nay, ye scurvy wretch, we be unruffled and sailing at full yards. We are men of dinkum honor, who settle all charges with cold, hard latinum!"

"Latinum, eh?" mocked the Nagus. "And I suppose you just happened to have a quarter-million bars stashed here in your hotel room?" The Nagus peered around, pretending to mock, but in reality quite anxious to discover whether Munk did, indeed, have a latinum mine.

Munk gestured expansively at the new "table." "Sit ye down, lads; give us a bit of sea room. Would ye crave yon tea, or something with a touch more hair?"

"Ah," said the Nagus, licking his lips, "if you could just replicate us a nice bottle of Ferengi spunk, I think the deal would go infinitely smoother."

The Grand Nagus and his chief financial officer sat at the table. Munk and Tunk seized the opposite seats, though Tunk looked a touch nervous and pink around the gills; the younger Ferengi allowed his gaze to roam everywhere but toward the Nagus.

Oddly enough, even the human, Fred Something, seemed to grow distinctly more nervous when they sat down.

"Look, be reasonable," said the Nagus. "Let's do this all legal and proper, according to our law. How much of a bribe do you want in order to take a hike?" He glanced quickly from Tunk to the cabin boy; alas, neither gave him a clue as to the source of their anxiety.

Munk smiled. "What makest ye think we'll depart for any number of Doubloons? We've a pretty wench here, and her name be *firepower.*"

"You're planning to bid on the photonic pulse cannon? Hoo-hoo! This'll be the funniest sight of the whole auction!"

Munk said nothing, merely smiling quietly. Tunk tried to imitate his father but could only manage a weak, sickly smirk. The Grand Nagus continued, squinting and trying to smile menacingly. *I'll let him know whom he's dealing with,* he decided.

"Listen, you old philanthropist; if you think that mass accelerator was expensive, just wait'll you see what the real stuff goes for! That's where we'll separate the marks from the Ferengi.

"You're no threat to me, Munk; you never have been. I was Nagus before you breached your first contract, and I'll be Nagus when death reposes your rotting carcass!

"But you are a bit of an annoyance to me just now; these are delicate negotiations, and I don't want any amateurs floating around and queering my percentages. I'm willing to buy out your options. How much do you want?"

Munk's nervous son sweated, squirming uncomfortably. *He definitely wants to grab the fast cash and make his exit.* When Munk said nothing, Tunk began to stammer. "Wha-wha-what exactly are you offer . . . offering, Grand Nagus?"

"Spoken like a true Ferengi!" congratulated the Nagus. "How about—"

"Not enough by half," interjected Munk.

"You haven't even heard my offer yet!"

"Aye, but I know that black heart of yours, ye lubber. I have it in me noggin that whatever ye're gang to offer, it's worth less than yer corrupt empire . . . and that's what I'm firing for: all that ye call yours."

The Nagus jumped up and pounded his fists on the table. The painting and tea set leapt alarmingly.

"That does it! That tears it! From now on, you're my sworn latinum-enemy!" The Nagus narrowed his eyes and lowered his voice. "If you try to withdraw money from any of your thirty-eight accounts at banks in Ferengi, Cardassian, or Federation space, you'll find them frozen because of 'pending litigation.' If you try to borrow money, you'll find your credit history full of creditors, bad debts, and unproductive little ventures that bankrupted everyone involved.

"If you try trading on the mercantile floor, you'll find your license is revoked. Your current loans are all due and payable immediately! And you can just tear up that letter of recommendation I wrote for your snivelling, little son for Acquisition University because I'll disavow all knowledge of its existence!"

The Grand Nagus suddenly leaned across the table, baring the windows of his soul. Tunk, who had been frozen in terror, his eyes gigantic, since the beginning of the outburst, cried out in terror and tumbled backward off his chair.

Munk, however, neither moved nor blinked; he faced the Nagus with the same faint half-smile he had worn since the conversation began and calmly adjusted the tablecloth, which the Nagus's outburst had skewed.

The Grand Nagus raised his walking stick, lowered his voice still further, and spoke in portentious tones. *"The mark of my cane is upon you, Munk. Feel it forever more!"*

Without another word, he turned and stalked out of the room, followed by his minions. He kept a brave exterior, but inside he knew he had lost the negotiation.

Oh well, he thought, *I win six and lose two . . . it's a good percentage overall!*

Cadet Wesley Crusher collapsed backward, letting his breath out in a rush. When the Nagus had slammed the table, a corner of the cloth had shifted, exposing one entire side of ersatz latinum! Fortunately, Munk had had the presence of mind to adjust it without giving away the show.

Munk burst forth in hearty, derisive laughter. He grabbed the picture frame and flung it, the cloth, and the tea set off the treasure hoard of glittering hectobars.

"We come not to praise the Nagus," he cackled, "but to bury him! Avast, ye scurvy knave!"

"Yes, cap'n?" said both Wesley and Tunk at the same time.

"Not you, ye addle-pated swabbie!" Munk grabbed his knobkerrie, but this time he thumped Tunk. "You there, Fried Kibble—sit ye down and hop to those knots, boy! I command another heap as grand as yon treasure trove before next the sun dawns."

Chapter Fourteen

WITH A STERN ADMONITION to stay and "keep yer eyeballs on the rigging," Munk sailed forth on yet another odyssey to the holosuites. Wesley silently counted to himself; he had reached thirteen when Tunk departed, calling over his shoulder, "You stay right there!" Munk had journeyed left to the north-going suites; being creative and independent, Tunk headed right for the south-going suites.

Wesley immediately left off his felonious activities to think for a minute.

During the argument with the Grand Nagus, Munk had inadvertently revealed his grand plan: He intended to use the counterfeit latinum to buy every useful item offered at the auction—in particular, the photonic pulse cannon—using them to seize the Grand Nagus's power, if not his title.

In fact, if even half the items worked as well as advertised, Munk could singlehandedly change the balance of power, not to mention the balance of payments, in the two explored quadrants of the galaxy. Either Munk would completely take over the Ferengi sphere of influence, or else there would be another major player to consider besides the Federation, the Klingon and Cardassian empires, the Tholians, and the Ferengi . . . or there would be civil war among the Ferengi.

Either way, Wesley could not allow Munk's scheme to succeed. Participating would be worse than counterfeiting: It would be treason. Whatever doubts Wesley Crusher felt about the entire rationale and moral legitimacy behind Starfleet, he was certainly not prepared to immolate his career on the altar of a supreme dictator, Ferengi courts or no.

I wonder whether the Ferengi courts would still rule in Munk's favor after he was denounced by the Grand Nagus? He shook his head. More than likely, the Ferengi would jail Munk and Wesley both, perhaps in the same cage. Either Wesley was an active collaborator or he was a contract-jumper; Ferengi authorities would consider both deserving of confinement at hard servitude.

He fished from his pocket the data clip containing his contract, popped it into a hotel reader, and perused it as closely as he could.

Cadet Crusher thought he had seen the summit of bureaucratic obfuscation when he memorized the Federation Space Training and Operating Procedures and Standardization technical manuals for eight increasingly complex fleet ships. Yet this theoretically simple Ferengi contract (to be hired as a cabin boy) was twice as long as the longest F-STOPS book!

One sentence in particular caught his attention:

INDEPENDENT CONTRACTOR(S) convenants and agrees that he, she, it, or they shall not disclose to third parties, including INDEPENDENT CONTRACTOR himself, herself, itself, or themselves, for use for its or their own benefit or for the benefit of others, wheresoever situated in physical space-time, whether normal space or subspace, and shall not set down or otherwise record any verbal or pictogrammatic description in any electronic or positronic device or mechanical storage device, any of CAPTAIN'S or CAPTAIN customer developments, confidential information, know-how, discoveries, production methods, hardware designs, software source code, software designs, technical goals or timetables, economic circumstances or plans, military schedules or armaments, philosophical inclinations, religious affiliations, business contacts, confidential conversations whether or not so-designated by CAPTAIN or CAPTAIN'S agents as confidential, notwithstanding or excepting any material in the public domain, which shall be deemed by this agreement to likewise be confidential unless specifically released by CAPTAIN as material-for-release, related materials, or the like that may be disclosed to INDEPENDENT CONTRACTOR or which INDEPENDENT CONTRACTOR may learn in connection with work to be performed under this agreement, including in particular and specific this agreement itself, including this nondisclosure clause; and further, INDEPENDENT CONTRACTOR agrees that any and all inventions, discoveries, developments, improvements, descriptions, or modifications that may be made by INDEPENDENT CONTRACTOR in performance of the work under this agreement or in respect to the specific subject matter thereof, shall be and remain the property of CAPTAIN and in connection therewith, INDEPENDENT CONTRACTOR agrees to execute and assign to CAPTAIN any and all rights and patent applications, copyrights, voting rights, mineral rights, action options, or privileges pertaining to or covering such inventions, discoveries, developments, improvements, modifications, descriptions, or any other creation, destruction, or alteration of existing or not-yet-existing materials, forces, space-time coordinates, whether normal space or subspace, involving matter or protomatter, energy in any format whatsoever therein mentioned.

Appended to the clause was an asterisk. Looking to the end of the contract, Wesley found a "rider" attached to the clause:

This clause shall remain active in all cases where it is not superceded by any clause mutually agreed upon which shall in legal effect render null and void any changes, emendations, iterations, alterations, or other adjustments to this or any other clause that is not so superceded.

He gave up perusing and took to skimming, trying to get a sense of what he might be able to do. After an hour, he began to understand the broad format of the contract he had been forced to sign.

First, the contract itself was considered confidential; according to the contract, it was a violation of the contract for Wesley to read the contract! Showing it to an attorney would probably be grounds for a firing squad.

Second, he was explicitly enjoined from relaying any information about Munk, Tunk, or their plans, including Wesley's own speculations (as an agent of Munk, anything Wesley Crusher did, said, or thought was covered by the nondisclosure clause), to anyone else.

The cadet's head ached. He had to talk to someone; but everyone he could think of was so wrapped up in the auction that he could spare no concentration for a befuddled, desperate Academy cadet.

What about Riker? Commander Riker was even more occupied captaining the *Enterprise* with Romulans, Cardassians, Tholians, and hundreds of other races drifting around in various orbits around a single, small planetoid, than he would have been bidding in the auction.

Well, then what about Data? The android was one of the few people Wesley knew with whom he truly felt comfortable. Data knew as much about technical subjects as Wesley, almost by definition; yet he was not constantly challenging the cadet to solve various technical "puzzles," as Geordi La

Forge tended to do. Data did not respond emotionally, did not treat Wesley like a kid (everyone on the *Enterprise* remembered him from when he *was* a kid!), and Data never judged the cadet . . . in fact, the android was incapable of judging.

Wesley tapped his shirt; then he smiled. He had fallen so much back into the habit of thinking of himself as a member of the *Enterprise* crew that he forgot he no longer wore a comm badge. He sat at the desk and used the hotel communicator instead.

"Wesley Crusher to *Starship Enterprise,* Commander Data."

After a moment, Data responded.

"Can you get a fix on my coordinates, sir?"

"I have your coordinates now. Do you wish to be beamed aboard the *Enterprise?*"

"Would that be against regulations?"

"A literal reading of the appropriate Starfleet orders regarding visitors would preclude my taking such authority. But I shall request permission from Commander Riker." A moment passed. "Commander Riker has given his permission; prepare to beam aboard, and welcome home."

"Thanks." Wesley felt a little uncomfortable about the "welcome home" greeting. He had not felt "home" on the *Enterprise* ever since he was admitted to the Academy; actually, the feeling was older than that; he had not felt comfortable on the *Enterprise* since he met the Traveler.

Then he felt his body begin to disassociate; the room became fuzzy, and intense vibrations rattled his brain. Feeling the chair disappear from beneath him, Wesley stood to avoid falling on his posterior when he appeared on the transporter pad.

Wesley waited in the transporter room, unsure of the etiquette. Technically, he was an ensign assigned TDS to the Academy—which meant that technically, he was AWOL. He had not applied for actual leave between semesters; he only had the limited liberty that all the students had, which did not extend to leaving the planet.

On the other hand, he was also the son of the chief medical officer; as a civilian, he would have the run of the ship except for certain places, such as the bridge.

It was too confusing; everything about Starfleet was confusing lately. Wesley waited in the transporter room, and Data strode through the doors momentarily.

They chatted pleasantly about nothing while heading for Ten-Forward; Data had been rewriting his "smalltalk" subroutines.

"So how come you're not down on Novus Alamogordus bidding for the Android Empire?"

Without warning, Data laughed insanely for two seconds, then cut off the awful racket abruptly. *Another laughing program,* Wesley realized.

"I am still refining the details, Wesley. Do you like the program?"

"Data, I think laughing would be more effective if you changed your facial expression. If you laugh hysterically while wearing the same expression you'd use to compute a navigational vector, people will think you're a homicidal maniac."

"How odd," observed Data, "Commander Riker used the identical term. This program is not working out as well as I had hoped; rather than set humans at ease, it appears to have the opposite effect."

"But seriously, folks, why aren't you down on the planetoid bidding, Data? I'd have thought you'd want to watch something so human as an auction."

"I was originally to bid for the Federation; however, Hatheby's rules committee decided that I was a piece of electronic equipment, not a person, and I was barred from participating."

"Data, that's terrible!"

"I found it quite objectionable, and I have already filed a strong protest with the Federation Chamber of Commerce. I have judicial precedent that contradicts Hatheby's."

Data's phrase rebounded through Wesley's brain: electronic equipment, electronic equipment. Not a person. It struck a responsive chord, but he could not quite . . .

Cadet Crusher halted in the middle of a corridor, struck by a sudden realization. By the nondisclosure clause of his Ferengi contract, he could not disclose to any person, by any means, his confidential knowledge; this strong prohibition would prevent any means of conveying information—but it only applied to persons.

On the other hand, regarding electronic devices, he was only forbidden from setting down the knowledge.

Wesley was stunned into awed silence: Data's entirely innocent recounting of a petty humiliation visited upon him by reactionary officials of a venerable, stuffy, old brokerage firm had accidentally revealed a loophole *in a Ferengi contract!*

Wesley was barred from using any verbal or graphic means of *telling* Data the information. But there was no rule stopping him from manufacturing circumstances under which Data would *guess* the situation all by himself.

There was also nothing at all in Wesley's contract forbidding him from using the Kimbal Clock himself; after all, he was the inventor, "Fred Kimbal."

"Data," he said, too quickly, "could you please teach me to play poker?"

Data cocked his head, looking puzzled. "Did you mean to ask me to teach you poker?"

"Yes. Can't you?"

"I can certainly do so. But this seems an odd moment for a sudden urge to play cards. Perhaps some other time would be more appropriate."

Cadet Crusher grabbed Data's arms, forgetting their respective differences in rank in his excitement. "No, you *have to* teach me poker, and you have to teach me tonight!" Bidding on the next major-ticket item would commence at 2030 that night . . . and Wesley suddenly had a great deal to do.

"If it is that important to you, Wesley, I shall make time and do so. Shall we meet at twenty hundred?"

"Nineteen hundred would be better."

"I will meet you in my quarters at nineteen hundred."

"Thanks, Data—you won't regret it!"

He started to dash away, but Data called after him. "Wesley, were we not on our way to Ten-Forward for a visit?"

"No time, gotta go!" He bolted back to the transporter room, leaving Data as nonplussed as it was possible for an android to be.

"Can you transport me back to the same coordinates I beamed up from?" Wesley asked the transporter chief.

The man looked up. "Did you forget something, sir?"

"Yes; I just remembered a sudden appointment. Can you beam me back up to the *Enterprise* at, uh, eighteen fifty-five?"

"Sure. Just contact me and let me know you're ready."

Wesley thought for a moment. The Ferengi would certainly be back by then, and just as certainly would be cracking the whip over his back to produce more "latinum." He considered asking Munk, *excuse me, you don't mind if I call the* Enterprise *and have them beam me back up, do you? I'll just be a moment . . . I promise not to tell anyone about the counterfeiting ring while I'm up there!*

The image brought a smile. "No, I won't have access to a communicator."

"Would you like me to replicate one?"

"Sure! Thanks. He thought for a moment. "Can you make me one that's completely generic?"

"Eh? Sure. Why?"

"Oh . . . uh, I actually wasn't supposed to come back alone, but I had something to show Commander Data. I'm with those Ferengi you picked up."

"Yeah, I heard about that. Wasn't on watch then. Heard you guys got out just before your ship blew up, sir."

"Well, it wasn't all that exciting. Hey, is that the comm badge? Looks sharp. Thanks!" Wesley reached over and plucked the badge from the replicator. "Well, gotta dash. Nice talking with you, Chief, ah . . ."

"Otto."

Wesley stared curiously at the badge. "You wouldn't happen to know what this thing is made out of, would you? It looks more silvery than the standards."

"Let me see, sir." Otto scrutinized the Bajoran comm badge. "Don't know. Could be titanium, could be chaseum."

"Thanks." Wesley retrieved the badge and stepped to the transporter pad. He pinned the badge on his loose clothing, behind a fold in the cloth where it would not be visible. "Energize."

A moment later, he was back in the room. He had just stepped over to the replicator when he heard the lock click back.

He abruptly realized he would have some fancy explaining to do: Where was the new pile of counterfeit he should have been producing while Tunk and Munk were in the holosuites?

He stood, looking guilty, as the door slid back. The minute the seal was cracked, he heard Munk and his son in the midst of a terrible hullabaloo. He listened in confusion, finally deducing that Munk and Tunk each tried to run the same holosuite program in opposite holosuites . . . but since the program was the most lavish, expensive, and *disgusting* Ferengi program available in the library, running it in two holosuites simultaneously overloaded the system memory and crashed the system.

Both Munk and Tunk found themselves in the middle of blank holosuites in a rather embarrassing condition of undress. Naturally, technicians immediately opened a comm link with the holosuites to ask if they were all right and apologize for the crash.

The tech for Munk's holosuite was female; the old Ferengi decided rather unreasonably that it was all a plot on Tunk's part.

From the way Tunk rubbed his head and cringed, Wesley figured Munk had been punctuating his diatribe with his usual shillelagh-work.

"Back! Back, ye sluggard, back to yer toil! Square the yards, furl the sheets!" commanded Munk, seemingly unaware that he had just issued contradictory orders.

"Aye, sir!" shouted Tunk, dashing Wesley out of the way in his haste to reach the replicator. Tunk reinitiated the chaseum-replication program and began shoveling the bars across to Cadet Crusher as fast as they materialized. Nobody remembered to ask Wesley what he had been doing for the past thirty minutes and why he had made no more counterfeit in the interim.

The cadet bided his time, falling into the routine of opening the face of the Kimbal Clock, inserting the newly minted hectobars of chaseum, twisting the dial, and dumping out the "latinum." Within moments, he felt his brain numbing as it always did when forced to perform boring, repetitive, and essentially mindless tasks at Starfleet Academy—which had happened more and more recently.

Or maybe the tasks aren't any more repetitive . . . I've just done them all so many times they seem mindless. Wes's threshold of boredom had unquestionably sunk during the last term; routine watches that used to excite or at least interest him now bored him so thoroughly that it was all he could do to not fall asleep. More than once, Wesley had disassembled and reassembled critical pieces of equipment or reprogrammed computers or sensors while on duty, just for something to do—knowing that if he got caught, he would be punished. Fortunately, he had not been caught.

Again and again, the *forbidden thought* rolled around and around his brain: *Maybe it's not for me, maybe I made a mistake, maybe I should just resign my com—*

Cadet Ensign Wesley Crusher clenched his teeth, wrenching his thoughts in another direction, *any* other direction. There are some verities cadets were not meant to question.

"Are you questioning Federation policy?" Wesley blinked; the words were so clear, he could swear he had actually heard them spoken.

Then he remembered he had, more than once: Instructors

asked variations of that same question over and over in his classes: department heads and executive officers asked it aboard training ships; he had even heard Starfleet admirals ask The Question of Captain Picard!

That, it seemed, was another Starfleet general order, one that perhaps even preceded "General Order Number One," the Prime Directive, in importance: Thou shalt not question the policy of the Federation!

Lately, however, Wesley had found himself questioning it a great deal. How could he continue on the path to being a Starfleet officer if he were not sure Starfleet, or even the Federation, had the right answers?

From history classes, he knew there were over seventy intersystem treaties, more than seven thousand *intra*system treaties, seven hundred thousand cultural, scientific, and economic pacts, programs, tontines, contracts, and general agreements, and surely at least seventy million private agreements in the two explored quadrants; nobody could even hazard a guess how many there might be in the Gamma and Delta Quadrants.

One small chain of those agreements, programs, and treaties made up "the Federation"; more than a third of all known species were involved, one way or another, in the Federation "treaty-chain."

But every single race, without exception—even human beings—were also involved in millions of other arrangements, agreements, and treaties that were not considered part of "the Federation."

Who could say, among all those interconnections between the hundreds of known races and millions of discovered planets, that there was not a *better system* for interlinking creative intelligence throughout the galaxy?

Lately, even while going through the motions of being a Starfleet Academy cadet, Wesley Crusher had developed a distinctly creepy feeling that the Federation, and Starfleet in particular, might actually be impeding the natural development of everyone. Perhaps by its very existence and by enunciating the Prime Directive, the Federation *broke* the Prime Directive.

Beyond all the politics, the threat of military force, the economic interlink; beyond the posturing, the threats, the great, charitable works; beyond the inevitable "crisis-of-the-moment," there waited the Traveler, the spiritual, almost mystic *direct connection* between the brain and universe.

For one brief moment, Wesley had actually known that direct connection. What he suddenly knew about himself and his destiny miniaturized the "Starfleet mystique" and the glorious Federation from a bright, floating palace in the sky to a child's sand castle on a crowded beach . . . even though he could not yet articulate what he knew of his destiny. There were no words; ultimately, there were *no words*.

Maybe I made a mistake. Maybe I should just resign my . . .

Cadet Ensign Crusher shut down the thoughts with such brutality that he actually made himself dizzy for a moment. He blinked and returned to the present time.

He waited, watchful for Tunk's inevitable loss of attention. It happened sooner than Wesley thought it would, but he was ready. He removed his chaseum Academy ring from his finger and slipped it in with the next batch of hectobars. A chaseum stylus followed; then he slipped his chaseum belt buckle off his belt and turned it into ersatz latinum.

It was not hard to find chaseum; since its invention, it had become one of the most popular metals throughout the Federation . . . all the metallic properties of latinum except color, density, and the fact that one could replicate chaseum.

The comm badge was trickier, since he could not afford to let the Ferengi know he had one. But Tunk soon wandered away to make himself some refreshments, and Wesley unpinned the badge and transmuted it.

Feeling unusually morbid, Wesley decided to simply explain to Tunk that what he was doing was illegal. The cadet did not expect it would do any good, but he was curious to hear what rationalization Tunk would use.

"You know this is out-and-out counterfeiting," he said.

"I'm not doing anything," whined the Ferengi. "All I'm doing is creating chaseum sculptures of hectobars of gpl. It's you—you're the one turning them into counterfeit latinum!"

Wesley rolled his eyes. "Do you really expect the authorities to buy that?"

"We won't ever have to find out," Tunk pointed out, "because you're in this up to your neck. If you get all legal about it, you'll go to prison yourself . . . and when you get out, *if* you get out, you'll immediately stand trial for contract violations in Ferengi court . . . and you'll wish you hadn't ever gotten out."

"Don't you think there's anything wrong with passing bad latinum in a deal? Isn't there something in the Rules of Acquisition about this?"

"Certainly there is!" sneered the Ferengi. "The sixty-ninth Rule of Acquisition states: Ferengi are not responsible for the stupidity of other races. We just drop your hectobars on the table . . . it's not our fault that Hatheby's stupidly mistakes them for latinum! No Ferengi would ever make such an elementary mistake."

"You're utterly devious," said Wesley, shaking his head.

"Why, thank you, hu-man. Apology accepted."

Fairy gold, thought Wesley; *that's what this is.* In fairy tales, people always grabbed at the fairy gold because they were so insanely greedy that they did not stop to ask how such a person—a beggar or a peddler—came by such a hoard.

Then, when the first rays of the sun struck the fairy gold, it turned back into leaves . . . leaving the greedy recipient utterly ruined.

How permanent was the Kimbal effect? Six months from now, would all the fairy latinum revert to chaseum?

Amazed at the depths of human greed and how thoroughly the glint of gold can blind the most astute businessman, Wesley kept at his task, slipping the hectobars of chaseum (and the occasional chaseum screwdriver or pocket knife) inside the clock face and twisting the dial.

With both Crusher and Tunk working, both more experienced than the previous night, the second pile of valueless specie grew more quickly than the first. At last, even Munk was satisfied that they had enough for that evening's game. Just as well; Wesley noted by his watch, now apparently made of gold-pressed latinum, that the time was 1855.

While Munk and Tunk gloated over the trove, dancing around the glistening pile like evil viziers around a magic lamp, Wesley casually rose and stepped into the bathroom.

He closed and locked the door, then touched his comm badge, now also made of "latinum." "Crusher," he whispered, "beam me up immediately, please!"

Munk and Tunk were so busy capering and singing little Ferengi nonsense-songs about limitless wealth, doubtless learned in Ferengi nurseries, that they heard neither Wesley's conversation nor his subsequent departure, not even with their sensitive Ferengi ears.

Materializing on the transporter pad, Cadet Crusher barely had time to notice that it was a different transporter chief, not Otto; he waved and mumbled thanks as he dashed off the platform and jogged along the corridors to the turbolift.

Data admitted him as soon as he touched the annunciator. "You are very punctual," observed the android. "My memory banks list two hundred and seven varieties of card game filed under the general heading 'poker.' Which particular variation interests you?"

"Oh, anything. Pick one, please, sir."

Data's quarters were inhumanly spotless, of course, despite the presence of Spot. The cat approached cautiously, not remembering Wesley at first. He inspected the hu-man gravely, sniffing Wesley's ankles; then, either remembering Wesley Crusher at last or simply deciding that the cadet was not dangerous, Spot walked around one of Wesley's feet and in between his legs. Spot rubbed his fur against the cadet's trousers, meowing plaintively.

"Geez, don't you ever pet him, Data?"

"I give Spot much attention, Wesley. He tells everyone that he is starved for both attention and food. Spot is a very deceitful cat."

Data removed a pack of playing cards from a drawer. He shuffled them so quickly that Wesley could not even follow the motions. "The simplest game is five-card draw, and it demonstrates the four basic elements of most poker games: dealing, drawing, betting, and comparing. Let us start with five-card draw poker. Let us adjourn to the card table."

Data led Wesley to a small, green felt table, hexagonal. He sat down in one chair and Wesley took the opposite.

"The first step is to buy into the game, receiving chips equal to the amount of money you paid. I will simply give you some chips; we may pretend that you purchased them."

The commander slid small stacks of blue, red, and white chips across the felt. "Thanks," said Wesley.

"Before playing, you must ante up. This means place a chip out as your initial bet, before receiving any cards."

Data slid a pair of white chips into the center of the table. But Wesley, instead of sliding out two of his own white chips, placed the "latinum" stylus on the table instead.

Data scrutinized the bet. "This is most unusual, Wesley. Generally, players use their chips to represent their bets. May I look at that item?"

"You mean to verify the bet?" asked Wesley, hope showing through. *I won't deliberately hand over counterfeits,* thought the cadet, still annoyed at the absurd Federation treaty chain that recognized the kangaroo courts of the Ferengi. *But can I help it if he wants to inspect my bet?* "Sure," said Wesley, gesturing at the stylus.

Data picked it up and examined it closely. "Wesley, this stylus appears to be made of pure gold-pressed latinum."

"Sure looks that way."

"Its value far exceeds that of the required ante."

"Are you saying you won't accept it as a bet?"

Data raised his eyebrows. "Making such a large ante is unproductive, because you are betting a large amount against a small amount at equal odds. But I will teach you a lesson by accepting it."

Wesley sighed in frustration. Data was so entranced by the absurdity of the bet that he failed to notice how incongruous was *the stylus itself*. Who would have a computer stylus made entirely of latinum, anyway?

The android continued. "Now we deal five cards to each player, all facedown." Data proceded to deal out all ten cards in less than one second. "You may pick up your cards and examine them. The possible hands are 'one pair,' which consists of two cards of the same denomination; 'two pair,' which consists—"

"Data, I know the hands. It's all right. I'll bet this." Wesley removed a "latinum" key from his pocket and tossed it on the table.

"We are not yet ready to bet again, Wesley," said Data, sliding the key back across the table to the cadet. "First, we must discard and draw cards. You may discard up to four of your five cards and draw an equal number; how many new cards do you want?"

Wesley stared at his hand. He had a pair of jacks—and three sevens.

"Ah, I'll take three," he declared, tossing one jack and two of the sevens on the table, keeping only the jack and seven of hearts. It was only the second time he had ever been dealt a pat, five-card hand in his "lengthy" poker career . . . and he had to throw it back into the ocean!

Data counted out three cards in a blur of motion. Wesley picked them up slowly, one by one: three of hearts, six of hearts, two of hearts.

Disgusted, he slapped the hand on the table. How was he going to get Data to examine the items unless he lost? And how could he lose when he threw out a full house, only to draw into a flush?

Data stared at the hand. "Wesley, I don't think you quite understand the goal. That is actually a very good hand."

"Is it?"

"Yes. In fact, the odds against drawing three cards to a flush are—"

"Ah, it's my deal, isn't it?"

Data nodded.

This time, Wesley removed his watch, now solid gold-pressed latinum, and placed it on the table.

"Wesley, once again your ante is much larger than the amount called for. Why do you not use your chips? You have plenty."

"Is there a rule against betting more than required?"

Data looked aside for a moment. "I do not find any specific rule against placing too-large an ante on the table. But it is not good form, and you reduce your expected payout."

Wesley reached out and nudged the solid-latinum watch. "Is this worth more than the ante?" he asked innocently.

Data stared; for the first time, he seemed to notice something odd. "May I examine the watch?"

"You need to verify its value for the record?"

The android picked up the watch and turned it forward and back, studying it. "Where did you get this watch? If this is gold-pressed latinum, it is worth considerably more than the ante . . . in fact, considerably more than all of these chips added together."

"I can't tell you where I got the watch," said Wesley Crusher, deliberately sounding as mysterious as possible.

"Do you mean you do not know where you got it, or you are not allowed to tell me?"

Wesley shook his head. "I can't tell you where I got it. Starfleet cadets are honest, trustworthy, brave, and true."

Data raised his brows in puzzlement, one of the few expressions he had mastered completely. He slid two white chips to the center of the felt table.

Wesley shuffled the cards expertly by splitting the deck and riffling the corners together, a shuffle he had practiced assiduously before the big game with Carl La Fong, Tunk, and the rest of the Academy riverboat gamblers. He dealt a pair of cards, one facedown and the second faceup. "Seven-card stud," he announced.

"I have a jack showing," said Data, "but you have only a six; therefore, I shall bet." He peeked at his hole card, then slid a red chip into the center.

Wesley kept a poker face; he actually had a pair of sixes. If he got extraordinarily unlucky, he would win the hand again. *Should have picked draw poker,* he berated himself; *I could have guaranteed a loss!* Then he remembered the last hand.

"I'll see that," said Wesley, matching the chip, "and raise you—uh, whatever this is worth." He plucked the comm badge, now seemingly made of latinum, from his shirt and dropped it onto the table with a muffled thunk.

This time, Data did not ask permission; he simply picked up the comm badge and inspected it. "Wesley, I must ask you where you got all this gold-pressed latinum."

"I'm sure you must."

"You did not answer the question."

"You noticed that. I can't tell you where I got the latinum comm badge."

"I have the feeling you are trying to tell me something without telling me something, Wesley."

"Me? I'm just playing poker."

"I do not have sufficient chips to call that bet, and it is probably above the table limit of most legal poker games."

"I'll take five blues as a call."

Data slid a small stack of blue chips into the center. Wesley dealt the next two cards.

"You received a queen, but I now have a king," said Data. Again, he bet a red chip; this time Wesley "called" with a solid "latinum" commemorative coin ("Zephram Cochrane —Three Hundred Years of Warp Drive—2361").

By the time the seventh card was dealt, facedown, Wesley had bet everything from "latinum" pliers to "latinum" bootlace tips. He had also accumulated another six along the way. Data had a pair of tens showing.

Wesley sweated the last round of betting; he had exhausted his supply of chaseum objects enchanted by fairies to resemble gold-pressed latinum and shoveled over a double-handful of chips instead. Data called.

"What have you got?" asked the cadet, anxiously.

Data turned over his hole card; it was a king, giving him two pairs: tens and kings.

Wesley swallowed. He looked down at his own hand and said, "Well, two pair beats a pair of sixes." Then he flipped his five faceup cards over and slid all seven at Data.

For an instant, Wesley was afraid the android would look at the hand. Instead, after a moment's hesitation, Data slid the pot to his own side.

"Whoops," said Wesley, "look at the time! Gotta dash. Thanks for the lesson, sir; I learned a lot."

Data frowned. "I think you need a few more lessons, Wesley. Here." He shoved all the ersatz latinum back toward Wesley.

"What? Are you calling me a *welcher?*" Wesley stood indignantly, folding his arms across his chest. "An Academy cadet never refuses a debt of honor or accepts undeserved charity."

"Wesley, this was just a lesson, not a real game. You may take back your property without dishonor."

"Nonsense! In a real poker game, wouldn't it have all been lost?"

"Yes, it would have. You played very erratically."

"Then since this is supposed to be a lesson, you should follow the rules and keep the property."

Data pondered for a moment. "All right, if you insist, Cadet. But I think it is an odd position to take." He thought for a moment. "Do you mind if I examine these items more closely, Wesley?"

The cadet shrugged. "I would never dream of telling a superior officer what to do with his personal property.

Uh-oh, I'll be late if I don't get out of here. It's been a real . . . learning experience, Data. We'll have to do it again sometime."

Wesley jumped up and motored toward the transporter room before Data could change his positronic mind and force the "latinum" back on the cadet.

Chapter Fifteen

As soon as Cadet Crusher had left the ship, Commander Data scooped all of the metal tools and objects, apparently and rather incongruously made of latinum, and brought them up to the bridge.

"Sir," he said to Commander Riker, "I just had a very strange encounter with Wesley."

"Ah, good old Fred Kimbal! How is young Kimbal getting on these days?"

Data calculated that this was a jest on Commander Riker's part, but a minor one; thus, the android confined his laugh program to a relatively short outburst of two seconds duration, rising to a peak volume of only twenty decibels.

"You're getting pretty good at that, Data; it's starting to sound natural."

"Thank you, sir. I am trying."

"Well? How strange was your encounter with Cadet Kimbal?"

"I was teaching him the rudiments of poker, sir."

Data was treated to a rather frosty silence, after which

Commander Riker remarked, "Why didn't he come to me for that request?"

"You would have been a more logical choice, sir; I am sure Cadet Crusher was reluctant to disturb you when you had command of the ship. To continue, he played erratically, as if he were trying to lose. And he did lose; he lost these six items, which he insisted I keep, despite my offer to return them."

Data spread the items onto a clipboard, which he passed to Commander Riker. The first officer pondered them for a moment.

"Data, this is . . . these are . . ." He looked up, his thick eyebrows lowering in suspicion. "Data, I've been in Starfleet for seventeen years, and I have never seen a comm badge made of gold-pressed latinum before. Something is very wrong, and for some reason, this is the only way Wesley can tell us about it."

Data nodded. "That matches my hypothesis, sir. He clearly intended me to win these items; when I requested permission to examine them, he said he could not control what I did with my 'own property.' He was quite insistent that they were now my property."

"Well, hadn't we better take them to the science lab and begin examining them, Data?"

"Aye, sir."

Riker and Data rode down the turbolift in silence; Data simulated thousands of possible scenarios in his positronic brain, trying to find one that resulted in Wesley Crusher ending up with latinum copies of several common artifacts. None had a probability higher than background noise.

"You know," said Commander Riker as they entered the lab, "we've been assuming that these things are really made of latinum."

"Yes, sir. I performed a full visible-spectrum, pseudo-Balmer-line scan on them when Wesley first bet them. They have all the gross characteristics of gold-pressed latinum."

"Appearances can be deceiving," said Will Riker. He picked up the commemorative medal, pretended to place it into his left hand; Data, however, saw him actually retain it in his right. "Here, Data, blow on this hand."

Humoring the commander, Data leaned over and expelled air over Riker's left hand, all the while keeping an eye on the other.

"Voila," said the commander, opening his left hand.

"Sir, you must practice that trick more assiduously; I saw you retain the coin in your other hand."

"You mean this one?" slyly asked Riker, opening his right hand; it was as empty as the left.

Data stared, replaying the scene several times through his visual circuitry. Try as he might, he could not see where his analysis had gone wrong.

"Are you looking for this, Data?" Commander Riker gestured casually at the specimen tray; there, sitting securely among the rest of the alleged latinum, was the medal.

"The point is well taken, sir," said Data. "Let us run a complete scan on the items using the positronal spectral scanners."

The positronal scanners were the most accurate in the lab, even more precise than the subspace scanners that ringed the *Enterprise* itself. Data placed the medal in the gravitic clamps and programmed the scan. "This will take approximately four minutes," he announced.

Even before the scan completed, Data already knew that the medal was not made of gold-pressed latinum. "Sir, please observe at this sequence here."

"Latinum," said Riker.

"That is the sequence of absorption lines commonly associated with gold-pressed latinum; but do you see the other pattern behind it?"

Faint "ghost-lines" appeared in the positronal spectrum. Data visually enhanced the image, increasing the contrast.

"What is that?" asked Riker. "I don't recognize the sequence."

"Perhaps it would look more familiar if I blue-shifted it back where it came from." He typed at the console, and the absorption sequence slid to the left.

"Chaseum?" asked the commander.

"Indeed, sir. It is my guess that these items are actually made of chaseum which has somehow been overlayed by the image of gold-pressed latinum."

"Fairy gold," breathed Riker.

"An apt description, sir. The counterfeit is excellent; there are only three positronal spectral scanners in this entire sector . . . and two of them are aboard the *Enterprise*. There is undoubtedly no other piece of equipment that would be capable of detecting the difference between this metal and latinum."

Riker stared at the display, rubbing his beard in agitation. "Data, do you understand the implication of this? You know why latinum is the standard currency of all three known quadrants, don't you?"

Data nodded. "Yes, sir; it is because it is one of only a few materials that cannot be replicated. The molecules of gold-pressed latinum are arranged in a nearly crystaline pattern that depends upon the precise orientation of eighty-eight 'fractal legs' of atoms. When the replicator attempts to duplicate the pattern, the second fractal leg induces a spontaneous reorientation of the first. Thus, each fractal leg recursively reorients its predecessor—"

"And you end up with chaseum, not latinum, in the replicator," concluded Riker. "It's like squaring a positive or negative number; either way, you end up with a positive square. But if you can alter the appearance of common chaseum to make it pass perfectly as latinum, then you hold the fate of the galaxy in your hand. Without latinum, there's no trade; and without trade, there is nothing to hold together the fragile alliances that prevent total war from breaking out."

Data turned off the scanner. The rest of the spectral absorbtion lines showed the same pattern: a strong latinum sequence in the foreground with the ghost of a chaseum sequence in deep background.

"Sir, if we are indeed dealing with a nearly perfect

latinum counterfeit, it is most urgent that we identify the perpetrator at once."

"Hopefully before he gets away with the photonic pulse cannon. Look, whoever is doing this needs a constant supply of chaseum. If we could tie into the chateau's computer system, we could see who is replicating chaseum by the ton."

Data tapped his comm badge. "Computer; establish a communications link with the Chateau Hotel Casino."

After a moment, they heard the voice of the chateau switchboard operator. "Good evening thank you for calling the Chateau Hôtel Casino located on scenic Novus Alamorgordus reservations are appreciated my name is Alison Swain may I help you sir?"

"This is Commander William Riker, first officer of the *U.S.S. Enterprise.* May I speak to the manager, please?"

"Certainly sir I'll connect you enjoy your stay here on scenic Novus Alamogordus thank you."

"Yes, Commander Reichert," boomed a boisterous voice with a distinct New Anglican accent, "Hugh Akston, Chief Concierge of the casino. I am at your service."

Riker hesitated a moment, then surprised Data by offering the manager a story: "We have reason to believe a known criminal is among your guests. We need to scan your replicator logs for the past three days to locate him."

The manager's pause was quite long. "I'm sorry, sir," he responded stiffly, "that information is private. Our guests do not come to the Chateau Hotel Casino in order to have their privacy violated."

"You don't understand. The Federation needs to examine your logs; this is an official request."

"No. No, it's quite out of the question. And we are outside the jurisdiction of the Federation, in free space; there is no Federation tribunal that has the authority to order us to hand over our logs."

"No, sir, you're right. I can't order you to hand them over. But if you do not, you will be aiding a very serious criminal enterprise, one that will almost certainly harm the very clients you're protecting."

"Commander Riker, this conversation is not getting us anywhere. You are welcome to beam down and try our nearly limitless diversions . . . Double-Dabo, a leafy-vine lottery, triple-odds craps tables, and the most beautiful Dabo girls in the quadrant. But we simply cannot authorize any computer link between the chateau computers and your ship. And if you try to take them by force, you'll activate a poison-pill virus that will overwrite them with random noise.

"I'm sorry, sir. Please do come down and join us, though, and please accept a free coupon good for six grams' worth of identichips, good in any restaurant or casino."

"Thank you." Commander Riker sighed. *"Enterprise* out."

When the comm link terminated, Data turned to the commander. "Sir, if you don't mind my asking, why did you not tell the manager about the counterfeit latinum?"

"The last thing we need right now is a specie-panic, particularly when we don't have much evidence to back up the charge. Hm . . . I wonder whether the counterfeiters were stupid enough to . . . ?"

Data caught on immediately. "Computer," he said, "has any crew member or passenger aboard the *Enterprise* replicated any items made of chaseum in the past one hundred and sixty-eight hours?"

"Affirmative," the computer replied. "Two Ferengi and Cadet Wesley Crusher have all replicated bars of chaseum within the past one hundred and sixty-eight hours."

"Bars? Did these bars happen to resemble bars of gold-pressed latinum?"

"Unknown; the bar designs of gold-pressed latinum are not contained within my memory banks."

"Of course not," muttered Riker. He turned to Data. "I was afraid of that," he said. "It seems our old friend, Cadet Fred Kimbal, is up to his earlobes in trouble with his two Ferengi friends, Munk and Tunk."

"He does have a remarkable propensity for getting into situations, sir."

Riker paced slowly to the spectral scanner. "So Munk is counterfeiting gold-pressed latinum. Aside from typical Ferengi greed, why? Why right here and now?"

"The most logical conclusion is the one you mentioned earlier, sir. He wishes to purchase items at the auction."

"The photonic pulse cannon? But why? That's what we need to determine, Data. That, and how we stop him."

"Perhaps if we informed the officials of Hatheby's about the deception?"

Riker shook his head. "Data, you've spent your entire life in Starfleet. You haven't lived until you've sat through a court trial . . . especially where a Ferengi is one of the litigants."

Riker held up fingers as he counted. "First, we're not disinterested parties; we're involved in the auction itself representing not only ourselves, but Betazed, the medical community, and the Klingon Empire.

"Second, Wesley—I mean Fred—used to be an officer of this very ship; he could claim that we breached crew privacy by reporting that he replicated the chaseum."

"Would Cadet Crusher make such a claim?"

"Of course not; but Munk or Tunk might make it for him. Third, we have no solid evidence linking any of them to the counterfeit latinum."

"I obtained it from Mister Crusher, sir."

"You won it in a poker game. And that doesn't indicate that he produced it, or that he even knows who produced it. He replicated chaseum, but so what? It's no crime to replicate chaseum."

"It might be considered probable cause to obtain a warrant to search the Ferengi's rooms."

Riker shrugged. "Fourth, whom do we petition for a warrant? As Akston said, we have no jurisdiction here. What should we do, beam the Ferengi up to the *Enterprise* and arrest them?"

"I see what you mean," said Data, raising his brows. "If we cannot warn the other bidders without initiating a lawsuit against Starfleet, and we cannot arrest the suspects without starting an interquadrant incident, what actions should we take?"

Riker's smile was grim, mirthless. "We simply have to stop them ourselves, Mister Data."

Data nodded, distracted by the test-procedures *daemon* he initiated. "I will attempt to devise a method of neutralizing the deception, Commander."

"Keep me informed. In the meantime, I think I'll put in a call to Captain Picard, Counselor Troi, and Lieutenant Worf. Always nice to keep in touch, eh, Data?" He smiled, indicating a mild jest; but Data's positronic brain was at maximum utilization and he had no room to initiate his "laughter" program.

In fact, he did not even notice when Commander Riker left the room. At a lull in the processing, he noticed that he was alone in the lab, standing near the display console, frozen nearly into physical paralysis by intense mental activity.

Data's problem was that he knew what had been done to make the chaseum look like latinum, but he did not know how it was done. The strong latinum absorption lines showed that chemically, it was gold-pressed latinum; but the residual chaseum ghost-lines showed that it was not.

Perplexed, he began to review all known chemical properties of the chaseum-class metals that could be checked.

Back on the bridge, Commander Riker opened a comm link with Captain Picard.

From long experience with the captain, Riker could tell that Picard was quite agitated, though few others could have detected the annoyance beneath the captain's calm voice. "Commander Riker, I am in the midst of a critical series of bids. What is it?"

Riker took a deep breath; the captain never called him "Commander Riker" unless he was very displeased. Tersely, he brought Captain Picard up to speed on the suspected Ferengi counterfeiting ring.

The change in the captain's mood was swift and gratifying. "This is grave news indeed, Will. Chairman Munk has taken to bidding silently with hectobars of latinum. Do you think they are all counterfeit?"

"Sir, I can't say for sure that any of it is. What does he say when he pulls out each hectobar?"

"Nothing, Number One; he simply drops them onto the table with a resounding thunk. In his twisted, criminal mind, he has probably convinced himself that this mitigates the crime, since he is not actually stating that he's bidding latinum."

"Would that work in a courtroom?"

Picard snorted. "I doubt it, unless it were a Ferengi courtroom. In this case, however, there is no place to try him anyway; Novus Alamogordus is outside Federation jurisdiction, yet not quite inside the territory claimed by the Cardassians. There is a Federation-Cardassian peace treaty currently being negotiated that may resolve this sector, but nothing has been finalized yet."

"Data is trying to find a way to reverse the illusion; I'll keep you informed, sir. In the meantime, I've got to contact Deanna, Beverly, and Worf."

"I must sign off, Number One; Gul Fubar has engaged the Grand Nagus in hectobar to hectobar combat over the plans for a stereographic sensor array, and I must enter the fray on behalf of Kahless the Unforgettable before he's forgotten. Picard out."

The warning to Dr. Beverly Crusher took only a minute; she was in her room, perusing catalogs of hospital equipment.

"It doesn't make any difference," she said, "he's not bidding on any medical lots, anyway."

Deanna took the information with typical steady calm.

Lieutenant Worf's reaction was typical.

"I will kill that earlobed Ferengi!" snarled Worf, forgetting himself for a moment. "He has insulted and dishonored . . ." Worf caught himself.

Worf and Geordi were not in the auction hall. They were in a corridor when they received Riker's call, and Geordi transferred the comm link to a public communicator with a viewscreen.

"Lieutenant," Riker said sharply, "you're not representing the Klingon Empire. You're representing the Federation, and we do not kill people for counterfeiting."

For an instant, Worf's anger flared so bright that Riker half-expected the gigantic Klingon to leap right through the comm link screen. Then it ebbed, and Worf was himself once again. "You are right, of course. I am sorry I lost my temper, sir." But his lip still curled in a dark Klingon snarl.

"Just keep bidding as if you don't suspect anything, Worf. We don't want to spook them just yet."

"But, Commander, surely we are not going to just let him outbid us on every item! Even without killing him, I can frighten him into fleeing Novus Alamogordus."

Riker shook his head. "That's the last thing we want. Worf, as important as this auction is, it's far more terrifying to think that a Ferengi has the means to counterfeit gold-pressed latinum."

"I understand, sir. I shall try not to spook him, though it will be difficult."

"Have you won any bids, yet, Worf?"

The Klingon frowned like a hired mourner at a skinflint's funeral. "There has been only one bid at the 'Senior-level' auction; Munk won it by dropping seventy-five hectobars of his fraudulent latinum on the table."

The commander chuckled. "Keep your eyes open, Lieutenant; Riker out."

Commander William Riker leaned back in the command chair and scratched his beard. *Needs a trim,* he thought, *starting to itch.* He tapped his comm badge. "Riker to Data."

Data had not moved at all since attacking the problem

except for the "involuntary" functions such as blinking and simulating breathing that occurred on their own timetables. Now, he seemed to wake up and answer the commander's call.

"Data here, sir."

"I know it's only been a half hour, but do you have any ideas?"

"Yes, sir."

"You *do?*"

"I am unable to deduce how the Ferengi are disguising chaseum as latinum; but I believe I have thought of a method that in theory, at least, will remove the disguise. I might be able to adapt the ship's phasers to produce a disphasic field which I can set to one hundred eighty degrees out of phase with the illusory latinum spectrum."

"You're saying that would cancel out the illusion?"

"I do not know for certain; but it is logical. In theory, the disphasic field should create an interference pattern where every wave is mapped to a trough and every trough to a wave. That should flatten the wave function, causing the illusion to vanish."

"How long would it take, Data?"

"I do not know. I would guess at least sixteen hours; and during that time, we would not have the use of the phaser banks."

"Let me think about this. Riker out."

The first officer thought of the danger posed by Munk and his fairy gold; then he thought of the Romulans, the Cardassians, and even the Tholians, all in various orbits around Novus Alamogordus. By a strict interpretation of Starfleet regulations, Riker had no choice whatsoever: Under no circumstances could a starship disarm itself in the presence of the three most aggressive empires in the quadrant.

He smiled tightly. *I guess I was never a one to follow regulations to the letter.* "Riker to Data."

"Data here, sir."

"Start working on that disphasic field and keep me posted. Riker out."

First Officer William Riker leaned forward, forearms on knees, pretending to study the viewscreen; but behind his eyes, he wondered whether he had just placed the *Enterprise* in deadly danger.

Chapter Sixteen

WESLEY ARRIVED BACK in the Munk-Tunk suite at a few minutes after 2100. He stepped out of the bathroom, shooting for "nonchalant."

He may as well have marched out with a brass band; the two Ferengi stared at him with curled lips, bared teeth, and suspiciously wrinkled noses. "Where were you, hu-man? Answer me!"

"Aye, and see that yer tongue be not flapping with the falsehood, or faith, but we'll lop it off!"

"What do you mean? I just—"

"You just transported out of the room for the last hour! The toilet was empty!"

"Th-that's what I was saying," improvised Wesley, feeling his face redden. Would the Ferengi notice his guilty expression, or were they telling the truth that all hu-mans look the same to them? "I was just . . . uh . . . beamed aboard the *Enterprise*, entirely against my will, I assure you." *The best lie sticks closest to the truth,* he remembered reading somewhere. "It's that Commander Riker, you know, the second in command? It turns out, ah . . ."

Wesley's mouth was dry, and he felt his pulse leap along at warp speed. Then, sudden inspiration. "There . . . there was apparently a transportation tax we didn't pay."

The Ferengi, who until that moment had been advancing menacingly, stopped as if hitting a force shield. "Er . . . tax?" asked Tunk.

"Yes! It's the, ah, Federation Council on Emergency Service Response Inter-Sector Revenue Enhancement Opportunity Tax. We were supposed to pay, um, a couple hundred bars of latinum. This Riker guy demanded that I pay for us."

"Hold, lad," said Munk, eyes narrowing again. "Why forsooth would yon admiralty make tae wring the tithe from me crew, not their skipper?"

"They . . . they . . . they knew they'd never get a gram from a Ferengi, that's why! They knew you'd be able to talk your way out of the tax. So they went after—poor Fred Kimbal instead, since I'm merely a human and unable to successfully negotiate my way out of this blatant piracy!"

"Ahhh!" said both Ferengi in unison, nodding sagely. "Scupper me, but that rings sooth," said Munk.

"So what happened, hu-man? Speak up, stop stammering!"

"Faith and the Profits!" cried Munk, "ye didn't fire a canister of our latinum at the lubber!"

Wesley blinked. "I would have if I'd had one with me. But I didn't." It was the simple truth; the Ferengi watched their fairy gold like paranoid leprechauns.

"Fray me ratlines!" swore Munk. "We canna cast yon bars adrift aboard ye *Enterprise*—they're spyglasses aplenty to prise the secret from our horde!"

"So how *did* you pay them?" demanded Tunk. "You haven't got two hundred bars of latinum!"

"I, uh . . ." Wesley looked from one unfriendly Ferengi face to the other. He realized he was rubbing his wrist, which felt quite odd without the chronometer he normally wore.

The chronometer . . . "I didn't have any latinum on my

person, so they, ah, they took my chronometer, my ring, my pendant, and entered a debt against me for the remaining amount."

Tunk reared back, face a caricature of astonishment. "They did? By the Profits, I didn't realize the hu-mans had such ingenuity!"

"Sink me, but 'tis an ambitious Ferengi solution! I'd not have sought it from the Federation landlubbers. *Decency*" — he spat the word—"clings to them like barnacles on a whale's belly."

Munk's hand lashed out, catching Wesley's wrist. He reeled it in like a fish on a line, then pointed to the paler, untanned spot left behind by Wesley's wrist-chronometer; at the Academy on Earth, the cadet found himself outside often enough to tan slightly . . . a side effect he silently thanked.

"Kimbal, 'tis a fine service ye hath rendered to yer maties," beamed Munk.

"Oh, yes," added his son, "very big of you. We're very proud." He smacked Wesley on the shoulder, bruising the cadet's arm. "Your generosity is a credit to your race."

"Certes, and of a surity, we sh'll gladly make it up to ye."

"With latinum and all the fine things money can buy . . . Dabo girls, holosuites . . ."

"Just as soon as we sail into safe harbor once begin."

"Aye—I mean, yes, just as soon as this little adventure is over! You have my *personal guarantee* on it."

"Now cease yer dancing and let's ship this booty to yon auction cabin."

Chortling, the two "supervised" while Wesley sweated and grunted the rest of the fairy latinum aboard an antigravity luggage pallet. While he worked, he noticed Munk sidle up to Tunk and mutter, "Sure as yer me ship's master, I've a task for your blade."

"My . . . blade? Sir?" Tunk cringed slightly, indicating reluctance to serve in any capacity requiring a blade.

"Aye. This'd be a deed for our two young scalawags, but they be scarpered. So 'tis a' up to ye. We needs make a scheme to vouchsafe yon clock, if the cannons loose their charges and it's every man for hisself."

"A plan? To protect the clock?"

"Aye . . ." Munk turned a suspicious eye on Wesley, who resumed loading. Leaning close, the old Ferengi whispered for several minutes into his son's ears; the cadet could not hear another word.

When he finally finished loading the latinum, he followed the Ferengi down the wide marble stairs into the main dining area.

The table, which ordinarily seated and fed two hundred, was reworked into a conference table that seated a mere eighty bidders who had posted a sufficient bond to qualify for the major-lot auction. Munk sat at his accustomed chair, Tunk behind him as advisor, two seats away from Lieutenant Worf, who was himself advised by Geordi La Forge. Further around the table, Wesley recognized Deanna Troi and Captain Picard, and at the far end, the Grand Nagus of the Ferengi, with about twenty advisors conveying messages in relays.

As the Hatheby's auctioneer explained the rules in tedious detail, rules that Wesley had heard explained in exactly the same tedious detail three times previously, he found himself nodding off. Small wonder: He had gotten virtually no sleep in the past forty-eight hours, unlike the Ferengi. He had not even "relaxed" in a holosuite or read for pleasure. All Wesley had done for two days, it seemed, was toil over a hot Kimbal Clock for hours on end, cranking out hectobar after hectobar of fake latinum, then attend Munk in auctions and feed him the hectobars ten at a time so he could toss them on the table and steal the show.

Dully, Wesley felt eyes boring into the back of his head. He turned around and finally spotted Counselor Deanna Troi observing him. *If she's reading my emotional state,* he thought, *I'll bet all she's picking up is exhaustion, frustration, and a hell of a strong desire to just go back to the Academy. Or better yet, ditch the Academy, the* Enterprise, *Starfleet, even the Federation.*

What Wesley Crusher really wanted was to leave everything behind and actually see the universe—not as a "representative" of the Federation or Starfleet, not in a starship bound by rules and regulations, even Standing Order Number One . . . not as "Cadet Crusher" or "Ensign Crusher," but simply as Wesley.

Once in his life, he had touched that sort of freedom, had felt liberated from decades of tradition and formalism: the few moments he had spent with the Traveler, where he actually touched universe, cosmos the known and chaos the unknown together, were the brightest points of his life. Those memories were the bright, hot flame at the tip of a long, gray candle.

I want those moments back, he thought. Someday, he knew, he would condemn everything else to hell and run away to join the Traveler. When he touched subspace and guided the *Enterprise* halfway across the quadrant, Wesley Crusher knew he had heard his true call; someday, he would answer it.

But not today, he added sadly. The bidding had begun.

Counselor Deanna Troi tried to look serenely confident as the bidding began; she managed only calmness, but it was safer than openly displaying the emotions that raged within her.

The bids began slowly at first; the auctioneer, Dmitri Smythe, had to coax each bid out of his reluctant suitors.

The first item was a personal force shield that supposedly absorbed and reemitted phaser blasts with near-perfect efficiency; the net effect, according to Dr. Zorka's abstract, which he published in lieu of an actual paper (he claimed he was too busy to write the paper itself), was as if phaser blasts were *perfectly reflected*.

Nobody could mistake the value of such an item; if it could be extended to a ship, the vessel would be invulnerable to phasers.

Even so, the mob seemed reluctant to even open the bidding. Mr. Smythe did not help matters by exercising his prerogative as "conductor" to issue a new ukase: In all bidding at the "senior level," which included every truly interesting lot, not only would the winner have to fork over the latinum . . . but so would the *runner-up.*

That is, if a Bajoran bid ten hectobars, and a Cardassian bid eleven and won the bid, then the Cardassian paid eleven hundred and got the item . . . and the Bajoran paid the thousand he had bid and got nothing!

At first, Deanna did not understand why anyone would enunciate such a weird rule; she had never before participated in an auction for anything but artwork and had never run across such peculiarities.

After she began to bid, however, she suddenly caught on. Having bid as much as she thought Betazed could afford, if another participant, such as the Grand Nagus, topped her, and no one else seemed likely to outbid—then Deanna was reduced to the quite enviable position of either overbidding the Nagus and at least getting something for her latinum or else sitting silent . . . and spending Betazed's latinum for nothing!

Needless to say, the bidding which began slow quickly escalated to wilder and wilder levels, as every participant caught on to the conundrum: Better to overpay for something than to pay and get nothing.

When at last Captain Picard topped Deanna's last bid, and Gul Fubar topped *that,* Deanna collapsed back into her seat in relief; Betazed (and Deanna Troi) had wriggled off the hook.

Don't use your epathy—don't use it! It's not fair! Deanna used her epathy in every round; she could not help herself. She could not turn it off except by drugs. *Hatheby's was right to refuse to allow full Betazoids,* she thought, then felt ashamed for thinking it . . . the rule virtually prevented her own home planet, telepathy-rich but latinum-poor compared to the mighty empires and the Federation, from effectively bidding.

She snuck another glance at her data-reader crib-clip, searching carefully one more time. The results were as negative as the last six times she had searched; there was no personal force shield listed in the catalog her mother had transmitted, and Betazed had not supplied her with any instructions on how much to bid for one. She was flying solo.

Across the table, Lieutenant Worf searched his own crib-clip to equally negative results. He leaned back to La Forge and spoke in what only a Klingon would call a whisper. "Sir, I find this entire affair immensely frustrating. Not a single one of the items which Starfleet particularly desired has come up yet, and not one of the lots that *has* been auctioned is on my list."

"Of course not, Worf . . . Starfleet probably assembled the list from the journal articles and abstracts that Zorka published. He claimed more basic inventions than Zephram Cochrane."

"Then where are they?"

The lieutenant commander chuckled. "They don't exist, Worf! That's what I've been trying to tell you all. It's illusory; Doctor Zorka never really invented anything worthwhile."

Worf rolled his eyes. "You told me he had invented several useful items. You said he developed a coupling shield for the nacelles."

"Oh, sure, twenty-five years ago."

"And he produced the first working model of a phaser attenuation lens."

"That was a long time ago, too."

"Doctor Zorka developed it after you graduated from the Academy."

"All right, so even a broken clock is right twice a day."

Worf turned his attention to the auction; the Ferengi called the "Grand Nagus" and the Cardassian, Gul Fubar, were slowly one-upping each other for the personal force shield. Then the Klingon furrowed his brow and turned back to Geordi La Forge. "How is a malfunctioning chronometer correct twice a day?"

"Well, when the . . . if the numbers . . . you know, I have

no idea, Worf. I've just always heard it, that's all. Anyway, you know what I mean."

"Commander, I am not sure that you know what you mean. I am positive that I do not." Feeling especially haughty at having finally won an argument from Geordi La Forge, Worf interjected a loud bid, topping the Grand Nagus by more than two hectobars. The Klingon decided that list or no list, he could not allow such a useful item to fall to the Cardassians because of simple, bureaucratic bungling.

The bidding paused; the Nagus and the Cardassian had gotten into a back and forth progression, and it was the Grand Nagus's "turn." Instead of bidding, he leaned forward and leered drunkenly at Worf.

At least, that is how the Klingon took the look. He stared back, vaguely repulsed by the Ferengi, but aware that his best response was not to respond.

"Eaww, looks like we have a newbie in the game. A virgin!"

Worf drew himself up. The "virgin" crack had struck home; it was, in fact, Worf's first bid on any of the important equipment. In awful tones, the lieutenant said, "I am bidding on behalf of the United Federation of Planets."

The Nagus stage-whispered to his cronies: "I am bidding on behalf of the United Federation of Planets!" in an annoying imitation of Worf's voice.

"Are you mocking me?" demanded Worf.

"Never let it be said that I mocked a Klingon," said the Ferengi with wildly exaggerated deference. His cohorts hooted with derisive laughter.

"Mister ah . . ." The Hatheby's conductor stared expectantly at Worf.

"Lieutenant Worf."

"Lieutenant Worf bids forty-eight hundred bars of gold-pressed latinum for the Federation."

After an embarrassing silence, the duel between the Ferengi and the Cardassian continued. Worf did not venture another bid.

At last, Gul Fubar's bids came slower and slower. He

hesitated a long moment at sixty-three hectobars; at sixty-five, he opened and closed his mouth as if gulping air, staring wildly.

Worf smiled; clearly, Gul Fubar had exceeded whatever amount he had alotted for the personal force shield, and now he was about to pay that amount and not get it after all. The Klingon understood the vicious beauty of the double-pay rule.

The conductor, Dmitri Smythe, nodded. "Then if there are no further bids, the lot will be purchased by the Grand Nagus for the Ferengi High Command for sixty-five hundred bars of gold-pressed latinum. One time, two times—"

A loud thud startled everyone at the table. Worf whirled, half-reaching for the phaser that he was not wearing.

It was the other Ferengi at the opposite end of the room, Munk. He had just dropped a huge stack of latinum onto the table—seven kilobars and five hectobars: *seventy-five hundred bars*. It was the largest amount of latinum Lieutenant Worf had ever seen in one place.

Gasps and astonished exclamations echoed around the conference table. The Cardassian looked stricken, but the Grand Nagus allowed his mouth to fall open in shock.

Munk said nothing, merely smiling.

The Hatheby's conductor frowned and nodded in appreciation. "The bid is now seventy-five hundred from Chairman Munk."

"Seventy-seven," bid the Nagus, only slightly recovered.

Munk slid the five hectobars back and dropped another kilobar.

"Eight thousand," intoned Smythe.

Worf half-stood, craning his neck to see from where the little, wizened, old Ferengi was pulling his kilobars. The Klingon saw a large, black satchel, but could not see how full it might be. It sat on a zero-gravity pallet partially behind Munk, next to the other Ferengi and the *Enterprise's* own Wesley Crusher, who had taken to calling himself "Fred Kimbal" for some peculiar reason.

"Where did you get that?" demanded the Grand Nagus, a

bit too jumpy. Munk's only response was to grab an earlobe and flap it at his nemesis, the Ferengi version of a universal gesture inviting an act that was anatomically possible for only six species in the quadrant (Ferengi not among them).

The conductor waited patiently, but nobody rose to challenge Munk's bid. Even the Grand Nagus, having by now recovered from his startlement, sat quietly with a grim smile frozen on his face while Smythe called for a bid once, twice, and finally gaveled the bidding closed. The Nagus paid seven thousand, seven hundred for the privilege of watching Munk pay eight kilobars for the personal force shield.

A sudden crack caused as big a reaction as Munk's thunk: The Grand Nagus, still smiling, held one broken piece of his walking stick in each hand.

Commander La Forge leaned forward and whispered to Worf, "It couldn't happen to a nicer pair."

"At least neither the Cardassians nor the Romulans got it," growled the lieutenant.

"Yeah," commiserated the lieutenant commander, "too bad. They could use a useless drain on their weapons budget."

Smythe unveiled the next lot, a stereographic sensor array that purported to be able to detect even cloaked vessels by the Doppler effect they produced in the subspace continuum.

Once again, Lieutenant Worf scanned through his list, then searched more slowly, line by line. "Sir," he announced, "it is not on the list again."

"Worf, you're really getting worried about this, aren't you?"

"What if we have been fooled, and this is not the real auction?"

"What do you mean, not the real auction? They just auctioned off a personal force shield."

Worf quickly looked left and right, checking to make sure no one was listening; everyone seemed engrossed in the bidding war between Gul Fubar and the Romulan representative, Legate Chirok.

"What if this is only a cover auction, and the real auction, where they are offering the items on my list, is happening somewhere else . . . where we have not been invited?"

"You're paranoid, Worf."

"Perhaps so; still, I wonder. Nothing matches the list I was given by Starfleet."

"Well . . . if you feel that strongly about it, Worf, why don't you investigate?"

The Klingon pondered for a moment. If he left, his place at the table might be taken by one of the alternates. On the other hand, he could certainly claim it back again at the next meal break; most of the bidders seemed like the types who would yield to a meaty forefinger tapping on the shoulder and a polite, but menacing, "pardon me."

"That is an excellent suggestion, sir. I think I shall take it."

Rumbling an evasive explanation, Worf rose and bulled his way to the door of the room, La Forge immediately following. The Klingon noticed Captain Picard watching him curiously, puzzled and concerned about his sudden departure; but it could not be helped.

As soon as they exited the room, Worf's comm badge beeped. "Worf here," he said.

"Riker," announced the voice.

La Forge joined the conversation. "Sir, we're right next to a public communicator; would you like visual?"

"All right; I'll wait."

A minute later, they continued with full audio-visual contact. Commander Riker brought Worf and La Forge up-to-date on the forged latinum, then signed off.

Worf breathed deeply for several seconds, regaining his warrior's calm. "I should have suspected them from the beginning," he berated.

"Oh, come on, Worf. Don't be so hard on yourself. How could you have known the latinum was counterfeit?"

Worf turned slowly to his friend, eyes cold and angry. "Because they are Ferengi!"

"You know, we don't know for sure that's fake latinum. It's all just based on Data's deduction."

"They are Ferengi!"

"I know how we could prove it, though."

Lieutenant Worf blinked twice and finally heard the comment. "How, sir?"

"Well, chaseum doesn't just fall out of the sky, Worf. You have to replicate it . . . which means there will be a record of the replication somewhere—somewhere in the casino's computer system."

The Klingon considered for a moment, then turned to La Forge. "Commander, can you access the memory banks?"

"If I can't, I'll demote myself back to ensign."

Geordi La Forge strolled down the corridor, hands behind his back flapping. He whistled a tuneless sequence of notes. Worf frowned. "Sir," he said as quietly as possible, "you may be the best engineer in Starfleet . . . but as a burglar, I believe you leave much to be desired."

"What's wrong?"

"You are whistling."

"I was trying to be inconspicuous, Worf."

"You are about as inconspicuous as a spiked *brazif* lizard in a gymnasium."

"I'm not acting like a successful intersector spy?"

"No, sir."

"Ah, then no one will suspect me at all, right?"

Worf rolled his eyes. *Human logic,* he told himself as they hurried along the corridor toward the turbolift.

Captain Jean-Luc Picard, bidding for the greater glory of Emperor Kahless, realized abruptly that he had slipped upward into the danger zone with his last bid. From that point on, each bid would be reluctant, fretful, for ending up the bidding as number two, thus paying but receiving nothing, would seriously weaken the Klingon finances.

At once, Counselor Deanna Troi of Betazed signaled her first bid on the warp coil redux damper; until that moment, she had sat silently while Picard and the Cardassian, Gul Fubar, one-upped each other.

It was the third time in a row that Deanna had suddenly begun to bid just at the moment that Picard started worrying, as if . . .

As if she's reading my emotional state, he thought, grimly.

It was ridiculous, unfair! How could he bid against an opponent who always knew when he was close to his upper limit? Immediately, Picard caught the irony. It was for precisely this advantage that Starfleet so often assigned Betazoids to starships.

If she didn't use her abilities, she would be failing in her duty to Betazed. Rough on me, though . . .

However much he might understand her motives, Picard was not about to allow his own clients to be "cheated" that way! *Time for a showdown,* he decided.

Captain Picard closed his eyes and let all the tension flow out of his neck and shoulders. He relaxed his face and imagined the cool vineyards of his native Labarre.

He felt his pulse and respirations slow; a soft, memory-breeze blew across his face, cooling him.

Picard opened his eyes, careful to maintain the feeling, and stared at Deanna until he caught her attention. She blinked, confused by the sudden change in Picard's emotions.

He smiled blandly. Deanna grew flustered, stammering out her next bid, "Seventy—seventy-eight!" she cried.

The captain sighed in relief; Deanna was so startled by the unexpected mood swing that she topped Gul Fubar's last bid by twenty hectobars. The gap was so wide that Picard found no temptation to follow . . . and neither did anyone else. *Just as well,* he thought; *I really didn't want the damned thing anyway.*

Deanna's face turned the color of a red giant star as she slowly realized her serious mistake. She was terribly overbid for such a minor improvement on warp field technology! The only thing that could possibly make it worse was . . .

Thud. Thud. "Eighty-three hundred is bid by Chairman Munk," intoned the conductor. In the Ferengi corner, loud guffaws spoiled the solemnity of the occasion.

Deanna turned white, and she clenched her jaw so tight that Picard winced in sympathetic pain. Now it was the counselor's turn to play number two with a hyperinflated bid.

The Hatheby's conductor counted Munk's bid out three times. Twice, Deanna opened her mouth to outbid the Ferengi; but she was obviously way over the line already with her bid of seventy-eight hectobars. Bidding higher would not ensure she got the warp damper; instead, Munk might merely top her again with latinum from his omnipresent sachel.

At last, she accepted defeat bitterly. Munk cackled, enjoying the consternation of the crowd. Deanna's debt was laid against Betazed.

For some peculiar reason, however, Jean-Luc Picard felt no joy or elation at having so tricked the Betazoid representative; no matter how minutely he examined the situation, it still added up to having defeated a friend.

In any event, the real problem was Lieutenant Worf, who despite representing the eight-hundred-pound gorilla in the auction, the Federation, had failed to capture even a single lot. In fact, the Klingon had offered virtually no bids at all.

Despite his own temporary loyalty to the Klingon Empire, Captain Picard fretted that the Federation did not have adequate representation in the auction.

The captain sighed; it made little difference. The Ferengi Munk and his cronies—including, for reasons he had yet to fathom, young Wesley Crusher—had won every bid anyway. He simply plopped down more and more "latinum" until each person had met and exceded his price ceiling. The only excitement came from the race *not* to be second place.

While the conductor droned on about the next lot to be

auctioned—a transporter subspace relay that allegedly boosted and repeated a transporter beam up to a thousand parsecs, abstract only, no working model—Picard leaned back out of the mainstream of conversation and tapped his comm badge.

"Picard to Riker," he said, speaking quietly enough that no one would likely notice or hear.

The voice response could only be heard by Picard, so the entire conversation was private. "Riker here."

"The situation is grim, Number One. Munk has won every single bid so far. He simply drops hectobar after hectobar onto the table until everyone else drops out. Has Commander Data readied his method of removing the latinum disguise?"

"I wish I could say he has."

"Then have we any other evidence we can present to Hatheby's? I'm sure if we could present a plausible case that Munk is bidding counterfeit latinum, he would be removed from the auction until his specie could be verified."

Picard could almost hear his Number One shrugging. "We could try to show that he's replicated a holdful of chaseum."

"Circumstantial evidence; it's suggestive but not conclusive. But if we coupled that with evidence indicating that Munk hasn't such resources on deposit anywhere, then at least we could force him to concoct an explanation of where he is supposed to have gotten it."

"I'll get right on it, sir . . . though I don't have any idea how we could tap into Ferengi bank records. They're not exactly forthcoming in that area."

"Hm. Keep me posted, Will. We have to do something fast . . . the photonic pulse cannon comes up for auction in a couple of hours, and I feel certain that as soon as Munk wins that bid, he'll disappear. Picard out."

The comm link severed. Jean-Luc Picard leaned forward, wearily resuming the frustrating game of "Who's on first, What's on second."

Geordi La Forge rested his fingers on the computer

console, trying to remember how to hack a VingeSys-666. "Haven't seen one of these things in ten years," he grumbled. "Worf, watch my back, will you?"

The Klingon muttered under his breath in Klingon; he did not seem to enjoy "black-bag" work. He did turn around and scan the lobby, his giant frame effectively hiding La Forge's unauthorized presence in the concierge's kiosk.

"Uh-oh," said Geordi, "there's a guard dog."

"Where? I will neutralize it."

"No, Worf, I mean a program designed to alert the management if someone's trying a forcible entry to the instruction segment."

"Are you able to bypass it?"

"Let me try a little trick I picked up from . . . never mind; you wouldn't know her."

Geordi wrote a small program in native code that wandered over to a main memory register, stored a particular, carefully chosen number, then left-shifted it two hundred and fifty-seven characters.

This pushed the original number far enough that it overflowed the register. In the 680-series VingeSys, such left-shifted overflows simply truncated, disappearing into nothingness. But in the older, 660-series, nobody had thought of leftward overflows. The numbers simply migrated to the left into a "system instruction" register normally inaccessible to data input.

Once there, the number was read as if it were a system program placed there by an administrator. The particular number Geordi had selected decoded into the instructions to give him access as a level-three administrator.

He instantly logged in and was then able to access all confidential records of the casino, including the replicator usage of the guests.

"Commander," rumbled Worf, "two Ferengi are approaching the kiosk."

"Uh-oh. Munk and Tunk?"

Worf squinted; they were a hundred yards away, and

Ferengi all looked the same to him, anyway. "I do not believe so. No, definitely not. But they are headed directly toward us."

"Give me just one minute . . ." Licking his lips, Geordi typed as fast as he could, having to backspace and correct every few keystrokes. First, he searched the replicator records and found one room that had made massive use of the replicator in the past twenty-four hours—a hundred times more usage than the next closest.

Alas, the data base did not bother to record exactly *what* was replicated; for that, he would need to service the machine itself. The data base did, however, list the room number.

Geordi quickly backed out, then entered the casino registry. He looked up the room and discovered that it had been rented to one "Brubrak & Party, 3 persons, 2 beds." The casino had also levied steep charges for heavy use of both holosuites on the same floor.

"Your minute is rapidly expiring," said Worf. "I suggest we leave immediately to avoid having to answer humiliating questions."

"Damn! They must have used an assumed name. Have you ever heard of a Ferengi named Brubrak?"

"No. Sir, we must leave *now.*"

"Wait, maybe I can access the holosuite records and see what programs they used. Wait . . ." Geordi La Forge looked back over his shoulder and realized that Worf had not been an alarmist. The two Ferengi were almost across the lobby . . . and they still headed directly toward the concierge kiosk.

They were arguing vehemently.

"Worf! Duck down here." Geordi dropped to his hands and knees, hiding behind the counter.

"I am not going to hide from a pair of Ferengi!"

"Worf, get down! We might hear what they're arguing about!"

"A Klingon warrior does not—*arf!*" Worf's last comment

was gargled as Geordi reached up and pulled him down onto his posterior. The Klingon warrior gritted his teeth and snarled; but Geordi hissed, holding a finger to his lips.

Fuming, Worf sat silently as the Ferengi approached. They paused on the other side of the counter.

"Where is that pig getting it?" demanded a Ferengi voice, high-pitched and reedy.

"Well, you've got about . . . eighteen minutes to find out, or he's going to slice your lobes." The second voice was deep for a Ferengi, dripping with menace and a sarcastic sneer that among Ferengi passed for command tone. He was obviously the senior.

"It's not my fault!"

"You were responsible for freezing them."

"But I did!" whined Reedy.

"Oh, really? And I suppose fifty kilobars of latinum just dropped from the sky into Munk's satchel. Just think it through logically, if you can," coaxed Sneery. "What are his resources?"

"Well, he had a couple of thousand."

"Where?"

"Fort Nagus."

Sneery laughed scornfully. "I'm pretty sure he didn't withdraw *that* in the last six months! Second guess."

"He must've sold his ship, what is it, the *Ferengi Indulging in All Possible Vices Simultaneously With Tremendous Satisfaction!* He arrived in that Federation ship, the *Business Venture.*"

"Hm. I hadn't thought of that. Well, I can check it with the Nagus's sources. Can't imagine he could get fifty keys for that heap of junk."

"Unless he sold it to a human. Maybe that Captain Picard." Reedy's voice dropped to a whisper; Geordi could barely hear it. "They say he's a . . . a *philanthropist.*"

"Shh! Even other races have ears. We don't want to start a war with the Federation!"

"Can I get back to the auction, Daimon? Please?" wheedled Reedy.

"Get your lobes out of earshot. Tell the Grand Nagus I'm checking maritime records for a ship sale . . . but if it doesn't turn a profit, you'd better be back out here in record time, licking my boots! And you'd better start thinking of somewhere else Munk could be pulling that kind of latinum, just in case."

Footsteps pounded away in a panic. After a moment, Sneery cursed and stalked away, muttering about a comm link.

Geordi looked across at Worf; the Klingon was glaring at him with bloodred eyes. "Are we through hiding like Ferengi digfish, Commander La Forge?" His voice was nearly as sarcastic as Sneery's.

"Just simmer down, *Lieutenant.* Sometimes . . . misdirection is the better part of valor."

Worf stood, straightening his uniform and rotating his metallic sash back to the normal position. "We have a slightly different version of that expression on the homeworld."

"I'm not surprised."

"Better twelve days of valor than twelve years of bowing."

Geordi tapped his comm badge and informed Commander Riker of the conversation they accidentally overheard.

"Geordi," said the first officer, "if we could get the Grand Nagus to give us a statement saying that he knows for a fact that Munk doesn't have access to that much latinum, then that plus the information you dug up about the heavy replicator use and 'Fred's' latinum watch and comm badge might just be enough for Hatheby's to haul that Ferengi in for questioning."

"Should we drop a hint to the Nagus?"

"I think you'd better. I'll inform the captain. Riker out."

Geordi smiled and spread his hands, as if to say *I told you so;* but Worf merely sighed and rolled his eyes. "On the homeworld, we could have resolved this entire problem hours ago."

"But think of all the fun we'd miss!"

Chapter Seventeen

WESLEY CRUSHER SAT next to Tunk, behind Munk, sweating and tugging at his collar. The room seemed infernally hot, as if the enviros were out of adjustment.

Or maybe I'm just feeling a preview of the penal mines on Abednego, he thought.

Munk's fairy gold had been so far sufficient to win him every bid; at the moment, the sly Ferengi owned title to every astonishing invention of Dr. Zorka, an arsenal of engineering and weaponry marvels that would probably buy him the entire Ferengi sphere of influence.

Wesley began to regret his bitter decision to strictly abide by all Ferengi laws, a decision which still kept his mouth taped firmly shut. He did not know whether or not Data had figured out that Munk's latinum was phony or what the android could do about it in any case.

The cadet made himself a promise: If the auction passed peacefully with no one discovering Munk's deception, then Wesley would turn himself in and confess . . . no matter what the consequences—and they would be severe. Ferengi courts did not distinguish between breaching a contract out of greed and breaching a contract because it was illegal; both led to swift and severe punishment, not limited to demerits or loss of leave-time, as at the Academy.

Still, Cadet Crusher could not sit idly by and watch Munk stroll off with a laboratory full of exotic propulsion systems, personal shields, and a photonic pulse cannon.

The next lot was announced, and Wesley jumped: It was, in fact, the photonic pulse cannon.

The one saving grace was that Munk had only thirteen hundred hectobars, one hundred and thirty thousand, left in the satchel, and that might not be enough. At least, Wesley could only hope it would not be enough.

Or was that all he could do? The cadet hawk-watched the Ferengi, waiting for an opportunity to sabotage his patron's bidding without actually breaching any terms of the labyrinthian contract he had signed (as Fred Kimbal).

Would they let me off just because I used a pseudonym? He shook his head: not in a Ferengi court, that was for certain! *Yeah, there's probably a clause in there that says if I use an alias, I'm legally applying to change my name to the new one.*

Worf looked brighter than he had during the entire previous part of the auction. He began the bidding confidently by announcing "ten hectobars."

Several of the other participants chuckled; the Grand Nagus snorted loudly. "Twenty kilobars!" he cried in a thin, avaricious voice.

"Twenty-*two*," declared Gul Fubar with finality, as if expecting the bidding to cease at once as a sign of respect.

"Twenty-three," said Captain Picard, his quiet voice cutting through the tumult.

The Cardassian glared at Picard. "Twenty-four."

The captain nodded at the conductor, who translated: "Twenty-five thousand from Captain Picard, representing the Klingon Empire."

"Six!"

Picard nodded again, but before Dmitri Smythe could translate, Gul Fubar overbid to twenty-eight.

Worf slapped the table so hard it rang. "Ten!"

Everybody stared. Smythe cleared his throat. "The bidding stood at twenty-eight thousand; does the Klingon gentleman from the Federation mean to bid thirty thousand, or raise the bid by ten kilobars to thirty-eight thousand?"

His face reddening, Worf clarified: "I will bid thirty-eight."

Deanna Troi, who was following the drama intently, let her breath out in a sigh of relief. *It just passed Betazed's threshold,* thought Wesley. Smiling weakly, Deanna sat back and folded her arms.

"Forty!" commanded Gul Fubar.

The Grand Nagus leaned forward, both hands on the table. He stared directly at Munk. "Fifty," he said, curling his lip.

Wesley swallowed hard. In a matter of moments, the bid had risen to fifty thousand bars of gold-pressed latinum.

An instant later, the Cardassian Gul Fubar gasped as he suddenly realized he was committed to paying *forty thousand* bars for nothing if the Nagus won his bid . . . but he could not quite bring himself to utter a bid in excess of fifty thousand.

Captain Picard, however, seemed to have a spine made of chaseum. He nodded, raising a single finger to the conductor, who translated it as "fifty-one thousand."

Lieutenant Worf and the captain proceeded to one-up each other until the price stood at an even eighty thousand with Worf holding. Gul Fubar sat without bidding, cracking his knuckles loudly. Picard and Worf, who sat right next to each other, had leaned forward almost imperceptibly with every bid, and they were now almost eyeball to eyeball.

The pair fell silent. The conductor intoned, "The bid is eighty thousand bars, one time, two times . . ."

Everyone turned expectantly to Munk. With an exasperated expression, as if much put-upon, he reached into his bag and hauled out an armload of latinum hectobars. He repeated the process over and over. When he finished, he had twenty piles of fifty hectobars each arrayed in front of him.

The crowd gasped; no one, apparently, had ever before seen one hundred thousand bars of latinum in one place.

Drymouthed, Wesley snuck a surreptitious peek at Tunk to see whether it was safe to flash a signal to Captain Picard.

The Ferengi was gone.

Startled, the cadet stared at Picard until he caught the captain's eye. Wesley gave him a tiny, microscopic headshake: *He's got more.* Captain Picard turned away, nodding slowly.

"And ten," announced the captain. Even without Counselor Troi's Betazed powers, Wesley could tell that Picard had stepped far out on a limb with the bid.

Munk pretended to start backward, cringing as if he had just been trumped.

The conductor counted it out. Just before he said "three times," Munk coughed in obvious glee.

As everyone watched, the Ferengi dug into his satchel and stacked the remaining hundred hectobars and twenty kilobars on the table.

Gul Fubar stared, glassy-eyed. Worf looked intense. Picard turned his head aside . . . but his eyes shifted directly to Wesley.

The cadet nodded faintly, just enough to convey the message: *That's it! Munk is broke.*

Picard's head glistened with sweat. He rubbed his chin, staring at the pile of one hundred and thirty kilobars of gold-pressed latinum.

Gul Fubar half rose to his feet. Reluctantly, as if regretting every syllable, he said, "One . . . one hundred and fifty!" He sat down hard.

Wesley stared around the table. Deanna Troi still stared at the pile of latinum, unable to tear her gaze away; Geordi stared at the Cardassian; Lieutenant Worf gripped the tabletop with both hands, squeezing so tightly Wesley wondered why the presumed wood of the table did not splinter.

221

Picard stared expectantly at Munk, then glared angrily at the Cardassian; he obviously did not want to see the cannon go to Gul Fubar. For his part, the Cardassian gritted his teeth, shaking like a dust mote in turbulence; the Grand Nagus seemed inordinantly jubilant, apparently relishing the thought of Munk being forced to pay out a planetary ransom for absolutely nothing.

Only Munk seemed calm and serene. Wesley watched him narrowly, knowing there was not another bar in the satchel; the cadet had packed it himself.

"Going one time," intoned Smythe gravely, "going two times . . ."

Gul Fubar leapt up, pounding his fists on the table, his face a caricature of glee.

Then, out of nowhere, Tunk loomed. The Ferengi pranced up to the table with yet another piece of luggage, upending it. Another fifty kilobars of ersatz latinum spilled out, making one hundred and eighty thousand in all.

"What!" cried Wesley, involuntarily.

With a sick expression, Gul Fubar sank slowly back into his seat, looking as if he had just tried Klingon food for the first time.

"One time." Long pause. "Two times." Dmitri Smythe glanced around the table, then raised his brows. "Three times. The lot is sold to Chairman Munk for one hundred eighty thousand; Gul Fubar of Cardassia is forfeit one hundred fifty thousand bars.

"Thank you very much; I declare this auction ended." Smythe produced a gavel and hammered on the table like the drumbeat of doom.

At once, Gul Fubar loosed a howl of despair as the situation finally parsed through his brain: The Cardassian Empire now owed Hatheby's one hundred and fifty thousand bars of gpl—for a handful of vacuum; and it was all Gul Fubar's fault!

With a sharky grin, the Grand Nagus rose from his own seat. "Moment please," he said, his quiet voice commanding instant attention. He turned his gaze directly upon

Wesley Crusher . . . at least, so it seemed to the cadet. The Nagus might have been looking at Munk.

"Yes, Grand Nagus?" queried the conductor.

"Regarding the last bid by *Chairman* Munk." The Grand Nagus emphasized the word *chairman,* turning it into a snide insult, emphasizing that the only thing Munk was chairman of was his own son and bodyguards.

"Yes, sir, one hundred eighty thousand bars of latinum."

"I formally charge"—the Nagus paused dramatically—"that Munk's last bid is a *fraud!"* His voice rose to a falsetto squeal, and he jabbed his walking stick at his fellow Ferengi as if it were a dueling sword. "He has no more ability to make good that debt than does his human servant!"

With these words, the Nagus did turn on Wesley, jabbing at him with the stick and making the cadet flinch.

Smythe stared in confusion. "But . . . Grand Nagus, sir, he has placed his bid in hectobars of gold-pressed latinum upon the table, in plain view of us all."

"Charity!" swore the aged Ferengi leader. "In my official capacity, I maintain records of every single Ferengi bank account. Chairman Munk has never had that much latinum on deposit in his life!"

"Perhaps in a non-Ferengi financial institution . . ."

"Philanthropic charity! I sent subspace messages to every financial-reporting center in the Alpha and Beta quadrants. Munk hasn't a gram more than ten kilobars anywhere in the galaxy!" The Grand Nagus nimbly hopped upon his chair, thence to the table. He strode its length, rushing Munk while the latter flapped his arms and squawked. "If that Ferengi now has one hundred eighty thousand, then he's trafficking in stolen latinum . . . and if you accept it, you're knowingly receiving stolen merchandise. If you take even one gram of that latinum, Smythe, then I swear by all the Profits I'll shut down your entire operation, quadrant-wide!"

"Moment please," said another soft voice. Wesley whipped his head around so quickly he pulled a muscle in his neck. The new speaker was Commander La Forge, standing at his own place.

"S-sir?" gaped the stunned conductor.

"We examined the replicator data base records of the *Enterprise*, and while we were transporting Munk and Tunk, they made extensive use of our ship's replicators . . . replicating these." Geordi reached down under the table, grabbed a metallic object, and threw it with a resounding thud onto the table. "Blocks of easily replicated chaseum designed to closely resemble hectobars of gold-pressed latinum."

Wesley felt an abyss open in his stomach; he recognized one of the chaseum hectobars he came to know and loathe over the last forty-eight hours.

The mob around the table began to get ugly as they saw the silvery bar of chaseum that, aside from its color, was an exact duplicate of the mountain of "latinum" in front of the Ferengi.

At last, Munk found his wits. "Avast, ye scurvy knaves!" he hollered, "but what witchery be this? I've cast me pearls before ye, and what giveth ye back? Libel and contumely!"

Tunk stood on his own chair; he started to step onto the table, but the Grand Nagus gave him such a ferocious scowl that he leapt back to his chair. "Yeah," said Tunk, echoing his father, "what lies are these? Sore losers, that's what you all are! Look—do these things look like that bar of chaseum? Are they the same color? Scan them! Use the best portable scanners you have . . . the scanners will all report that *these hectobars are latinum!*"

Captain Picard rose to his feet, awesome as a judge. "I offer the services of the *Enterprise* science lab; we have much better scanners than any portable machines you may have with you."

"Never and nay!" cried Munk. "An' we ship yon bullion back to yer ship, what should we gamble? Certes, your scanners will say 'tis not genuine—yer entire crew fronts for some foreign power or other that savors the goods we've bought by the sweat of our forebrows!"

His son clarified, for those who did not speak pirate. "Of course the *Enterprise* scanners will back up the captain . . . he's obviously rigged them to report false information."

"Perhaps I can help illuminate the situation," said the uninflected, unemotional voice of Commander Data from the doorway.

"Foul!" shrieked Tunk. "That's a foul! Hatheby's formally ruled that this electronic android shall not be allowed to participate in any way in the auction . . . *get him out of here!*"

Data raised his eyebrows. "As I understand the rules, once the conductor has declared the auction ended, it is ended. Thus, there is no longer any reason I cannot transport into a public room in this public casino."

"He's got a point," said Dmitri Smythe, nodding vigorously, pleased to be able to make at least one ruling.

"You were saying, Data?" prodded Captain Picard.

"Allow me to activate this device. I assure you that it is not physically harmful to any beings present here."

The Cardassian, Gul Fubar, jumped to his feet again and fumbled at the holster where he usually kept his sidearm; he grabbed a handful of air, since Hatheby's had disarmed each participant before the auction began.

Before anyone else could react, Data pressed a touchplate; Wesley's hair stood straight up off his head and he felt "phantom ants" crawling up and down his skin.

The enormous pile of fairy gold in front of Wesley shimmered blue, along with the single bar of untransmuted chaseum. Data released the touchplate, and the blue glow stopped.

The hundred and fifty participants leaned forward and sucked in a breath as one organism: Every single bar of "latinum" had reverted to its original appearance. Eighteen hundred bars of worthless chaseum hulked in front of two pink Ferengi and one green Academy cadet.

The entire room sat in paralyzed silence—except for the conductor. Dmitri Smythe raised his hand and gestured a genteel "come-hither." From the shadows where they had lurked, a pair of massive, reptilian Skamis approached. One grabbed the back of Munk's neck, the other captured the upper arms of both Tunk and Wesley.

An enormous ham-fist clamped around Cadet Crusher's biceps, squeezing like a vise. Clenching his teeth to stifle a yelp, Wesley bounced to his feet and hustled along next to the creature; his alternative was to allow his arm to be pulled from its socket.

The sauroid Simaks stood a mere eight feet tall, but they must have massed a metric tonne each. They wore brightly colored feather outfits and carried meat cleaver cutlasses that could carve a young cadet in twain with a single blow; Wesley decided not to test the hypothesis.

He stared frantically at Captain Picard, willing him to look up and notice what was happening; the captain was still contemplating the treasure hoard of fairy gold that had turned, in the wink of an eye, into scrap chaseum.

"Hatheby's has sustained the Grand Nagus's motion to reopen the bidding," said the conductor. "We declare Chairman Munk's last bid of one hundred eighty thousand bars of gold-pressed latinum to be null and void. Bidding will resume where we left off . . ." Smythe glanced down at his data reader. "The bid is held by Gul Fubar for the Cardassians at one hundred fifty thousand."

Wesley still stared at Picard, but the captain was busy huddling with Lieutenant Worf. Worf shook his head vehemently; then Geordi joined in the discussion. It looked quite animated, but Wesley could not hear a word.

"Come on," he muttered, "glance up, *notice* this monster holding my arm, put in a word with Smythe . . ." But the captain's telepathic powers were at a low ebb, and he did not glance at Wesley.

"One time . . ." Dmitri Smythe glanced around the room; the bidders seemed more interested in the metal mountain of chaseum on the table or their three erstwhile competitors in custody than in the final lot of the auction. Wesley was not surprised, since only Munk had been able to outbid the Cardassian—and that was with fairy gold.

The cadet's heart pounded, and his arm began to ache from the Simak's grip. As soon as the auction was over, he had a terrible feeling he knew where he was headed.

"Two times . . ."

Gul Fubar stood so suddenly he bowled his chair over; it fell with a clatter, and everybody jumped. The Cardassian's eyes opened so wide, Wesley thought they would fall out of their sockets.

"Three—"

"One hundred eighty!" announced Captain Picard, also rising. He smiled at Gul Fubar.

The Cardassian did not seem to understand what was happening. He nodded vigorously, slapping the table with a resounding thunk.

The conductor frowned, stabbing at his data reader. "Has the Klingon Empire that much latinum on deposit, Captain Picard?"

"No," admitted the captain, "but the Klingon Empire *combined with the Federation* has over two hundred thousand bars on deposit."

Worf stood up next to Picard. "It is a joint bid between our two clients," he confirmed.

Gul Fubar was still pumping his head up and down, as if he could not stop. But he wore the expression of a man who has just swallowed his own foot up to the kneecap.

He began to laugh, a chuckle at first, rising to a hysterical cackle. Gul Fubar dropped heavily back into his chair, leaning his head back and howling like a lunatic.

The conductor's "once, twice, sold" was anticlimax; the other competitors were already packing up their notes, communicators, data clips, drinks, snacks, and catalogs and heading for the door. Smythe announced that the other lots would be reauctioned at a later date, beginning at the last bid before Munk won each round.

When the room was almost empty, Captain Picard finally

looked over at Wesley. "Mister Conductor," said the captain, catching Smythe's attention, "I appreciate your diligence, but it really isn't necessary to treat the boy so roughly. I'm sure he's learned from his mistakes."

"Undoubtedly, Captain Picard." Smythe nodded vigorously, emphasizing his agreement. Then he turned to the Simaks. "Proceed, ladies."

"Put me down!" shrieked Tunk in abject terror. "Picard, you blackguard, *I'll ruin you if it's the last thing I ever do!"*

Wesley turned his head toward the Ferengi. "Where's your sense of humor, Tunk? It's just a harmless 'phrank'!"

The Ferengi fell silent, glaring phaser blasts at Cadet Crusher.

The Simaks strode toward the door, swinging left, then right like dinosaurs.

"Mister Smythe!" called the captain. Wesley craned his neck to look back over his shoulder, reminding himself of the pulled muscle. The jailers did not stop, but they were slow enough that it was taking them quite some time to reach the door.

"Yes, Captain Picard?"

"You may release Mister . . . ah . . . Cadet Kimbal into my custody; I shall assume full responsibility to ensure he shows up for . . . well, whatever hearing you plan to hold. There's really no need to lock him in a jail cell."

"A most excellent suggestion, sir. I shall take it under advisement." The Simaks continued on their ponderous way.

Wesley eyeballed the captain, waiting for him to do something, until the jailers passed through the door; one slammed it behind them with her tail.

I'm actually being arrested! thought the cadet frantically. Somehow, no matter how many times he had told himself this was the likely outcome of his Ferengi adventure, Wesley had never quite accepted the fact that he could end up inside a jail cell.

Jail cell . . . even the words sounded sinister; he envisioned a horrific dungeon with barred rooms and devices to put him to the question.

The reality was not far removed from his fantasy. The Simaks carried the two struggling Ferengi and Wesley along the corridor, down the stairs, and right through the lobby in full view of everybody. A procession padded along behind them, led by the Grand Nagus.

Tunk, like Wesley, seemed too numbed to speak. But Munk sputtered and flapped his arms like a captured goose. He was trying to speak so quickly, the words fell against one another like a verbal waterfall, cascading impotently into the marble floor. The Simak jailers paid him no attention.

The Grand Nagus caught up to them, cackling and hooting at their discomfort. "I've waited for this day for so many years, I've lost count!" he exulted. "I hear they still use thumbscrews and pressing on Novus Alamogordus . . ."

The Simak with Munk opened a door in the far wall, since she had a hand free. It led to a landing and a spiral stair, which wound down and down, wrapping so many times that Wesley became completely disoriented not only as to how deep they were, but which way he was pointed. They passed at least four landings, but it might have been as many as six.

Led along a narrow corridor with bare, metal walls—made of chaseum, Cadet Crusher wryly noted—they came at last to a series of cubicles, each of which had a solid back wall, ceiling, and floor; the other three sides were indeed bars.

Each prisoner was placed into a separate cell; there were no other prisoners.

Wesley stood in the middle of his cubicle, staring forlornly at the departing backs and tails of the Simaks. Then, filled with melancholy and despair, he sat on the fold-down bunk, hands on his knees. He decided to allow himself at least a couple of hours to wallow in self-pity before doing something constructive. *I've earned that much, at least,* he told himself.

Instead, he found he had the giggles, almost like Gul Fubar when he took second place for the second time in the auction. He sat on the bunk guffawing, watching Munk and Tunk pound the bars and demand to see their advocates; it was unquestionably the funniest thing he had ever seen in his life, though he could not have said why.

Chapter Eighteen

"HEY, HU-MAN!"

Wesley Crusher did not respond.

"Hey, you! Huuu-man . . . you'll *fry* for it in a Ferengi contracts tribunal! Don't even think about turning ears on us."

"Aye, laddie, unless ye'er wanting to be scuppered and skewered and hauled below yon keel."

Ferengi have an uncanny sixth sense, thought the cadet, *that warns them when they're about to be sent down the mine shaft.*

In fact, turning "ears" on Munk and Tunk was precisely the path Wesley was trying to argue himself into.

He had always imagined that sitting in the jail cell would drive him mad, that he could not live in a cage. But in reality, it was the first time in many days that Wesley Crusher had had a chance to just sit down and think about right and wrong, actions and consequences.

According to Federation law, he was certainly not bound to any contract with Cap'n Munk. Signing under the alias

"Fred Kimbal" clearly indicated he never had any intent to enter into a contract; there was no "meeting of the minds," the most basic component of an enforceable contract . . . in Federation space.

Ferengi law drew no such fine distinctions, unfortunately; according to their laws, his current name on a contract in his own hand was unassailable proof that the contract was valid—and if he chose to sign with an alias, well, who were they to pry into his reasons?

It was irrelevant whether Wesley really wanted to sign the contract, or whether he had been bullied or threatened into it; a deal was a deal! If one party happened to have the upper hand in negotiations, for example, by threatening to put the other party out the airlock if no agreement was reached, then that was simply the Ferengi Way.

By a carefully worked-out treaty, the Federation of Planets agreed to accept all Ferengi judgments about cases within their jurisdiction, which the Ferengi defined as any deal involving a Ferengi as one party.

However, even according to Federation law, the Ferengi held jurisdiction, since the deal was signed aboard a Ferengi-flagged vessel. No matter how Cadet Crusher examined the puzzle, there was no logical solution: He was caught in a Ferengi legal web.

Hatheby's was the aggrieved party, and they operated under Federation law; thus, Munk and Tunk had to be allowed access to Ferengi advocates . . . which meant there was no way to prevent word of Wesley's breach from reaching the Ferengi High Council, which would then demand extradition. Much as complying would cause Captain Picard personal pain, Wesley was under no delusion that the captain would defy the treaty and refuse to transport the cadet. Wesley Crusher was *en route* to the Ferengi system no matter which angle he examined . . . unless Munk and Tunk could be persuaded not to talk.

The cadet sat quietly on his bunk, watching the jailhouse door and waiting for his interrogators, whom he called "inquisitors" to himself. They would certainly arrive soon, though Wesley would be perfectly content to have them show up a week later. The delay would give him more time to think through the problem.

Precisely on cue, he heard footsteps along the corridor; they echoed off the chaseum walls, sounding deep and hollow like drumbeats in a French cathedral.

"Remember, Kimbal—remember!" warned Tunk, sliding his finger across his own throat.

The door slid open noiselessly; a pair of inquisitors entered, followed by a Simak, then Commander Data.

"I hope you do not mind," said the android, "I took the liberty of informing the Hatheby's investigators that I would act as your legal counsel."

Wesley nodded wordlessly. The Simak opened the cell door and gestured at Wesley to exit and precede her.

"If there are any questions you feel might incriminate you, Wesley, please alert me and I will object to them."

"Hm." Wesley was deliberately noncommittal.

They returned along the same corridor the prisoners had been brought along six hours earlier; but this time, they entered a small white room with a single desk and four chairs. Wesley and Data sat at one end, while the two inquisitors, private police officers hired by Hatheby's, took the opposite. The Simak remained *en garde* by the door, watching for any monkey business.

Wesley Crusher faced the two humorless inquisitors; his stomach crumbled into a ball, his pulse pounded, and he still did not know what he was going to say, if anything.

But before the first question, a curious peace and calm suddenly descended upon him.

It's right and wrong . . . forget all the rest! Forget the contract, forget the threats. Wesley looked at Data, preparing to defend the cadet as best as Data's positronic brain could do.

There is really only one question: When do the lies stop?

At once, Wesley knew exactly what to say. "I would like to turn plaintiff's evidence," he said.

"Yeah?" asked one of the inquisitors, a short man with a

belligerent scowl and an accent reminiscent of Captain Picard's, but harsher. "What's yer deal?"

Wesley laughed and shook his head. "No, you don't understand. No deals. I just want to tell you exactly what happened."

"Are you sure this is wise?" asked Data. "I would certainly not suggest you lie about your involvement, but perhaps you need some time to think out exactly what defense you—"

"Sorry, sir. I know you're trying to help me. But it's time that somebody, at least, just sat up and said what really happened."

Data pondered for a moment, then finally nodded. "You are determined to 'come clean,' as the police used to say, even if it means implicating yourself?"

"Even if, Commander."

"Very well, I cannot stop you."

Wesley Crusher licked dry lips, swallowed, and proceeded to tell the entire story, from the start at the poker game to the moment he was dragged away to the cells.

The inquisitors quietly wrote down every word, every so often interjecting a question to clarify a particular point.

"Well, that's it. That's the whole thing," concluded Wesley.

The inquisitors glared a bit suspiciously, then withdrew across the room, conferring among themselves.

"What's going to happen to me?" the cadet asked Data.

"I cannot say for certain, Wesley. You are fortunate that most of your counterfeiting activity was carried out here at Novus Alamogordus, since that is outside the jurisdiction of the Federation. The only crime you committed within jurisdiction was the small amount aboard the *Enterprise.*"

"Isn't counterfeiting Federation-standard bars of gold-pressed latinum within the Federation jurisdiction period, no matter where you do it?"

Data stared into space for a moment, accessing his memory banks. "Curiously enough, no; it is not."

"It *isn't?* Why not?"

Data raised his eyebrows and frowned, indicating a shrug, a very humanlike facial gesture. "For the simple reason that it is impossible to do so, Wesley. At least, until now it was impossible.

"Federation specie is tied to the gold-pressed latinum standard; one gram of pure latinum pressed into nineteen hundred ninety-nine grams of gold is one bar of gold-pressed latinum, regardless of what image is stamped on the obverse. Likewise, a hundred grams of latinum pressed with nineteen hundred grams of gold filler is a hectobar, and a kilogram of latinum pressed with a kilogram of gold is one kilobar.

"The external structure is irrelevant to the value; a gram of latinum embedded in a silver coin is also worth exactly one bar of gpl, as is a gram of pure latinum. Only the latinum has value.

"The only Federation crime is *passing* counterfeit latinum within Federation jurisdiction or to Federation citizens, which includes Hatheby's Brokerage."

"And I aided and abetted Tunk and Munk when they did that."

"I am certain that a Federation tribunal would take into account your motivation; but it is not a defense. By all the laws of the Federation and the regulations of Starfleet, covering up for the transgressions of a fellow citizen or cadet does not justify participation in a criminal enterprise."

"Great. So as soon as I finish my extended vacation at a Federation fleet prison, I can look forward to being extradited to a Ferengi court to be tried for breach of contract."

"I am afraid that is the most plausible outcome, unless we can persuade Hatheby's to drop the charges and the Ferengi not to report the breach."

The pair of inquisitors returned, their faces stone masks behind which Wesley could glimpse only contempt and scorn. They gestured to Data, who joined them for a quick conversation Wesley couldn't hear.

Data turned to Wesley. "I have made a deal," he said. "Produce the clock, and they will drop the charges."

Great, thought the cadet; *now what? How am I going to figure out what Tunk did with that damned thing when the Hatheby's inquisitors came up with a big, fat zero?*

He tried to swallow again, but he had no saliva. His only hope was that he knew Tunk well enough from personal contact to guess where the wily Ferengi might have stashed the Kimbal Clock.

On their way back to the above-ground section of the casino, Wesley, Data, and the inquisitors stopped off at the cells again to ask Tunk what he had done with the clock. It was a vain hope; naturally, the Ferengi expressed puzzlement, as if he had never heard of such a thing.

"If you will release Cadet Crusher into my custody," suggested Data, "I will accept full responsibility for him."

The inquisitors looked at the commander as if he were crazy. The inquisitors, Wesley, and Data trooped upstairs, then up the turbolift to the Tunk and Munk suite.

An hour's search finally convinced Wesley that there was no Kimbal Clock to be found. Curiously enough, all of Munk's and Tunk's possessions were also gone . . . only Wesley's remained in the otherwise empty rooms.

The bath towels were also missing.

"All right, Data, assume I'm telling the truth."

"I never questioned that," said the android.

"So what could he have done with it? There's no way he would destroy it—he wouldn't kill the goose that lays the latinum eggs."

"Did Cadet Kimbal also manufacture an *anatidae* that lays latinum eggs?"

"No, Data, it's just an expression that means—"

"Ah, yes, I have just referenced the fairy tale in question. A most apt analogy."

"Thanks. He wouldn't destroy it, but he obviously was expecting to leave directly after the auction and he didn't want to have to run back up here. But he wouldn't leave it anywhere where it might be found, either. So?"

"Since the Ferengi had no ship, perhaps they intended to buy or rent one?"

Cooper grunted, then touched his wrist-chronometer, opening a comm link. "Coop of Hatheby's to the Palace concierge."

"May I help you, sir?" oozed an obsequious voice from the air.

"Check Fanny's, Lazy-Eight's, and Bourbaki for any Ferengi renting spaceworthy vessels in the last couple of days. Did Tunk or Munk file a flight plan?"

"No, sir. The Grand Nagus's pilot filed a flight plan this morning, but no other Ferengi."

"Nobody else?"

"No, sir."

"Get back to me with that rental information."

"Yes, sir."

"Cooper out."

"You know," mused Wesley, "I'll bet he stashed it out in the lobby. It's the only room directly en route from the banquet hall to the exit."

Cooper scowled. "You saying we gotta go back to the lobby?"

The cadet folded his arms and glared at the Hatheby's rent-a-guard. "We can't let that stupid thing just lie around here; somebody's sure to find it and figure out what it does."

"Maybe they won't."

"And if they do, this can happen again and again, only on a larger scale. Imagine if the Cardassians or Romulans got it!"

"Hrm."

"Yeah, go ahead and say 'hrm.' You know we have to find that damned clock."

"All right, all right, I was just saying."

The casino lobby was mobbed. All the bidders swarmed around the front desk, trying to pay their bills simultaneously. Most of the quality were staying an extra day, just to avoid the stampede; but the smaller delegations, co-ops, representatives, and consortia preferred to blitzkrieg the bellhops and crowd the cashier rather than pay for another exorbitant night at the Chateau Hôtel Casino.

Hatheby's Agent Cooper clamped Wesley's biceps as tightly as had the Simak; the inquisitor narrowed his eyes and pulled his snap-brim hat tighter onto his size-nine head.

"Skooze me, Mac," said a slurry voice behind them, "but canoe direc' me to the turb . . . turpo . . . the lif'?"

Wesley, Cooper, and Data turned to take in the suspicious character. The cadet stared in amazement; "D'Artagnan! I mean, uh, Simon . . . what are *you* doing here?"

D'Artagnan's eyes narrowed; then he recognized Cadet "Fred Kimbal" at last. "Fred, my buddy my pal my man! Hey, I follied yer advish, an' lookit! Lookit!" He reeled drunkenly and stabbed out his finger to point at his Klingon friend, poking the behemoth in the eye. The Klingon muscle gripped a valise to his chest, stuffed with latinum bars.

"Thash four hunnert bars!" bragged d'Artagnan, breathing ethanol fumes upon the cadet.

Wesley gagged, waving his hands to clear the stench. "You *won* at Dabo?"

"Followed yer system!"

"But *nobody* wins at Dabo . . . it was invented by Ferengi!"

"Four hunnert bars!" He leaned close, winking at the cadet. "An' you know whut? Here . . . thish ish fer you, as a kine-a royalty. Here!" D'Artagnan reached into the valise and fished out a pair of dekabars. "Thas' fiffy percent!"

"Five percent," muttered Wesley.

"Use it in—" He hiccoughed violently. "In good healt'. Now we're off . . . off to th' wild, blue yonder."

"Where?"

D'Artagnan winked again. "We're gonna be *gennlemen farmersh* on a planet on the Cardapsian and Frederation frontier—we're retired! See ya in the holotoons!" With a final hiccough, d'Artagnan and his Klingon partner trooped away to find a turbolift.

"Who was that?" growled Agent Cooper.

"Another benefactor of Ferengi generosity," said Wesley. "C'mon, kid; let's hop to it."

Wesley scanned the room. There was no Kimbal Clock, but he did see a brochure stand, several ash trays, replicators, fifty or sixty couches, Louis XIV chairs and love seats, tables, some communications devices shaped like antique "telephones," a suggestion box, and of course a thousand pieces of luggage.

"Do those replicas work?" asked Data, indicating one of the telephones.

"Damned if I know," said Cooper. "I don't know which end you tap."

"These are similar to the telephones that Dixon Hill uses in Captain Picard's holodeck programs," said the android. "I am reasonably familiar with their working."

He picked a black cylinder from a cradle and held it to his ear; then he leaned close to the conical mouthpiece. "Hello?" he ventured, "can anybody hear me?"

After a moment, he replaced the earpiece. "I can hear a comm link opening; presumably, the telephones function as normal communications devices. The computer asked me to whom I wished to speak."

"Why is that one different?" asked Wesley. He pointed at one that was approximately half again as big and dark blue, instead of flat black.

"I do not know. Perhaps it is reserved for special clientele."

Wesley placed the earpiece against his ear. "I don't hear anything."

"Joggle the cradle switch," suggested Data.

"Look, son, this is all interesting, but we've got about fifteen minutes to find that clock or you're back to the cell."

Wesley joggled. "Nope, still nothing." His backbrain sent warning signals: something important about this particular telephone.

"It must be out of order," said Data.

Wesley stared at the telephone. "Commander . . . this

would be pretty easy to spot from across the room, wouldn't it?"

"I believe its visual uniqueness would be detectable from some distance."

"And no one's likely to steal it. What would you do with it?"

"I do not see your point, Wesley."

The cadet stared speculatively at Commander Data. "Sir, perhaps we've been looking for the wrong clock."

"I do not understand what you mean."

"Commander, the only important part of the Kimbal Clock is the internal guts, the electronics . . . the clock itself is completely irrelevant, and Tunk knows it!"

"Yeah, what's yer point, kid?" Cooper checked his wrist chronometer again.

"There's a replicator right there, about ten feet away."

"I believe I understand your thinking now, Cadet Crusher; it is very probable."

"Let's give it a shot."

Wesley found the plug and removed it from the base of the instrument. He placed the telephone into the replicator bay, twisting the long stem to get it fully inside. "Remove the entire outer casing," he commanded the machine, "but leave all internal electronics."

The telephonic exterior shimmered and disappeared. Wesley stared at the mess of hand-built circuits and fiberoptics . . . it looked all wrong! Then a piece slid sideways, no longer contained by the metal walls of the telephone base. At once, the image rearranged itself in Wesley's head and he finally recognized his own handiwork.

"Cooper," he said quietly, "you got any chaseum on you? I'd like to show you something."

Fifteen minutes later, Cooper returned Wesley to his cell. When the agent left, Wesley held a whispered conversation with his counsel.

"Commander, is the Federation going to file charges?"

Data considered for a moment. "I do not believe so,

Cadet Crusher." He spoke with exactly the same intonations and quality of voice, but he turned down the volume, giving him the disconcerting effect of speaking normally from ten meters distant. "You certainly acted under duress from the moment you were kidnapped aboard Munk's vessel; arguably, everthing you did after that point simply marked time until you could safely speak to the authorities."

"Data, I'm not sure that's entirely truthful."

"Perhaps not; but that is the conclusion Starfleet will probably draw."

"I took an oath, sir, and so did you. I will not lie, cheat, or steal, nor tolerate those among us who do."

Data nodded, raising his brows. "The oath requires you to always answer truthfully, but it does not require you to answer questions that no one asks.

"I advise you to say nothing unless you are directly asked. The law *as written* does not always fit every possible circumstance . . . not even in Starfleet."

"Hm. All right, what about the Ferengi contract court?"

"Perhaps it would be better to utilize that connecting ramp when we arrive, Wesley."

The cadet puzzled for a moment. "Cross that bridge when we come to it?"

"I have an idea about that charge as well; but I do not wish to speak of it before checking the thermal level of the liquid."

"Sir, do you do that on purpose?"

"Yes. I find that restating common idioms in a convoluted manner gives me an affect of ingenuous naivete."

"You mean all these years . . ." Wesley trailed off.

Data nodded. He started for the door.

"Commander," called Wesley, "aren't you going to tell me not to deviate from these coordinates, because your return is imminent?"

"Do not go away, Wesley. I will be right back."

When Data left, Tunk, who had sat quietly, suddenly

grabbed the bars and pressed his face against them. In the third cage, Cap'n Munk snored like the red-alert claxton on the *Enterprise*.

"So, didn't find any clocks, did you? Heh-heh!" Tunk nervously tugged at his ears, trying to look confident.

Wesley looked at him and smiled knowingly.

A thought tickled the cadet's forebrain, a memory from the past . . . a rule—a new Rule of Acquisition: *The sheep want to be fleeced.*

He suddenly remembered. All he would need to "phrank" Tunk and pay him back a little of his own coin was the complete cooperation and sanction of the victim.

Tunk tried more Ferengi subtlety. "I told you you wouldn't find anything . . ." He stared wildly about the room, obviously imagining hidden microphones and holovision cameras. "After all, *there was nothing there to find! Yes, that's what I said! I don't know why you made up that ridiculous story about counterfeit latinum, Kimbal!*"

At the word *latinum,* Munk snorted in midsnore and sat up groggily. "Closer to the wind, boys," he muttered. "Show us some sheet. Arrr." He fell back onto his bunk, snoring again before his pink head struck the hard pillow.

"Speaking of latinum," said Wesley, "I have a payment for you."

"Eh?" Tunk looked nonplussed at the change in subject . . . but curiously interested in the new and promising direction taken by the conversation.

"Here." The cadet withdrew the pair of dekabars given him by d'Artagnan and chucked them through the bars into Tunk's cell. "That's from my human friend, the real Fred Kimbal," said the cadet, "and that completely squares his poker debt to you."

One of the dekabars fell on Tunk's rack, but the other dropped to the floor. With a sudden snort, Munk came fully awake at the sound of the ringing latinum. "Arr," he commanded, "fetch that hither, boy!"

Glaring reproachfully at Wesley for being such a lousy

shot with latinum, Tunk handed over the bar that had dropped to his father.

"Good thing the other one landed on the bed," said the cadet, loudly enough that Munk could have heard him upstairs in the casino.

Casting a furious glare back through the bars, Tunk forked over the other bar as well.

After a moment, Munk collapsed, clutching his last remaining booty to his chest as if at any moment he would rise and begin singing sea chanties.

Now, thought Wesley, *how to play Tunk against himself?*

At once, the cadet recalled a Ferengi racial characteristic: Imposter-Syndrome, the nagging belief that any moment, *They* are going to *Find Out Everything!*

Wesley leaned close, winked at the Ferengi. "Don't worry," he said, "a good advocate can even beat physical evidence."

Tunk started; then he sneered, exposing sharp, rotting teeth. He sniffed haughtily, but the effect was spoiled when Tunk nervously began chewing on his lower lip. "Ah, ph-physical evidence? Whatever could you mean? Heh-heh." He wiped the sweat from his brow with his sleeve.

Wesley smiled vacuously at Tunk, giving the Ferengi no certainty about whether they had or had not found the Kimbal Clock. *Let him stew,* thought the cadet; *in a few more hours, I'll say something casual about a telephone.*

Thus began Wesley Crusher's own, subtle "phrank" . . . one that could be milked for hour after hour, leaving Tunk in an exquisite agony of ambiguousness and mounting terror about his possible trial.

Data did not return for almost twelve hours; by the end of that time, Tunk was nearly frantic. Wesley dropped more and more hints about finding the device, carefully keeping his remarks just ambiguous enough that he drove the Ferengi wild.

"It's a phrank!" shrieked Tunk, shaking his finger through the bars at Wesley. "You're trying to phrank me . . . but I'm the king of the phranks! Nobody phranks Tunk the Monster-Lobed!"

"Phranking Tunk the Monster-Lobed would certainly be something to call home about," agreed Wesley.

"Call? Did you say *call?* What did you mean by that?"

"If someone did pull it off, he certainly couldn't replicate it."

"Couldn't what?"

"Certainly couldn't duplicate it; no sir."

"You didn't say duplicate—you said *replicate!*"

"They'd have to have slipped in a ringer."

Tunk groaned, resting his monstrous head in his hands and sinking back onto his bunk. Wesley grinned . . . he had had Tunk's full cooperation and sanction for the last half-day of victimhood!

Commander Data suddenly walked into the room. "Cadet Crusher," he began, "I have a pleasant surprise for you."

Data stepped aside, and the Grand Nagus himself waddled into the prison, leaning on his disselboom, followed by an angry Agent Cooper and Conductor Smythe.

"This is ridiculous!" insisted Smythe. "I won't hear of it."

"Bah! Away from me, hu-man!" The Grand Nagus waved his walking stick like a club; Wesley concluded it was a common debating tactic among leathery old Ferengi men.

"It is an elegant solution to all of your problems," argued Data.

Wesley followed the discussion avidly, trying to catch the gist.

"But what's *he* want with them?" demanded Cooper, gesturing in exasperation at the Nagus.

"What do *I* want with a pair of thieving Ferengi traitors and turncoats?" The Nagus scratched his ears, pretending to ponder the problem deeply. "Let's see now . . . would I want to elevate them to daimons? Tempting, but no; I don't think there are any openings. Would I want to—hmm . . . sign over our most lucrative trade routes to them? Oh, charity! I forgot to bring my official seal along.

"Oh, well, I guess the only thing left to do is flay them

alive and use their internal organs for spare parts. But first, I think I'll let them serve my harem girls as live-in slaves for a few years . . . after we make Munk and Tunk into *eunuchs,* of course. I wouldn't want my property damaged!"

"But . . . but what's in it for Hatheby's?" Wesley noted wryly that Smythe did not seem particularly concerned with the fate of Munk and Tunk; he only cared about his employer's stake.

"If I may make a suggestion," ventured Data. He leaned over and spoke into the Grand Nagus's gigantic ear; the cadet could not hear what he said.

The Nagus scowled. "Are you *really* sure that's necessary?"

"All things worth having are worth paying for—as a last resort," said the android.

The Nagus stepped back, staring at Data with new respect. "I didn't realize they taught the Rules of Acquisition in Starfleet!" He shrugged elaborately. "All right . . . Smythe, I'll pay you one gram on the hectogram for all amounts that Munk paid with counterfeit."

Smythe drew a data-reader from his belt like a Klingon drawing a disruptor. He tapped away for a few seconds. "That's three thousand, five hundred and fifty grams of latinum," said the conductor.

"Exactly! Let's round it up to an even thirty-five hecto-bars."

"Thirty-*six.*"

"Whatever, whatever. Is it a deal?" The Grand Nagus grinned like a shark.

Smythe frowned. He stared back and forth between Munk and Tunk, then back to his data-reader. "Oh, all right," he grouched at last. "What about this Kimbal?"

The Grand Nagus shrugged. "I have no use for hu-mans; I don't think the girls would like it." He cackled as if he had just gotten off a whizzer, slapping Smythe on the back.

The conductor stiffened at the familiarity, but the Nagus continued, oblivious. "But I guess I bought it, so it's mine."

"Fine. Hatheby's shall expect payment in the morning

. . . in latinum." He leaned down and curled his lip. "In *real* latinum!"

"Of course! What do you take me for?"

"A Ferengi," muttered the conductor, tossing him the key. Turning away, Smythe marched back up the corridor, Cooper in tow.

The Grand Nagus did not hear; he had turned back to Tunk and Munk and was contemplating the pair.

The younger performed several standard Ferengi cringes, unable to decide which was more subservient. "Please, your Grand Nagusness. Mercy, kind sir! Spare my life, oh, great avaricious one! It's not my fault . . . *it's not my fault!* It's him! He did it!" Tunk pointed frantically at his father.

Munk just scowled belligerently; *give the old man credit,* thought Cadet Crusher; *at least he doesn't belly-crawl, like his son.*

"If it's booty yer after having," whispered the old man with a sly wink, "I ken the path to latinum like grainules of sand . . . millions o'bars, an' I'm or altruist!"

In his thin, reedy voice, the Nagus spoke. "I think I'll let you two stew in your own juices for a while, while I think of something truly unique for each of you!"

The Grand Nagus threw back his head and howled with laughter, shaking his shillelegh like a wrathful godling.

Simmering down, he started to leave the room, still giggling.

"Sir," called Data, "have you not forgotten something?"

"Oh, yes, where are my manners! Until we meet again, Commander."

"Sir, I believe you agreed to release Wesley Crusher into my custody."

"So I did. Where is he?"

"He is here, Grand Nagus. In the far cell."

"Nope; Fred Kimbal. It says so right in the charge sheet." The Nagus fished a data clip out of one of his dozens of pockets. "I made no promises to liberate any Fred Kimbals!" He leaned forward, stage-whispered behind his hand to Data. "But, you find me a Wesley Crusher, and he's off, free as a curse!"

"Sir? Commander? May I handle this?"

"If you wish, Wesley, though I am your counsel."

"Just this one time, all right?" Wesley stared at the Grand Nagus, who watched him back. "You have no particular objection to releasing 'Fred Kimbal,' do you?"

"Not at all, not at all! If the price is right, that is."

"Would, um, thirty-six hectobars of gold-pressed latinum be a fair price?"

The Grand Nagus grinned. "Now *that* sounds like a worthy reason to let you go, young man."

"Do you mind if it's fairy gold? You know, chaseum altered to give the illusion of latinum?"

"Wesley," said Data, "I urge you to reconsider. You are in plenty of scalding liquid already without adding another charge."

The cadet waved his counsel to silence. "Do you mind?" he repeated to the Nagus.

"Why . . . why no, not at all, *if* you'll allow me to help you produce it; after all, I certainly wouldn't want to overtax you, after all you've been through."

"It's a deal. For thirty-six hectobars of counterfeit latinum. Now let me out, please."

"Well, since you put it that way . . . how can I refuse?" With a smirk wide enough to dock a shuttlecraft, the Grand Nagus brought the key within two meters of the cell and activated the unlocker.

"And just in case you were thinking of grabbing my new toy away from me . . ." added the Ferengi, trailing off into silence. He held up a vicious, Ferengi phaser. "I can draw and fire this thing faster than you can say *Dophu wox almuqti woxas!*"

The Nagus ushered them all into the interrogation room, where Smythe, Cooper, and Dobbs prodded the erstwhile guts of the Kimbal Clock. As they entered, Smythe poked it with one fat forefinger.

"Out of the way, hu-mans!" barked the Ferengi merchant-prince.

The three Hatheby's agents looked up, annoyed. "Please take your prisoners and leave, sir."

"Take your hands off of my device!"

"Your device?"

"Cadet Kimbal has given me temporary custody of the device; as you have no legal right to confiscate it, take your grubby paws off."

"We, ah, we need it for evidence," suggested Agent Cooper.

"For the investigation," appended his shadow, Dobbs.

"What investigation? I bought full jurisdiction! I need it for my—I mean *our* trial!"

Data ventured his own opinion. "Since you sold complete jurisdiction on this case to the Grand Nagus, on behalf of the Ferengi High Council, I would advise you not to withhold potential exhibits."

Smythe and his two seconds stared at the Nagus, at Data, finally at Wesley Crusher; then the Hatheby's men conferred privately. After a moment, they broke down and vacated the room, leaving the transmutation device behind.

"Yes," breathed the Nagus, "yes yes yes yes! Hurry now, hu-man—tell me how to work it!"

As Wesley pushed past Data, he whispered almost inaudibly into the android's ear, "Follow my lead, sir."

The cadet stepped up to the table opposite the Grand Nagus. "Well, first of all, sir, you have to have some chaseum. That's what it turns to latinum."

"Chaseum, ah yes . . . of course! Of course, chaseum . . . ah, yes!" The Nagus fumbled in his numerous pockets, finally fishing out a Ferengi ear-pricker tool for picking locks. It was made almost entirely out of chaseum.

"Now place it on the pad there. Careful, don't touch the pad! It's very dangerous."

The Ferengi yanked his hand back; then, from a distance, he tossed the ear-pricker onto the transformation pad. Wesley continued. "I rigged that stem to activate the device;

we need a power source, a battery or something. Pretty low power. Um, Data?"

"I believe I can supply the necessary power without draining my own electrical cells," said the commander. He reached across and gripped a pair of electrodes, and the operation LEDs glowed cherry-red.

"Ready, Grand Nagus? Twist the clock stem. But be very cautious! We wouldn't want you to receive a dose of . . ."

"Of *what*, hu-man?" croaked the Grand Nagus.

"Well, never mind. If you're careful, nothing will happen this time."

"This time?"

Wes tapped the stem. Brow glistening with nervous sweat, the Nagus bared his pointed teeth, gripped the stem between his leathery fingers, and twisted.

The chaseum ear-pricker shimmered and flowed . . . the "melted butter" effect marked the transformation. The "pie plate" pad heated red-hot; but sitting within it was an ear-pricker that now appeared to be made of pure, twenty-four-carat latinum.

The Grand Nagus stared. "By all the Profits!" he gasped, stretching out his hand. Awed, he plucked the still-hot "latinum" from the pie plate, bouncing it from hand to hand to cool it.

Wesley stared in horror. He staggered slightly, as if he had just seen a ghost, clutching Commander Data for support. "He *touched* it!" cried the cadet.

The Grand Nagus looked up, confused. "Touched it?"

"He touched it . . . *with his bare hands, as I'm an ensign!*" Wesley turned a shocked gaze on Data.

The android cleared his throat. "Wesley, I am afraid you neglected to inform the Grand Nagus that he should use rubber gloves so soon after the transformation."

The cadet retreated, shaking, until he bumped into a chair, into which he dropped heavily. "I . . . I never thought a man would be so foolish as to *touch fairy latinum with his bare hands!*"

"What? Why? *What did I do?*" The Nagus flung the

"latinum" tool across the room, frantically wiping his hand on his clothing, the wall, the table.

"Data, is there an electo-decrystalizer aboard the *Enterprise?*"

"I do not believe so, Cadet."

"Oh, no!" Wesley leapt to his feet and staggered about the room, hands clutching his head. "What are we going to do?"

"Hu-man! Quick, what did I do? What's going to happen?" The Grand Nagus hopped up and began flapping his arms like a bat with a broken wing.

"Why, Grand Nagus, don't you even know how that machine works? It's a distribumorphic isolinear recrystalizer! By God, when you picked up that latinum, you recrystalized your entire arm! And you know what that means, don't you?"

"I do?" squeaked the Ferengi, eyes as wide as wagon wheels.

"Darn it, Nagus, you might lose the whole arm! Data, Data, what can we do? We have to do something quick, or . . ." Wesley made a snikking noise, sliding his finger across his neck.

"We must get the Grand Nagus to the nearest decrystalizer," suggested the commander.

"Sir, that's . . . that's brilliant!"

"It is?"

"Of course! It's our only chance—we'll build an emergency decrystalizer right here!"

"Please, I beg you . . . hurry!" The Nagus grabbed his arm and stared at the hand. "I can feel it crystalizing already!" He looked up at Data with a wild surmise. "Can you wrap a tourniquet around it?"

"Of course," said Data, calmly.

"Would it do any good?"

"None at all. But if it will make you feel better psychologically, I will do so anyway."

The Nagus groaned and sank into the other chair. "I'm slain! Oh why, oh why did I ever get so greedy?"

How do you think you became Grand Nagus? thought the

cadet, but aloud said only, "Hurry, sir . . . the emergency decrystalizer!"

"What do I do?" demanded the Nagus in a falsetto screech.

"We have to get a crystalization processor . . . now, where could we find one?" Wesley pretended to ponder, glancing every now and again at the transmutation device on the table.

Unconsciously, the Ferengi's own gaze followed the cadet's, settling upon the clockless Kimbal Clock. "Isn't there a crystalizer, decrystalizer, whatever-it-is processor in . . . in there?" The Nagus pointed gingerly at the device as if afraid it would jump up and bite off his finger.

Wesley slapped his forehead. "By all the Profits and Rules of Acquisition, that's *right!* How could I be such a chowderhead? Of course—we can use the crystalization processor in the transmuter itself!" He stared in awed wonder at the Ferengi. "How did you know that, sir? Have you studied subcrystaline tomographic discrepancy theory?"

"Well, I-I-I guess I've, oh, fooled around with it a bit . . . Ferengi science is quite advanced by human standards, you know." The Nagus grinned, accepting the accolades which were his natural right. He bobbed his head, eyes tightly shut, until he suddenly remembered his predicament and stopped abruptly.

"Hurry! There's not much time left . . . you don't, um, feel any tingling in your arm already, do you, Grand Nagus?"

The Ferengi moaned, staring at his arm again. "All up and down, from fingers to elbow! Is that a bad sign?"

Wesley shuddered and turned his attention back to the device. "There . . . take that cover off, sir."

The Nagus absently started to pick up his ear-pricker, then yelped and yanked his hand away.

The cadet reassured him, "No, no, it's all right! The crystals have set by now."

The Grand Nagus gingerly picked up the tool, holding it

from the extreme edge, and unlocked the frequency clamps at each corner of the transmuter's grounding plate.

Quietly, but with increasing urgency, Wesley Crusher talked the Ferengi through the steps necessary to remove the main processor . . . the custom-built original that Fred Kimbal himself had concocted. Wesley still had no idea how it worked.

But he had a pretty good idea how to make it *stop* working.

"Quickly now—fast!—put it on your arm . . . no time, no time! Just rest it there and hold it down with your finger!"

The Nagus did as he was told. Wesley leapt up, grabbed the pair of copper wires . . . for what he planned, the fiberoptic cables were no good at all. When overloaded, they would simply shunt the excess power off as visible light.

"Data, grab these two ends!" The android complied, and Wesley issued his final instruction. "Now reverse the polarity, Commander, and give it all the juice you've got! Do you understand, sir?"

Commander Data nodded. "I believe I do, Cadet."

For an instant, the copper wires glowed hot red, then yellow, then white, so bright Wesley had to turn his face away. At once, a sudden crackling noise echoed through the room like thunder, hurting the cadet's ears.

The Nagus howled like a banshee as the burning hot processor sizzled his forearm. He yanked his limb away, clutched it with his other hand, and ran around and around the interrogation room, swearing like a drunken sailor.

On the Nagus's third orbit, Wesley Crusher caught hold of him. "Let me see your arm!" he demanded.

The Ferengi shoved the requested body part forward viciously; Wesley held it steady and stared at it. "By God, but you have the luck of a Ferengi!"

"You—you—! I do?"

"Yes . . . Grand Nagus, we actually caught it in time! See?" Proudly, the cadet pointed at the distinct mark of the processor, branded into the Nagus's arm. "You've now got at least nine square centimeters of recrystalized flesh . . . you're going to be all right after all!"

Shaken, the Ferengi sat down at last. He stared in dismay at the blob of bubbling goo that had once been the Kimbal fairy-gold processor before Data fried it. "Gee, thanks," said the Grand Nagus without true conviction.

Wesley collapsed back onto his own chair, mopping his brow with his shirtsleeve. "Thank God; I thought it would *never* work!" Surveying the fried processor, Wesley said, "It's so sad that such a valuable invention—to which I own full rights—should have to be destroyed just to save the life of the Grand Nagus."

"Er . . . you weren't thinking of any court actions—were you, hu-man?"

"I don't know; in my present state as a slave to you, I just can't think at all. I'm liable to jump to the first action plan I happen upon."

"Ahhh . . . what the heck. I don't think I could get anything for you, anyway. If you'll call us square for the clock, I'll release you for now."

The cadet stuck out his hand. "Data, you witness the deal, all right?"

"Of course, Cadet."

"Then it's a bargain, Grand Nagus: You let me go—"

"For the moment," clarified the Nagus.

"For the moment, and I won't press a claim on the Kimbal Clock."

The Nagus grumbled and bit, but in the end he finally agreed. Wesley walked out of the Novus Alamogordus jail cell a free cadet . . . for the moment.

"Ah, well," said Cadet Crusher, "all's well that ends."

Data spoke up. "I believe the exact quotation is 'all is well that ends well,' though the Bard uses a contraction for 'all is.'"

Wesley smiled. "I think I like my version better, Commander."

253

Chapter Nineteen

COMMANDER WILL RIKER waited more or less impatiently for Wesley Crusher to beam aboard the *Enterprise* again. Data had already transmitted a full report of the deal. With Munk and Tunk in custody, the only potential catastrophe for the errant cadet would be if the Grand Nagus filed an action for the breach of contract . . . a contract he now owned under Ferengi law.

Out of the frying pan, thought the first officer. Still, it would not impair the learned lesson if Riker were to let the boy know he was still considered one of the crew.

Wesley opened a comm link to the transporter room, requesting beam out. He had returned to his room and gathered up the few possessions he had with him. Riker acknowledged and beamed the cadet up himself.

When he materialized on the transporter pad, Riker was all smiles. "Why, Fred Kimbal, haven't seen you in days! How was the auction, Fred?"

Wesley had the decency to wince at the name. "It was very illuminating, as Commander Data would say."

"Actually, he used the term stimulating."

"That, too. But it's good to be back, sir. I haven't really visited my moth— Doctor Crusher since I arrived."

"Speaking of Beverly, I have an offer for you, if you'll swear on your honor as an Academy cadet that you won't tell her . . . Wes."

Wesley relaxed. He nodded briskly as he shouldered the clothes he had been wearing when he was kidnapped.

"I understand you were trying to get Data to show you some of the manly art of poker. Well, Wes, you've tried the rest, now learn from the best."

"Sir?"

"Why don't you drop by my quarters after you've gotten settled in and spent some time with you-know-who? I'd be happy to teach you a thing or two about poker that would even startle an android." Riker winked and elbowed the thin, haggard-looking cadet in the ribs.

Cadet Crusher stopped so suddenly that the first officer almost ran into him. The cadet whirled, staring at Riker as if the latter had just suggested a bombing run on Betazed. "No!" he shouted, eyes wild, taking on a belated "sir" as an afterthought. "No, no, that's very kind of you, sir, I must decline." Wesley resumed a quick-march to his temporary quarters, leaving a puzzled Will Riker in the corridor.

The commander shrugged finally and headed back toward the bridge, shaking his head.

Lieutenant Worf silently piloted the shuttlecraft *Nāmeme,* while Professor Raymond Redheffer, representing the Federation, Commander Kurak, representing the Klingon Empire, and Lieutenant Commander Geordi La Forge, representing nothing but his own reputation huddled together in the passenger section, which had been hastily converted to an auxilliary cargo hold.

Behind the *Nāmeme*—far behind it—they towed the newly built photonic pulse cannon by tractor beam; Commanders Data and Kurak had spent four full days assembling the device from the data clip plans jointly purchased by the Federation and the empire. The *Nämeme* also towed a pair of small equipment-asteroids for targets, brought along by Professor Redheffer.

Raymond Redheffer was a tall, muscular, gray-haired old man—he claimed to be one hundred and twenty, but he looked not a day over one hundred—who had joined them from a small, one-person scoutship sent out from Starbase 6. He was a technician sent to test the pulse cannon by the Federation Association for the Advancement of Science, which had stolen an orbit on the rival Federation Exo-Vironmental Research Council.

Raymond Redheffer had greeted them with a hearty clap on the back that staggered both Geordi and Kurak. He regaled them with incessant poetry as they transferred the hastily assembled observation equipment from the scoutship to the *Nämeme,* offering to buy a drink for anyone who could quote a line from a poem that Redheffer could not identify within five minutes. Geordi tried and ended by owing the good doctor three drinks.

Commander Kurak fixed the human professor with curled lip and suddenly barked out a short line in Klingon.

"Invincible is the enemy, but you are merely invulnerable."

Redheffer blinked rapidly. He stared at the mohawked Valkyrie, saying nothing.

"I appear to have stumped your Federation professor," she declared, grinning.

"Only because you misquoted Tyrdak the Battleflag," retorted Redheffer.

"I did not!"

"Didn't you?"

"No!"

"Doesn't this sound a little closer to the original?" Redheffer cleared his throat, then recited in harshly sonorous Klingon: "Invincibility comes from your enemy, but invulnerability comes from within/To attack invincibly, the enemy must move from his place/In that moment, he becomes vulnerable."

Worf grunted, almost grinned. "My memory of the poem matches Professor Redheffer's recitation," he ruled.

Commander Kurak gasped, raising her fist; then she turned the attack into a polite bow. "I yield to the human's superior learning," she oiled. She smiled . . . but the cold glitter in her eye as her gaze caught Geordi's made him shudder. *Thank goodness I'm not Ray Redheffer,* he decided.

Professor Redheffer wore a kind of visor, and Geordi felt an odd kinship; the visor allowed Redheffer to plug his eyes directly into the broad-band scanner, giving him an even greater visual range and acuity than Geordi had.

"Commander," said Worf, "you should participate in designing the experiments. You know more about Doctor Zorka than anyone else here."

"The Klingon's right," said Redheffer, "I've never studied Zorka. I was just the only techno near enough to get here in time."

"Mm-*mm!*" grunted Geordi La Forge, shaking his head emphatically. "I'm in enough trouble already. Everyone knows I think Zorka was loopy. If I'm involved, they'll just say I set the experiments up to fail."

"Suit yourself." Redheffer shrugged. He began barking orders to Kurak and Worf, who glowered but finally obeyed. Neither one of them had any experience with testing weapons systems.

The equipment stuffed into the *Nämeme* filled practically every cubic meter of both the cargo hold and the erstwhile passenger section; nobody knew how many shots the crew could get from the pulse cannon, and they wanted to make every possible measurement. The crew was jammed in almost as an afterthought, left to fend space for themselves. Geordi had had to argue for several minutes with Commander Riker to be allowed to waste precious space by accompanying the expedition.

At last, they reached a position one light-year away from Novus Alamogordus and the two orbiting ships, the *Enterprise* and the *Hiding Fish;* Redheffer and Kurak agreed that the distance was sufficient for safety.

Worf launched the first target satellite and waited while it maneuvered into range approximately three hundred thousand kilometers distant; then he delicately used the tractor beam to rotate the pulse cannon into position.

Geordi watched, helpless and anxious, as the other two engineers carefully armed the pulse cannon, then began powering it up. Twice, he almost interjected himself, correcting a sloppy reading or lending a hand in calibration; but each time he stopped himself, desperately afraid of tainting the experiment by his biased participation.

I'm just an observer—nothing more!

During the final five minutes of critical testing, Geordi La Forge literally sat on his hands to keep them to himself.

Come on, baby, he coaxed; *just one little, total failure for Daddy . . .*

Geordi felt like a traitor to his profession and his oath for his attitude; but he realized that if the photonic pulse cannon were a raving success, he might as well kiss his reputation good-bye.

At last, the test countdown picked up, and Kurak counted slowly from eight to zero in Klingon. At zero-seconds, she touched the trigger plate.

A high-pitched whistle shattered the silence aboard the *Nämeme,* and all four crew members clapped their hands over their ears. After a moment, Commander Kurak had enough presence of mind (and threshold of ear pain) to reach out with one hand and disengage the triggering pulse. The noise ceased.

For five or six minutes, all Geordi could hear was a persistent ring echo; apparently, no one else could hear either, because Kurak, Worf, and Redheffer simply sat quietly, rubbing their ears. At last, Redheffer began checking the circuit, finding the short at last.

This time, before she actually fired the weapon, Kurak performed a low-amp test of the triggering circuitry, verifying that there were no more breaks. She turned to Geordi. "Was that what you humans call a wolf whistle? I did not know I was so attractive."

It took La Forge several seconds to realize that Kurak had actually *made* a joke—a rare event indeed for a Klingon!

"Fire two," she said, then counted down from eight again. Just before she pressed the plate, the other three testers poked fingers into ears.

Two. One. Zero. Commander Kurak pressed the touchplate, and for an instant, the entire shuttlecraft seemed to draw a breath. Every gauge pegged as far to the right as it could register: The shuttlecraft power cells were nearly sucked dry.

A loud *pop* inside the cargo bay sounded like the world's largest champagne cork. Geordi ducked involuntarily.

A thin green beam of energy lanced from the end of the cannon to the satellite target; Geordi adjusted his visor's scan-speed and discovered the beam was, indeed, pulsing.

It touched the satellite and bounced off, so low-energy it barely even registered on the sensitive instrumentation.

Geordi sucked in a breath.

Kurak spoke hesitantly. "The energy . . . must be going someplace."

"It's not in the beam," confirmed Redheffer, his own detachable visor locked into the sensors. "Of course, if it's not still in the shuttlecraft, and it's not in the beam, there's only one other place it could be."

"Shields up!" shouted Geordi.

Worf barely had time to raise the shields before the vaunted photonic pulse cannon, for which the Federation and Klingons had jointly paid one hundred and eighty thousand bars of gold-pressed latinum, blossomed into a silent, white flower of violent disintegration.

The shuttle, struck by the force of the explosion, tumbled like a cast die for several moments until Worf could reassert control, by which time Kurak, Geordi, and Redheffer, as ballistic projectiles, had managed to tear apart much of the delicate equipment the professor had brought from Starbase 6.

Kurak quickly checked out the two humans; Redheffer had broken a finger, but Geordi sustained only a few bruises.

The political officer snorted. "Hmp. Trust a human to design weaponry that attacks itself!"

Geordi could not help grinning, however; in fact, he barely restrained himself from shouting *Yes!* and pumping his fist in celebration. *Saved by the supernova!* he silently exulted.

Then he noticed that all three of his crewmates stared, dumbfounded, at his entirely inappropriate jubilation. "Ah," he improvised, "I'm just, um, pleased that we're all still alive."

Kurak snorted again, staring at the *Enterprise* engineer with new respect. "Remarkable," she muttered; but whether she meant his successful, gut-feeling prediction that the cannon would not work or his peculiar glee when proven right, Geordi could not tell.

Worf spoke more quietly than usual. "Perhaps we had better return to our ships to make our reports."

"Oh, well," said Redheffer, shrugging fatalistically; *"and all at once they sang, 'Our island home/Is far beyond the wave; we will no longer roam.'"*

Captain Jean-Luc Picard had luxuriated for four days with nothing to do while Data and the Klingon science officer Kurak built the cannon, then towed it off for testing.

Picard spent his brief respite of free time perusing two new books received in the last subspace cultural broadcast: a new analysis of the Mayan-like language found on a three-hundred-thousand-year-old Vulcan etching, and a vaguely amusing time travel conceit about King Arthur. Halfway through the latter, Picard grew bored by the author's ponderous style and bloodthirstiness, and erased the novel from the memory banks.

At last, his annunciator chirped. It would have to be Geordi La Forge, since the *Nämeme* had just returned . . . somewhat the worse for wear, according to Commander Data.

"Come," said the captain, in his mind's eye still figuratively crawling on hands and knees through the ruins of a Vulcan culture three thousand centuries old.

The door to his quarters slid open; Geordi La Forge stood triumphantly in the doorway, data clip in hand. "Results of the photonic cannon tests," he proclaimed.

With regrets, Picard saved a pointer in the archaeology book and turned off the data-reader. "Can you give me a brief synopsis?"

"Yes, sir." Geordi grinned, making no effort to hide it this time. "It's a complete dud, Captain. It sucks power like a leaky containment field, it's so loud it shakes its own structure half to pieces when we fire it, and if we had three of them, we could produce a photonic pulse beam that was almost as powerful as a regular phaser. That is, if we could manage to build one that didn't vaporize itself as soon as the energy bulidup exceeded the maximum storage capacity."

Captain Picard sat in shocked silence for nearly a minute. Geordi had not made any report by subspace after the tests, insisting on delivering the news in person . . . and now Picard knew why.

At last, he cleared his throat. "Ahem, perhaps I had better review the entire report before you send it off to Starfleet, Geordi."

"I thought you might, sir." He placed the data clip on the captain's desk.

Picard stared ruefully at the data clip as if it were some sort of betrayer. "Let me review this tonight; I'd like you and the rest of the senior staff, and Wesley, to assemble in my ready room at zero-eight hundred."

"Aye, sir, I'll tell the first officer."

"Dismissed."

Geordi left, still smiling, leaving Captain Picard wondering how he was going to explain to both Starfleet and the Emperor Kahless a very, very large bid on a very, very big pail of air.

The next morning, Commander Riker arrived at the ready room fifteen minutes early, as was his wont; he was surprised to see Wesley Crusher already waiting.

"You're here early, for a change."

"I got used to it at the Academy, sir. They wake us up by

playing reveille at zero-five thirty; by zero-five thirty-five, we're expected to be dressed in PT clothes and outside, ready for a morning run or PT."

Riker grinned. "Really! They actually do that?"

"Whoops . . . I guess I don't need to tell you what they do in the Academy." His face reddened, but he smiled.

"Nah, back in my day, we got all our exercise chasing dinosaurs off the drill field."

"Good heavens," said Captain Picard's voice behind them. "Then I must have attended the Academy around the time blue-green algae began producing oxygen."

Riker and Wesley stood respectfully as the captain entered the ready room, followed by Data, Geordi, Worf, Beverly, and Deanna Troi. Picard sat, and the crew followed suit.

"Well, it's a bit early, but since you're all here, we may as well begin. Geordi, perhaps you'd care to fill us in on the results of the testing?"

Geordi cleared his throat. "Well, I assume you've all read the report by now. Basically, they tested models where they existed and attempted to build them where they were only vaguely described.

"The results were . . . well, I hate people who say they hate to say I told you so, so I'll cheerfully gloat that I *did* tell you so. In a nutshell, nothing works. All of Doctor Zorka's junk turned out to be, well, junk."

Riker muttered, "And we're stuck with the biggest piece of junk of them all."

The captain steepled his fingers. "Strategic analysis of our position, Mister Data?"

"To put it bluntly, sir, we are up the proverbial aquatic waterway without an oar."

"Data!" objected Beverly, grinning.

"Um," said Geordi quietly, "that expression is a little scatological in its original form, Data."

The android raised his eyebrows. "Indeed. I meant only that we have severely compromised the security of both the Federation and the Klingon Empire by paying an amount likely to cripple defense spending for some time for what turns out to be a valueless fantasy. The only consolation is that Cardassian will also have to pay a large amount, their own losing bid . . . assuming they choose to honor the debt."

"What if they don't?"

"There is little we can do to force the issue. We have virtually no commerce with the Cardassian Empire; we have no formal diplomatic missions; trade talks are already sporadic; and the Cardassians have shown a proclivity toward canceling debts and payment schemes owed to the Federation upon small pretext.

"Besides, we are in the process of negotiating a treaty over the exact borders of the Federation and the empire, and the Cardassians need only demand debt relief as a condition of signing.

"On the other hand, because we live by the rule of law, we cannot so easily discharge our own debt to Doctor Zorka's son, Bradford Zorka, junior."

"I thought Doctor Zorka's first name was Jaymi," Beverly Crusher said.

"We've already been through that," said Geordi, cryptically.

Hesitantly, Wesley decided to join the discussion. "May I speak, sir?" Picard nodded, and Wesley continued. "Commander, why can't we simply refuse to pay on the grounds that the merchandise was not as advertised?"

"It is not as easy as that, Cadet. In order to participate in the auction, the Federation representative, Lieutenant Worf, signed a contract obligating us to honor all bids, no matter who won or whether subsequent developments rendered the lots obsolete. Captain Picard signed the same contract on behalf of the Emperor Kahless."

"Basically," clarified Will Riker, "we agreed that if we developed our own photonic pulse cannon tomorrow that was better than the one Zorka supposedly developed, we wouldn't use that as an excuse to back out of our bid."

"Unfortunately," continued Data, "Hatheby's wrote the

clause ambiguously enough that we cannot use our own test results to retract the bid, either."

"Sounds like a Ferengi contract," Wesley said. *And I beat a Ferengi contract,* he thought—*maybe I can beat this!*

"If it were," added Data, "then at least we could be sure the Cardassians would pay their own bid. The Cardassians have commerce worth several million bars of latinum with the Ferengi, and they would not jeopardize it by defaulting on a debt of one hundred and fifty thousand."

Wesley furrowed his brow; Riker knew the look: It meant that another intricate scheme was running through the cadet's brain. "Data, are you saying that if the Cardassians owed the latinum to a Ferengi company, rather than Hatheby's, they would *have* to pay it?"

"That is most likely true. The Ferengi are their primary trading partners, and the Cardassians cannot afford to devalue their credit by defaulting on a debt."

"Wes," said Riker, leaning forward, "do you have an idea?"

"Almost, sir. Let me keep thinking for a few minutes."

Picard nodded. "To continue, is there anything we can salvage from the tests?"

"Jean-Luc," said Dr. Beverly Crusher, "I should point out that the medical equipment I purchased on behalf of Admiral Dyreal of the *Luqtan* Research Facility does work; I tested it myself."

"I'm not surprised," said Geordi, "in his early days, Doctor Zorka really was brilliant. His reputation wasn't built on vacuum. In fact, there are some interesting principles in the photonic pulse design; they learned a lot from playing with the cannon."

"Just not one hundred and eighty kilobars' worth," said Picard ruefully.

"Right."

"There is one consolation," said Riker.

"Yes, Will?"

"At least we've got the Cardassians thinking we have a photonic pulse cannon. Worf, is there any way we could fake a test that would leave the Guls convinced we've got a planet buster?"

The Klingon considered for a moment. "If Kurn cooperates, I believe we can produce a fraudulent test firing. But I do not like the idea, sir."

"What's wrong with it?"

Worf fell silent, obviously reluctant to criticize his superior officer's suggestion; but his warrior's heart did not take kindly to victory by deception.

"Seriously, Worf, if there's a problem, I need to know it."

"Sir, if we stoop to such chicanery, we are no better than . . . *Romulans."* He spat the last word as if tasting something nauseating.

Picard spoke up. "I can give Worf's unease a concrete image, Number One. Suppose we did fake some test results and convinced the Cardassians we had a superweapon. What then?"

"First, they would be driven to develop their own version of a photonic pulse cannon . . . one that might actually work.

"Second, suppose they then claimed to have done so, and as proof presented a test quite similar to the one we had rigged. Should we believe it? Or should we assume they are just as capable of trickery as we? Once you start down the road of disinformation, you begin to fundamentally doubt all information and fear to take any action. You become paralyzed with indecision.

"Third, if word of the trickery leaked to the Cardassians —and make no mistake, Will, it would—they might be tempted to doubt any future announcements of new weaponry we had supposedly developed. After all, if we were willing to lie once, why not again?"

"And besides," added Riker, yielding with a smile, "I think I agree with Worf: I hate victory by deception. The only thing worse is losing."

"The Cardassians would find out within a matter of months, Will. Trickery is not a viable option."

"Well," said Wesley, uncomfortably, "at least not that kind of trickery."

"How's that idea of yours, Mister Crusher?" asked the first officer.

"I think I have a suggestion, Commander. But you may not like it . . . there's some trickery involved. In fact, I think Tunk would call it a *phrank.*"

"Never let abstract theory get in the way of a good plan, Cadet. Fire away!"

"All right, sir. You have a problem and I have a problem. Your problem is that you paid almost two hundred thousand for a worthless piece of junk . . . that's ninety thousand bars from the Federation, ninety thousand from the Klingon Empire."

"Wesley," said his mother quietly, "if you have an idea, just tell us."

He continued logically; it was the only way he knew how to proceed. In fact, he was still working out the solution as he spoke. "My problem is that the Grand Nagus is dangling a major threat over my head: prime blackmail material. All he has to do is bring charges against me on behalf of Munk and Tunk in a Ferengi court; the Federation extradites me and I spend the rest of my life shoveling coal or serving alcohol at Ferengi orgies."

"Wesley!" cried Beverly, scandalized.

"Sorry, Mother. The Grand Nagus has a problem: He laid out thirty-six hectobars for Munk and Tunk, and they haven't got a gram between them. Or rather, they have only twenty grams." He smiled at the memory of the jail cell payoff.

"The Cardassians have a problem: They lost out on the bidding, and now they don't have a nice, new photonic pulse cannon."

"Great," said Riker, "everybody's got a problem."

"No, sir. Everybody has *different* problems; so I asked myself . . . what would a Ferengi trader do? Specifically, what would Tunk do?" The cadet smiled, sitting back in his chair. "It's pretty obvious. Tunk would pull the biggest 'phrank' of his career."

"I am unfamiliar with the term *phrank*," said Data.

"It's a term Tunk made up. I think it means a prank or a practical joke—one based entirely on the cooperation of the victim. In this case, we would simply give the Cardassians the opportunity to make suckers of themselves."

Picard said nothing; he looked at Riker. The first officer shook his head. "I don't get it, Cadet."

"I do not like the idea," rumbled Lieutenant Worf. Counselor Troi and Wesley's mother merely looked puzzled.

Only Geordi began to grin, perhaps beginning to glimpse the plan—the *phrank*.

"It's really straightforward," said Wesley. "We just get the Grand Nagus to steal the pulse cannon and sell it to the Cardassians."

"Cadet Crusher," said the captain, "I don't see how that helps us any."

"He sells it to the Cardassians for an even two hundred thousand bars of latinum and gives us one hundred eighty."

Geordi sat forward. "And the Grand Nagus keeps the other twenty thousand as profit!"

"Which solves *his* problem," added Wesley. "In exchange, he gives us jurisdiction over Munk and Tunk and their contract—which solves *my* problem."

Data spoke up, sounding puzzled. "But eventually, the Cardassians will test the cannon and discover that it does not work."

Wesley shrugged. "Hey, that's *their* problem! That's why it's a phrank . . . they'll know it was a phrank, but they'll also know that they were the ones who bought allegedly stolen merchandise. We have their sanction. They can't accuse us without simultaneously accusing themselves of a far more serious offense: receiving stolen property."

They sat in silence for a moment until Commander Riker began laughing. Geordi and Deanna joined in, while Beverly merely smiled. Data activated his laughter program, though it was set too slow and sounded like a coughing fit.

Only Picard remained serene. "Mister Crusher, if you can pull this off, I will personally write a letter of explanation to Admiral Boxx and Captain Wolfe."

At the mention of the commanding and executive officers of the Academy, Wesley sobered instantly. He looked at his newly replaced wrist chronometer; classes would begin in three days . . . if he were not back, he would be marked as "missing ship's movement," exactly as if he had not shown up for a starship assignment.

Another few days after that and he would be officially listed as AWOL. The former could result in a reprimand and two weeks double duty; the latter could buy him thirty days in the stockade and expulsion from the Academy.

Whatever he was going to do, he had to do it quickly, then somehow get the captain to return to earth at warp five.

Riker finished chortling and leaned forward on the conference table. "Should I hail the Grand Nagus and see whether he wants to play?"

Picard nodded. "Make it so."

The negotiations actually took eight hours; the Nagus drove an adamantine bargain. In the end, Picard and Worf each had to sign a written agreement giving the Grand Nagus full authority to negotiate with the Cardassians on their behalf, making any representations he chose. The Federation and the Klingon Empire would split the first one hundred eighty thousand the Nagus received, plus ten percent of any amount above that with no upper limit.

At Wesley's urging, Picard made one big concession a deal buster: In the event of a dispute in terms, the contract would be interpreted by a Federation court according to the Federation code of civil procedure . . . not by a Ferengi court or by Ferengi rules. The only reason the Grand Nagus agreed was because he had already discovered that Gul Fubar had received authority to double his credit line . . . rather belatedly.

With the contract signed, Wesley sprang his photon torpedo: "Commander," he requested of Riker, "I'd like to be the only person on the away team with the Grand Nagus."

Riker raised his eyebrows. "I wasn't planning to send an away team. I assumed the Nagus himself would handle the details."

"I've been thinking about this. There's a flaw in the whole operation; how is the Nagus supposed to have gotten the plans for the cannon?"

Riker shrugged. "He stole them."

"How did he even get into the computer? And why aren't we after him?"

"Hm. Well, maybe Gul Fubar will be so greedy he won't even stop to ask."

"And maybe he will ask. We'd better have an answer, sir, and I've got one. I'm a spy, a turncoat . . . I made a copy of the operational plans and I'm willing to hand them over to the Cardassians in exchange for latinum—lots of it. The Grand Nagus is acting as my agent."

Riker stroked his beard. "Well, Gul Fubar did see you working for the Ferengi, Tunk and Munk."

"And by now, he knows that Data tried to get Hatheby's to hand over jurisdiction to them, but the Grand Nagus bought me, along with Tunk and Munk."

"All right . . . so how did you get into the computer?"

Wesley smiled. "I hacked it."

"He's going to believe that?"

"He will after I hack his computer."

"Can you?"

The cadet shrugged. "I don't know; I've never tried. But how hard can it be?"

Will Riker closed his eyes. It was a dangerous assignment . . . and if anything happened to Wesley, Will shuddered to think what Beverly would do to him.

Besides, he thought, *no matter what the kid does, he's still part of the family.* If Gul Fubar did anything to Wesley, Beverly would not have the opportunity to slay Riker: He would beam over to the Cardassian ship, phaser in hand,

and get to Gul Fubar before the Cardassian soldiers could cut him down.

"All right, Crusher; you're the away team. But I want you to get a comm badge before you leave." He smiled. "One made of chaseum, not latinum."

More hours passed; now the Grand Nagus was privately negotiating with Gul Fubar, trying to persuade the Cardassian that a human defector had actually stolen the long-sought plans for the pulse cannon.

The Gul had a hard time buying the concept. Obedience to the state was so ingrained in Cardassians that whenever the Gul tried to contemplate not only betrayal, but betrayal *for profit,* he became so enraged that he could not rationally bargain with either the "traitor" or even the Ferengi.

Had the Nagus been trying to convince another Ferengi, the concerns would have been reversed: The Ferengi would have no trouble understanding an insider who turned spy for money . . . but they would be highly suspicious that the plans were not bonafide.

One sticking point was that the Gul was not stupid; he knew that anyone could fake plans and call them "a photonic pulse cannon." Thus, he would be satisfied only with the original plans themselves, just as they had come from the auction.

They were stored on a security data clip, one with latinum identifiers that could not be accurately duplicated by replicators or any other means of copying.

The Grand Nagus, playing the game to the hilt, became highly agitated and doubled his price, bringing the total tab to well over the anticipated two hundred thousand. This time, however, Gul Fubar was ready with a large enough line of credit.

They finally agreed on the deal, with the Grand Nagus warning the Cardassian that he had better immediately take off for Cardassian space at top warp the instant he transferred the kilobars and received the plans . . . a double blessing, since it meant that Gul Fubar would not be able to test the cannon until he was far, far away.

The interior of the Cardassian ship was cold, gray, and dreary; even Klingon ships were more colorful.

Wesley's role was easy: He simply had to play the part of a nervous, frightened, anxious traitor who wanted nothing more than to unload his data clip, pick up the latinum, and "get the hell out of here," as Picard's favorite literary detective, Dixon Hill, would have put it. Except for the "traitor" part, the rest of the description was perfectly accurate: It was quite an easy role for the cadet to play.

Gul Fubar was one of the "long-necked" Cardassians, his head rising half a meter above his shoulders, the neck muscles sloping down from the jawline to the tips of the arms. Out of the blue, Wesley wondered how such Cardassians could ever turn their heads to look at something.

The Ferengi and the Cardassian finalized the deal in furtive whispers, despite being alone with the cadet in Gul Fubar's sterile quarters.

"You, ah, got the thing?" asked the Cardassian.

"You have the money?" countered the Grand Nagus.

"I *might* have; then again, I might *not* have. What about the . . . you know?"

"Well," cackled the Nagus, "I *might* know; then again, I *might not* know."

"The thing!"

"It *might* be a thing, but it might *not* be a thing."

The two of them strolled around the barn a few more times before Gul Fubar finally admitted that, yes, he did in fact have the money.

He had a junior officer bring it in on a pallet, a small, symmetrical mountain of 225 hectobars of latinum, the price agreed upon. The Grand Nagus managed to conceal his avarice, an amazing act for a Ferengi, considering that the sum represented a clear profit to the Nagus of forty-five thousand bars.

Wesley fished around his shirt pocket and handed Gul Fubar the original Hatheby's data clip.

The Cardassian grinned nastily, holding the clip as if it

contained the philosopher's stone, the elixir of life, and the Great Word of Power. "It may have taken half the yearly weapons development budget," he whispered, more to himself than to his visitors, "but it's worth every last gram . . . I'll stake my career on it!" His eyes lit up with a holy glow, a missionary who has just discovered the promised land.

Then they narrowed in suspicion. He glared back and forth from the clip to Wesley Crusher. "Is it ready to review?"

"There's a password," improvised Wesley.

"Yes?"

"I'll tell you when we're safely out."

Gul Fubar grumbled a bit but finally relented. At last, one standard day, almost to the hour, after Wesley first thought of the idea, they loaded the pallet of latinum into the Nagus's personal shuttle and launched from the Cardassian cargo bay.

As soon as they launched, Wesley hailed Gul Fubar. When the frequency opened, he broadcast only a single word: *swordfish.* It was the first password that popped into his head. Then the Grand Nagus hit the impulse engines, and they were gone.

Before they made it halfway to the *Enterprise,* Gul Fubar took his own ship out of orbit and exploded back toward Cardassian space . . . at warp 9.5.

"So much for the environmental warp treaty!" said Wesley, chuckling.

The Grand Nagus began to snicker. "That was truly clever, human . . . that was Ferengi-clever!"

"Really?"

"Absolutely! What did you call it? That was one of the best *phranks* I've ever participated in. And highly profitable, of course, for all parties concerned."

"Except the Cardassians."

The Nagus turned to the cadet, winking and leering hideously. "Nonsense! They bought an expensive but very valuable lesson!"

Wesley bowed his head. "Well, if it was Ferengi-clever, it's because I learned from the cleverest and sneakiest Ferengi in the quadrant."

"Why, thank you, hu-man. That's quite a compliment . . . and completely true, too." After a moment, however, the Nagus began to scowl; then he looked puzzled. "Wait a minute—did you mean me, or that altruist Tunk?"

Just at that moment, however, Wesley saw something on the instrument panel that absorbed his full concentration; after a while, the Nagus became distracted by the mind-numbing sum beside them and forgot all about his question.

Chapter Twenty

Show me the way to go home,
I'm tired, and I want to go to bed . . .

WESLEY HUMMED THE ANCIENT SONG to himself as he stood outside Captain Picard's quarters, steeling himself to the task of touching the annunciator and bracing the captain for a favor.

His pulse and respirations were elevated, and his palms were sweaty. *Jeez,* he thought, *I might as well be asking for a date!*

Finally, he decided he had sufficient self-control. He touched the plate and was rewarded by an instantaneous "come" from the interior.

Captain Jean-Luc Picard sat behind his desk, trying to fit together what looked like the broken pieces of a vase.

"Oh, ah, did you drop something?" asked the cadet.

Picard smiled without looking up. "Not exactly, Wesley."

"Can't you just use the replicator to repair it?"

"This water gourd is over seven thousand years old . . . can you believe that?"

Wesley stared curiously. "It's wrecked."

The captain finally looked up; his face was calm and

274

peaceful, definitely a good sign. "I wonder," he said, "what you will look like seven thousand years from now."

The cadet frowned, considering the shards. *Isn't it more interesting to understand the universe as it is, rather than study the broken remnants of dead cultures?* But he said nothing aloud . . . he wanted a very big favor from Picard and decided it was probably not the best strategy to begin by insulting the captain's first love: archaeology.

"Sir, classes start tomorrow. My first class is not until thirteen hundred."

Picard put down the pottery shard and looked up politely. "I know. I keep abreast of my entire crew's duty assignments."

Wesley held up a small data-reader. "I performed a few calculations, sir. We could just make it back without exceeding the environmental speed limit. If we leave fairly soon, I mean."

"How soon?"

Wesley grinned disarmingly. "Oh, within the next half hour, forty-five minutes."

Captain Picard smiled. "No," he said.

"I'm sorry?"

"No."

"Uh . . . when can we leave?"

"We're leaving immediately. But we're not going anywhere near Earth." Wesley said nothing, and the captain continued. "Did you actually think I would deviate the assigned cruise of a Galaxy-class starship just to ferry an errant schoolboy back to his classes?"

Wesley stared, opening and closing his mouth.

Captain Picard watched and waited. Wesley remained speechless—not because he thought the captain should ferry him back to the Academy, but because he had never even thought about the possibility that he would not.

Picard smiled. "Think of it as my own 'phrank' on you. This is the real world, Ensign. When you make a decision, you must accept all the consequences, whether you thought about them at the time or not."

An enormous pressure built up inside of Wesley, as if his warp coils had breached and filled him with ultrahot, pressurized steam.

Of course he wouldn't! He didn't drag you out here; you're not under orders; you're out on a crusade, a juvenile lark, light-years from where you're supposed to be! What in the universe made you think the Enterprise *would drop everything to charge back to the Academy, just to drop you off?*

Picard was right; unconsciously, Wesley had expected somebody else to take responsibility for getting him back. Without thinking, he had slipped into the Tunk-mode, expecting the sanction of the victim for any inconvenience the cadet might cause by running off on his holy crusade to save Fred Kimbal's career.

"You're right, sir. I shouldn't have asked; I had no right." Wesley took a deep breath; for the first time, he understood he really was in serious trouble with Starfleet. "Missing ship's movement" was bad enough; but if he did not find some quick way back, he would be a wanted felon.

"Sir, I need some advice. I got myself into this, and I won't make excuses. Do you have any idea how I can get back to Earth before they declare me AWOL?"

"I don't suppose a shuttlecraft would help, and I can't spare one anyway."

"Too slow. I'd be back sometime in the second week of classes."

"Computer," said Picard, raising his voice, "request flight plans of outbound vessels from Novus Alamogordus. Are any of them headed near Earth?"

"Captain Kurn's ship will pass through Sector Zero-Zero-One on its way back to Klingon space," said the mellifluous voice of the computer.

"Cadet, I suggest you begin negotiating with Kurn. Once you're in the first sector, you can certainly find a merchant ship headed toward Earth. Perhaps Kurn can put you off at the starbase nearest his route."

"Sir, I would be happy to bargain with Captain Kurn . . . but what do I have to offer him?"

Picard considered. "For your service to the Klingon Empire, in my capacity as representative of the Emperor Kahless, I will ask him as a personal favor to take you."

"Captain, that's very generous; but the only deal we made was for you to write me a letter of explanation to Admiral Boxx and Captain Wolfe."

The captain smiled. "That was in my capacity as captain of the *Enterprise,* thus a representative of the Federation. I will only ask Kurn to take you aboard and drop you off en route; it's up to you to get back to the Academy from there."

"Thank you, sir. I appreciate it."

"It was no trouble, Wesley . . . or I wouldn't have done it. You had no business coming out here in the first place—and you violated your Starfleet orders by not taking the first opportunity to steal the device, jump ship, and return. Just be thankful that you came up with a clever scheme to get the Federation and the empire out of a serious problem, or else I would have cheerfully abandoned you here on Novus Alamogordus to work your own way back."

"Aye, sir."

"Go back to your quarters and pack everything; be standing by in the transporter room in ten minutes. Dismissed."

"Aye, sir. Thank you again, Captain. I hope to see you again soon . . . this time on official leave."

Wesley exited smartly and was standing by in the transporter room, ready and waiting, three minutes early.

He remained standing by for an additional two hours before Kurn was ready to break orbit and leave. Riker, Data, and Geordi dropped by separately to say good-bye and wish him luck with the "Big, Bad Wolfe."

"I served with Wolfe on the *Hood,* when we were both lieutenant commanders," the first officer reminisced. "He was a real hard case then, too. Good officer, but we all hated his guts."

Data spoke up. "I would strongly suggest you attempt to bypass Captain Wolfe and get Admiral Boxx to hear your case."

"Data's right," agreed Riker, "it's always better to go before the captain than the first officer. We get paid to be hard cases!"

"I won't say a word," said Geordi with a grin.

"Outside, Geordi! Get a mop and pail and start swabbing the outer hull. Give a shout when you're finished."

Data looked puzzled for a moment; then he activated his laugh program, chuckling lightly.

"That was perfect, Data," said Geordi.

"Thank you, Geordi. I have worked hard on the program, but I do not think I will continue using it. It seems to disconcert human beings more than it sets them at ease."

Riker pulled at his beard, frowning. "I think they're just not used to hearing you react in a way that would be considered 'emotional' in a human, even knowing it's just a program."

"Anyway," said La Forge, "good luck."

"Give Wolfe one for me."

"I'll tell him you said to, Commander."

"I wish you well, Wesley; I hope the next time we meet, it will be under more fortuitous circumstances."

Cadet Crusher sat in the transporter room, alternately filled with ennui and anxiety. After another half hour, Lieutenant Worf and Deanna Troi entered the room.

Deanna almost hugged the cadet, but satisfied herself with a hearty handshake instead. Worf glowered, congratulated him on his bravery in volunteering for the mission to Gul Fubar's ship, and advised him to straightforwardly and forthrightly admit his actions and accept the consequences.

As they left, Wesley noticed a curious connection between them, almost as if there was more to their relationship than mere professional colleagues . . . and as if their simultaneous arrival might be more than timely coincidence. The impression was too nebulous for the cadet to name, however, and he said nothing. Besides, it was none of his business, though he could not imagine why Deanna Troi would be more attracted to Worf than Riker.

His mother was the last to arrive and wish him well. At

their request, the transporter chief departed temporarily and they were alone in the room.

Beverly Crusher did not hesitate to embrace him; he hugged her back, feeling somewhat embarrassed and thankful that the others had already left.

"Wes, what's going to happen? Is there any chance that you'll be expelled from the Academy?"

He shook his head. "I didn't do anything other than miss the beginning of class—I mean I *will* miss it. That's not an offense they expel cadets for. The most I might have gotten was a letter of reprimand anyway . . ." Wesley grinned lopsidedly. "And being kidnapped by Ferengi counterfeiters is a heck of an excuse."

"Are they going to believe you?"

"Captain Picard put it all in his letter; he sent it to me on the data-reader before I went to see him."

"Then there's nothing to worry about? You're not going to be in hot water?"

Wesley was silent for a moment. Years ago, he routinely shared with his mother all his feelings, fears, worries; but starting back when he first became "acting ensign" aboard the *Enterprise* and began learning about adult responsibility, he had felt a curious reluctance to share his private pain with anyone . . . especially with Mom.

"I'm not going to be in hot water," he said. She did not notice that he only answered one of her two questions.

"Do you want me to put in a word for you with Admiral Boxx? I've known him for . . ." Beverly Crusher stopped, her face turning red. "Oh, son, I'm sorry. I didn't mean that the way it sounded."

"Sure you did; it's a Mom-thing."

"I've been your mother for twenty-two years; it's hard to break a habit you've had that long."

"Don't even try, Mother. I'd rather have you as my mother than my doctor anyway."

Beverly made sure no one had crept into the room, then tousled his hair. She performed a passable impersonation of Lwaxana Troi, Deanna Troi's mother: "You never call, you never write! You're such a stranger, I don't even know where you are half the time." They both laughed. "Try to drop by once in a while, kid," she said, "only not quite so dramatically, all right?"

"See you."

Beverly Crusher left; leaving was hard enough and she only wanted to do it once.

At last, Kurn's ship, the *Hiding Fish,* broke orbit and tore away toward Klingon space, dropping its shields just long enough to beam Wesley Crusher aboard as it passed.

Aboard the ship, he was greeted not by Captain Kurn himself, but by a beautiful, muscular, hard-edged commander named Kurak. Despite her very pronounced fore-ridges, savage uniform, and mohawk, Wesley felt a powerful attraction toward her.

She was extremely intelligent but Commander Kurak had an intuitive, abstract grasp of subspace that almost equalled that of the Traveler . . . though she could not turn her theoretical knowledge into direct physical control as he could.

He decided the feeling was mutual; else, how could he explain her especial delight in shoving him around, boasting of her superior fighting skills, and offering to wrestle him, man-to-man? She offered to "show him her holomorphic model," but Wes decided he was not quite ready for what she obviously meant by *that* invitation.

During the night, while the *Hiding Fish* crawled along at warp five—even the Klingons had temporarily accepted the "environmental speed limit," though privately, Wesley thought it a ridiculous conceit, an excuse to avoid facing the problem and coming up with a real solution—he lay on Kurak's own bed in her own quarters, wishing she were with him and simultaneously thanking his lucky stars that she was not.

Two hours before, Wesley discovered that all the extra racks in the *Hiding Fish* were occupied by the Klingon observers who had arrived with the Federation technician on the *Heisenberg*. The cadet was so exhausted and haggard that he found a quiet corner of the engineering division and tried to sleep.

Kurak nudged him awake and brazenly insisted, "You must share my bed, human."

Wes stammered, attempting to refuse; but she grabbed his arm and propelled him to her cabin—whereupon she pushed him into the bed and left.

Chagrined, he realized she meant share her bed literally: He could sleep in Kurak's rack while Commander Kurak stood watch—then when she returned to sleep, she booted him out as politely as a Klingon female commander is capable of ejecting a hu-man cadet.

Wesley felt incredibly ambivalent toward the sexy, frightening Klingon girl: she was older, at least twenty-eight; and she exuded a confidence and sense of self that so far eluded Wesley. Kurak *knew who she was* and *what she wanted to become:* a warrior and a scientist, both.

By contrast, Wesley was completely unsure of both questions, holding only partial answers . . . and negative ones at that. He was sure he did not want to be a scientist stuck on a research base somewhere; but he was becoming more certain with every passing month that he also did not want to be a Starfleet officer, like his father, Jack Crusher, like Will Riker—and the growing knowledge gave Wesley the cold sweats.

Why am I even going back? The only answer he could find was because he had given everyone his word. He was not a "slave to duty," like Frederick in *The Pirates of Penzance,* which he had studied two years earlier. still, he had no reason to believe his word was coerced or his agreement forced . . . yet.

He lay all night in the dark, eagerly awaiting his Klingon warrior Kurak, dreading the possibility. She finally did come, but only to shake him awake roughly and tell him he had fifteen minutes before he would be beamed to Starbase 2—again *en passante.*

Maybe if he caught her by the shoulders and kissed her hard, right on the lips—

Wesley rubbed his eyes, canceling the fantasy. It was silly, adolescent schoolboy stuff. He would never see Kurak again, and she would forget he existed ten minutes after he disembarked.

"Kurak, I think you're really—great. It's too bad we couldn't have—I mean, would you have ever—did you think about anything?"

She smiled. "Here, human." Reaching up, she raked her claws across his face so suddenly he had no time to flinch.

Shocked, he touched his cheek and brought his hand away bloody.

"There," she said, "now you can never forget me."

Hurts like hell, he thought in wonderment. He forced himself not to grimace or show any sign of pain. "Commander Kurak. I won't forget you . . . beautiful."

She was gone, and Wesley grabbed the duffel bag he had never unpacked and headed toward the transporter room. When she met him to say a formal good-bye, she made no reference to his gouged cheek or the unwiped blood; in fact she did not even look at it. The soldier manning the transporter noticed but said nothing.

Wesley paced his small quarters on Starbase 2 for two days before a merchant ship agreed to return him to Earth. He angrily refused medical treatment for his cheek, secretly hoping it would leave a scar when it healed. Alas, after a day, he could barely see Kurak's claw marks, and it was obvious that it would leave behind a cheek as unblemished and unscarred as the rest of him.

The great worry he had refused to reveal to his mother concerned not himself, but Fred, the *real* Fred Kimbal.

For all his brave words and his intellectual knowledge of their truth, Wesley was more than half convinced that Starfleet and Captain Wolfe would find some way to throw Wesley Crusher out of the Academy. In a way, it would be a relief: He felt like a victim of the old torture, arms and legs pulled in opposite directions by separate teams of horses. He could not in good conscience stay and accept his commission in Starfleet; he could not honorably depart unless Starfleet proved itself a fraud.

But either way, he knew he would survive. His self-worth was not bound up with being a Starfleet officer. The sense of self he sought would not be found in a red, yellow, or blue uniform; of that much, he was sure. When Wesley Crusher discovered who he was, the matter of being a commissioned officer or an Academy reject would be completely irrelevant.

But the same blow that would liberate Wesley Crusher would probably destroy Fred Kimbal.

Their lives were not at all parallel. Fred was the most brilliant young man that Wesley had ever met . . . in some areas, so much brighter than Wesley himself that Kimbal could hardly survive without burning himself out.

Unfortunately for Kimbal, he was brilliant in precisely those areas in which Starfleet and the United Federation of Planets held the monopoly.

Wesley's destiny lay *somewhere Out There,* beyond the hull. Fred Kimbal lived only to see the interior of a starship or starbase; what was outside did not concern him.

Wesley gripped a handful of stars in one hand and a personal connection to humanity in the other; he was the bridge between his species's reach and its grasp.

Fred lived so far beyond the farthest star that trying to live outside the hull of Starfleet would be the equivalent of sucking vacuum. He needed the structure, the goals, the hierarchy; Kimbal needed external direction, since he had no moral compass; he required somebody to hang onto his feet while he reached for quasars with both hands.

The only "somebody" with that much strength was Starfleet; if they cast the boy out, he would be lost forever.

"I'll just have to make them see it," swore Wesley, standing in the observation lounge and staring at the star that spawned his race. It was so close he could touch it, almost see it as a disk; but he could not seem to catch a falling ship.

I'll make them see. I'll make them understand. I'll put it in terms that nobody can mistake: If Fred goes, I go!

283

Chapter Twenty-one

CADET WESLEY CRUSHER stepped forward with his left foot, centering himself in the doorway. He executed a left-face, then raised his right hand and pounded three times on the doorframe.

No response. Though he could clearly see the executive officer of Starfleet Academy, Captain Lyle Wolfe, sitting at his desk working—and though Captain Wolfe could just as easily see Cadet Crusher—the executive officer did not respond.

After a minute, Cadet Crusher raised his hand and again pounded the pine three times.

"Do I hear some kind of bird pecking on my chamber door?" asked the captain rhetorically, looking up as if he did not see Cadet Crusher.

Cadet Crusher pounded the pine three more times, bruising his palm with the force of the blows.

At last, Captain Wolfe focused on him. "Enter."

"Sir, Cadet Wesley Crusher reporting as ordered."

"You're a little late, aren't you?"

"Sir?"

"You're a little late, Cadet."

"Sir, Cadet Crusher received a message to report immediately upon disembarking from the *Kings of the High Frontier* Lonatian merchant vessel. The cadet reported immediately from the landing field."

"Yes, but it still seems to me that you're about, oh, *two days late!*"

"Yes, sir."

"Well, do you have any particular reason for being two days late? Couldn't get out of bed? Late night out with the boys? Just couldn't get motivated, eh?"

"No excuse, sir!"

"No excuse, sir! No excuse, sir! Do you really think I'm so stupid that I don't know what 'no excuse, sir' really means? Well, are you just going to stand there and refuse a direct question?"

"No, sir! The cadet does not think the executive officer is stupid at all, sir."

"So you think I *do* know what 'no excuse, sir' really means?"

"Yes, sir."

"What?"

"Sir?"

"Sir? Sir? The lowest damn enlisted man knows enough to at least try to answer a question! He doesn't let his eyes bug out and say 'sir?' with that vacuous expression you jerky little cadets use that implies you never even heard of such a thing as answering a question! Now let's see if you can spit it out."

"Aye, sir. 'No excuse, sir' means that the cadet understands the gravity of his off—"

"DON'T YOU MOVE! You are at attention! Get those damned thumbs along your trouser seams and stop running your eyes over me!"

"Aye, sir. 'No excuse sir' means that the cadet understands the gravity of his offense and offers no . . . and does not attempt to excuse his actions, sir."

"Oh that's *much* clearer, cadet. Well, the cadet obviously

doesn't understand much, so I'll illuminate him. 'No excuse, sir' means that the cadet was told somewhere by some senior cadet that that's what he's supposed to answer whenever somebody in his chain of command asks him why he did something *stupid,* even if he didn't know until that moment that it was something *stupid.* But what it really means is that you think I'll be *impressed* by you taking responsibility for your actions! Oh, Cadet, I'm just shocked at how responsible and honest you are! Why, with just a dozen more like you, we could abandon the entire Starfleet Judicial Advocate General office, since everybody would be so honest, loyal, brave, thrifty, trustworthy, and true that no one would ever stand captain's mast again!"

"Aye, sir."

"Aye, sir? Are you responding to an order, Cadet?"

"No, sir! The cadet meant 'yes, sir,' sir!"

"Oh! You think I'm soliciting your *opinion* on my suggestion?"

"No, sir!"

"So now you're *contradicting* my suggestion?"

"No, sir! The cadet was confused, sir."

"My God! You *are* an honest little cadet, aren't you?"

"Yes, sir!"

"No excuse, sir! Well, let's just start all over again, shall we? Why were you two days late for classes?"

"Sir, the cadet was kidnapped by Ferengi counterfeiters, Munk and Tunk, and taken to an auction on Novus Alamogordus."

"Kidnapped! My, how exciting for you. But . . . I thought you were kidnapped by *one* Ferengi, Tunk?"

"Yes, sir. Tunk kidnapped the cadet from the landing field; then later, Tunk's father, Munk, continued the kidnapping to Novus Alamogordus."

"Oh, very glib. So tell me, Cadet . . . how did Tunk happen to kidnap you? Did he abduct you at phaser-point from your quarters?"

"No, sir."

"Did he chloroform you in one of our passageways?"

"No, sir."

"Well, how did he manage this dastardly deed?"

"Sir, the Ferengi ordered his bodyguards to prevent the cadet from leaving the Ferengi's ship before it launched."

"But . . . before this Tunk could *prevent* you from leaving his ship, you had to be *aboard* his ship—or am I missing something?"

"The cadet was aboard the Ferengi's ship, sir."

"Well, how did the cadet *board* the Ferengi's ship?"

"Sir, the cadet . . . snuck aboard the Ferengi's ship in order to retrieve a device."

"My, goodness! So you're telling me that you *burglarized* Tunk's ship, and he caught you and took you along with him to Novus Alamogordus!"

"Yes, sir."

"So he didn't really *kidnap* you at all, and you lied to me!"

"No, sir."

" 'No sir' which? That he kidnapped you, or that you lied to me?"

"Sir, the Ferengi kidnapped the cadet, and the cadet did not lie to the executive officer."

"You know something? I don't think we're getting anywhere on this one, Cadet. You're just too clever for me. Gosh, I just can't remember when I've heard so many great excuses. I'll have to write a few of them down so I can remember them in case I accidentally shoot down my own wingman! I've submitted a letter to your file, which is my right as your supervisor; and it's not a very nice letter. In fact, it's what we call a *letter of reprimand,* and it means you're going to have an awfully hard time getting a good billet from your detailer when you graduate. That's all I have to say to you, Cadet Crusher. Now get your butt inside to do a little tap dance for the admiral. Dismissed."

"Aye, sir!" Cadet Wesley Crusher took a step backward, executed an about-face, and exited the office. He executed a left face, walked to the next office, centered himself in the doorway, turned to face the closed door, and pounded the pine three times.

"Enter." The door slid open.

"Sir, Cadet Wesley Crusher reporting as ordered by the executive officer."

"As you were. Take a seat, Cadet."

"Aye, sir."

"This is just an informal meeting, Cadet. We'll have to hold a formal captain's mast next week; but I'll tell you now what we're going to decide. Unless you'd rather request a formal court-martial."

"No, sir."

"Wise decision, Cadet. According to Captain Picard's statement on your behalf, you have admitted to leaving Academy grounds without authorized liberty, gambling with civilians and other cadets, and breaking and entering the ship of a civilian. Do you contest any of this?"

"No, sir."

"Good, let's stay ahead of the power curve, Cadet. I know why you burgled the Ferengi's ship, and under the circumstances, I'm inclined to dismiss the charge as an example of initiative, rather than criminal action."

"Thank you, sir."

"I like the fact that you didn't just sit back and let the Ferengi have a latinum-counterfeiting machine. You rolled up your sleeves and solved the problem. It took some ingenuity; good job. I do *not* like the fact that you built the latinum-forging machine in the first place. Where was your head, Cadet? Didn't you think?"

"Sir, the cadet—"

"You can drop the third person rule for this meeting, Cadet, and for your mast next week."

"Aye, sir. Sir, I didn't know what the machine was until it was built. I considered destroying it immediately; in retrospect, I should have."

"Yes, you should have. Innovation is all well and good;

I'm all for progress. But there are some things we just weren't meant to know, such as how to counterfeit latinum."

"Yes, sir. I weighed that against the scientific value gained by studying—"

"Are you qualified to make that decision?"

"Ah . . . no, sir. I'm not, sir."

"All right, there you go. Let's keep ahead of the eight ball. But I'm really not concerned about you. Look, son, I know about the big poker game; I know who was there, I don't need you to tell me."

"Thank you, sir."

"I could reel off the names: La Fong, Axel, Lees, DuBois, Jantzen, Ackermann; I always know when the big game is on, and everybody involved gets a slap on the wrist. Do you know how long that tradition has lasted here?"

"No, sir."

"Neither do I. I played in a couple of big games when I was a fourth year cadet, lo these many years ago. Did Captain Wolfe tell you about a letter of reprimand?"

"Yes, sir."

"Well, don't worry too much about it. We call it the Poker-Chip Slapdown. Nobody pays much attention to it in the fleet . . . unless you get into trouble and they decide they want to boot you; then your commanding officer can use the Slapdown to show a pattern of unofficerlike conduct.

"I really don't want to talk to you about *you*, Cadet. I don't think you're a problem; you're a good man, and you'll make a good officer."

"Thank you, sir. I appreciate having your confidence."

"I admit I had my doubts when I assumed command; I read about that incident in your first year and wondered whether you were really fit to be at this Academy. I watched you very closely over the next year, Cadet; but I've changed my mind. I think you were incredibly stupid to pull that starburst thing, but you showed some guts later when you broke the code of silence. Wish we had more like you."

"Thank you, sir."

"Son, this is a very important lesson. I want you to listen closely and remember this throughout your entire career: Starfleet is not about never making a mistake. Everybody makes stupid mistakes! Starfleet is about taking responsibility for your mistakes—and not just saying 'it's my fault' or 'no excuse sir,' but actually fixing the problem. Even if it wasn't your mistake in the first place, but your crewmate's."

"I understand, sir."

"No, you don't. But you will, given a few years out in the fleet. I'm not worried about you; I'm worried about one of your crewmates. You didn't say anything, but I can tell from your face that you know exactly who I mean.

"Crusher, I'm very concerned about Cadet Fred Kimbal. I don't know if he's really officerlike material; and I don't know if the Academy can afford to keep him. But I'll give you a chance to change my mind."

"Thank you, sir. Sir, I . . . I need to speak frankly."

"What you say will not leave this office, Crusher."

"Sir, I think you're very wrong about Kimbal. I think he would make an excellent officer, and I would be proud to serve with him."

"Continue."

"No, sir. Sir, Kimbal is the most intelligent cadet at the Academy, bar none. He understands warp theory, uh, postgravitational fluctuation, the gravity wave equations, subspace . . . everything better than anyone else here. He has an incredible, intuitive understanding of exactly how subspace really works; not even Commander Sur knows it from the gut the way Kimbal does."

"That's great; he can go to Keynes and be a physicist. I want you to tell me why he'd make a good Starfleet officer, Cadet."

"Sir, he's learning. He's coming along. He's showing definite improvement."

"Kimbal's admission was questionable to begin with, Cadet Crusher."

"But he's getting a lot better at—at leadership and

command and all the qualities that go to make a good Starfleet officer."

"So he's what, about up to admission standards now? At the end of his second year?"

"He's better than that, sir."

"Let me tell you my standard, Cadet. I don't expect cadets to learn how to be officerlike while they're here; I expect them to *already be officerlike* when we accept them to the Academy. If I decided to just commission everyone tomorrow, I would expect every single cadet to be a solid, reliable, dependable Starfleet officer . . . immediately. Son, there is no time to 'grow into' being an officer; the day I pin that dot on your collar, you had better already *be* a Starfleet officer.

"Now frankly, I would have no hesitation pinning you right now, or La Fong, or Cadet Lees. You don't have the experience to pilot a Galaxy-class starship yet—no, not even you, Crusher; what you did on the *Enterprise* isn't enough, and it's no more than half the cadets here have done before they came here—but you were already officer material when you came to us . . . in fact, like a lot of the cadets, you were already an officer.

"We don't make officers here, Mister Crusher. We refine them. The Academy isn't like a factory, turning out cogs for the big Starfleet machine; it's like a latinum mine, chipping away the useless mass to find the valuable latinum that's already there, just hidden.

"Now throughout your whole defense of Cadet Kimbal, there's one question you haven't answered. You've been dancing around it. Based on what you know about Cadet Frederick Kimbal, would *you* say it is in Starfleet's best interest to graduate him."

"Sir, I—"

"Take your time. Wait a moment and think about it. All right, go ahead and answer."

"Yes, sir, I do."

"You do?"

"Yes, sir. Fred is definitely not poured from the same

mold as most of the cadets here; I won't argue that! He's quirky, he's different, and he doesn't always do what you expect him to do.

"But it's not right to say he's not officerlike. We can't let the 'standard mold' of a Starfleet officer become a prison that traps us into being one specific type of person and keeps out anybody who might give us a fresh perspective.

"I agree . . . Fred Kimbal is no Jean-Luc Picard and no William Riker. He's not even a Carl La Fong or a Locarno.

"But neither am I! Not really. Every one of us is different; we all bring our unique perspectives to being an officer in Starfleet . . . and if we didn't, then you may as well fire us all and replace us with seventy-three million copies of Commander Data, like Starfleet wanted to do before.

"That was wrong then, and it's wrong now. You're right, sir; Starfleet isn't a huge machine, and we're not cogs. We don't all look alike, act alike, or think alike. Fred Kimbal looks just a little further outside the norm than the rest of us, but *he knows what he's doing*. He has the most important skill of all for a Starfleet officer: He genuinely, desperately, *wants* to lead his crew and accept his responsibilities. There aren't many people left in the quadrant with that quality.

"Sir, Kimbal is committed, devoted to Starfleet, and willing to accept the consequences of his own actions and those of his crewmates. He is brilliant, he *is* reliable—you can rely upon him to solve problems that the rest of us can only dimly understand—and he is an honest, decent man. He has all the qualifications to be a strong, successful Starfleet officer. And yes, I would be proud to serve alongside him."

"How about serving *under* him, Mister Crusher?"

"If necessary, yes."

"If necessary? Why the qualification?"

"Well, I just meant . . ."

"Mister Crusher, you gave a very strong defense. You caught me by surprise; you changed my mind about several things anent Kimbal."

"But I didn't change your mind about the most important thing."

"No, son. You didn't."

"Sir, please reconsider. I know I can make Kimbal more officerlike . . . he's improved so remarkably in the last year, since La Fong put us together, that I know he'll make a first-rate officer."

"No, son. He won't . . . because if he hasn't by now, he never will. With apologies to Mister Kennedy, ask not what the Academy can do for you . . . ask what you can do for the Academy. I'm afraid we've just hit an irreconcilable difference between your view and the Academy's view: Fred Kimbal simply does not come across as a Starfleet officer."

"Sir, are you saying you're going to dismiss him because he doesn't *look and feel* like an officer?"

"No, son, and I don't like that tone. I'm saying I've decided to dismiss Kimbal because I would not feel comfortable serving under him . . . and neither would you, whether you'll admit it or not. You already told me that when you hesitated when I asked whether you would be willing to serve under him."

"Does that mean that anyone who is the least bit different from the 'Starfleet norm' will get bounced from now on?"

"I didn't invent the norm, Mister Crusher; and I'm not enforcing it any more rigidly now than it was enforced last year, or ten years ago, or back when I was a cadet here. I'm not willing to throw it out the airlock just for one extremely smart misfit."

"Sir, I almost feel like saying if Kimbal goes, I go."

"I hope you don't say that, Mister Crusher. I would hate to see you leave. But that's a decision that each one of us must make on his own.

"I will caution you about one thing, Cadet: Before you accept your commission, you had better be *damned* certain that you're willing to carry it on your shoulders; because if you're not sure, I guarantee you those collar dots will get heavier and heavier with every passing day until they finally drag you down to the bottom.

"Now do you have anything else to say before I dismiss you?"

"Yes, sir."

"Speak up, son."

"Sir . . . if your decision is final, then I request permission to be the one to inform Cadet Kimbal."

"Granted. Go ahead and tell him; he may as well start making arrangements. Ask him to come speak to me before he leaves and to swing by the PDP to arrange his flight home and mustering-out pay. They'll have a few forms for him to ident, and they'll tell him what equipment he can keep and what belongs to us."

"Aye, sir."

"I'm appointing you his mustering-out liaison. Any problems or disputes, he goes through you straight to me. You understand?"

"Yes, sir."

"The chain is from Kimbal to you to me from now on. Dismissed."

"Aye, sir. Thank you, sir."

Wesley walked across the quadrangle, his steps slow but still too fast, too certain. *They've turned me into one of them,* he thought morosely. *If I'd had any guts, I would have told them I refused to accept their moral authority to tell Kimbal he wasn't officerlike, and if they wanted to cashier him, they would have to do it without my sanction. But I have no guts. I'm complicit in everything they do to Fred. I'm just as guilty as Bernard Boxx.*

He avoided the turbolift and walked up two flights of stairs, then slowly marched down the passageway with a measured tread.

Wesley thumbed the pad and opened the door, then stopped. Fred sat on his already-packed suitcase, wearing civilian clothes.

"Heard you had landed and gone to see the old man," said Kimbal.

"I'm sorry, Fred. I tried."

"I know. I knew you wouldn't turn them around, too. Wes, they're right, you know."

"They're not right."

"I'm not cut out to be an officer."

"You don't know that, and neither do they. They *think* they know it; but nobody knows anything about anyone until he's actually in the line of fire. Maybe I'll freeze up on my first command. Maybe I'll turn left when I should turn right and drive into my wingman. Maybe I'll win the bronze nebula on my first tour of duty . . . *nobody knows*. It's insane to pretend that you can know from how the uniform hangs whether a cadet will make a good officer."

"Wes, I'm really not destroyed by this. I really thought I'd make it, but I'm not going to stick a phaser in my mouth."

"You have any ideas?"

Fred shrugged. "Harvard, Stanford. I can probably get a scholarship anywhere."

"It won't be Starfleet."

"I don't know whether to say 'too bad' or 'thank God.'"

"You have to go to the PDP."

"I already called and made an appointment. Do I go through you or La Fong?"

"I'm the liaison."

"Good. I hate that arrogant, strutting Carl La Fong, capital-*L*, small-*a*, capital-*F*, small-*o*, small-*n*, small-*g*, Carl La Fong."

"I don't know what to say, Fred. I'm going to miss you."

"I'm actually going to do my best to forget you and everyone else here, the whole damned Academy."

"Sorry."

"Not your fault, Wes. I just want to concentrate on tomorrow, not yesterday. All right?"

"Fair enough. Good-bye. I hope after a while you can write and tell me where you are."

"Leave word with Boothby where you get posted."

Then Wesley blinked, and Fred Kimbal was gone.

Wesley Crusher lay down on his bunk, not even bothering

to throw his civvies into the replicleaner and put on his uniform.

If he rushed, he could still make his last class for the day. He did not rush. If he changed, he could attend evening chow in the mess hall. He did not change. If he got up, he could wander to the O-club and down some synthehol, toast Fred Kimbal, remember his friends on the *Enterprise*, laugh about his close scrapes with Ferengi and Cardassians, and tell lies about his encounter with the commander Kurak aboard the *Hiding Fish*. He did not get up.

It's a damned giant squid, its tentacles wrapped all around us, and it eats people like Fred alive. It's cold and leathery, and it cares only about spreading its tentacles farther and farther into the universe until they stretch infinitely far, their moral fiber stretched infinitesimally thin. It's paradise. It has everything . . . peace, plenty, power; replicators to feed the hungry, holodecks to feed the spiritually dead; and an obsessive fascination with the past to feed dreams of yesterday. It is sterile, unsympathetic. The moral compass spins free, pointing neither north nor south. Starfleet has lost its way.

The sun set; the room grew too dark to see. But Wesley saw perfectly well.

Do I have the courage to do what I was called to do?

In the morning, he rushed, he changed, he got up and ran downstairs by 0535 for PT. His first class was History of Moral Philosophy, and if he missed one more lecture, Captain DuBois would have his hide.

About the Author

Dafydd ab Hugh—raconteur, troubadore, and bon vivant—is the celebrating author of *Fallen Heroes,* the *Deep Space Nine* novel where everybody dies, as well as the justly unforgotten *Heroing* and *Warriorwards* (the Jiana Chronicles) and the equally unappalling *Arthur War Lord* and *Far Beyond the Wave*—a vaguely-amusing time-travel conceit about King Arthur.

Mr. ab Hugh is found under the H's (for "Hugh") in the science-fiction section, where he startles inattentive browsers by sudden movements.

Mr. ab Hugh assures his readers that he is not now, nor has he ever been, Peter David.

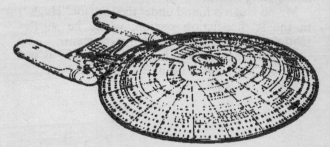